Praise for Penny Parkes:

'Hugely enjoyable' **Catherine Isaac**

'Larkford is still my happy place' **Katie Fforde**

'Delightfully warm' **Jo Thomas**

'Has everything: warmth, humour, drama,
laughter and a few tears' **Milly Johnson**

'A pure delight' **Julie Cohen**

'Vivid, evocative and beautifully written' **Holly Miller**

'I very much enjoyed this thoughtful and
absorbing novel' **Kate Eberlen**

'Clever, warm and funny, Penny writes with a big heart,
a light touch~~ and supreme confidence~~' **Veronica Henry**

ALSO BY PENNY PARKES

Out of Practice
Practice Makes Perfect
Best Practice

eBook only:
Swept Away (eBook short story)

PENNY PARKES

Snowed In With You

**SIMON &
SCHUSTER**

London · New York · Sydney · Toronto · New Delhi

First published in Great Britain by Simon & Schuster UK Ltd, 2019 as *Snowed in at the Practice*
This Paperback edition published 2021

3 5 7 9 10 8 6 4 2

Simon & Schuster UK Ltd
1st Floor
222 Gray's Inn Road
London WC1X 8HB

Simon & Schuster Australia, Sydney
Simon & Schuster India, New Delhi

www.simonandschuster.co.uk
www.simonandschuster.com.au
www.simonandschuster.co.in

A CIP catalogue record for this book is available from the British Library

Paperback ISBN: 978-1-3985-0843-9
eBook ISBN: 978-1-4711-6404-0
Audio ISBN: 978-1-4711-7733-0

Excerpt from *The Power of Intention* by Dr Wayne W. Dyer.
Published by Hay House, 2004. Reprinted by permission of Hay House.

Typeset in the UK by M Rules
Printed and bound by CPI Group (UK) Ltd, Croydon, CR0 4YY

For The Ginger Ninja

my sanity-saving,
cushion-stealing,
Post-it-chobbling,
sounding-board
& perfect writing companion

Always

'When you change the way you look at things,
the things you look at change'

DR WAYNE DYER

Chapter 1

Dr Holly Graham swirled the pancake batter onto the Aga hotplate with almost surgical precision; just another one of the imperceptible ways she was subconsciously keeping her eye in while on maternity leave. Taffy wrapped his arms around her waist and lovingly rested his chin on her shoulder. 'Can I just have one really huge one?' He paused, weighing up the likelihood of success. 'With lots of chocolate chips?'

Holly arranged a stack of perfect circles onto his plate and shook her head with a smile. 'Keep dreaming, Taffs. We're leading from the front, remember?'

They both glanced over at the huge oak kitchen table, round and stocky, their four children marking out the four points of the wooden compass that had dictated virtually every moment of Holly's universe for the last twelve months. Typically, Elsie had stationed herself between Lottie and Olivia, seemingly oblivious to the mangled rusks that now adorned her silk dressing gown, perfectly happy to spoon dollops of apple-sauce-swirled yoghurt into their willing mouths as she embraced her role as honorary 'Grandmother'. Ben and Tom, on the other hand, their appetites growing as quickly as their gangly six-year-old legs, wanted none of it.

They were holding out for pancakes – gazillions of pancakes, to be precise – with lashings of maple syrup.

'Well, at least the maple syrup's organic,' offered Taffy, his own tendency towards mainlining junk food having been brutally curtailed in his quest to become a decent role model, and to stand a chance of fitting into his morning suit for the wedding.

'Do top up my coffee, there's a darling,' said Elsie, having recently decided that life was just too short to drink camomile tea, whatever her consultant may say. As a result, the entire household had been cunningly and covertly switched to decaf and Holly's mood was suffering a little as a result.

'Anything good on the cards today?' Holly asked Taffy, as she flipped over another batch of Scotch pancakes to top up the rapidly diminishing supply on the table. Her tone was almost wistful with enquiry; she was missing her patients and the cut and thrust of practice life far more than she was willing to concede. Of course, it didn't help that they seemed to be coping so indecently well in her absence. All her offers to step in, help out, lend a hand, had been politely but pointedly declined by the team at The Practice.

'Don't worry about it,' Dan said. 'Enjoy your babies,' Alice said. 'Make the most of your time off,' they all repeated ad nauseam. Her grip tightened on the spatula at the very thought.

Time off!

Who were they kidding? Being at home with newborn twins had hardly been a picnic in the South of France.

Throw in another set of twins, five years ahead, and bouncing with all the energy of Duracell bunnies, a timeshare labradoodle and an increasingly needy (and enormous) piglet and Holly's slate was full. Speaking of which, Nineteen grunted at the French windows for his breakfast, still seemingly disgusted at no longer being allowed into the kitchen, on the sofas, basically wherever he pleased – but weighing nearly seventy pounds, Nineteen was no longer an adorable, snuffling piglet: he was a hog in all senses of the word. Every attempt to give him more room in the meadows nearby had resulted in him making a break for home. It was yet another thing on Holly's mental To Do list that needed attention.

Taffy swallowed his mouthful of pancake and took a slug of coffee for good measure, looking at his mug in confusion when it failed to deliver that morning boost he had come to rely on. 'Not much on today, really. Same old, same old.'

Holly sighed, realising he had no idea how appealing the notion of 'same old' was to her right now. Not that she hadn't adored this special time with her babies – and they were an absolute delight – she just sometimes felt as though her brain was turning to Play-Doh and her conversation to mindless jibber-jabber. Thank heavens for Elsie's ongoing vacillation about her living arrangements. Although duly installed at Sarandon Hall – the retirement destination for the blue of blood and heavy of wallet – she still seemed to spend most of her days, and quite a few of her nights, here at Number 42 being generally eccentric and inspiring. Although once Elsie's own family home, ensuring that Holly's growing brood could now call it *their* home had been one of the greatest acts of generosity that Holly had ever witnessed. Spending the first few weeks of Olivia and Lottie's lives quite literally holding Holly's hand, as Taffy had been subsumed gradually back into work, had been another. From where Holly was standing, Elsie's presence was a reassuring constant she'd be lost without.

'Tell me,' Holly said. 'How's the Major doing? Is Alice coping with her new clinic hours with Coco? What happened about Pru's mammogram in the end?' She wasn't so much firing questions at him, as machine-gunning them into the room, the way Ben and Tom did when they were on a mission for information, snackage or attention.

Taffy just nodded. 'It's all good. Hey, haven't the boys got a concert rehearsal this afternoon?'

Holly swallowed her frustration, along with a bite of pancake. At this rate, she'd be the size of a house before she found her balance. She nodded. 'Dress rehearsal today, boys,' she reminded them.

Ben and Tom looked at each other and scowled, perfect mirror images of disgruntlement. 'I hate stupid Guy Fawkes,' Tom said firmly, always the more outspoken of the twins, 'and this stupid concert.'

'I hate my costume and Tarquin is a big meany,' Ben continued. 'He keeps tripping me up when we do our stupid song.'

Holly frowned. She'd initially been quite on board with the new head teacher's plan to add a performance by the primary school pupils to their traditional Larkford Bonfire Night festivities, until that is, she'd realised the commitment required to persuade twenty-eight children, each seemingly with two left feet, into their costumes and into the limelight without anyone being trampled, roasted or embarrassed to death. Even accounting for the little sod that was Tarquin Holland and his painfully right-on mother, Cassie, these Guy Fawkes preparations had quickly become a labour of love for all the parents of Larkford Primary. Of course, for some, the love had been somewhat enhanced by the very presence of said new head teacher. Mr Alec French had certainly swayed the pyjamas-to-mascara ratio on the school run in the opposite direction since his arrival.

The front door swung open and Alice and Coco barrelled

through the parquet hallway and into the kitchen. Since her boyfriend Jamie had taken a temporary work placement in Ireland, it had become Alice's custom en route to The Practice, to call in at Holly's for the first coffee of the day – Elsie's kitchen providing the central focus for most of their socialising these days. At times, Alice seemed quite lost without him, and Holly was only too delighted to provide company, coffee and distraction, in exchange for a little update now and then.

'Morning! I hope you haven't eaten already – I picked up Danish pastries,' said Alice chirpily, her assistance dog Coco at her feet, as she carefully hung up her beautiful velvet coat. No longer one to keep things for best, she was a close contender with Elsie for the role of Larkford's style icon these days. Not that Elsie seemed to mind.

'I hope one of those pastries has my name on it!' Elsie said, deliberately ignoring the look that passed between Holly and Taffy. 'I'm in need of decadence today. All this puréed fruit is giving me a glimpse into my future and I'm not sure I like it.'

Holly noticed that Taffy, Ben and Tom had quickly squirrelled away all evidence of their pancake extravaganza and were holding out their plates expectantly. Seriously, thought Holly, it was like feeding an army in this kitchen most days.

Needless to say, Alice had thoughtfully picked out a dairy-free offering for Ben and soon contented yummy noises filled the room, to the accompaniment of Olivia banging her fists on her high chair in excitement at the sliver of buttery goodness heading her way.

'Stick the radio on,' said Alice, as she poured coffee for everyone, and Holly handed out orange juice in a tried and tested manoeuvre of choreography. 'Lizzie had me in stitches just now. She's on cracking form, have you noticed?'

Holly had in fact noticed that giving her best friend, Lizzie, ready access to a microphone and a Nespresso machine had been a masterstroke in her recovery from anxiety, not to mention with all three of her children now being at school, Lizzie was indeed generally on the up. It was fair to say that, in their small community, the 'anonymous' part of Lizzie's Agony Aunt phone-in show on Radio Larkford was really anything but. Nevertheless, Lizzie's advice was often on message, despite being off the cuff, and generally hilarious in its bluntness.

'All I'm saying,' came the emotional tones of today's unwitting caller across the airwaves, 'is that I'd just like a small break from my children climbing all over me, before my husband starts, you know?'

Holly and Alice both snorted their coffee across the table as they burst out laughing, recognising only too clearly the voice of Hattie from The Deli in town. Taffy merely looked perplexed.

'But, surely it's nice that he still fancies her—' began Taffy, unwittingly stepping into a barrage of abuse from the women at the table.

Lizzie clearly had no scruples when it came to telling it like it is, even when on the airwaves. 'You're not a cappuccino machine,' she said with feeling. 'He can hardly expect you to be on the go with kids and The D— I mean, with work all day and then get hot and steamy at the flick of a switch.'

Taffy swallowed his laughter in a moment, when he saw how intently his beloved was listening to the answer. Holly offered him a watery smile in reassurance, but Lizzie was on a roll.

'Seriously, any new dads out there feeling all hard done by because they're not getting much duvet action need to take a long hard look at themselves. You can't be Mary Poppins one minute and Jessica Rabbit the next. Your wives may be mothers now, but that doesn't mean you should stop wooing them. When's the last time you ran them a bath, or cooked them supper? Maybe looked after your kids for a bit so they could regroup? Hat—, I mean, our caller has a point – there needs to be a transition from mother to partner and you guys need to make that happen!' She spoke with feeling and gusto and Holly laid odds that there were women all over Larkford cheering her on, not to mention husbands curling their toes. 'Ask them what they want! And now here's Journey with a little reminder.' As the lyrics of 'Any Way You Want It' blasted out around the kitchen there was an uncomfortable silence for a moment.

Ben looked around the table in consternation. 'Aunty Lizzie gives weird advice on the radio. If they like climbing so much, she should just tell them to buy a climbing frame—'

Alice excused herself from the table as orange juice spurted from her nose and Holly held her sides laughing.

'Out of the mouths of babes,' said Elsie drily, as her magpie attention was caught by Alice's vintage necklace, as she passed around handfuls of napkins to deal with the problem.

Taffy took Holly's hand as she went to stand up and clear the table. 'Tell me what you want,' he whispered with a smile, taking Lizzie's advice to heart.

Holly's eyes flashed at the possibilities. 'Anything?'

Taffy smiled wolfishly. 'Anything at all.'

She sat back down beside him and kissed him. 'Can I take your diabetes clinic today? You could stay with the girls?'

Taffy laughed. 'Oh, Holls, you're so funny.' He stood up and dropped a kiss on top of her head. 'Think about it, though, I'm serious. Dinner? A spa day with Lizzie maybe? Whatever you need, just say.' He kissed Olivia and Lottie, somehow escaping their outstretched sticky grasp, and chivvied the boys to get their school shoes on.

Holly mutely watched as he turned away, momentarily speechless. 'But I just *did* say,' she managed, only for her words to be drowned out by the chaos of locating last-minute school clobber and performance paraphernalia.

She bent down to kiss both the boys as they swung their arms around her thighs and to check their faces were free of maple syrup. She couldn't quite face a 'friendly chat' on the tiny chairs from the glorious Mr French just yet. It would surely be better to meet him properly before her first official dressing-down.

'I'd best be off too,' said Alice, as everyone realised the time and hustled together. Even Elsie wandered through into the hall to prepare for her morning ahead. Another class with the Silver Swans, no doubt, reliving her misspent youth at the barre and brushing up her pliés.

In fact, in less than three minutes, Holly's kitchen went from being a hive of sociable activity to the front door swinging quietly shut behind them with a dull *whumpf.*

She turned to the girls, their hands outstretched and their faces smothered with sticky pastry crumbs. 'Well,' she said after a moment, mustering a cheery smile, 'as I'm obviously not playing doctor today, you two are going to be my partners in crime, okay?' She kissed their foreheads adoringly. 'Now, what do you two little poppets want to do this morning?'

Chapter 2

Holly glanced down at her vibrating mobile as she attempted to insert a reluctant Olivia into the pushchair. Three missed calls, all from the same number. She ignored them, as Olivia arched her back grumpily and made a bid for freedom.

There was only so much pep that a person could take at this time of the morning and Patricia, her return-to-work co-ordinator from the local Commissioning Group was just two degrees south of a California cheerleader – not to be taken without prior preparation, to wit, a glass of wine in hand.

Holly allowed the voicemail to play out loud, as she looked around her at the scene of devastation from simply getting all three of them washed, dressed and ready for Toddler Tambourine. Getting back to work was clearly going to require a lot more organisation and even less sleep!

'Go-ood morning,' trilled Patricia, with approximately two hundred per cent too much gusto for this hour on a Monday morning. Voicemail had definitely been the right call. 'It's Patricia calling again. I just need a moment of your time to discuss your return-to-work strategy, Dr Graham. We've some lovely workshops coming up for our ladies wishing to return to General Practice and I thought of you.'

Holly took a deep breath, trying not to rise at the

incredibly patronising, not to mention sexist, tone that young Patricia always chose to adopt. She was sick of explaining that a year's maternity leave hardly qualified as a 'career break'. Holly truly felt that shadowing someone for a fortnight to remind her what to do in her own practice was taking the mickey. A simple concept that seemed to elude her nominated case-worker.

'So,' continued Patricia, 'if you'd like to call me back, I can talk you through the Return to Work Protocol again.' She paused, the doubt at Holly's willingness to comply almost voluble down the line. 'You will need to comply with the four steps, as we discussed before, Dr Graham. I'm only here to help and it's my job to guide you through, one step at a time. No need to over-face ourselves. So, well, call me back.'

Patricia seemed to subscribe to the notion that an upbeat, positive attitude may not solve all of life's problems, but it would annoy enough people along the way to make it worth the effort.

Holly couldn't help a small smile of satisfaction that Patricia's bounce had considerably less amplitude by the end of the message. Bureaucracy was such a farce sometimes.

Lottie began to whimper and, like dominoes, Olivia swiftly followed suit. Holly sighed, knowing that there were hoops she needed to jump through and ignoring them was seemingly no longer an option. But it made more sense, to her at least, to get her familial ducks in a row first.

Holly offered Lottie a conciliatory teething cracker to gnaw on, rather than her sister's outstretched fingers, and for a moment there was silence. Poor Patricia was only doing her job – she did realise that – but surely, as an experienced doctor Holly could be trusted to look four steps ahead without throwing in the towel?

'Knock, knock, coo-ee!' called Lizzie, opening the front door and letting herself in. 'I must seriously love you, Holly Graham. I've barely got my own kids off to school and you're making me endure bloody Toddler Tambourine all over again!' She grinned to show that she was joking but there was a certain amount of truth in her words. She scooped Lottie up into her arms and covered her with kisses. 'Who's ready to go and sing some songs,' she said, before turning to Holly with a smile, 'and then who'll be ready to go and drink some gin?' she continued with the same upbeat sing-song delivery.

Holly burst out laughing as Olivia clapped her approval at this plan of action. 'I seriously owe you one for this, Lizzie. It's almost impossible to do these classes with only one pair of hands. God knows what it will be like when they start running everywhere.'

Lizzie blew a raspberry on Lottie's tummy. 'Well, hopefully you'll have a nanny all sorted by then and you can have a little balance between work and home. I'm still reeling that it's actually cheaper to have a proper nanny than pay four sets of childcare fees. That has to focus the mind a little.'

Holly nodded, feeling oddly choked up at Lizzie's instinctive understanding of her situation – no judgement, no comment – it was obvious that she'd already walked several miles in her shoes.

'Any progress on that front?' Lizzie asked, as they made their way through the streets of Larkford, the autumn sunshine lambent across the Market Place, picking out the pastel-fronted buildings and giving Holly just the boost she needed.

'I've a few booked in for interviews next Monday, but to be honest that may not be my biggest hurdle anymore ...'

She outlined the delightful Patricia's plan and was gratified to see Lizzie's face pucker in consternation. 'Bonkers, right?'

'Completely,' Lizzie agreed. 'What does Taffy say about all this? Surely there's a sneaky shortcut for partners who've been away less than a year?'

Holly's cheeks flushed suddenly and it had nothing to do with the swift breeze lifting her hair. 'I may not have mentioned it, actually. He seems so happy having a stay-at-home mum for the girls and it's not as though they're exactly shorthanded at work now, is it?' Not for the first time, Holly felt a shiver of regret for having found such wonderful maternity cover in the form of Tilly Campbell. Outspoken, compassionate – young, but experienced – Tilly had seemingly slotted into life at The Practice like an old friend. Which of course, to Alice, she was.

'Do you ever feel superfluous to your own life?' Holly asked quietly, as they ambled through the sunshine, ochre leaves drifting to their feet as they crossed the park, watching a team of volunteers add yet more timber, branches and old furniture to the ever-growing town bonfire under the Major's roaring supervision.

Lizzie looked at her sharply, only too familiar with the swirly rabbit hole that was negative thinking. 'You are anything but superfluous to these gorgeous girls though, Holls. You're just too close to see it, right now. And don't forget, I'd have been lost without you, during my whole going-completely-fecking-mad phase.'

Holly nodded, stroking Olivia's precocious blonde ringlets that bounced in the pram in front of her and smiled at Lizzie's irreverent take on life. 'I know. I do. And I count myself incredibly lucky to have options, but I can't help thinking I would appreciate all of this so much more with a little professional challenge thrown into the mix. A little light and shade? Rather than everything changing at once?'

'Ah well, you know what Elsie would say? "Adapt or die, my darlings. Darwin was right all along."' Her off-key impression of their favourite octogenarian was so on-point, it gave Holly just the boost she needed.

'Point taken,' Holly said with a smile. 'As long as we agree that I'm no Galapagos Tortoise?'

'Hmm,' said Lizzie impishly, 'then maybe we should talk moisturiser?'

Any time for silliness and gossip disappeared the moment the two women stepped inside the chilly church hall, hearts sinking in tandem at the sight of Cassie Holland with her trusty guitar and basket of maracas, 'shaky eggs' and, of course, the eponymous tambourines.

'Dear God, shoot me now,' whispered Lizzie none too quietly, provoking a flurry of titters from the new mums already seated on the floor in a circle, their various offspring perched on their laps.

'Ladies, ladies, take your seats for baby's welcome song,' said Cassie, her chirpy voice oddly reminiscent of Patronising Patricia. Since when did having a baby mean that women had to be treated like children too, wondered Holly. Even as Cassie's enthusiasm roused the room into a cheerful rendition of 'The Wheels on the Bus', Holly's attention was wandering. Not only because Lizzie was making snarky comments in her ear about the likelihood of any of these well-heeled children ever having to take the bus anywhere – except possibly at the airport – but also because, not so very long ago, the women in this room had been her patients. She could glance around the hall and do a quick visual check of Kerry's rosacea, Victoria's progress with her battle of the bulge and, judging by the animated tambourine-bashing, Lara's chronic migraines were now well under control.

Holly pulled her attention back into the moment, revelling in Olivia's tenacious grasp on her 'shaky egg' and her seemingly instinctual sense of rhythm – something she could only have inherited from her father! Holly breathed in deeply, watching Lottie's face light up with excitement and glee as she bashed on a bongo drum with determined fists, despite Lizzie wincing with each percussive blow.

She was exactly where she was supposed to be right now, she reminded herself, taking pleasure in her daughters' delight at the cacophony.

It was odd how she'd experienced none of this conflict during the first few months, excitedly – if exhaustedly – embracing the role of motherhood and the constant demands of two sets of twins. It was only as they'd found their daily pattern and their sleep had improved that Holly's existential angst had emerged. She was a mother first and foremost, of course, but being a doctor wasn't just a job for her, it was a part of her identity. Without it, she felt as disoriented as if she'd lost her own shadow.

As Cassie took a break between songs to pour forth her traditional breast-is-best-only-organic-for-baby lecture, Holly bit her lip and tried not to smile. Lizzie's impression of this very monologue had the ability to reduce her to tears of laughter after a glass or two of rosé. As mothers cracked open their mini Tupperware and doled out dutifully healthy snacks under Cassie's watchful scrutiny, Holly began to wonder when parenting had become so regulated and restricted. The irony, of course, being that Cassie was the biggest local advocate of free speech and individuality – so long, apparently, as it dovetailed nicely with her own beliefs about child-rearing.

Holly paused, an odd sensation prickling her scalp. Instinctively, she leaned forward to check both Lottie and Olivia, ignoring Lizzie's queer look of concern. It was the faintest whisper of a noise, but Holly's hearing was long honed over the years of medical practice and she knew that her ears weren't deceiving her.

She slid Olivia gently into Lizzie's arms and stood up, holding out a hand as though directing traffic. 'Stop, stop—' she said gently, turning within the circle until her gaze alighted on Mims, the vet's wife, and their darling baby boy, Henry. A hubbub of conversation grew around her bizarre behaviour as Holly dropped to her knees and held out her arms for Mims's baby.

'Hello, darling,' she murmured calmly, clocking the grapes in Mims's Tupperware pot with alarm. Cut in half, the way everyone advised, but not lengthwise and so still a miniature grenade . . . His weak, whistling breaths and the hint of blue to his lips told her everything she needed to know.

In that moment, Holly was oblivious to the people around her, even her girls balanced on Lizzie's lap, and the murmurs of consternation building in the background. She took Henry, slight for his age, and checked inside his mouth, before laying him along her forearm, face down, at an angle, making sure that her fingers supported his neck and chin. Five adept blows between his shoulder blades with the heel of her hand elicited no sound from Henry, only the sharp intake of breath from the women surrounding her.

Holly murmured a running commentary to Mims, as she turned Henry onto his back and placed two fingers in the middle of his breastbone, positioning them carefully in line with his nipples before giving five firm thrusts.

Still nothing. And Holly's heart began to race.

It was all very well being the doctor on site, but emergency measures were always stressful in any scenario, let alone with a full audience and a fleeting suspicion that she might be a little more out of practice than she'd realised. Turning Henry over onto her forearm again, it was the third blow that did the trick – a mangled grape flying from his mouth and the reassuring gasp of air, and then tears, that followed.

From beginning to end, less than a minute.

To Mims, and to Holly, it felt more like a lifetime.

Henry's puce and screaming face was the most welcome sight Holly could possibly imagine.

'Why don't we call it a day here and head over to The Practice? I think a little reassurance that young Henry here is none the worse for his adventures is a good idea, don't you?' Holly said, amazed that her voice could still sound so calm and reassuring, while her heart was pounding and sweat prickled in her hair.

'There's nothing to worry about, but it's definitely time to call it a day,' said Holly calmly, as she helped Mims to her feet and scooped up Lizzie and her girls in less than a minute, leaving Cassie mouthing vaguely at the front of the class.

Leaving the church hall, the low sun was almost blinding, and Holly squinted her eyes to refocus.

'Well,' said Lizzie with feeling. 'Say what you like about a morning with you, Holls, but it's never dull. How did you even hear this little tyke wheezing above all that noise?'

Mims nodded, still mute with shock, as she cradled Henry to her chest. 'I can't believe I didn't—'

Holly shook her head. 'No recriminations, Mims. It happens to all of us, sooner or later. Although grapes are the very devil and I spend more time cutting them in quarters than I care to imagine. Ben choked on a piece of apple, Tom choked on a— now, what was it?'

'Malteser, I think,' said Lizzie matter-of-factly. 'And my Jack has been banned from eating those bastard lollies with the round balls on a stick. The number of frights he's given me . . .'

Mims looked at each of them and then back again in disbelief. 'You mean, it's just something I have to get used to. Choking?' She clung ever tighter to little Henry until he squawked in protest.

Holly nodded. 'I mean, it's not a weekly occurrence or anything, but kids do shove things in their mouths and it does happen more often than you'd think.' She leaned forward and smiled at Henry's pink cheeks and steady breaths.

'Maybe a baby first-aid class wouldn't be the worst idea,' Mims said, her brow still concertinaed in concern. 'I still can't believe I hadn't even noticed there was a problem before you were across that room like a gazelle.'

Lizzie snorted with laughter at the notion of there being anything gazelle-like about Holly these days. 'And don't forget, as another bonus,' Lizzie chimed in, 'you get a guilt-free pass on Tambourine Torment. It's been a win-win situation really.'

Mims nodded, as they followed their feet to The Practice. Even as Mims watched Henry like a hawk, Lizzie leaned in close to Holly. 'Hey, Miss Marple, you did well back there. I hate to think what would have happened if we'd skived off and gone to The Deli instead. It's probably just as well I pissed off Hattie on the radio this morning, or that's exactly what I would have suggested.'

Holly managed a smile; the suggestion had been on the tip of her tongue too. It was only the ever-present guilt trip about socialising her babies that had propelled her into the church hall that morning.

Pushing open the door to The Practice, she was assailed by the sights and sounds of her professional life and she had to confess that she craved it like a drug. Even briefing Alice as she reluctantly handed over care of Henry and Mims in the middle of a heaving morning surgery felt like a primeval wrench.

Their Practice Manager, Grace, gathered Holly into an impromptu hug in reception. 'Aren't you a sight for sore eyes?' she said affectionately. 'No pressure from me, but it's properly lovely to see you.' She dropped her voice. 'We're in danger of letting the lunatics run the asylum if you stay away much longer.' She nodded towards the Staff Photo wall, where Taffy, Dan, Alice and Tilly smiled down benevolently, albeit with the recent addition of moustaches and devil horns. Grace hugged her again. 'But it's good to know you haven't lost your touch. Good save with young Henry.'

Reluctantly saying goodbye, Holly returned to Lizzie and the girls outside. It was only then that she realised: there'd been no hesitation, no need for work-shadowing or retraining that morning. She had been a doctor, pure and simple. A doctor in mum's clothing, to be sure, but nevertheless her instincts had been fast and faultless. She allowed herself to smile.

'Now, how badly did you piss off Hattie, or can we have a celebratory cappuccino at The Deli without threats of violence?'

Lizzie shrugged. 'Let's live a little and take a chance. I only suggested she might like to experiment a little in the bedroom—' She paused. 'And I may have accidentally let slip who she was ...'

Holly shook her head. 'For what it's worth, we were all listening over breakfast and it was a hoot and a half. You've got a real skill for the radio.'

Lizzie clasped her arm in excitement. 'That's what we should do! You've just proven you've still got your head in the game – stuff Patronising Patricia – come on air with me. We can be a duo to contend with and, frankly, I know the producer would leap at the chance – he keeps saying I need more credibility. Madness, right? Apparently raising three children isn't enough experience to advise Janet not to let her hamsters sleep in her children's beds!

'But still, Holly – come on … You know you want to. I can be the Agony Aunt and you can be the Doc of the Airwaves!' Lizzie's voice had risen in excitement with each suggestive sentence. 'Seriously. Let's do this.'

'Well …' hedged Holly.

Lizzie fixed her with a look and adopted her best radio announcer intonation. 'Dr Holly Graham – Radio Larkford needs you …'

'Well, it is always nice to be needed,' laughed Holly. 'But seriously, what on earth could I possibly talk about?'

'Come and talk about the hazards of choking on a grape, talk about toddler biting, or immunisations, or whatever the hell you like – it's never stopped me. Say yes!'

Holly paused and then slowly nodded; there was more than one way to be a doctor, it seemed. Might this actually be enough to placate the clamouring medic inside her?

'Woohoo!' cried Lizzie, making Holly jump and the twins clap in excitement. 'Big morning all round!'

Holly paused, her mouth a perfect O. 'Lottie clapped! That was the first time! Did you see that? She clapped! Oh you clever, clever girl.'

Lizzie fidgeted uncomfortably for a moment. 'Probably not the best time to tell you that she did it in class this morning too. While you were holding Henry, she watched Olivia do it and then just copied. It was terribly sweet actually . . .'

Holly felt the glow of accomplishment from her morning's efforts quickly extinguish, to be replaced by a thud of guilt. She'd missed it. Another milestone in her babies' lives and she'd missed it. And if it felt like this now, how on earth would she cope if they decided to take their first steps while she was at work, or their first words while she was covering the evening shift?

Maybe frightful Patricia had a point and there was more to be figured out about going back to work than she'd realised?

Chapter 3

Alice pulled the door closed behind her and allowed herself a smile; it had been so lovely just now to be back talking medicine with Holly, however fleetingly. And thank God she'd been so on the ball about little Henry Hallow; sometimes a matter of moments could make all the difference with an airway obstruction, especially in one so young.

Right now though, she had her own patient to concentrate on and this conversation wasn't going to be easy.

'Lady Peal. Thank you so much for coming back in,' said Alice, as she ushered the formidable, yet delicate dowager into her consulting room. The way Coco sat instantly beside her and laid one paw on her thigh yet again confirmed what the hastily drawn blood tests had already confirmed; there was something seriously amiss with Lady Peal's immune system.

'All this fuss just to get some decent travel insurance,' said Agatha with a nervous laugh. 'Although I can't fault the NHS – I've seen you more of late than my own children, Dr Walker.'

'How are things at home?' asked Alice tentatively. Since the passing of Lord Peal a few months previously, she knew only too well the frustrations and grief that had been dogging one of her favourite patients. Wandering alone through the echoing halls of Peal Hall – or The Big House, as it was affectionately known locally – couldn't be easy, and knowing that neither of her high-flying, career-driven children were keen to return couldn't help.

Agatha Peal shrugged, a world of eloquence in her tweed-clad shoulders. 'Well, I must admit everything's a little easier now everyone's stopped tiptoeing around me. It's hardly as though the old bugger's passing was a surprise to anyone.'

'Still,' said Alice, a little blindsided by her matter-of-fact approach. 'Bereavements, not to mention funerals, can be stressful—'

Agatha shook her head. 'We had plenty of notice, Dr Walker. I suppose it makes me sound callous, but Mary and I had stocked that freezer with enough vol-au-vents and sausage rolls to feed his entire regiment, although he was an absolute pest for trying to eat them before we could get them frozen,' she said fondly. 'Old sod.'

'Right,' said Alice, trying to recalibrate; the older Larkford residents really were cut from a different cloth. 'And your children?'

'Well,' continued Agatha, 'I'm more convinced than ever that there's very little point in me spending my dotage keeping the home fires burning, if my little darlings have absolutely no intention of actually coming home.'

Alice nodded sympathetically, all too familiar with the burden of family expectation and the pressure of the looming line of inheritance. 'Maybe they'll change their minds when they see Larkford in all her Christmas finery?' she suggested. 'Perhaps they might like The Big House as a weekend retreat from the city?'

Aggie snorted unappreciatively. 'The Big House is no weekender, Dr Walker. She's a lifetime's commitment. Frankly, if they can't step up, I've half a mind to sell her to the highest bidder – no need for a fortnight in Florence if I can move there indefinitely, is there?'

Alice faltered; Aggie's plans for emigration would clearly be under threat by the news she was about to impart. 'Well, let's get you hale and hearty before you make a break for the Uffizi, shall we? How's the tiredness been?'

'I would suggest that tiredness would be somewhat of an understatement. I just can't seem to rally. I know they said grief was exhausting, Dr Walker, but I can't help thinking it's disproportionate to how much grieving I've actually been doing.' She looked up at Alice and her hands clenched repeatedly around her long strand of pearls. 'I rather think there might be something else going on.'

'I agree,' said Alice quietly. 'In fact, I'd like to refer you over to one of my colleagues at the hospital in Bath. In the absence of any obvious symptoms to point us in the right direction, I think a scan might be in order. Your tiredness and the weight loss, we could obviously put down to what's been going on in your life, but your blood tests do suggest there is, as you rightly suggest, something else going on.'

Aggie looked down at Coco, still sitting vigilantly at her side, her specialist skillset no secret, and the gentle but considered demeanour of her doctor. 'So, it's cancer then, I suppose.'

'Let's not make any assumptions, before you've seen Mr Choudari. He really is the most wonderful consultant and I know you'll like him. Let's get the ball rolling at least. The sooner we know what's what, the sooner we can have you sipping Campari in Florence. How does that sound?'

'It sounds as though I should have sold the house and buggered off years ago—' began Agatha, her voice quavering slightly before her stiff upper lip was able to reassert itself. 'You're not in the market for a very beautiful, rather crumbly

but historically important money pit, are you, Dr Walker?'
she said, as she left the room on shaky legs.

'Let's keep in touch,' suggested Alice, as she held open
the door to reception and wished, as always, that there was
something more she could do.

'Was that Aggie Peal?' asked Dan, emerging from his
consulting room and joining Alice as she headed to the doctors' lounge for a much-needed caffeine infusion. He was,
of course, the only one who dared call Lady Peal that – all
the other doctors being too intimidated by her status even
to attempt familiarity. Dan, on the other hand, wasn't fazed.

Alice nodded. 'Not great news, I'm afraid. Coco seems to
have a hundred per cent track record at this point.'

'Bugger,' said Dan succinctly. 'And you can bet your last
tenner that her spoiled kids won't be coming back to hold
her hand.'

They pushed open the door to the lounge only to find
Taffy guiltily necking a triple espresso. 'Don't tell Holly,' he
said by way of greeting.

'Oh the power . . .' grinned Dan. 'Now, dance my puppet,
dance!'

Taffy just shook his head in bemusement. 'Blackmail's
hardly your strong suit now, is it? What are you two whispering about, anyway?'

Alice shrugged. 'Looks like The Big House might be on
the market if you know anyone with a few spare million to
fling around?'

'Is that what it's worth?' Taffy asked, clearly out of step
with local property prices.

'Three point four, I reckon,' replied Dan, who had made
something of a habit of devouring every single property paper
since he and Grace had decided to shop for a doer-upper

together. Sadly, even the most neglected of townhouses in their chosen area seemed to be completely out of their price bracket. It was lovely that Larkford was on the up, quietly recognised by those in the know as one of the most aspirational market towns in the Cotswolds, but it did also mean that their community was in danger of succumbing to a nasty outbreak of weekenderitis – houses standing empty all week, only to be overrun by retreating Londoners every weekend. Even boosting local tourist appeal was in jeopardy, as picture-perfect cottages were snapped up as second homes, rather than holiday cottages.

'Listen, while it's just us,' said Taffy, blushing wildly at whatever he was about to say and looking around, 'I really think somebody should have a word with Tilly. It's just that, well, there seems to be a trail of lovelorn young men propping up the bar at The Kingsley Arms every weekend—'

'Oh, let the girl have her fun,' interrupted Grace, walking in mid-conversation. 'If she was a bloke, you wouldn't be having these worries, now would you?'

Taffy shrugged. 'I might, actually. It really is getting a little out of hand. I mean, I know we all thought it might take her a while to settle back into a normal routine after all her far-flung doctoring, but it's been months and she's still behaving like a sailor on shore leave. People are talking.'

'So let them talk. She's a big girl and she can make her own decisions. It's not as though it's affecting her work, now is it?' Grace said firmly.

Dan and Taffy looked at each other. 'I suppose.'

Alice sipped her coffee thoughtfully. 'You don't think that maybe it just means she doesn't see Larkford as a permanent position? I mean, if you're just passing through, you might care less what people think, right?'

Dan nodded. 'Makes sense. And we should probably talk about that too. We have no idea how long we need her for, do we?' He turned to look at Taffy. 'We all want Holly to take as long as she needs. I'm certainly not going to be the one who pressures her back to work—'

'Even if we do seriously need her steadying hand on the tiller,' finished Grace wistfully.

Alice looked from one to the other in confusion. 'But she *is* ready to come back. It's obvious she's missing her working life. She even turned up here with an emergency patient from the Toddler Tambourine class!'

Taffy shook his head. 'Well, that's Holly for you. Even when she's off duty, she can't help looking out for her patients. We all know she's an amazing doctor, but right now she's allowed to just be a mum.'

'But have you actually asked her, I mean, properly talked about it?' Alice persisted, realising she was slightly overstepping the mark as she did so.

Taffy sighed huffily. 'I think I'd know, don't you, Alice? She's just had twins. It's hard to even begin explaining what that's like. She's going to need more time at home with them and they *have* to be the priority. Let's not put any pressure on her. Please.'

Alice frowned, unused to Taffy being anything other than open-minded, and certainly caught unawares by his (to her ears) slightly condescending explanation. From where she was standing – childfree obviously – Holly was showing every sign of wanting to come back to work. In fact, she'd seemed almost upset to be handing over Henry's care earlier. Alice sighed; if Holly could see the almighty juggle that was going on in her absence, she reckoned it would seal the deal. Sure, they had four doctors, two of them female, but she was the first to admit that neither she nor Tilly had Holly's experience, intuition or rapport with the mothers of Larkford.

And she had to think that a conversation between the partners was long overdue. Obviously Tilly had no idea whether she was coming or going – it was hardly the optimum scenario for her to put down roots.

'If Tilly thought she was staying longer, do you think she'd go out with Teddy at the pub? His crush on her is almost painful and it has to be killing him seeing her go home with a different bloke every Friday night,' Taffy said, his compulsion to couple up all of his mates growing ever stronger since he got married himself.

'I'm not sure you can base our entire business plan on getting Teddy the girlfriend of his dreams, Taffs. He might have to step up and actually ask her out—' Dan began.

'Oh God no,' interrupted Alice. 'If he really wants to stand a chance with Tilly, he needs to be as unavailable as possible. I'm not saying it's logical, it's just *really* effective.'

There was a flurry of activity and conversation about coffee as Tilly made her way into the room, texting at warp speed as she walked and somehow avoiding colliding with every obstacle in her path. 'Hi,' she mumbled, as she clicked refresh on her Twitter feed and pored over the latest news headlines. Tilly's world on Twitter was so tightly curated as to give her an extremely focused view of current affairs, Alice had recently decided. She would have no clue of any events in the local vicinity, or indeed on TV and radio, but she could tell you exactly how many children were being affected by the famine in Somalia, or the bombings in Aleppo, or indeed under the purview of social services in the UK. 'What's new?' she asked, yawning widely after another night on the tiles – a Sunday night at that.

'We were just wondering who was up for staffing Big Bertha at the Sixth Form Health Day?' Taffy blurted. Their Health in the Community initiative had gone from strength to strength and the addition of Big Bertha, their big yellow bus that housed a mobile health unit, had become their crowning glory.

'Yup, I'll do it,' said Tilly easily, tucking her mane of blonde hair behind one ear and ripping open a bag of what might have been parrot food. 'Anyone want some Chia seeds?'

Grace made wide insistent eyes at Dan across the room that Alice struggled to understand.

'Oh, you're sweet for volunteering, Tilly, but the boys need to take their turn with Bertha too – no fobbing it off all the time,' Grace said eventually, her visual semaphore missing its mark entirely.

Tilly smiled. 'I don't mind. The students are lovely. And the headmaster said I was a big hit with the sixth-formers last time I went in, so . . .'

Dan's gaze flickered between Tilly's microscopic skirt, endless forty-denier legs and Grace's face until slowly the penny dropped. 'I'm sure you were,' he said with feeling, 'but Grace is right. Some of those sixth form lads don't have much by way of a male role model, so Taffy and I need to take a turn at the helm as well.'

'Okay,' she said easily. She popped her empty wrapper in the bin. 'I mean, you wouldn't want me flirting with the underage lads as well as a different bloke every Friday night.' She gave a little wave as she left the room, leaving them in no doubt that she had overheard every word of their earlier conversation.

'Well, that went well,' said Alice drily.

Dan and Taffy looked at each other and blushed. 'Are you

going to make us take the Tactfulness in the Workplace sem-
inar again, Gracie?' asked Taffy ruefully.

'Well, it wouldn't be the worst idea, now would it?'
answered Grace, looking just as uncomfortable for her part in
the proceedings. 'I mean, it's hardly any wonder the girl can't
settle down if she still feels like she's under scrutiny all the time.'

Alice couldn't help thinking Grace had made a valid
point. The issue from her perspective was somewhat thorn-
ier: professionally she couldn't wait for Holly to return, she
missed her guidance and her company, but personally, there
was also the risk that Holly's return would mean that Tilly's
time in Larkford might be over and Alice wasn't yet ready
to relinquish her best friend to the jungles of South America
again, especially with Jamie still gadding about in the wilds
of Donegal.

Not for the first time, she wondered whether it had been
some kind of madness to put their fledgling relationship to
the test like this. A nine-month placement ought to be man-
ageable, shouldn't it? But then, why did she miss Jamie quite
so very much, or become so easily perturbed by thoughts of
him meeting new people, new clients, new friends . . . After
all, hadn't she been one of his clients when they met?

She turned and emptied a packet of Jammie Dodgers onto
a plate – little point searching for a biscuit tin, the whole
lot would be scavenged in moments – before deciding that
pushing the agenda for Holly might have to take a back
seat for a while. After all, Holly had her husband on staff to
communicate her wishes, didn't she? Who did Tilly have on
her 'team', except Alice? And possibly, right now, vice versa.

'Got any new pictures of the babies, Taffs?' Alice asked,
in a sure-fire manoeuvre to change the subject, for her own
benefit as much as Tilly's.

Chapter 4

'I can't believe you get to be on the radio!' said Elsie the next morning. 'Did you not tell your Lizzie that *I* was available?'

Holly smiled. 'I imagine she thought Radio Larkford might be a bit of a comedown from what you're used to.' She had a point; far from being the hi-tech studio of the local BBC, or indeed Media City where Elsie had last been interviewed, Radio Larkford occupied a nondescript office suite above the fishmonger's. Quite regularly, the echoing shouts of the boys downstairs for 'another bag of scallops, Bill' could be heard in the background, not to mention the pervasive smell that seemed to cloak Lizzie whenever she'd been on air. Holly wasn't quite sure why she hadn't mentioned this morning's plans to Taffy earlier – perhaps it was because, secretly, she wondered whether he'd consider being a radio phone-in doctor a bit of a comedown too?

'Do I look okay?' asked Holly nervously, doing a twirl for Elsie's benefit. 'I don't want to wear anything too nice or it'll end up stinking of halibut.'

Elsie snorted. 'Does my halibut look big in this?' she laughed. 'Nah, you look fine – besides, my darling, this is radio, remember? You could turn up in your pyjamas and nobody would notice.'

Holly grinned and rolled her eyes. 'Well, if you'd told me that an hour ago ...' She turned and settled Olivia and Lottie into the pram, holding her breath as the inevitable tantrum failed to materialise. 'Wow,' she whispered under her breath, unwilling to jinx whatever magic was making her morning run so smoothly. 'And are you sure you want to come and watch?'

'I wouldn't miss your radio debut for toffee,' confirmed Elsie. 'The girls and I will hang out in the Green Room with some refreshments and be your entourage for the day. You should always have an entourage, darling.'

'I always do,' said Holly, managing a wry smile; the days when she could scoop up her handbag and keys and follow her feet were long gone.

'And now, we have a very exciting addition to our line-up this morning,' crooned Lizzie into her microphone an hour later, as Holly fidgeted nervously beside her, sipping water from a plastic cup. 'Dr Holly Graham is joining the show to offer some words of wisdom on the medical front – so if you call in today, you can have two opinions for the price of one. Good morning, Dr Graham. Thanks for joining us.'

'It's lovely to be here,' Holly said, holding herself stiff and trying not to let her voice wobble. She glanced up to see Elsie watching her through the glazed partition and swallowed her laughter at the hastily handwritten sign she was holding up: *Just remember not to bloody well swear, when you're talking live on the bloody air.* She felt her shoulders drop and a smile spread across her face and into her words. 'I'm delighted to have the opportunity to connect with our Larkford listeners.'

Lizzie nodded her approval and flicked a switch on the

complicated-looking control panel in front of her. 'Well, if you want to talk to Dr Graham or myself – Lizzie, your Agony Aunt – then get dialling and in the meantime, let's start as we mean to go on. Here's Robert Palmer with a "Bad Case of Loving You".' She faded in the song and sat back in the swivel chair with a grin on her face as Mr Palmer called repeatedly for the doctor. She held up her hands. 'See? Easy peasy. And if that light's showing, we're off air and can talk privately, okay? I've got a whole doctor motif running in my play list this morning.' Her face puckered for a moment and she went a slightly sickly colour.

'The fish smell getting to you too?' asked Holly, who had been breathing through her mouth for the last five minutes.

Lizzie shook her head. 'I don't think so. It's just something I ate; it's the last time I'm being adventurous with the curry menu. I was so sick last night and I've still got awful tummy ache.' She winced again, waving away Holly's concern. 'Bloody Will and his competitive spiciness.'

'And here's hoping Mr Palmer makes a speedy recovery,' Lizzie said, back on air, in her upbeat-radio-DJ voice that made Holly want to giggle despite her concern. 'Let's take our first caller, shall we, Dr Graham? Hello, caller, you're on the air.'

'Hi,' said the caller, her voice tentative and quiet. 'I wanted to ask about restless legs? I'm finding it really hard to sleep at night and I keep kicking my husband.' She sighed. 'We're both exhausted and grumpy and to be honest it's causing a few marital issues. I wondered what you'd recommend?'

Before Holly could even formulate a response, Lizzie had dived right in. 'Well, it seems to me, caller, that we might be looking at this from the wrong angle. Which came first, the chicken or the egg? I mean, if there are unresolved tensions in your marriage, might the kicking actually be your subconscious way of expressing your frustrations?'

'Oh,' breathed the caller, utterly winded by the suggestion. 'Well, I didn't *think* we were unhappy. We've been together so long, you see, and barely a cross word. But we do both love our sleep, so I put the recent problems down to that.' She sounded really concerned now. 'Maybe I was just kidding myself?'

Lizzie nodded. 'It's always easier to be objective from the outside looking in.'

'If I could just ask,' Holly interrupted, unable to sit idly by while this poor woman's apparently happy marriage was taken apart on live radio, 'have there been any other changes in your life of late? Moving house, hormonal milestones?'

'Not really,' replied the caller. 'I'm too young to be menopausal, if that's what you're suggesting.' She sounded a little peeved actually and Holly rallied quickly.

'What about dietary changes?' she offered.

'Oh, well, yes. I suppose. I became a vegetarian about six months ago. I couldn't stomach the idea of food–with–a–face anymore.'

Holly watched the colour leach from Lizzie's already pale and clammy face with concern. 'Are you okay?' she mouthed silently.

Lizzie nodded, waving her hand at Holly's microphone to continue.

'The reason I ask, caller,' said Holly, completely relaxed into her zone now, nerves eclipsed by the distraction of Lizzie looking increasingly awful, 'is that iron deficiencies can be one of the triggers for restless legs at night and, if you're not making sure to get enough iron from your new meat-free diet, it may be a contributory factor.'

'You mean, me giving up steak might have caused this?' the caller clarified in bewilderment.

'Well, obviously, it's hard to say exactly without meeting you, but it would seem like a promising place to start, before you begin looking for problems in your marriage that might not even be there. Have you been feeling guilty about this, by any chance?'

'Yes!' exclaimed the caller. 'So weirdly guilty about all sorts of things actually.'

'Okay, so when you go to the doctor's, it might be worth asking them to check your Vitamin B12 levels, as well as your iron. Guilt is a recognised symptom of B12 deficiency and can often go hand in hand with anaemia. In fact, to everyone listening, it's worth remembering that your body's engine can only run efficiently if you give it the fuel it needs – a balanced diet, plenty of fruit, veg and protein and don't forget to drink some water.'

'Good advice in theory there, Dr Graham,' said Lizzie. 'And maybe we should have a call-in one day about how to eat well in practice?'

Holly grinned. 'Good idea. But my general advice still stands – give yourself a good foundation and then a little of what you fancy does you good.'

'There you have it, folks, your doctor agrees that a glass of wine and a bar of chocolate may actually be good for you.'

Holly laughed. 'Well, dark chocolate *is* an excellent source of iron—'

'And now it's time for the news and traffic from our partners at Bath Radio,' Lizzie said, clearly using up the last of a very deep breath. She flicked the switch and the 'off air' light pinged on. 'We've got five minutes now if you need a wee. You're doing great, by the way.'

'But you're not feeling so good, are you?' Holly said. 'Come and get a breath of fresh air. I need to look in on the twins anyway.' She stood up and held out a hand, wondering how anyone could spend hours each day in this sweaty, stinky little cubicle.

To Holly's absolute amazement, the twins were happily sitting in their pram, legs swinging contentedly and gurgly noises a-go-go. 'Wow, check you out, Elsie – you must be the baby whisperer.'

'Oh, I just pop a splash of gin in their bottles; it keeps them ever so good,' laughed Elsie wickedly, clearly enjoying the flash of alarm on Holly's face. 'Oh calm down, it's just the water from your baby bag. It is very hot up here and I thought they might get dehydrated. But they seem to enjoy hearing your voice on the radio. I have to say, darling, you do seem to be a natural.'

'You might need to be, today,' said Lizzie with another grimace, bending forward from the waist and clutching her stomach. 'I do not feel good. Bloody super fancy phaal curry – I'll kill Will when I get home. Do I care if it's all the rage, do I heck?' She winced again and checked her watch. 'We should really get back in there. If I keep pressing buttons and doing the links, can you keep talking?'

'Sure, no problem,' said Holly, looking to Elsie for support. 'But if you feel this bad, maybe we should cancel the show?'

Lizzie shook her head and the very action made her sweat. 'Can't have dead air, Holls. Not on my watch.'

By the time they'd taken several more calls, Holly was beginning to wonder whether all was entirely well with Lizzie's marriage. So far she had managed to persuade an older gentleman that his wife's sudden interest in tennis meant she was having an affair, a teenager just starting at university that long-distance relationships were doomed to failure – she crossed her fingers that Alice wasn't listening – and even a nervous young bride that she could relax, safe in the reassurance of knowing that a first marriage was just a good place to learn the ropes.

'Hey, Lizzie,' Holly said as they switched through to the travel update again, 'what's with you this morning? Are you and Will having a fight?'

Lizzie swallowed another wave of nausea, pressing her hand to her side. 'He's just being a stubborn old goat, that's all. He reckons I'm spending too much time with Connor.'

Holly sighed; she could actually understand Will's perspective on this one. Connor Danes, although recently widowed, still carried the panache and good looks of the world-class rock star that he was. Despite being old friends with Will, it was Lizzie he had been turning to over the last year as he attempted to rebuild his life, Lizzie he spent hours talking to over a bottle of wine in the afternoon, Lizzie who had become his confidante. Now, he was on a mission to move to Larkford permanently and Lizzie was skittering around the countryside looking at fancy houses with him. It was all totally innocent. Apparently. But still . . .

'Can you believe he was furious that I went house-hunting with Connor? Just because the newspaper caught a picture and ran some dodgy headline about Connor's "mystery blonde" doesn't mean Will has anything to worry about, does it?' Lizzie said angrily, her face increasingly bearing a sheen of perspiration from each wave of pain. Pain that, to Holly's eye, seemed to be growing in intensity.

Lizzie shook her head and flicked the switch. 'And now we're back with Dr Holly Graham to answer your questions, but first, a little Aqua with "Doctor Jones".'

The moment Lizzie hit play, her face crumpled. 'Jesus,

Holly, this isn't right. It hurts like hell.' Within moments she had comprehensively hurled into the waste bin, as she clutched her abdomen.

Holly yanked off her headphones and was around the desk in moments, laying Lizzie down on its surface and gently palpating her stomach. 'On a scale of one to ten, how bad are we talking here?'

'Ten!' screamed Lizzie, as Holly evidently zeroed in on the problem. 'It's been so much worse since I had those antacids,' she groaned. 'Even the hot-water bottle didn't help.'

Holly looked up as Elsie banged on the window, some kind of Morse code that completely eluded her. Well, Elsie was a parent herself, albeit long out of practice; she could certainly deal with the twins for a moment while Holly got Lizzie the help she needed.

'Okay, Lizzie. So I'm going to call you an ambulance. I think you have acute appendicitis, actually. And there's a chance that those antacids may have tipped inflammation over into a possible rupture. So keep still, keep breathing and we'll get you to the hospital.'

She rested a hand on Lizzie's forehead and was shocked to feel the burning temperature of her skin, even as she dialled 999 and conveyed the necessary information.

'You're going to be fine,' she reassured her friend, as the next song looped on to play in the studio. 'A little op and a few weeks taking it easy.'

'Last time I eat spicy curry,' Lizzie groaned.

Holly managed a smile. 'It won't be the curry. It's more likely all those apple cores you insist on eating.'

'Waste not, want not,' breathed Lizzie, aiming for humour but sounding a little delirious.

Holly checked her watch; the ambulance should be due any

moment. Elsie hammered on the window again and Holly pulled open the studio door. 'I'm going to have to get Lizzie to hospital. I think her appendix may have burst.'

'I know,' said Elsie, 'and so does the whole of Larkford!' She pointed towards the 'on air' light; the music may have been playing, but their mics had been live the whole time. 'The switchboard's lit up like Christmas. What do you want me to do?'

A banging door downstairs followed by running feet preceded the arrival of the paramedics.

'No dead air,' called Lizzie from her supine position on the desk. 'Not on my watch.'

'Right,' said Holly. 'Elsie, you're up. Can you handle the show for the last hour?'

'Handle it?' said Elsie with aplomb. 'I have every intention of rocking the airwaves.'

It was some testament to how bad Lizzie was feeling that she didn't even blink at the suggestion, or attempt to flirt with the dishy paramedics. Even as she was bundled into the ambulance, with Holly wielding the twins in their pram and promising to meet her at the hospital, all Lizzie could keep muttering about was finding the perfect house for Connor. It gave Holly a small insight into Lizzie's subconscious and, for the first time, she conceded that Will might have every good reason to be worried.

Chapter 5

'Seven children is definitely too many!' exclaimed Holly the next morning. Tired, dishevelled, but ultimately relieved, she had spent the night in a state of anxious unrest waiting for the phone call from Will to confirm that Lizzie's surgery had gone well. Having Lizzie's three worried children to stay had been the obvious solution, as Will had rushed to his wife's bedside. Thank God they'd got her into surgery before the ruptured appendix could lead to peritonitis. It had been all Holly could think about all night long – she knew too much, perhaps, about what could go wrong.

At least now they'd spoken to Will on the phone, Archie, Jack and Lily seemed a little more at ease as well – happy to go to school and continue their day as normal. Getting everyone fed and dressed on time had been a different story.

Elsie laughed. 'Well, only four of them are keepers ...' She lined up five juice boxes, five morning snacks and five packed lunches, rallying in a crisis as always, and Holly made sure everyone was wearing the right uniform and had their trusty book bags packed. She couldn't be more grateful to Elsie for ditching the Dinner Dance at Sarandon Hall to stay the night with her and lend another pair of hands, as Taffy, seemingly piqued about her radio heroics, had made himself scarce yet again: the 'mental load' of running this household increasingly falling on Holly's shoulders, since she 'wasn't working'. Still, there was no time to be riled about that now; there were too many children to be considered.

The hustle to the school gate was farcical in the extreme, as Holly shepherded her own expanded crocodile through the streets of Larkford, Eric weaving between her legs and one strap of her dungarees continually making a break for freedom. 'Okay,' she said, crouching down in the playground. 'Has everybody got everything?'

'Do I need my sports kit if I've got gym first lesson today?' Lily suddenly wondered, wide-eyed and innocent. Holly didn't have the heart to remind her that she'd asked them all, repeatedly, at home about their kit requirements. Tears slowly welled in the corners of Lily's eyes. 'I don't want to get a detention!' she began to wail.

Holly looked around helplessly, wondering if there was time to nip home and get what she needed. 'You won't get a detention, darling, I promise,' she said rashly, distractedly waving off Jack and Archie who dived into the football-hive in the playground with barely a backwards glance. 'I'll pop back and get your kit, okay, Lily?' Ben and Tom hovered beside her in their duffel coats, rather unaccustomed to such a chaotic school drop-off and awaiting their hugs.

Naturally Lottie and Olivia chose that exact moment to kick off, Ben and Tom jostling for Holly's attention as she crouched down beside the pram to settle them and Lily worked herself up into a snot-bubbling state of drama.

'It's tooooo laaaaaate . . .' she sobbed. 'You won't get back in time!'

It wasn't exactly how Holly had foreseen speaking to the new headmaster at Larkford Primary for the first time, but then nothing about this morning was going the way she'd planned. Deprived of sleep, worried about Lizzie, and doing her best to be upbeat and chirpy for the kids had clearly taken its toll and she was now being singled out for pastoral care!

'Can I help?' came Alec French's deep gravelly voice, as he too crouched down beside their little huddle, his well-worn brogues and soft dark moleskin trousers Holly's first proper introduction to the man himself. She looked up from settling Olivia and stalled, her decaffeinated brain no match for his piercing blue eyes. His heavy tortoiseshell glasses seemed to be the only thing stopping his fringe from tumbling into his eyes completely and, as he offered her his hand – partly by way of greeting, partly as they both made to stand up at the same time – Holly found it hard to align everything she'd heard about their new headmaster with the man standing here before her.

'Everything okay?' he continued. 'I got an email from Mr Parsons updating me on the situation, so I thought I'd pop out and offer my support. Tricky times all round.' He bent low and rested a hand on Lily's shoulder. 'Don't cry, munchkin, I have special plans for you today. How would you like to be my special assistant – are you any good at blowing a whistle, I wonder? And I need a little help setting up an obstacle course, for gym class.'

Lily's tears dried instantly, to be replaced by an almost visible hero worship. No wonder Ben and Tom had been so much happier at school lately, with this switched-on and empathetic head at the helm. It was a far cry from the ramshackle situation last year under the old regime. In fact, listening to him chatting easily with the children about what books they could recommend to him, Holly realised that the only way he could be a more perfect head teacher in her eyes was if he'd been a woman.

Almost as though he was reading her mind, Alec French left the three children chatting about Paddington Bear and turned to hold Holly's gaze, intrigue and interest in his eyes. Well, maybe not a woman, exactly, Holly reconsidered. From where she was standing, he was doing a pretty good job just being a bloke.

'I have to say, it's lovely to meet you in person at last, Dr Graham,' he said with a smile. 'Your boys have certainly been keeping me on my toes. It's actually a delight to have two such enquiring minds in our little school.'

Holly smiled. 'Well, I hope you still feel that way by the end of term,' she joked, knowing only too well how many questions her twins could cram into a day and hoping that Alec French's patience was as long as his eyelashes. She blushed furiously at the very thought. 'Well, I must get going. Are you sure it's okay that Lily doesn't have her sports kit?'

He nodded, his gentle empathy warming his expression. 'I think you've got your hands full enough for one day, don't you? Send Mrs Parsons our love won't you, Dr Graham?'

'Of course,' she said. 'And please, do call me Holly.'

'Holly,' he said, almost experimentally.

She flustered a little when he made no reciprocal offer, before he leaned in a fraction and dropped his voice. 'I have to be Mr French at school; I hope you understand. Otherwise, I'm Alec.'

Holly was still slightly thrown off her game by the time the school bell had rung and the tide of children and teachers had surged into the old stone school-house. Standing in the playground, suddenly adrift, Holly shook her head to clear her thoughts. Surely she was imagining it? With her hair hurriedly stuffed into a bun, a chunky roll-neck older than the twins and her ancient dungarees hardly making an erotic ensemble, she was not exactly the most alluring of mummies on the school run, but she was quietly convinced he'd been flirting with her. Maybe he had a thing about *The Good Life* and her Felicity Kendall look was actually ticking his boxes?

'Oh, Mr French,' she murmured as she pushed the pram out towards the Market Place. 'Perhaps we should put *you* in detention?'

'Are you talking to yourself, there, Holls?' called Alice cheerfully, striding across towards her, with Coco trotting neatly at her heels and a coffee in her hand, neat bob swinging with every step.

Holly glanced down at her own hurried attire, noticing for the first time the dribble of raspberry jam on her top and sighed. It was one thing to know you were dropping the ball, it was something else entirely to be spotted doing it.

'Morning,' she said, gratefully accepting Alice's heartfelt hug. 'You're looking super bouncy this morning.'

Alice grinned. 'Well, Jamie Skyped first thing and woke me up, so I had time for a run. Perked me right up – you should join me sometime? You were talking about getting back into it, weren't you?' Her heart was in the right place, bless her, thought Holly generously, but it was also obvious she had no idea of the metaphorical marathon that Holly had already run this morning, just to get to this point.

'I see you've met the dishy Mr French?' Alice continued. 'He's perking up the mummies of Larkford a treat.' She looked around as though imparting state secrets. 'You wouldn't believe how many have signed up for the "Fit Over Forty" programme since he arrived.'

'Whatever it takes, I guess,' Holly said, mortified that only seconds after meeting Alec French, she too had been considering the Pilates class in question.

'I've got to dash,' Alice said, apologetically checking her watch. 'I've poor Lady Peal coming in early for a chat.' She sighed, clearly wanting to share but professionalism holding her back. Holly may still be a doctor by name, but until she was back on the roster, it still felt like a breach of confidentiality. 'I don't suppose you know someone with money to burn and a fondness for Georgian architecture, do you? It looks like The Big House might be looking for a buyer.'

Holly shook her head. 'It's a little rich for my pockets. Gorgeous house, though – I have to confess I thought that one would stay in the family for ever.'

'I guess you never know, right?' shrugged Alice. 'You heading back home for a lovely coffee?' she asked, having clearly bought into Taffy's beliefs about how Holly spent her day.

'Something like that,' Holly managed with a smile, unwilling – or possibly unable – to burst Alice's bubble about her idyllic 'time off'.

'All right for some!' Alice laughed as she bounded across the Market Place, Holly's heart sinking further with every tap of her three-inch heels.

Holly took a breath and determinedly turned the pram away from home, away from the lure of the biscuit tin and the six loads of washing demanding her attention, and along the lane to Blackleigh Farm. She told herself, as she hummed to the girls in the pram, that they were stretching their legs, enjoying the somewhat bracing fresh air, getting a little exercise. But even in her head it sounded unconvincing.

Ever since Charlotte Lansing and Jessica Hearst had been so badly injured in the incident at the Larkford Show, Holly had taken it upon herself to keep a casual eye on them. In her opinion, the mental scars took much longer to heal than the physical ones and she'd been rather moved to find that Charlotte and Jessica had struck up an unusual friendship, the decades between them no barrier, along with the Major – no bitterness or blame for his decision to hire the little biplane that had caused so much pain and drama in their lives.

A little stroll up to Blackleigh Farm every now and again could easily be classed as exercise, should anyone look closely enough to ask. And Holly had to admit that the riot of red and gold leaves celebrating their last hurrah was incentive enough to get walking; the drifts of colour already forming by the roadside blanketed Holly's path and brightened her morning with each crisp, satisfying step. Was there anywhere finer to be on an autumn morning than here in the Larkford valley? She thought of Alice at her desk, with a patient beside her, and pushed the mental image away – she had never felt so conflicted.

'Helloooo!' Holly called, as she pushed the pram up into the stable yard at Blackleigh Farm twenty minutes later and wildly out of puff. The slope up out of town caught her una-wares every single time, but the view along the way made the effort worthwhile.

'In the kitchen!' called Charlotte, well used to Holly's impromptu visits by now.

What Holly still struggled to adjust to, however, was the row of empty stables – no horses looking out and whickering in greeting, no longer the sound of metal-shod hooves on the lane. Selling her eventers had been a heart-wrenching decision for Charlotte, but after narrowly avoiding losing her arm, she'd quickly found that, while she'd saved the limb,

she'd comprehensively lost her nerve and couldn't be persuaded to do more than amble around on her retired hunters.

Swinging the pram around to the French windows so the
girls could slumber on peacefully in the fresh air, tucking
them in tightly under their blankets, Holly wandered into the
kitchen and stopped dead in her tracks. Charlotte, the Major
and young Jess were all sitting cross-legged on the flagstone
floor, looking up at her expectantly.

'Err—' managed Holly in confusion. 'I think you had the
tumble dryer too hot. You seem to have shrunk your horse.'
She looked at each of their beaming faces again in turn and
then returned her attention to the beautiful, perfectly-formed
miniature horse in Charlotte's kitchen. Eric froze in the
doorway, his face a picture of confusion, tail clamped down
with uncertainty.

'He's called Banana,' said Jess happily. 'Because he's a
palomino.'

'Okay,' said Holly, still completely lost for words, as she
tentatively held out a hand and Banana trotted over to
say hello, his velvet muzzle snuffling into the palm of her
hand, and his withers barely reaching mid-thigh. 'He is just
adorable.'

'Clever too,' said Charlotte with a smile, pulling herself
up and putting the kettle on. 'What do you think? Will the
stable yard sound like home again when I've a stud full of
these little beauties?'

Holly couldn't help the spontaneous smile that lit up her
face. 'Are you serious? A pony stud?'

Charlotte nodded, glancing over at the Major. 'We've
decided to go into business together. They're all the rage
among people who love horses, used to ride maybe, but life
has kept them from pursuing their dream.' She paused, only

too aware that she herself fell firmly into that category. 'And they're not ponies,' she said firmly. 'They're proper horses – just a lot smaller.'

'So you can't actually ride them?' Holly checked, as Banana leaned easily against her legs and harrumphed happily as she affectionately scruffed his mane.

The Major shook his head. 'No, no. They're more like a dog than a horse, really. Only, you know, with hooves and whatnot.'

'Look,' said Jess excitedly, by way of demonstration, 'Banana! Banana! Kisses? I'm doing a project on him for my tutor.' It was the first time Holly had heard Jess be anything but disparaging about her time being home schooled.

The little horse turned away from Holly and ambled straight over to Jess, reaching up to nuzzle her ear and making her giggle. 'Isn't he wonderful?'

'He truly is,' said Holly, grateful that Taffy and the boys weren't with her, as they would no doubt start campaigning for a miniature horse to be joining her own menagerie the moment they knew of Banana's existence. 'And you're going to breed them?' she asked Charlotte, delighted to see the colour in her cheeks and a sparkle in her eye at long last. She'd even forgotten to pull her sleeve down over the hideous scar on her arm in all the excitement.

Progress indeed.

In fact, now Holly came to think of it, as she listened to Charlotte outlining her plans, it had been a long time since she'd seen the three of them as animated, happy and relaxed. She stroked Banana's soft palomino coat as he contentedly explored his new surroundings. Therapies came in all shapes and sizes, she decided. In this case, around thirty-two inches of brown-eyed, shaggy-maned, equine enjoyment.

'I just need to find someone who wants to rent out my paddocks,' Charlotte continued. 'These little chaps won't even make a dent in sixty acres of prime pastureland. I wondered whether to offer it to the school as playing fields, but apparently there's all sorts of liability issues, according to that lovely Mr French. And then Lizzie mentioned she might know of someone who'd be interested, but he needed the house as well, so . . .' She shrugged her shoulders. 'I guess it's the last thing on her mind at the moment.'

Holly nodded. 'She's making a good recovery though, and then I can guarantee she'll be bored to tears and more than happy to meddle.'

'I heard you on the radio yesterday,' said the Major quietly. 'We were all on the edge of our seats, hearing your little drama play out on the airwaves. You're in danger of becoming a local hero, Holly.' He shrewdly watched her blush. 'Nice to see your fine medical instincts being put to good use while you're taking a little time off.'

Holly just about mustered a smile, focusing on the compliment in there somewhere. Not too shabby for a woman with no eyeliner and a recent penchant for dungarees, she thought, as she sank onto the floor and Banana lay down beside her and presented his tummy for scratching, much to Eric's disgust.

There were certainly worse ways to spend a Wednesday morning.

Chapter 6

Grace Allen closed down her computer, already mentally cataloguing the contents of the fridge and deciding that, after such a long day, she and Dan could surely justify supper at The Kingsley Arms. Being Practice Manager came with its own unique set of challenges, and while Dan had spent the day talking to patients, she herself had nothing so rewarding to report.

The Committee for Rural Affairs had given them both a seat at the table, but a bi-annual meeting was hardly enough to count as professional fulfilment for either of them, no matter how pleasing it was to have a voice for once.

'Do pass on my best to Dr Graham, won't you?' said Pru Hartley, stopping by reception on her way out, interrupting Grace's train of thought. 'She is a wonder, isn't she? All those babies to take care of and still saving lives. We were glued to the radio in the bakery, I can tell you. And I gather Lizzie's surgery was a success. So all's well that ends well.'

Grace managed a smile. Trust Holly. Always the right person to have around in a crisis – or every day, for that matter. Grace found it difficult to express how much she missed her calming presence at work.

Obviously she wasn't the only one. 'Do you know,' Pru

continued, 'I can't wait for her to be back at work. That Dr Campbell isn't quite the ticket, is she? I mean, I told her I'd been feeling rather dizzy of late and her reply? Had I ever had vertigo? Well!' Pru huffed. 'I told her I was a Scorpio and that her Third World medicine wouldn't wash with me, but she just laughed.'

By the time Grace had soothed Pru's ruffled feathers and sent her on her way, trying not to laugh, Grace felt rather more relaxed herself. You could always bank on Pru's confuzzlement with words to lighten a deadly dull afternoon. Not that things were all bad . . .

Grace looked up as Dan wandered through from his consulting room, his eyes seeking hers automatically. She couldn't quite believe that she got to go home every night with this gorgeous, funny, thoughtful man. 'Hey, you,' she said, affection laced into each syllable. 'Nearly done? I thought we might treat ourselves to a pub supper? You know how Noodle and Doodle love a bit of scampi.' It was second nature now, for Grace to plan her leisure time around the vagaries of her two adorable miniature dachshunds and Dan was quite used to it.

He leaned his forehead against hers, a rare moment of intimacy as The Practice wound down for the evening. 'I can meet you there if you like? I still need to see the Lawton baby. He's off his food and his mum's worried, so I squeezed him in. No point them worrying all night if they don't need to.'

Grace cupped his face in her hands and kissed him on the lips, her thumb smoothing the tired lines around his eyes. 'You're such a softie. And I don't mind waiting. Come find me in the doctors' lounge when you're done, okay?'

He nodded gratefully. 'It's the right thing to do.'

'It is,' she agreed, as she watched his face carefully, his

reaction to the gurgling unhappy baby arriving in his mother's arms telling her everything she needed to know.

It really didn't matter how many times they talked it
through; there was no denying the fact that Dan was desperate to become a father. At forty-two, and with two grown
sons, Grace felt his longing in an almost visceral way, but
that didn't mean she could promise something so big without
taking her own position into account. Did she really have it
in her to go through another pregnancy, two decades after
the first?

She watched him lift little Billy Lawton easily into his
arms. 'Well, hello, young man. Your mummy says you're not
wanting your food. How about I take a look at your tummy?'

It didn't take too much imagination to see that raising a
child with Dan would be an incredible experience, if only
there was a way to skip ahead, to jump over the part where
her uterus was expected to step up and provide room and
board for the best part of a year. But as long as Dan's DNA
was making a play for the future, there was little point even
mentioning the thorny issue of adoption.

As the door swung closed behind them, Grace caught sight
of the look on Billy's mother's face – part admiration, part
concern – Dan certainly knew how to put his patients at ease.
And, she imagined, that was part of the problem.

It had taken so long for her to find this wonderful – blissful – relationship, that she found herself worrying more than
she would like about how it might end. After all, just because
her child-bearing years were drawing to a close, that didn't
mean Dan couldn't look elsewhere for his happy-ever-after.
God knows, enough of his patients carried not-so-secret
crushes for their somewhat flawed, but nevertheless appealing
GP; Grace was perfectly aware that the man had options.

'Penny for them,' said Dan, making her jump. How long had he been standing there, in the doorway, watching her mental gymnastics, she wondered.

She stood up and smiled, unconsciously echoing his yawn. 'Long day. How's little Billy doing?'

'He's good and his mum's happy. Just a little constipation. Hopefully they'll both rest easy tonight.' He yawned again. 'I called the hospital, by the way, but they said Lizzie already has half the ward in uproar with her visitors, so I guess I'd be superfluous.'

Grace nodded. 'Maybe phone for a chat later? Put your mind at rest so you can rest easy too?' She knew how close Dan and his cousin were.

Dan smiled gently. 'Good plan. When I think how differently that could have ended, if she'd been home alone, or on the radio with anyone but Holly. I mean, how was she to know that the pain had only eased off a little because it had ruptured? Do ordinary people know that kind of thing?' He shrugged, as he looped his arm around her shoulders. 'It certainly makes you think, doesn't it? About seizing the day?'

'It does,' said Grace, an increasingly familiar feeling of panic sweeping over her chest in hot needles. She knew only too well where this conversation was heading. 'Did you give any more thought to the local council elections? They're seriously keen to have you as their candidate.'

Dan just shrugged. 'I guess it would be better than this feeling of treading water. I just can't shift it. Everyone around me is making a difference and all I'm doing is sending out Bertha the Bus with a fistful of leaflets and my fingers crossed that a little health education might go a long way.'

Grace laced her fingers through his own. 'Let's pick up a pizza, light the fire and eat it in our pyjamas?' she suggested.

'You look too tired to even prop up the bar tonight. I'll take the dogs out for a quick stroll while you have a bath?'

'Maybe an early night is just what the doctor ordered,' smiled Dan, leaning forward to draw her into a lingering kiss. 'Maybe we could seize the day on that front too? Throw caution to the wind?'

Grace simply kissed him. Some conversations really were best kept for the privacy of their own home.

'I was thinking, actually,' said Dan, as they worked in practised tandem to flick off all the lights, 'that we should go away this weekend. Give the bonfire festivities a miss? I don't know about you, but I'm not sure we're the target audience of this year's events.' He tried to smile, he really did, but his sleepless night was catching up with him.

'Oh, I don't know,' said Grace easily, 'I'm not averse to a few fireworks and a bit of candyfloss in the right circumstances. But yes – let's find a gorgeous hotel and hibernate for a few days.'

'Give the little ones the run of the town . . .' Dan said, unable to conceal the hint of wistfulness in his voice and Grace's heart sank.

Dan's biological clock had always ticked louder than most, indeed it had been the catalyst for his awful break-up with Julia Channing, but the arrival of Holly's latest twins seemed to have thrown oil on the flames. A spark of interest in becoming a father was now in danger of becoming a raging inferno and insidiously affecting every part of Dan's life. It seemed as though 'losing' his best friend to the demands of fatherhood had simply compounded the problem.

'Let's spoil ourselves. What's that fancy restaurant-with-rooms that's always in the press? The one near Oxford?' Grace suggested, hoping to distract Dan with the promise of culinary perfection and a roll-top bath – so long as he was focusing on quail's eggs, not her own, they could at least unwind and rest up a little.

He paused, able to read her like a book. 'Adults only get-away it is then.' He kissed her gently. 'I do love you, Grace Allen. I hope you know that.'

'The feeling is entirely mutual,' Grace said with a smile. 'And you know how I love a mini-break.'

'Come on then, Bridget, let's get home and PJ'd up. All the glamour for us tonight. We'll schedule saving the world for another time, then, yes?'

He pushed open the door into the car park, caught un-awares by the wind that was picking up, and Grace stilled for a moment, as two figures emerged from the darkness. It wasn't as though she consciously thought about the night she'd been attacked at The Practice after-hours; it was more that a subconscious part of her brain was always on alert for warning signs these days. Her grip on Dan's arm tightened and an involuntary gasp of fear caught in her throat.

'Hey, it's okay,' Dan reassured her, knowing exactly how her mind worked. 'They're just sixth-formers. It's okay.'

'We're not okay,' cried one of them in the twilight. 'Can you help us?'

Grace pushed the door wide open so the last light in the building flooded out to illuminate a wedge of the car park and two girls with tear-stained faces, their school uniforms awry, one of them clearly supported by the other. Conscious but rambling, one of the girls was finding it hard to stand and had a trail of vomit down her school tie.

'Jesus, Laura? Is that you?' Grace cried, recognising the supporting girl as their neighbour's seventeen-year-old daughter. 'Come in, come in. What happened? Have you been drinking?'

'It's Vicky! Her heart rate is going mental and then she couldn't breathe.' Laura sobbed. 'We weren't drinking,' she said, her pupils vast and dark, amidst the smudges of electric blue mascara.

'What were you smoking?' asked Dan, as he deftly laid Vicky down on the treatment bed in his office. 'Does she use marijuana a lot?'

Laura fell silent, staring down at her hands.

'I need to know,' said Dan. 'I need to know what she's been taking or using so I can help her.'

'Laura,' said Grace encouragingly. 'You brought her here for help. Let us help.'

'It was just one roll-up,' Laura whispered. 'And I know Dr Campbell said it only takes once to be dangerous, but everyone was doing it. We just wanted to join in with our friends. One puff, honestly, that's all she had.'

Dan caught Grace's eye, wondering whether they were ever going to get through to their teenage patients with all the outreach in the world. Apparently, they heard the message and then ignored it anyway.

'Different people react in different ways,' said Dan quietly, as he measured Vicky's heart rate and blood pressure, noting the slight blue tinge to the tips of her fingers. 'And you're sure it was a cannabis roll-up? No pills? Nothing else?'

'Just a joint,' said Laura, still unable to meet his eye. 'But I remembered about the leaflets from the bus, you know, Bertha. So I knew we had to get her here ...' She burst into great swallowing gulps of sobbing. 'She has allergies.'

Grace wrapped her arms around Laura and allowed her to sob against her shoulder. Dan worked quickly and quietly, assessing the situation before him. He crouched down beside the bed and took hold of Vicky's hand.

'Am I going to die?' Vicky asked, as she gasped for air. 'I can't feel my fingers. They were tingling, but now . . .' She broke off and her gasping got worse as she cried, pressing her knuckles into her chest and keening disconsolately.

'Vicky,' tried Dan again, 'I want you to look at me. I know your heart is racing and that's scary, but you need to look at me.' He lifted her chin very gently until she could no longer avoid him. 'You're having palpitations because of the drug. And that's scary, I know that. But the panic is what's causing your fingers to go tingly. I need you to breathe with me, okay, nice and steady. Match your breaths to mine.'

Grace watched as Dan matched her accelerated breathing to begin with, until they were in rhythm, then slowed gently, bringing her with him, until Vicky's entire focus was on matching him too, breath for breath.

'I need my inhaler,' she said, after a while, when even the slower breaths revealed a rattling wheeze.

'Can you even be allergic to cannabis?' asked Laura, the tears and rivulets of mascara making her eyes seem even larger and more vulnerable.

'More likely mould,' said Dan. 'You're smoking a dried plant, remember. But the panic and the palpitations? That's no allergy; that's a powerful drug messing with your body.'

Grace glanced at the clock on the wall, stunned to see the time nearing ten o'clock. How long had they been here, soothing this troubled girl? More to the point, what would have happened if they hadn't been here? If they'd slipped out to that early supper and these girls had had nobody to turn to?

'You did good tonight,' she said gently to Dan as they made cups of tea for everyone. 'I guess Holly's not our only local hero this week.'

Dan smiled. 'Ah but at least I didn't do it live on air. Talk about attention-seeking.' He shrugged. 'I guess sending out Bertha isn't entirely without merit.'

'So you weren't treading water this evening?' Grace asked, genuinely intrigued.

'No water. Pure adrenalin,' Dan replied thoughtfully. 'And frankly just grateful I could help. Kids, eh? Who'd have them?'

Grace felt his arm tighten imperceptibly around her shoulders. She thought they both knew the answer to that one.

Chapter 7

'Well, the storm's blown through in the night and the bonfire's still standing, so I'm calling this progress,' said Taffy
with a grin, as he pushed back their bedroom curtains that
Saturday morning and peered out across the Market Place,
the last few branches stripped bare in the night to give them
a perfect view of Larkford's rolling parkland. 'I don't think
I could have smiled through another debacle like last year.'

Holly stretched, her eyes still bleary with sleep. 'I still
have nightmares about it,' she yawned, incredibly touched
that he'd thought to bring her a cup of tea in bed, even if he
had eaten the accompanying toast on the way back upstairs.
Sometimes it was the smallest things, she thought. Of course
they were both tired, stretched pretty thin; perhaps it was just
too much to expect smooth sailing in a relationship once four
children were in the mix? She smiled at him, sipping her tea
contentedly, enjoying this brief moment together, before her
thoughts, as always, returned to practicalities. 'Do you think
there's any chance of this performance going smoothly?' she
wondered aloud. 'I mean, I know the kids are keen and Mr
French has got them all wound up about it, but isn't it far more
likely they'll all end up distracted by the fireworks and hopped
up on sugar instead?'

'Just as long as Tarquin bloody Holland is nowhere near a firework,' growled Taffy with feeling, making her laugh. Oh, how she'd missed just having a silly chat with him – no stresses, no juggling, just the two of them on the same song-sheet. And where Tarquin was concerned, they were definitely of one mind: Tarquin's mother, Cassie, was renowned for her 'alternative' parenting style and, as a result, half of the residents of Larkford were ready to string the obstreperous little darling up by his ankles.

'But still, at least this new head teacher seems to have taken a firm hand with all of them,' she said. Holly swung her legs round and got out of bed before Taffy could see the ridiculous blush that coloured her cheeks at the very thought of Alec French taking a firm hand with anyone.

She stood in the bathroom, staring at her bleary reflection and wondered when it had come to this: yesterday's make-up never removed, hair left to dry naturally and run wild, wearing Taffy's pyjamas and blushing like a teen at the very mention of her sons' head teacher? Grateful for just a few moments of her husband's undivided attention. Babies, or no babies, she seriously needed to get a grip.

'Holly?' came a plaintive call from the bedroom. 'Where's my shirt? The nice one with the stripy bit inside the collar?'

'Try the airing cupboard,' she called back, rubbing at her eyes with the last few drops of make-up remover, too little too late.

Taffy appeared in the doorway. 'I can't find it.'

Holly took a deep breath. 'Well, have a good look or wear the nice checked one instead?' she suggested, as her alarm pinged again, her window of opportunity for peeing without an audience of children rapidly shrinking. It was going to be a long day with seven children in tow, five of them in costume. Holly had to grab her moments of peace where she could.

Pulling on her warm layers, one eye on the clock for the girls' tandem awakening, Holly jumped as her mobile rang.

'Just wanted to wish you luck,' said Lizzie, the smile in her voice giving Holly a boost that her friend was firmly on the mend. 'I'm coming home later today, but my bossy consultant says coming to the show would be too much. Are you sure you're going to cope?'

'Of course,' said Holly, wondering if she needed to cross her fingers at this blatant over-estimation. 'I've got this covered. Taffy's off duty and looking after the four boys; I've got my girls and Lily. We have a plan, so you can just relax and get better.' She paused; even with this plan in place she knew they were outnumbered, and her upbeat reassurance was only able to go so far. 'You gave us all quite a scare, so please – take the time you need to get well and then we can stop worrying about you.'

'I forgot to say,' said Taffy poking his head around the door as Holly hung up, 'Dan and Grace have popped away for a little mini-break. So I said I'd cover his afternoon shift today. That's okay, right? I'll probably be there until five or six, but you've got this bonfire thing under control?'

Holly blinked hard, re-running the conversation on this very topic only forty-eight hours ago: Taffy's reassurances of help, an extra pair of hands, a steadying hand on Lizzie's excitable boys in the crowds while she focused on the babies. 'You are kidding?' she said slowly. 'We talked about this – remember? Five kids, two babies, one Holly?'

Taffy guiltily scrunched up his face. 'Yeah, that does ring a bell actually. But Dan was never going to cope with seeing everyone playing happy families, was he? I think it's a good thing they've gone away.' He paused, frowning. 'I thought you'd understand.'

'I do,' said Holly simply. 'But I also think that Alice, or Tilly, might have been available to cover – you know, since they have no children and this is actually a school event now?'

Taffy shook his head, as he began ferreting through the pile of neatly folded laundry, crumpling up every item in his quest to find either of his favourite shirts – one of which Holly had just spotted, dirty and discarded under his side of the bed. 'They've been working really long hours, Holls. They need their weekends too.'

'So do I,' Holly said, her words falling on deaf ears, as he yanked a jumper over his head and made for the door.

'Have fun today!' he called from the hallway, waking every sleeping child in the house as the front door slammed behind him.

'Remind me again why I love you,' Holly muttered angrily in his wake.

It was amazing to her still, after more than a year of married life, how her affection for her husband could turn on a sixpence. Obviously she loved him, there was no question of that, but with every day that passed, Holly began to wonder whether men and women were actually designed to live together in peace and harmony.

She wouldn't necessarily confess it, even if pressed, but she was delighted that Elsie was spending so much time back at Number 42, although she still wasn't to be drawn on why. It had started with vague grumblings about how her laundry was being handled by the Sarandon Hall housekeeping staff, their disregard for her delicates causing a disproportionate amount of grump. Still, the fact that Elsie's silk what-nots now adorned the Pulleymaid suspended from the utility-room ceiling at Number 42, at least gave Holly an excuse to see her lovely friend for pep-talks and common-sense advice. Even if she was reluctant to drag her into the niggles and peeves that seemed to be stockpiling by the day as Holly and Taffy navigated the transition to parenthood this time around.

Holly couldn't help but smile as she walked into the kitchen, a baby in each arm and saw Elsie squashed into the corner of the sofa by a blissfully contented Nineteen, Eric beside them on the floor looking most put out. It was an incongruous sight at best: Elsie stylishly layered in her designer 'active wear' for one of her classes, gently scratching the giant porker's belly as he snuffled and grunted appreciatively, trotters tucked up like paws.

'When is this pig of yours going to realise that he's not actually a dog?' Elsie said affectionately. 'I only opened the door to give him some breakfast and he was on the sofa before I could blink.' It was true; for one so cumbersome, Nineteen had a remarkable turn of speed when it suited him. If the sofa was unavailable, he was just as likely to be found lying stretched out beside the Aga, dozing contentedly.

Holly laughed, settling the twins into their high chairs. 'I've taken him over to Clive Shaw's water meadows every day this week, I've shown him his new little pig sty and Clive has checked all the boundaries, but still he turns up here every morning.' She couldn't be annoyed with him though, her fondness for his tufty face at the window still strong even in the face of Nineteen's adolescent confusion. 'I found him on the dog bed with Eric yesterday. I think Eric got the poorer part of the deal, to be honest.'

Elsie tried to extricate herself and failed. 'I know how he feels.'

'I think you'll just have to surrender to his affections. I

didn't even realise you'd slept over again; I'd have brought you a cup of tea in bed,' Holly said.

Elsie shook her head. 'Don't you worry. Your glorious husband already made me one, actually. He's really very good about me being underfoot and imposing on your hospitality – didn't bat an eyelid.'

It was true – another point in Taffy's favour was how incredibly accepting he was about the comings and goings here, with Elsie, Alice, Lizzie, not to mention all their various livestock. Holly tried not to frown; as always, she was left feeling like the bad guy after one of their tiffs – maybe he was right and she should just have been more understanding of Dan's situation? He needed a mate in Taffy, just as much as she did in Elsie . . .

And then she looked around the kitchen, pulling out every melamine plate they owned to accommodate the extra mouths to feed, deftly slicing up bananas and fingers of toast for seven hungry (and noisy) mouths, and swallowed hard. Was it really too much to ask for her needs to come first occasionally, though, or at the very least, to be considered?

'Since I'm here, why don't I make myself useful?' Elsie volunteered, clearly not missing Holly's reticence to praise Taffy's tea-making skills, but astute enough not to open that particular can of worms during the proverbial feeding time at the zoo.

Nineteen grunted unhappily as Elsie made a bid for freedom, Eric leaping up to claim her spot as soon as it was vacated. The labradoodle and the Gloucestershire Old Spot were like siblings at times – they clearly adored and riled each other in equal measure.

Elsie laid a gentle hand on her shoulder as she passed and Holly felt instantly soothed, her worries fractionally allayed. Such a small gesture of support, but it meant so much. Today was going to be challenging – today on five hours' sleep was quite the ask – but somehow Holly felt a little more capable simply from knowing Elsie had faith in her.

'Now, I'm off to my Pilates class,' Elsie said. 'Do speak up if you want me to stay and help, because I can easily—'

A volley of vibrating thumps from next door drowned out the last of her words and Lottie promptly burst into tears.

A number of swear words sprang instantly to Holly's mind, yet she restrained herself. 'Seriously? Who on earth are these new people next door? It's the weekend, for goodness' sake and they're still knocking seven bells out of the place.'

Elsie looked worried for a moment. 'You're not going to go round and cause a fuss, are you, darling? Only, I'm not sure you're in the most, well, tactful of moods . . . And they will be your neighbours soon enough.'

'But still!' Holly insisted, as she settled Lottie with a beaker of juice and a kiss. 'All day, every day. Is it any wonder the whole street wants to hammer their door down and tell them where to go? They haven't even come round to introduce themselves, or apologise.' She dropped her voice in case the boys overheard her. 'I reckon it's just another couple of London wankers, come down here to play at country weekends and marvel at the Georgian wainscoting, assuming there'll be any original features left by the time they've finished mangling the place.'

Elsie pulled Holly into her arms and gave her an uncharacteristically maternal hug. 'You can't blame the new owners for their builders, darling. Maybe they're on a tight schedule, or a budget? Who knows, maybe they'll be just wonderful and you'll end up the best of friends?'

'Hmm,' said Holly, withholding judgement until she'd actually met them, even though Taffy and Lizzie had both said much the same thing. A little fun, fresh blood in the street, might be just the boost she needed.

Elsie looked over her shoulder in concern as she left, clearly not convinced by Holly's protestations that she could cope, and clearly not missing the fact that, yet again, her protégée appeared to be slipping down the list of her own priorities. She closed the door with a thoughtful sigh, wondering how best to help without outstaying her welcome.

It was times like this, when Holly felt overwhelmed by the task ahead of her, that Larkford came into its own, Holly decided later that day. Her pride almost definitely about to come before a fall, she was already kicking herself for turning Elsie's offer of help away. She needn't have worried though – it wasn't as though her shattered appearance was a cry for help, more a warning flag to the women around her that all was not quite going to plan.

By the time she had handled the drama of persuading five recalcitrant children into their costumes, coats and mittens, Holly was ready to wage war on 'stupid Mr French' for planning this fiesta, Dan for his over-sensitivity to all things 'children' and her very own beloved for always, always wanting to do the right thing – even though that increasingly meant doing the wrong thing by his own nearest and dearest. Indeed, by half past four, standing at the edge of the Market Place, Holly was as close to a man-hating, militant feminist as she was ever going to get.

Only the clear skies, a light spackling of stars already peeking out around a gibbous moon, and the exuberant excitement of every child around her stopped Holly's mood from descending further. Watching Gerald, the resident Larkford goose, honking indignantly at the PTA mothers as they attempted to string bunting around their cake stall, gave rise to a tiny smile. Watching snooty Cressida Bourne being chased towards the river, as Gerald took umbrage at her flapping at him with her weighty peacock scarf, actually elicited a bubble of laughter.

Sometimes, it was all about perspective, she thought. The Major and his terrier Grover were sharing some candyfloss, Pru Hartley was looking down her nose at the PTA brownies and slagging them off, causing floods of tears from ten-year-old Persephone Monk, who'd spent the entire morning baking them. Tact was never a strong point in the Larkford ensemble, but somehow, thought Holly, weren't they all the closer for it?

It pleased her no end to see most of the nurses from The Practice all huddled together, gossiping about their Big Night Out the night before, munching on toffee apples — living together, working together, having fun together.

Holly breathed out slowly, trying to take in the moment, reassured, as the nurses laughed and bickered. It seemed as though Holly was the only person who expected this level of intimacy to happen without a few road-bumps along the way. Certainly poor Jason was being lambasted for his choice of daffodil-yellow Doc Martens and he didn't appear to be taking offence.

'Holly!' said Alice, ambling over towards her, with Coco, Noodle and Doodle trotting obediently beside her on a clever three-way lead, and a latte in the other hand. 'Are you okay? I thought I had my hands full with three dogs and the fireworks this weekend, but just exactly how many children are you attempting to wrangle there, anyway?'

Holly smiled, surprised to find that her bad mood had ebbed away, and her smile was actually genuine. 'Panic not – it's only temporary. Three of them are Lizzie's on short-term loan.'

Alice nodded. 'Phew! I did wonder whether I'd blinked and missed a batch for a minute. And where's that daft husband of yours anyway? He's normally fairly handy on the wrangling front.' She gently pushed her wayward bobble hat back from her face, sun-kissed strands of hair falling forward artfully. The very picture of relaxed après-ski. There was no guile in her question; she clearly had no idea that Taffy was working so she wouldn't have to.

'Well, he's being handy at work instead, covering for Dan.' Holly tried to keep the judgement out of her voice, she truly did, but a smidgen crept in, making her feel small and petty.

Alice frowned. 'But why?'

Holly shrugged, at a loss for an answer momentarily. 'Because that's who he is,' she said in the end. And – the little voice in her head reminded her – one of the very reasons she fell in love with him in the first place.

How ironic.

Chapter 8

As the hand on the clock tower moved slowly towards five o'clock and the crowd assembled around the crackling bonfire began to look about in expectation, Cassie Holland arrived, huffing and puffing under a sequined, quilted poncho that surely was no match for the increasingly chilly evening, regardless of its eco-friendly ethnic credentials. She barged her way through Holly and Alice's conversation and shoved a reluctant Tarquin forward into the group of children, all of whom seemed to be intent on picking the little buckles off their costumes and getting their white stockings as muddy as possible before show-time. Alice stepped back, bemused, automatically sheltering Coco from Tarquin's unpredict-able reach.

'That Mr French is all full of good ideas and plans, but does he ever think about the parents?' Cassie cursed to anyone within range, causing a flurry of eyebrows to shoot up at her vehemence. 'It's all very well being an idealist, but you have to back it up with your actions, not delegate responsibility.' Cassie's habit of speaking in media sound bites and memes could get a little wearing, but Holly had long since decided that her heart was in the right place. Tarquin, of course, was the only one whose white costume hadn't been hurriedly bought from the internet; instead his was an elderly pair of harem pants cropped at the knee to make breeches and what appeared to be a hand-quilted waistcoat several sizes too large. Poor kid never stood a chance, thought Holly privately.

'Evening, everybody,' said Alec French, as he checked his clipboard to see that all his little performers were indeed present and correct, seemingly unaware of the ripples his arrival caused among the female contingent. His *Blackadder*-esque seventeenth-century ensemble really should have been off-putting, not to mention the accordion casually slung over one shoulder, but somehow nothing seemed to dull his natural charisma. It was actually a little concerning how the crowd of mothers seemed to react to his very presence.

Cassie, on the other hand, was unmoved and merely fixed him with an utterly filthy glare before storming off into the ever-growing crowd. Alec French stared after her for a moment, but made no comment.

'Hi,' said Holly simply, feeling as though someone ought to fill the awkward silence that hovered in Cassie's wake.

'If you need a hand with the Parsons kids later, just shout,' he replied easily. 'I can't quite believe the turn-out actually, but it's certainly going to be, err, interesting, corralling all the children into line.' He gave her a warm, encouraging smile and turned back to the group of children, clapping his hands once and gaining their instant and silent attention. Well, apart from Tarquin, who twirled in circles on the spot. 'Easy, tiger,' said Mr French and, impressively, Tarquin too fell silent.

As Mr French continued to give his pre-performance pep talk, Hattie walked over to Holly, waving at her own girls in the huddle as she did so. 'He's like the child whisperer, isn't he? Ellie actually *wanted* to do her homework last night! Maybe he's hypnotised them with those stunning blue eyes?'

She grinned at Holly's shocked expression. 'Oh, come on, don't say you haven't noticed them?'

'Well, they are *very* arresting,' chimed in Elsie, joining them with pink cheeks and a throaty chuckle, seemingly swathed in enough cashmere to single-handedly keep the Mongolian economy afloat. 'In fact, I cannot understand why that Cassie woman seems to have taken against him so. Surely making a few costumes is a small price to pay for such a feast for the senses?'

You could take Elsie off the stage, Holly realised, but her vocal projection didn't seem to come with an off-switch. She hurriedly leaned forward to tuck the blankets more tightly around Lottie and Olivia, as Mr French's gaze turned enquiringly in their direction.

'Ah, you know Cassie,' Hattie replied. 'She doesn't need a reason to take against someone.' And Hattie would know – Cassie was barely civil to her since discovering that the chocolate sprinkles used at The Deli weren't fair trade. The coffee was. The chocolate was. But the sprinkles . . .

Everyone settled quickly as Mr French turned to the microphone provided. 'Good evening, one and all, and welcome to our Bonfire Night celebrations. We have food, we have a beautifully clear night and we have the children of Larkford Primary School to entertain you. Please do feel free to spend their pocket money and indeed your own, as every penny raised today will go to support the remarkable Young Carers here in our very own community.' He nodded his head towards Matthew Giles in thanks for his amazing work and the crowd broke into spontaneous applause. 'So, with a nod to artistic licence, not to mention health and safety, let the Guy Fawkes Gaiety begin!'

Holly grinned widely as Matthew made his way through

the crowds to say hello, her earlier mood eclipsed by the groundswell of good-feeling, and the company of friends. She clasped the lanky young man into an embarrassingly maternal hug. 'I'm so bloody proud of you!' she exclaimed. It had been such a leap of faith for Matthew to abandon his degree last year and come home to care for his mother, Molly. To be afflicted with young-onset Parkinson's had been an ongoing battle for her for years now, and having Matthew at home had been both a blessing and a worry for Molly. But now he had found his niche, and his enthusiasm and commitment to helping other Young Carers had started a dialogue in the town that helped everyone. More than that, he was putting plans into action that the GPs could only have dreamed of – ongoing, face-to-face support for some of their most vulnerable youngsters. Being a child was hard enough in this day and age, without taking responsibility for an ailing parent as well.

Matthew grinned, embarrassed of course, but also clearly touched by Holly's words. 'I can't get over how much your babies have grown!' he said, peering into the pram.

'Well, it does happen,' laughed Holly. She pointed across the Market Place to where Ben and Tom were dutifully awaiting their turn in the circle of bunting that marked out their performance space, looking utterly adorable in their historically questionable costumes and taking it all very seriously. 'And before you know it, they're off to school and plotting to blow up parliament. Or, you know, setting up a charity and changing people's lives.' She gave him a nudge. 'Your mum's so proud of you too, you know.'

Matthew nodded, secure in Molly's love and estimation. 'I know. She's even more chuffed since Bath Rugby came on board as a sponsor. Reckons she'll get try-line tickets for all the big matches.' He grinned. 'She's probably right – she can still charm anyone with a smile, my mum, even from her wheelchair.'

Holly agreed; Molly was a delight to work with – one of her most afflicted patients, yet easily one of the loveliest. 'Well, maybe don't tell Taffy and Dan that's even an option, or we won't see them until spring!'

Holly tried not to stare as Tilly wove her way towards them through the crowd, only to seemingly spot Matthew and do an abrupt U-turn. Obviously married life wasn't the only option that came with a few hurdles; being footloose and fancy-free on the dating front was clearly no walk in the park either. Thankfully Matthew's attention was focused elsewhere and he missed the knowing look between Alice and Holly. For all his maturity in setting up the charity and caring for his mum, Matthew had clearly missed the lecture at university about Playing It Cool 101.

Alice made her excuses and followed Tilly through the crowd and, again, Holly felt the slight give in her shoulders from the reassurance that Larkford was the kind of town that never left a man, or woman, down. It was The Larkford Way.

As the older children finished their song about gunpowder, treason and plot and the crowd clapped enthusiastically, Holly stood on tiptoes and managed to capture the perfect image of Lizzie's two boys beaming with pride – it was all the more appealing for the way that Gerald the goose had been weaving his way around the children as though guarding his territory, yet somehow in time with the music. She pinged it over to Lizzie as a text, knowing how much she resented missing out.

Matthew waved in the air, almost jolting Holly's phone from her hands with his gangly enthusiasm. 'Holly, Holly, wait here. I want you to meet someone. He's a huge fan of yours,' said Matthew over the opening strains of the next song, as he plunged into the crowd and ushered a man towards them, a man whose shoulders were so wide he had to slide sideways through the cheering parents.

'*The* Dr Graham?' he said. 'I'm Mike Urquhart from the Rugby Club in Bath. We're the ones sponsoring young Matthew's group? But actually, I just really wanted to say how impressive you were on the radio the other day. We were all listening in the gym and the boys let out quite the cheer when you saved the day, I can tell you. And when Matthew here said he knew you ... Well, I wanted to pass on our regards. Impressive work indeed. Your patients are very lucky to have you.'

Dear God, thought Holly for a moment, as she felt her neck begin to warm unattractively, she was clearly having some kind of midlife crisis. First, there'd been amorous thoughts about the boys' head teacher, despite his obvious fondness for an accordion, and now she was involuntarily having blue thoughts about some random rugby player she'd only just met! This latest development tossed Taffy's habitual but harmless flirting with the lass in the fish'n'chip shop into a cocked hat.

She seriously needed to get a grip, or possibly get laid – assuming she could somehow engineer for her and her husband to be awake in the same place, at the same time.

'Well, thank you, but I'm actually on maternity leave at the moment,' Holly blustered, unused to such effusive praise, or indeed such intense scrutiny from such a bear-like man.

Mike paused, almost as though he had a cartoon thought bubble ballooning above his head. 'Really?' he said slowly, appraisingly. 'Not working at all?'

Holly shrugged, waving a hand at the double pram and the sleeping twins beside her. 'It's not exactly a holiday.'

'But, aren't you missing it?' Mike asked, intrigued and not

missing for a moment the look of longing on Holly's face as she began to talk about her patients and her community.

'So, I'm lucky in many ways – there's lots of ways to be a doctor,' she concluded, realising that although he hadn't asked for her life story, she'd somehow felt the need to make sure that he knew she was a serious professional, not just an exhausted-looking mother. It wasn't just vanity, so much as professional pride, she told herself.

He reached into his coat pocket and pulled out a business card. 'Come and have a chat with me, Dr Graham. We've been talking about having a dedicated GP on staff for the club and, you know, I have a really good feeling about you. Part-time, full-time, we're open to suggestions at this point, but I really want you to think about how we might fit together.'

'You mean as a *private* GP?' Holly said, completely blind-sided by his offer and pushing aside any thoughts whatsoever about anyone fitting together.

Mike nodded. 'Hell, you can bring the kids if you like. We pride ourselves on being family-oriented. Have a think and then call me ...' He paused, as he made to walk away back into the crowd. 'When you know, you know, right? And I really think you'd be an excellent fit.' He smiled as he left, Holly mouthing like a goldfish and feeling completely caught off balance.

'Blimey,' said Matthew. 'Mike doesn't make offers like that every day. He's normally all about the due diligence and number crunching, not so much the spontaneity. He must really want you on board.' He laughed delightedly. 'Just wait until Dan and Taffy hear about this. You just got offered their dream job!'

Holly blinked. The offer sounded genuine enough; it was the circumstances that threw her. She managed a smile, grateful for the fact that Ben, Tom and Lily were now taking their turn to enter the performance circle, getting ready to begin, offering the perfect excuse not to reply. As the music struck up, she watched the younger children step into their much-practised routine, the older pupils now waving glow sticks in generous loops from the front row of the audience, sparklers having been roundly poo-poo'ed by the PTA on health and safety grounds. Seeing the flying ponytails and exuberant gyrations of some of the pupils, Holly was forced to admit that they may have had a valid point, no matter how overly officious it felt.

Somehow, despite all logic, everything fell into place with none of the drama or confusion every parent in the crowd was braced for. Was this some visual metaphor, Holly couldn't help but wonder, as the chaotic routine ended with everyone exactly where they were supposed to be. Or was she just looking for a little order in her own life and seizing on anything that endorsed the notion?

As she quickly snapped several photos to send to Lizzie and Taffy she couldn't help considering the serendipity of the offer. Maybe, it might prove just enough to ease her back into her working world? Maybe it was actually exactly what she needed, if only to *be* needed, professionally speaking?

Holly knew she wasn't really making sense, even to herself, at this point. She loved her job at The Practice, didn't she? She just felt so discombobulated by how her evening was unfolding. She seriously needed to get some more sleep, she decided, or they'd be carting her off to the funny farm. Monday's nanny interviews couldn't come soon enough.

'You know,' said Elsie quietly beside her, almost as though she could read her mind, 'good things happen to those who show up. And you, my darling, show up and step up every single day.

You deserve this opportunity, and don't let Dan and Taffy tell you otherwise just because they quite fancy it for themselves. They weren't here today, you were. Just remember that.'

A lone, pre-emptive Roman candle exploded overhead as Holly's breath misted in the chill evening air and the crackle of opportunity – or was it an illicit sparkler? – sent tingles down her spine.

Chapter 9

It was somewhat of a baptism of fire, Connor decided, to make this bizarre celebration his first foray into the carousel of high days and holidays that seemed to populate the Larkford calendar with almost alarming regularity.

Perhaps it was a sign that he was finally starting to heal – his recovery now a tiny green shoot, able to withstand a little more than a huddle of close friends in The Kingsley Arms, or his almost constant occupation of The Big Chair at the end of Lizzie's kitchen table.

He couldn't help feeling a little saddened that she wasn't here beside him; her reassuring presence and her total lack of respect for his rock-star alter ego had been the one constant that kept him on track, kept it real. He knew, deep down, that he pushed it too far sometimes, irritating Will despite his best intentions – he couldn't quite put his finger on the date that his allegiance of 'best friend' had transferred from husband to wife, but he was still able to take a hint at least.

'If you want to be useful, mate, go and help Holly with the kids and stop hovering around here,' Will had declared, as he brought Lizzie back from the hospital just now. It wasn't really the kind of request that you could argue with, even though seeing Lizzie in a hospital gown brought back more memories than he was really prepared to deal with right now.

Being useful would be a good distraction, he decided. If only he could find Holly and her tribe among the throngs of red trousers, tweed coats and highlighted blonde mummies. He glimpsed Holly in the distance at last, decidedly unglamorous in jeans and a ponytail, outnumbered by children, quashing a moment of panic as her band of happy helpers drifted away to deal with their own families, or simply to grab a hot chocolate and a doughnut to soften the full-on spectacle of Mr French's Guy Fawkes vision, which was clearly some kind of *Hamilton* homage if the cringe-worthy attempt at rapping was any kind of guide.

The whispers followed him, as always, as he made his way through the crowd towards her, at the same time keeping an eye peeled for Dan, or Taffy, or another comforting face. Their camaraderie and ridiculous japes had been one of the few things to make him properly, achingly, laugh in the last twelve months and he had to confess that he looked forward to their bets and shenanigans more than anything else these days. It may not be cool, or trendy, but watching them trying to best each other at eating as many chocolate oranges as they could in under five minutes had been the highlight of last weekend at Lizzie's. Five minutes in, five seconds out. It was a wonder that Lizzie was still speaking to any of them.

He paused for a moment, sheltered from view by a pack of strangely equine-looking women in perfectly tailored jackets, conflicted between helping Holly out and saving her dignity. To be fair to her, she'd probably been coping brilliantly all evening, wrangling seven children into line with good grace, so it was Sod's Law that Connor should turn up at the very moment she appeared to be on the verge of completely losing her rag.

He hung back a little, hoping that the situation might resolve itself. The last thing he wanted to do was make Holly feel under scrutiny; he was already kicking himself for not even considering the children as Lizzie was whisked into hospital – his only focus had been on her, on what he could do for her. Turning up at the hospital with Lucozade and magazines and a lovely new robe had been the extent of his consideration. It was not something he was especially proud of now, watching Holly and the extent of her support for her best friend.

Maybe blokes were just wired differently, he thought, before chastising himself – or maybe he really was just as much of a self-serving, egotistic wanker as his bandmates? It made for an uncomfortable train of thought.

Action was required.

As he approached, both Lottie and Olivia had begun to wail from the pram, having been abruptly awakened by the less-than-tuneful Junior Choir Ensemble mangling a madrigal, and Holly was hastily attempting to untangle Ben, Tom, Jack and Archie's interlocking glow sticks from each other's, where an impromptu mid-match huddle had ended with a ruinous entwining of neon, hair and buckles.

To be fair, the spectacle of four miniature Guy Fawkes attempting a Haka was one he would never forget, but still . . .

'Need a hand?' said Connor, unable to hide the amusement in his voice, or written all over his face, at these lads and their antics and realising too little, too late, that Holly felt he was laughing at her predicament.

Her face flushed scarlet as he calmly knelt down beside them and tried to extricate her hair from the worst of the tangle. He could hear people around them whispering and the occasional click of a camera as Connor's very presence encouraged attention as it always did. When would the residents of Larkford ever get used to having him strolling in their midst, he wondered. It wouldn't be quite so bad, but he was perfectly aware that in half of the tabloid photos, Holly and Lizzie had not fared so well.

'Hive front-man strolls with ailing companion,' screamed the headlines as Holly had joined him for an early morning dog walk sans make-up last month.

'Bereaved rocker seeks solace with old friends,' proclaimed an internet blog, going on to feature a series of blurry candids of Holly and Lizzie, which had been cropped at the least flattering angles imaginable. The one featuring a full 'moon' of Holly's denim-clad bottom had been angled to perfection for maximum acreage, as she bent down to retrieve a discarded teddy bear. He knew from Taffy that it had been enough to precipitate a post-baby crash diet, doomed to failure through lack of sleep alone, and his guilt on that front was a small taste of how his fame affected the people around him, the people he truly liked, or even loved.

He didn't want anyone to feel persecuted just for being his friend – after all, nobody wanted to be photographed every time they went anywhere together, least of all him.

Holly gasped in surprise as the flick of his penknife opening inches from her hair caught her unawares and he realised he'd been so deep in thought that he hadn't even warned her of his basic untangling approach.

'Keep still,' Connor said quietly. 'You're just making it worse.'

'Wow!' breathed all four boys in unison, making no attempt to hide their hero worship. Rock star. Guitarist.

Pen-knife-Wielder. Clearly they deserved equal billing, as far as the boys were concerned.

Connor's wide and easy grin put them all at ease and Holly appeared to breathe a sigh of relief as one and all were separated without loss of blood or limb. Despite a few glow stick casualties, they had all emerged intact, with the possible exception of Holly's dignity. As the boys pestered to see every single function of the fancy Swiss Army knife, from the corner of his eye Connor noticed Holly watch in fascination and attempted to smooth the bird's nest on her head.

On his knees like this, kids around him, and randomly showing them clever penknife permutations, he felt a gut-wrenching twist. His baby would have been much the same age as Lottie and Olivia now. He swallowed hard and forced a smile onto his face. Still, at least he was making progress, not only coming here today, but intent on finding a new place to call home, somewhere beyond Lizzie's kitchen table to make a step towards his fresh start.

He straightened up as the boys' interest was claimed by the arrival of a large box of doughnuts and lollipops – Mr French's strict discipline clearly not extending to nutrition.

'Nice save,' said Holly, generously with a smile.

'It's all part of my Move To The Country Plan,' he said, laughing at how ridiculous and hipsterish that sounded. 'Used to be a plectrum and a spliff, now it's a penknife and a Barbour. Who knew?' He shrugged self-deprecatingly and saw Holly instantly drop her guard; she really must have thought he was judging, he realised.

'Suits you,' Holly replied, and Connor couldn't help but agree. Not quite the improvement he was hoping for, it had to be said, but at least he was looking a little brighter these days, thanks to a little Larkford fresh air.

Progress indeed.

No time like the present, he thought, taking Holly's hand and pulling her gently to one side, shaking his head as she looked questioningly at his fingers entwined with her own.

Somehow, this in itself was more shocking than anything else. Connor was known for his effusive hugs, his frankly ridiculous and lovey way of kissing cheeks not twice, but three times on greeting and always, always being the last soul standing at every social gathering, but holding hands? This was new, he realised – and not entirely unpleasant. But at least it accounted for the blushing surprise on her face.

He guided Holly away from the crowd, one hand in hers and one guiding the cumbersome pram where Lottie and Olivia were somehow now back in deep slumber despite the chaos.

'I need you,' he said simply, *sotto voce*, as soon as he turned to face her. Seizing the day.

'At last, I've got you alone,' said Connor intently, oblivious to Holly's apparent self-conscious confusion. 'Can this be just between you and me? Just us for now. I don't want to get Lizzie involved.'

'Wha—?' managed Holly eloquently, as his intense blue eyes stared questioningly into hers.

'Elsie tells me you're the one I need to talk to.'

'Elsie?'

'For the inside line on houses around here? Come on, Holls, you can tell me: debt, divorce and death. It's the only way I'm ever going to find what I'm looking for, isn't it?'

Holly's eyes widened instinctively at his cavalier words and he blanched. His grief therapist had warned him that the events of the last year had, to an extent, inured him to loss of life, that not everyone would be comfortable with his blunt-ness – a little tactful tiptoeing around other people's feelings might be a good idea, rather than jumping in with both feet and waving his cheque book. Until he saw the expression on Holly's face, he hadn't really thought it was a valid point.

He did now.

Maybe he shouldn't have been quite so hasty in quitting his regular sessions?

He leaned in closer, eager to explain himself. 'It's just that I've been to every single estate agent in a twenty-mile radius and they've got nothing. Loads of fancy houses, but farms are in short supply. I guess they just stay in the same family for generations, but how can I start building a legacy if I can't even pass "go"?'

Holly squeezed his hand and let go. 'It's not going to happen overnight, Conn. You've got something really specific in mind, and that's great. But sometimes that makes it harder to find.' She paused and bit her lip and he could tell she was weighing up how blunt to be with him – it was a look he was now accustomed to. People here didn't seem to have the measure of him yet – he was hardly the snowflake diva the popular press seemed to imply.

Rock star, or widower.

Those were his two roles and he felt a quiet ripple of disappointment that only a very few people here had taken the time to get past that, to the real him. He had thought, until that moment, that Holly was one of them.

'To be honest, I rather thought you'd already bought the house next door and were just keeping it quiet because you knew you were pissing off all the neighbours,' she said, after a moment, raising her gaze appraisingly to his. No tiptoeing at all. She offered a small smile, an opening to confess and he was almost disappointed not to give her the response she was so clearly expecting.

Connor shook his head and gave her his best, most effective grin. 'Now, would those be the same neighbours you thought had more money than sense? And probably no taste either?' Connor asked wryly.

Holly laughed, taking him by surprise. 'Oh. I did say that, didn't I?'

'Not me, though, no matter how well your artful description applies.'

Holly sighed. 'Well, somebody has to know who they are. It's ridiculous to think that no one has even met them yet, but their builders have been terrorising us all for weeks!'

'But that's not true—'

'Oh-ho, it bloody well is—' Holly interrupted crossly.

'No, I mean, Elsie's met them. Twice at least, I've seen her coming out of their front door. All smiley, friendly-like.'

Holly's glare zeroed in on him like a hawk. 'It must be one of her red-trousered, chinless cronies then. Someone she's met through Sarandon Hall, maybe?'

Connor shrugged, his interest in the comings and goings of Larkford's pensioners, property owners or not, was fairly limited. 'Unless you think one of her cronies might be selling a nice farmhouse, with about a hundred acres?' Connor tried to bring the conversation back on track, but he could tell he'd lost Holly's attention the moment he'd, possibly rather tactlessly, let slip that Elsie knew more than she was letting on. 'You know, for me to buy . . .?'

Holly wrinkled her nose guiltily. 'Sorry, yes. Got a bit distracted.'

It was unusual, he realised suddenly, for Holly to drop the ball, even for a moment. They'd been talking for a while now and even while he felt that she was hearing every word, focused on him, her eyes would still casually log in with all the various children in her care – no drama, no fuss, just multi-tasking at an Olympic level. Was that why she was widely considered to be the best, most empathetic GP at The Practice, he wondered. Because she had an innate skill to make everyone she spoke to feel heard and understood? He could certainly do with a little more empathy in his life, and a little less sympathy.

'You know,' Holly said, proving his point without even realising it, 'what if you just took a step back, stop listing bedrooms and outbuildings and acreage to these estate agents and actually think, really think, about what matters the most to you? You never know, the perfect house might be waiting for you and you're not hearing about it because you only wanted en-suite bathrooms or something?'

His hand sought hers again, again with the unintentional and confusing double meaning to his every word. 'Tell me what I need.' His tone was almost plaintive. 'If I want to rebuild my life and have a family like yours, Holly, tell me where to start.'

She shrugged, closing her eyes briefly, deep in thought.

She'd been there, after all, Connor recalled. Starting over. Divorcing Milo had certainly been no picnic, if Lizzie's indiscreet tales were any measure.

'You need a home, not a house,' she said eventually. 'It actually doesn't matter if it would look good on the pages of a magazine; you need the comfort. For me, it starts with a kitchen I never want to leave – you know, long suppers talking nonsense, lazy Sunday breakfast ...' She sighed deeply. 'But then, we both know it's not bricks and mortar and fancy worktops that make a kitchen welcoming. You need to live there, really inhabit your space and make it yours.'

Connor nodded, taking in every word. 'A great kitchen, okay. Got it. What else?'

Holly laughed. 'This isn't *my* wish list, you doof. It's yours.'

'Did you really just call me a doof?' Connor said, shocked and amused in equal measure. He shook his head and laughed. 'You know this place – Larkford? I can just be me here. And this is where I want to live. Nobody calls me a doof in LA. Shocking, right? And it turns out, I hadn't realised that I missed that.'

'So there you go,' said Holly with a smile. 'Number one on the list: has to be in Larkford. And for the record, I'm happy to call you a doof as often as necessary. Then you just need to work out what else means the most.' She shrugged. 'Maybe you won't find it all in one house, though. I mean . . .' She looked around, catching sight of Charlotte and Henry Lansing holding hands as they watched the Bonfire Night celebrations unfold. 'Maybe you just find the perfect home and then rent a few acres from the Lansings – they've about seventy or eighty acres going spare last time I looked. You know, mix and match? Pick'n'mix?' She grinned. 'I bet they don't have that in LA either.'

Ben and Tom charged across to swing around her legs, hyped up on sugar, and scrambled excitedly for her undivided attention. 'Did you see us, Mummy? Did you see?'

'I didn't even trip over,' said Ben solemnly.

'And I remembered all my words,' countered Tom, his competitive one-upmanship with his twin still running strong. 'Mr French said I was brilliant,' he said modestly.

'Come on!' shouted Ben, the doughnuts and applause having clearly gone to his head. 'Jack and Archie are doing the next song. The hard one.' The two boys were gone again, weaving through the legs of the crowd, hands automatically connected, as always.

'One day some horrible child is going to point out that

holding hands isn't cool. That their natural urge to connect is weird, or gay or something equally cruel, and I think my heart will break a little,' Holly said out of nowhere, a confidence that Connor felt he really had no right to have earned.

Connor leaned over and kissed her cheek spontaneously. 'You're a lovely mum,' he said. 'And even, possibly, a bit of a genius.'

'I am?'

Connor nodded vigorously. 'Pick'n'mix,' he said vehemently, claiming another kiss on the other cheek and pulling her into a hug. A full, no-holds-barred, genuine hug of friendship, leaving Holly flustered and blushing.

'Looks like I got here just in time,' said an amused voice beside them in the crowd. 'It's a good job I'm not the insecure type.' Taffy clapped Connor on the back in greeting, somewhat more forcefully than normal. He leaned down to kiss Holly fleetingly on the lips, his whisper all too easy for Connor to hear: 'I turn my back for five minutes, Wifey, and you're smooching with a rock star.' He was joking, of course he was, but there was still that tiny boost to his very Welshness that only happened when he was feeling on edge. 'Anything else I've missed? Like, for example, why the Guy Fawkes effigy awaiting a fiery death appears to be wearing my favourite shirt?'

Holly's eyes widened in surprise, but she kissed him firmly in greeting, dodging his question, instinctively covering for the boys. Connor noticed there was no mention of her earlier struggles to keep all the children in check and get everyone 'show ready'. Maybe, to her, it was already old news? Or maybe, she was just too proud to let Taffy know that him bailing out on her today had actually been more of a problem than she was willing to admit. He allowed himself a private smile; she certainly didn't seem too set on chastising the twins about the impending incineration of Taffy's clothes.

Every marriage was different, and who was he to comment?

'Oh,' Holly said, as the thought just occurred to her, 'there is one thing that'll make you both laugh. I've been offered a job!' She grinned and folded herself into Taffy's side as she chattered away about Matthew's charity and The Big Cheese from the Rugby Club hearing her on the radio, almost laughingly telling them both of the plump, juicy offer on the table.

It seemed to Connor that she'd already made up her mind. Perhaps she was just so easy and comfortable in her decision not to accept, that she didn't seem to notice Taffy's reaction, so keen to share the joke that she completely missed the tightening of his jaw and the peeved flash in his eyes.

But Connor didn't. From where he was standing, there was trouble brewing and he could only hope that Holly's diplomacy extended into her own life as well. It looked like she was going to be needing it.

'Still,' Holly concluded happily, 'it's always nice to be asked.'

'Yes,' Taffy replied stiffly, turning away as the firework finale began in earnest, lighting up the Larkford sky. 'I imagine it must be.'

Chapter 10

'Well!' exhaled Elsie loudly, a few days later, the roll of her eyes almost audible as Holly showed Bettina von Harden to the door, trying desperately to keep a straight face.

'If I'd known being your wingman for nanny interviews would be this exciting, I'd have joined in weeks ago,' Elsie continued, topping up her cup of tea.

Holly closed the front door and returned to the sofa, shaking her head. 'Seriously, what the actual fudge?'

Elsie snorted. 'I see the no-swearing plan is going well?'

Holly frowned. 'You try interviewing all these vapid girls without a few choice expletives up your sleeve.' She glanced at her watch, grateful for once that Lottie and Olivia had gone down for their nap without complaint. Of course, it had been an exhausting morning of constant stimulation to make it so, and now Holly had two more interviews to conduct before she could officially call the afternoon's offering a bust.

'Should we switch to wine, darling, just to be sure? This amount of stress can't be good for either of us. I mean, what on earth was Bettina von Clueless even going on about? You could tell from the moment she walked in the door that she'd never even got close to an infant!'

Holly agreed wholeheartedly, but she didn't dare tell Elsie

the reason why. The nanny agency had already forewarned her that the notion of a fine Georgian townhouse, two doctor parents and a semi-resident movie star were proving irresistible to their applicants. Despite all their best efforts, there were one or two muppets slipping through the net to interview stage and it was now, apparently, Holly's job to weed them out.

No such worries with their next contender though, as she bustled inside at Holly's behest, her starched brown uniform its own calling card of sorts in the world of professional nannies. 'I'm Melva Cumberland. How do you do?'

'Melva?' said Elsie, with a twinkle, unable to resist meddling. 'That's an unusual name.'

'Yes, well, um . . .' For a moment the professional façade dropped and a flurry of discomfort tweaked her features. 'My father was called Melvin and he, er, wanted to keep the name in the family. So to speak.'

'Fascinating,' said Elsie. 'And not a name that's easily forgotten, I would imagine. I wonder, was he hoping for a son?'

Melva turned her attention to Holly, almost imploringly, hoping for the actual interview to start. None of these candidates seemed to realise that, for Holly and Elsie, the chit-chat part of proceedings was where they gleaned the information that made all the difference. Their personality, after all, was often just as important as their CV.

'So,' Holly said, taking pity on her. 'Your résumé is beyond impressive. I wondered, have you any experience with twins?'

The relief on Melva's face at being back on solid ground was nothing compared to the five-minute monologue she launched into, clearly pre-prepared. She was obviously determined to show that, although none of her charges to date had been twins 'per se', that didn't mean she was fazed by the prospect.

Melva leaned forward, elbows on her knees, brown

uniform almost crackling. 'I think the most important thing, is to start as you mean to go on. One must really be very firm with Baby from the outset. Or indeed Babies, I should say. Baby needs to know his or her routine and to fit around the family, don't you agree, Mummy? There's no need for the entire family to be disrupted during their early years, after all.'

Holly nodded and sipped her tea, desperately trying to regain her composure and determinedly looking away from Elsie for fear of total and unprofessional collapse. Although, come to think of it, she wasn't here in a professional capacity, was she? This was her home, her children, her rules.

'And if the family in question wanted a slightly more, well, laid-back approach. After all, if I'd been at work all day, I would like to see my children—'

'After bedtime?' Melva cut in. 'Oh, Mummy. Routine is everything – *especially* with twins.'

Elsie's snort was quiet but unmistakable.

There was no doubt that Melva was qualified – overqualified probably for what they needed – but Holly was beginning to realise that it wasn't letters after their names she was after. Given a decent amount of experience – unlike the dreadful Bettina – they needed someone like-minded to slot into their already chaotic lives.

Showing Melva the door was easy.

Working out what to do next to narrow the search was somewhat harder. A squawk from the baby monitor meant their time was up. The last candidate would very much have to take them as she found them.

Nuzzling both of the girls into her arms at once was a skill that she had carefully honed over the last twelve months. Olivia and Lottie settled so much more happily if they were together and Holly could also do away with the constant tally chart that ran in her subconscious to check she was dividing her time equally.

It had been the same with Ben and Tom and nothing had really changed.

There was still only one Holly to go around, only this time she was stretched in four directions.

Wiping ineffectually at the sweet potato purée stain on her blouse, Holly gazed down at her girls adoringly, their starfish fingers reaching out and grasping anything within reach. After every meal, it was cuddle time.

Family law.

Admittedly, it was a little cosy on the sofa when everyone was home, but it also gave Holly a real opportunity to spend time with her kids. It was also the time that Ben and Tom were most forthcoming about their day at school. If she asked as soon as they got home, she was lucky to get a 'yeah, good' in response. If she wanted to know how they were really doing, then cuddle time was it.

Perhaps the same could be applied to Elsie, she wondered, whose behaviour had become increasingly squirrelly of late. 'So, any news on the noisy neighbours?' she asked, all innocence, determined not to let on that Connor had already dropped her in it.

The doorbell rang, setting off a cacophony of barking from Eric and the odd, snuffling grunty greeting that Nineteen had adopted since being relocated to the garden full time.

'Crap, she's early,' said Holly, looking around at the scene of devastation that had taken a mere twenty minutes to evolve. There was also no hiding the look of relief and guilt that flitted across Elsie's face and Holly briefly wondered whether

Elsie was in fact having an amorous affair with some ageing lothario on the other side of the party-wall.

'Don't you dare tidy up for the staff!' said Elsie firmly, regaining her poise. 'I'll get the door; you stay put.'

Holly fidgeted uncomfortably, every part of her screaming out that just a quick tidy, a gathering of muslins and onesies would surely be okay – her contentedly settled children staring up at her said otherwise. Stay put, don't move. If she was here to judge, then Plum Castigliano was not the help that Holly needed.

Holly smoothed the tiniest perfect ringlet from Olivia's forehead, finding a more serene sense of purpose simply from following their lead. She glanced up to see Elsie practically fizzing with excitement in the doorway.

'Come through, come through and meet Dr Graham,' Elsie said impishly, mouthing something to Holly that looked like 'way too hot'. Holly frowned for a moment before Plum walked in behind her and the mystery was solved.

Plum walked across the sitting room, looking for all the world like a young Sophia Loren. 'Oh, hello, bambinas,' she said warmly, tossing her well-worn Tods bag onto the floor and sitting down beside Holly on the sofa, eschewing the carefully positioned 'interviewee' armchair. 'Oh, Dr Graham, they will be heart-wreckers when they are bigger, yes?' She held out a finger and Lottie instantly clasped it tightly. 'This is good. Girls need to be strong, Dr Graham, don't you think?'

'Hi,' said Holly, 'I'd shake your hand, but—'

Plum laughed easily. 'You have them full, no?' She leaned in and brushed feather-light kisses on each of Holly's cheeks. 'So we say hello the Italian way.' She crossed her endless legs and her slender pencil skirt moved with her body as though it were tailored to fit her personally.

'I have here my *documenti* and my references ...' She

reached down and pulled out a sheaf of papers held together with an expensive tortoiseshell hairclip. 'But you know, the most crucial things cannot be written on a piece of a paper.'

Holly's glance flickered over to Elsie, who was looking equally spellbound. 'We were saying just the same thing, only moments ago,' she confessed, not even looking at the paperwork. 'Why don't you tell us a little about yourself?'

Plum smiled. 'Well, this is no problem. I talk a lot. You need to know this about me.' She glanced down at the gurgling babies in Holly's arms. 'So there is also no problem with the cell phone and the iPad. With my babies, we do the talking – in English, in Italian, as you prefer.' She smiled, blushing prettily. '*Così* – about me. I am the middle child of seven in my family. You know Italians! So from a very early time I was taking care of my little brother and sisters. Then I trained with a lovely family in Florence – they had three nannies and eight children, from babies to teenager. I had to learn fast, you know? And then I like to travel, so I work with this company who lend the villas – very big, very beautiful – a lot of very spoiled children, though. It is sad, I am thinking, to have so much, but appreciate so little. But I realise, you see, my English needs the work and so I am arriving this month, with all my letters of support and you can phone these families too if you want.'

Plum stopped for a moment, guiltily smiling as she realised she had barely taken a breath. 'I am not looking for tempo-rary, Dr Graham. I look for a home in England, with a nice family, like when I was beginning in Florence. I look to grow with the children, you know.'

'Wow,' said Holly after a moment. 'And how do you feel about animals? Dogs, pigs, occasionally geese ...' She was feeling her way here, waiting for the flaw, the crack in the porcelain of perfection.

Plum laughed. 'My home in Toscana is a farm, so I'm okay if you want me to milk a goat.' She shrugged apologetically. 'I'm okay to butcher your pig, but I do not like to do the killing, I'm sorry.'

Holly gasped. 'No, no, he's a pet – the pig. He's part of the family. No killing required.'

'Oh, okay! *Uff!*' said Plum prettily. 'Sometimes the English can be a little ...' She made her deep limpid eyes go wide. 'You know?'

'Oh, I do,' said Elsie, nodding her head, as though she herself weren't one hundred per cent Union Jack through and through.

Holly shook her head and laughed. 'Okay, so you're good with animals, you're used to a little chaos and you're happy for me to call your references?'

'Of course,' said Plum firmly as if this were the most obvious thing in the world. It was indeed a world away from the evasive, canny manoeuvrings on this very point that they had witnessed of late.

Lottie began to squirm and fidget and Holly moved to quickly adjust.

'May I?' asked Plum, as she caught Lottie before she could slide any lower on Holly's lap. 'Well, hello there, I'm Plum,' she said very seriously. 'It is most wonderful to be making your acquaintance.'

'That's Lottie,' said Holly, watching Plum's deft and easy manner with interest.

'This is such a pretty name,' Plum said. 'You are a very lucky girl, Miss Lottie. My true name is *Vittoria*, but my brothers and sisters they called me Plum, like in the books. And also it is hard to say, no? Can you say *Vittoria*, little Lottie? You see – *complicato* – too tricky.'

Holly looked up at Elsie, eyes questioning. She was so strongly tempted to hire this girl on the spot. Yes, she was gorgeous and Elsie was right, way too hot to be a sensible hire. But then, what did that say about Taffy if she turned away this perfect woman on the strength of a possible flaw in his willpower?

'Plum?' said Holly. 'Do you drive? Can you cook?' Her common sense reasserted itself in the face of this woman's charisma. But in all honesty, who was she kidding? She knew instinctively that Plum would simply gel with their household, that Ben and Tom would adore her and that she'd match Elsie banter for banter.

Plum shrugged. 'Of course. I have a clean licence and I can cook for the whole family if you like. You like lasagne? Risotto? Maybe a little roast pork?' She gasped in horror. 'Not your little piglet, of course! I can go to the butcher!'

Elsie was working hard to find reasons to find fault too. 'Ben – he's six – has a severe allergy to dairy. How would you handle that?'

Plum considered for a moment. 'It will be difficult for him, yes? With friends and play-days after school? I think I must teach him to cook delicious things that have no dairy. Teach him where to look, which dishes are safe, so he can eat with confidence. Invite his friends for a meal, you know. Show them that different isn't bad. Different can be good. But we must be careful too – your other boy, and these girls, they need their calcium. I am thinking lots of seafood and the – how do you say? Legumes?'

'How would you feel about a trial period?' Holly said after a moment.

'To live with you here?' Plum queried.

Holly nodded. 'I have some time before I go back to work. Things are a little, well, uncertain on that front, but I thought perhaps we could overlap?'

Plum's face lit up. 'You could show me the rope! I would love this. Sometimes, when I start with a new family, they just give me a *list*.' The disdain in her voice for this approach was unconcealed. 'You can show me how you like things to be. I am not their mama, after all. But I need to follow your lead.'

Holly paused, taking in the chic, beautiful young woman before her. She had no doubt that she would treasure and nurture her children. And, in a way, wasn't it complete discrimination to turn her away simply because she was so stunningly beautiful? She tugged briefly at her sleeves, wondering whether as part of her acclimatisation programme, Plum might be persuaded to take her shopping. There was a time and a place for dungarees and Taffy's jumpers, but if she were going to pick up the mantle of Dr Graham, rather than simply 'Mummy', then where better to start?

Lizzie's advice flickered through her head: 'You feel good; you look good.' She made a concentrated effort to ignore her other, more salient, pearls of wisdom – 'Never invite a beautiful woman into your home unless you plan to be there.'

Holly watched Lottie's reaction to Plum, her peals of laughter and her open smile. 'Plum, do you have any personal commitments? A boyfriend? An all-consuming love of drums or tap-dancing?'

Plum laughed, her raven hair reflecting the beams of sunlight that filtered through the window, as she leaned forward to clasp Holly's forearm affectionately. 'Oh, Dr Graham, you make me laugh. But no – there is nothing, nobody. I am footloose and fancy-free. Did I say that right?'

'You did,' said Holly, knowing it should make a difference, make her pause, but her heart was ruling her head in making this decision. 'When would you like to start?'

Chapter 11

Alice passed the box of tissues across the desk to Margaret Harwood and gave her a moment to compose herself. It was almost as though the Universe was having a little laugh at her expense this afternoon.

Seriously, she thought, what were the odds that—

'And I know she's busy,' sobbed Margaret, 'and they've got a lot on, but that doesn't mean she couldn't visit! I am her mother, after all.'

Alice tried so hard to empathise with her patients, to look past the medical sometimes, to the personal issues behind their symptoms, but this one was seriously testing her. Although it wasn't poor Margaret's fault that her appointment came hot on the tails of three increasingly bulldozing voicemails from Alice's own mother.

'Well,' said Alice, 'why don't *you* go and visit *them*? I'm sure that Kim would love to see you, even if she can't swing a visit to you here. I mean, if she and her husband are both working, and the kids have schools and clubs and commitments, that's five people's diaries to wrangle. Whereas, if you went to stay with them, you could slot right in. Granny on site? From what you've said, it seems like Kim has her hands pretty full?'

Margaret looked at her sharply. 'Did she call you? Did she tell you to say all this?'

Alice shook her head. 'I just like to look at situations from both sides. And, to be honest, Margaret, I don't want to be prescribing you anti-anxiety medication just because you've asked for it. Anxiety is a clinical diagnosis, Margaret. It's more than a bad mood, or feeling panicky or angry—'

'Well, I phoned that Lizzie woman on the radio the other week and she said that misplaced anger could be a sign of anxiety,' Margaret countered, looking very pleased with herself.

Alice sighed; there were some patients who were never going to be happy unless they walked out of her consulting room with a prescription in their hand. Sadly, she had yet to find a way to prescribe what Margaret really needed on the NHS. She saw it a lot; older women who seemed to have forgotten how challenging it was to raise a young family, and that was even before the concept of 'having it all' had translated into 'doing it all' for most women. And, of course, like poor, much-maligned Kim, the later they were starting a family, the more likely they were to be juggling a demanding career, young children and increasingly challenging elderly parents. And the geographical spread hardly helped.

Alice sighed. There wasn't a prescription for empathy, although rarely a day went by when Alice didn't wish otherwise.

Even three patients later, Margaret's obvious distress still left footprints in Alice's mind.

Was there a similar story being shared with her own mother's GP back in Orkney, she wondered, trying to follow her own advice to walk a mile in someone else's shoes. Particularly where her own mother was concerned, it was easier said than done.

Freya Walker was Orkney born and bred, never having entertained for a moment that her mainlander-husband would have done anything except follow her back to the islands and make his own life there too. Since his passing, she had become gradually more and more resolute in her belief that life began and ended in the wilds of this Scottish outpost. Her moods were mercurial at best, her disposition towards Alice changing with the direction of the wind, or so it seemed.

She had taken Alice's decision to head south as a sign of rebellion, accusing her of going 'soft' but always, always believing that she'd be back.

Alice took a deep breath, picked up the phone and dialled, wondering which version of Freya Walker would be on parade today: loving mother, demanding tyrant, Orkney's greatest proponent or simply a tearful old lady appealing to her daughter's compassion to come home?

'Mum, it's me.'

'Whitna wey is tha ta say Aye te tha mither?' came her mother's garbled response, her words a mongrel combination of English and Orkney's distinctive dialect. As always, it took a few moments for her mind to change gear when her daughter phoned from '*aff sooth*'. Alice could almost hear the cogs whirling. 'How are ye, Alice?'

'I'm okay, Mum. Just at work and thinking about you, so I thought I'd call.'

'Ah, well tha's alwis nice to hear,' replied Freya, her tone softening more and more with each syllable. 'I was talking about ye only yesterday. Magnus Droll from the castle sends his best. Offered to find a job for your Jamie if you're ready to come home? Assuming he is still *your* Jamie with this daft job in Donegal keeping him away.' She always spoke as though Alice were away from the islands under sufferance, a nuisance to be tolerated until she could be home again. Freya Walker had never understood Alice's desire to flee the somewhat overwhelming reality of island-life and she really couldn't understand why Jamie had made his choice to be away from her daughter.

Alice smiled through slightly gritted teeth. 'You are lovely, Mum. And do please thank Magnus, but I'm not sure there's much call for training assistance dogs at the castle.'

'Ach, he's adaptable, isn't he, this lad of yours? He likes dogs, and they're in need of a gamekeeper.' She paused. 'Dr Sjorgen is retiring next year, you know . . .'

Alice did know.

She'd been receiving the countdown to Dr Sjorgen's retirement in every phone call for the last three years. It felt like a large *Countdown* clock ticking in the background of every phone call and the resulting tug of obligation and guilt was a cocktail that left a bitter taste.

In Alice's opinion, it was no coincidence that the Orcadian expression for common sense was '*mither witt*' – it was absolute doctrine that mother knew best, an uncomfortable relic of her island education that refused to release its tenacious hold on her belief system no matter how far south she moved.

Never had Alice been so delighted about one of Tilly's dramas as she was after ten minutes of this circular conversation with her mother, going nowhere but wearing her down nonetheless. And her mother wondered why she didn't call more often?

'Help me?' wailed Tilly, abruptly letting herself into Alice's consulting room and closing the door behind her, leaning against it for good measure. No matter how calm and professional she was as *Dr* Campbell, out of hours, she was still the same old Tilly Campbell from med school, who left a trail of devastation and broken hearts in her wake.

With plenty of promises to call her mother again soon, Alice disengaged herself from the guilt-train and turned to Tilly with a smile. 'Ten out of ten for timing. But dare I ask who you're hiding out from this time?'

Tilly shrugged. 'Just, you know, a chap in the waiting room.' Tilly's expression brought a whole new layer to her habitual mortification about crossing paths with her romantic conquests and Alice felt a moment of disquiet.

'Tills, is he here with his wife?' she queried, wondering whether they were about to have a scorned-spouse-on-the-rampage type moment.

Tilly blanched. 'Worse,' she whispered. 'His mother!'

Alice's eyes widened in shocked disbelief. 'No?' she breathed. Surely it hadn't come to this? Tilly's fuck-it-all attitude to relationships was one thing, but picking off young men who simply weren't old enough to know better was quite another. 'Is he . . . ?' she ventured. 'I mean, is he still at school?'

It wasn't such a stupid question. Some of the sixth form boys at the local college looked like adults, and they all knew that Teddy Kingsley had a fairly relaxed attitude to under-age drinking at The Kingsley Arms. Just because this lad had been propping up the bar at the weekend with a pint, didn't necessarily mean he was of legal age.

Tilly shook her head. 'I don't think so. But seeing him with his mum, I'm suddenly not so sure. He was at the bonfire thing too. Can you look him up on the computer?'

Alice took a breath, wondering how to tell her friend that due diligence should really come *before* she leapt into bed with them, not after. 'Okay,' she said reluctantly, knowing full well this was not what patient records were designed for. 'Who is it?'

The awkward pause spoke volumes.

'Bloody hell,' cursed Alice uncharacteristically. She pushed back her chair and left the room only to return moments later with a smile.

'What?' Tilly said, her awkwardness making her stroppy. 'What are you smiling about?'

'It's Matt,' said Alice simply. 'Matthew Giles?'

Tilly looked blank.

'You're fine. I mean, obviously not, or you wouldn't be shagging anything with a pulse without finding out their name, but you're not about to end up on the sex offenders' register. He's twenty-one. Moved home to take care of Molly last year. He's actually rather lovely and far too nice to be one of your sexual discards.'

'Oh,' said Tilly.

'Yes, oh,' replied Alice, shaking her head.

Tilly paused. 'He looked older.'

'Don't you think we should be talking about this?' Alice persisted. 'I mean, it's a different bloke every weekend, almost. And if you didn't even know his name ...'

'It's easy for you to say,' Tilly said churlishly, 'spending all your time pining over Jamie, happy with a long-distance relationship. I'm just not in that place. I just want a bit of fun and I'm not sure there's anything wrong with that. I've been doing it for years. Not *everybody* wants a rela-tionship, Al.'

'Not everybody does. But you used to,' Alice said gently.

'People change,' Tilly said under her breath. She stirred herself and plastered on a smile. 'Sorry about barging in. Just panicked a bit when I saw him – boys and their mothers, eh?'

'Maybe it was timely? I mean—' Alice attempted, before being cut off mid-conversation.

'Do we have to go over this again? I like it here. But it's hardly challenging medicine, is it? You all keep looking at me as though I'm about to bolt, but I'm still here, aren't I?'

'You are,' Alice conceded, 'but even you have to admit that shagging your way through half the patient roster suggests a certain ambivalence to your future here?'

'Well, when you put it like that . . . Look, it's fine. I'm fine. No laws have been broken. Crisis averted. If you can even call it that. It's always First World problems around here anyway, isn't it?' She set her jaw in a way that told Alice everything she needed to know – a classic Tilly-ism of old. It meant that she knew she was in the wrong, but was prepared to go down fighting.

Alice nodded, her defusal skills well honed. 'You're absolutely right. But then, you're never going to see anything more than that, if you never take the time to look beneath the surface, are you?' She clicked through various windows open on her computer screen until she found the one she was looking for.

'Have you even been to the Pickwick Estate in all the months you've lived here?' Alice challenged her friend, knowing only too well her weakness for a cause and suspecting strongly that all her risky behaviour of late had been an attempt at filling the adrenalin void that her MSF days had previously occupied.

'What's that?' asked Tilly with a raised eyebrow. 'Another one of the stately homes around here?'

'Another kind of estate; it's social housing,' Alice replied, refusing to rise. 'Families living on benefits. Health problems, drug and alcohol problems. We see kids with malnutrition, mums with depression … and that's just the obvious. Ask people. If you're looking to make a difference, you could do worse than starting there.' Alice hit print and watched as a report form churned its way out of the printer beside her before handing it to Tilly.

'Why don't you go and do this home visit, hmm? May Fowler, sixty-three. She's raising her granddaughter, while her daughter, Keira, is in hospital having her third round of chemo for ovarian cancer. May's arthritis is flaring up and she's struggling with the stairs, but the Council won't repair the lift because it keeps being vandalised. So when I can, I go to her.'

Alice watched Tilly flush uncomfortably, May's circumstances chiming in direct contradiction to the picture of bucolic happiness in Larkford to which Tilly still seemed so firmly, and erroneously, wedded. Of course, Alice knew only too well that the same issues affected some of their wealthiest patients too, but somehow she felt that the Pickwick Estate might appeal to Tilly's altruism and fondness for the underdog in a way that Georgian townhouses and cute cottages might not.

'Is May retired?' Tilly asked after a moment, scanning the document in her hands.

Alice nodded. 'Been a teacher for forty years. In the state sector. She really is one of the good ones, Tills. Deserves better than this for her retirement. I gather she used all her savings to help Keira get by when she was first diagnosed, hence the social housing and the surrogate mum.'

'You kind of imagine that if you work your whole life and do the right thing, that you get to enjoy your retirement in a lovely cottage with roses round the door, don't you?' Tilly mused.

Alice said nothing for a moment, Tilly's question only echoing her own.

'Tills?' she said, as her friend distractedly stood up to leave. 'Let Matthew down easy, won't you? He doesn't have the easiest time, but he makes such a difference to all the Young Carers around here; he doesn't deserve the Campbell Brush-off.'

Tilly nodded. 'I'll talk to him. Maybe, you know, cut down on the dating for a bit. At least locally ...' She attempted a laugh, but its pitch was off-key and unconvincing.

Alice didn't feel good about it, but somehow she was hoping that, by opening Tilly's eyes a little more to the good people around her, she might start to finally put down some roots. After all, it wasn't just people in the war-torn corners of the planet who needed the drive and determination of doctors like Tilly. And the sooner Tilly herself realised that, Alice thought, the more likely she was to settle in Larkford. She actively chose to ignore her own vested interest in Tilly staying put, as she picked up the phone to call Jamie, her mother's unsettling opinions still rattling around in her head.

Chapter 12

Dan knocked on Lizzie's front door and waited, hearing the scuffle and swearing that accompanied Lizzie's every attempt to stand up since her op. 'I'll be there in a— Oh, shit! Hang on, I just— Bloody hell!' Lizzie yanked open the front door, one hand pressed firmly against her appendix scar and looking somewhat green in the face. 'Sorry.'

'Are you sure you should be going out and about?' Dan asked, eyeing up his cousin apprehensively.

'It's a mental health issue at this point,' said Lizzie fiercely.

'No change there, then,' teased Dan affectionately, reaching out a hand to steady Lizzie as she wobbled. 'So, what am I? Your back-up, back-up plan?' Dan asked. Not known for her patience at the best of times, Lizzie was finding her enforced recuperation somewhat of a challenge. 'Let me guess: Will's at work, Connor's finally realised what a pain in the backside you are when you're bored and Holly's busy juggling all of your various offspring?'

Lizzie pouted, hating her predictability. 'Do you want to go and nosey around The Big House or not? Did you even *know* it was on the market? I mean, I thought they'd carry Lady Peal out of that house in a box!'

Dan sighed; as was so often the case in Larkford, he

knew more than he was able to share. If anything, he was
impressed by the determination of Aggie Peal's decision-
making process. She certainly wasn't letting the grass grow
under her feet.

And Lizzie had known full well that he wouldn't be able
to resist the chance for a snoop – his recent interest in the
local property market was in danger of becoming a full-
blown obsession. 'Come on then,' he said, avoiding her
question. 'Connor said he'd meet us there and he'll think
we've forgotten at this rate.' He held out his arm for Lizzie
as she wobbled. 'I can't believe how quickly Connor moves
when he puts his mind to something. Unlike you – you
slow poke.'

The front door to The Big House was barely fifty yards
away, though to look at the expression of intense concentration on Lizzie's face, you'd think it was a mile, but as
recuperative outings went, Dan had to admit this was far
more enjoyable than he'd imagined. There was something
rather restful about strolling along at the snail's pace that
Lizzie could just about manage, rather than dashing everywhere like a blue-arsed fly. There was a stubborn layer of
frost underfoot and a recent heaviness to the blanket of cloud
overhead that boded the arrival of winter, but the freshly
baked bread from Pru Hartley's bakery still scented the air,
bringing a familiar comfort. It was good to be home, he
decided, no matter how lovely his mini-break with Grace
last weekend had been.

He gazed at Peal Hall – The Big House – as they
approached. It really was one of Larkford's finest gems: a
Georgian rectory standing squarely at the head of the town,
its rear lawns rolling down to meet the grassland of Blackleigh
Farm and its front door facing the Market Place. The best of

both worlds. It would, no doubt, have cost Connor a small fortune, Dan realised.

A cacophony of high-pitched barking greeted their arrival. 'Jesus, how many dogs has she got in there?' Dan asked in surprise.

Lizzie shook her head in despair. 'Too many. There's a Yorkie, a chihuahua and a chorkie – no guesses where that little mongrel came from, all a bit Heinz 57. Not to mention a fluffball, a setter, oh, and a beagle, I think. They just kick off whenever anyone walks by, which is basically every five minutes. You get used to it after a while.'

Connor pulled open the glossy front door, as though he had been poised for their arrival, its glossy myrtle paint adding yet another touch of class to the honey-coloured stone façade. 'Come in, come in,' he said, holding out an arm to Lizzie, 'let's find Witchy a sofa, shall we? She's gone that attractive green colour again.'

Dan and Lizzie exchanged amused glances; the money had barely changed hands but Connor was already morphing into his new persona as Lord of the Manor. 'Where's Aggie?' whispered Lizzie. 'I feel a bit weird just letting ourselves in.'

He ushered them through from the flagstone hallway into the kind of kitchen Dan had only ever seen in movies, or on the pages of a glossy magazine. It was simply stunning. The kind of place that he and Grace could only ever dream of.

The huge Aga took pride of place, of course, throwing out heat and facing a vast Georgian dresser that reached up to the ceiling and had clearly been in situ from the very beginning. French windows stood ajar overlooking the sweeping garden, clearly planted for every season to enjoy its moment; a swathe of winter jasmine released its heavy, luxurious scent into the air.

The scrubbed oak kitchen table, which could easily have seated twenty people, was covered in unrolled plans, their corners weighted down with pewter jugs and silver fruit. 'Oh, how divine to see you both,' said Aggie Peal from her carver chair at the head of the table. 'And such perfect timing! I was just mixing a little Friday cocktail or two.' It was obviously assumed that they would be joining her. 'What a lucky boy you are, Connor, to have such lovely, supportive friends.'

Lady Peal blew a kiss to Lizzie, as Connor settled her onto the kitchen sofa, shuffling a yawning Irish setter out of the way to make space. 'Oh my darling, you do look sore. Do you want some of my pain pills?' she offered without missing a beat. 'I've got some really good ones, now.' She caught Dan's eye and blushed. 'Ooops.'

Dan shook his head, his personal affection for her only just covering his professional irritation. 'Are you determined to move from one "Big House" to another? I hardly think pushing drugs is the best career choice at this point, Aggie,' he said sternly.

'Sorry, Dr Carter,' she said meekly, clearly not giving two shits about the concept of serving hard time. It was some measure of how she was responding to her recent diagnosis that she really was living like there was no tomorrow. Her tomorrows, very sadly, being in short supply.

'And how are the kids taking the news of the sale, Aggie?' Dan asked quietly, as he helped their hostess by tonging ice cubes from the crystal ice-bucket on the kitchen worktop. 'I half thought they might change their minds and move down here, once they knew what was going on.'

Agatha sheepishly twisted a strip of lemon rind around a spoon handle. 'Well, to be honest, Dr Carter, I haven't *exactly* mentioned it. We both know they don't want to be living out here in the sticks; the last thing I want is for them to do so under some misguided sense of obligation.' She shuddered lightly. 'Or worse still, play along to humour me and sell up before the grass has grown over my grave. I'd like to choose my successor, thank you very much.'

'But you told them about your health?' Dan said, wondering why he was even surprised by Aggie's disingenuousness.

Lady Agatha Peal just shrugged and tossed him an apologetic smile as she raised two Martini glasses in the air. 'Cocktails, my darlings.' She took a sip, clearly savouring the first aperitif of the evening. 'Besides, as I was just explaining to Connor, I've been pining for a little European adventure for a while and since this blasted leukaemia is a bit of a lottery anyway, I thought I'd just head for Switzerland.' She shrugged eloquently.

Lizzie's mouth dropped open. Dan simply gaped. 'Aggie? Seriously? Dignitas is a bit extreme . . .' he began, floundering.

Her laughter brought them both up short. 'Not like *that*. I just decided that if I'm to suffer through the indignities of chemo, I'd rather head for the Alps and one of the amazing clinics over there. Thanks to lovely Connor here, I can afford to shell out for a little expediency and a view to die for. No pun intended.' She sipped her Martini gently. 'And I always rather liked the thought of skiing,' she added impishly, enjoying Dan's reaction. 'SKI-ing, darling. Spending the Kids' Inheritance.' She smiled affectionately at Connor. 'All thanks to this one,' she concluded dreamily, obviously rather enamoured with the idea of Connor and his plentiful resources taking care of her beloved money pit.

'And you can blame Holly, actually,' said Connor. 'She made me realise that if I couldn't buy a lovely house with land, then I could put the package together myself. And since

Lady Peal, sorry, Aggie, has kindly agreed to allow me the honour of making this beautiful house my new home, I've taken over the lease on the land at Blackleigh Farm. Charlotte and Henry Lansing are going to stay in the farmhouse and keep enough land for those teeny tiny ponies they seem to love so much and I get the one thing Larkford didn't have – a country estate. Happy days indeed.' An odd look flickered across Connor's face as he raised his glass that Dan couldn't quite discern.

'Happy days!' cried Agatha enthusiastically, downing her cocktail with such fervour that a trickle of Martini escaped and ran down her chin. 'But you must remember, Connor darling, you are now the guardian for the next generation: with great property, comes great responsibility.'

'Spiderman?' queried Dan.

'I rather think he stole it from me, actually,' Agatha retorted. 'Now, where was I? Oh yes. To Peal Hall and the future!' she toasted, only to freeze in horror. 'Oh dear God, did you know it's bad luck to toast with an empty glass?' She clearly believed the superstition far more than any of her doctors' cautions about combining alcohol and pain meds.

What a generation!

He'd take the Elsie Townsend and Agatha Peal approach to his twilight years any day of the week, Dan thought. It certainly made you think, he realised, sitting here and marvelling at the shelves on the dresser, which positively bristled with a lifetime of family photos – was this ever going to be his? Was he going to be able to look back and see a life well lived and a family raised, or was his sole contribution to this life going to be as their family doctor? He couldn't get past the notion that, for him, it simply wasn't enough.

He smiled and laughed and joked along with his companions, but his head and heart were still in an Oxfordshire hotel room with Grace. Grace's openness and honesty was persuasive, he knew, but part of him still wished she were prepared even to consider having a child together. A child that was truly theirs. They weren't *that* old, for God's sake. Forty-two was the new thirty-two when it came to fertility, after all.

He glanced over at the photos once more, Agatha's features reflected over and over again in the faces of her children, and sighed. If his career was to be everything, then right now it wasn't enough and changes needed to be made. Just as soon as he'd worked out what they were.

'Oh, and you'll be wanting to let me know about Mary?' Agatha said suddenly, frowning as though trying to remember what else she had meant to discuss and jolting Dan from his reverie. 'Will you be keeping her on, Connor darling? She's a very good maid-cum-housekeeper and Benedict and I have always found her adequate.'

'Damned by faint praise,' muttered Lizzie under her breath, earning herself A Look.

'But I thought your housekeeper introduced herself as Janet?' Connor checked. 'Do you have two?'

'Ridiculous girl,' said Agatha with feeling. 'Undermining a perfectly satisfactory system. We've always called all our staff Mary, saves one having to remember new names, you know?' She huffed. 'I suppose you could go all modern and call her Janet, is it, if it suits you?'

Agatha yawned and closed her eyes, as though having lost interest in the conversation and Connor nodded to Dan and Lizzie. 'Do you want to have a little look around?' He got to his feet and a pack of dogs appeared from various corners of the kitchen at the faintest prospect of entertainment.

'And you're quite sure about the dogs, Aggie?' Connor queried as they lined up like the von Trapp children at his heels.

'Oh yes, especially if I'm making a break for it. They'll be so much happier here with you,' Aggie said sleepily, before nodding off in the grand carver armchair, her heavily coiffured hair tipping forward like a quiff.

Dan was perhaps the only one who could see the expression of forbearance on Connor's face as he left the room, extolling the virtues of the sash windows and original mouldings.

'So, exactly how many dogs come with the house?' Dan whispered to him, knowing only too well how Noodle and Doodle had tweaked the pecking order in his own home.

'Seven,' said Connor quietly, his answer almost eclipsed by Lizzie's snort of amusement, as they made their way into the main entrance hall.

'One setter, one spaniel, a beagle and four little fluff balls,' said Connor in resignation that his beautiful new home apparently came complete with a built-in menagerie.

'Shih-poo,' offered Lizzie, glancing down at the smallest one, jumping up at her legs.

'Bless you,' said Connor with a grin, as he bent down to pick up said fur ball and tuck it into his waistcoat. 'The other three are related, but I'm not sure how.'

'You know,' said Dan with a smile, as Connor continued to play it cool, even as he affectionately stroked the little dog under the chin. 'I think you're nearly ready for your red trousers now.'

'Ooh,' said Lizzie. 'I like it. Don't worry, Conn, we'll get you kitted out in no time.'

'Anything else I need to know?' Connor asked in concern, as the Irish setter leaned herself against his thigh and refused to budge. 'There seem to be even more strings attached to this deal every day and I haven't even moved in yet. Your Holly might have a lot to answer for, you know? Although I just might forgive her if she gets me some decent tickets to the rugby.'

'The rugby? Holly?' Dan queried. 'What did I miss?'

'Oh, it's nothing,' Lizzie reassured him, looking increasingly tired by this early evening decadence. 'Just a funny job offer that Holly got the other day. Can you believe the Rugby Club in Bath want her on staff? A private GP, no less, and access to all those lovely firm thighs – can you imagine?'

'Holly?' double-checked Dan in disbelief.

'I know, right?' agreed Connor. 'Your mate's just great, Witchy, but she can't tell one end of a rugby pitch from another.'

Lizzie snorted indelicately. 'I bet she can tell one end of a rugby player from the other, though.'

Connor gave a filthy laugh but Dan couldn't even muster a smile. Dear God, if Holly was ready to come back to work, then why the hell wasn't she at The Practice and sharing the load? He knew, deep down, that his disproportionate anger had nothing to do with Holly and everything to do with her apparently casual dismissal of the kind of job he had often dreamed of, always assuming he could ignore his pesky moral compass long enough to actually seek out some job satisfaction for himself.

Well, that and his quiet suspicion that he would trade places with Holly in a heartbeat, not truly understanding why she felt the need to return to work so soon when she had those glorious babies at home.

Obviously, he would never dream of saying that aloud – far too controversial – but he couldn't help but wonder whether paternity leave would be everything he hoped for. Or indeed, whether he would ever have the chance to find out.

'And she's considering it?' Dan asked quietly. 'Going into private practice, I mean?'

Lizzie shook her head. 'You know Holly, she's all about the right thing to do. She won't even think twice about what a cushy number this might turn out to be. She'll carry on pining for her patients until you guys let her back.'

'*Let* her—?' Dan began, confused.

'Do you know,' interrupted Lizzie suddenly, clapping her hand over her mouth. 'I'm not sure I should have drunk that Martini . . .'

Dan's thoughts were rudely shoved to the back burner, as he helped his queasy cousin to a chair and fetched her iced water, before ruinous thoughts of babies and rugby crowded his thoughts, his ambitions seemingly thwarted on every front by the women in his life.

hearing Jamie's tales of Padraig and his incorrigible attempts to wind up the *Limey* and it was only too clear to Alice, listening to the commitment in Jamie's voice talking about Minty, that her sacrifice here was small, not to mention temporary, but the difference he was making over there was lasting.

Wandering through the Market Place later, Coco at her heels, further dented Alice's mood. Watching all the other families and couples flitting from stall to stall, the first few Christmas vendors boldly staking their claim on all things sparkly, made it so much harder to be endlessly unwavering in her support. The very thought of Christmas was yet another topic that Alice had been choosing to avoid. She sighed. It may have been the phone call from Jamie, or possibly the slightly passive-aggressive care package that had arrived from her mother. Of course, it was thoughtful of her mum to send down her favourite Tracy Chapman record on vinyl, 'in case she was missing it', but they both knew that her beloved record player was still up in Orkney, in the unchanged room that awaited her return. It was the latest in a series of gentle nudges, followed up by less than gentle phone calls – conversations best avoided if feeling fragile about Jamie's absence. As far as Alice's mother could see it, there was no future in the relationship if he was prepared to accept a job overseas, and her words had the ability to stick in Alice's mind like bindweed and bring torment in the wee small hours.

'You look shit,' said Tilly cheerfully, bounding over and throwing her arms around Alice's shoulders from beside her.

'Aw, you flatterer, you,' said Alice with a smile, thanking God, and Holly and her prodigious fertility, that Tilly had come back into her life, just as Jamie had left. 'Always knowing just the right thing to say.'

'Well, we can't have you pining for that lanky pooch-hustler all the time, can we? Plus, you know, it's Saturday, so I'm guessing the Mad Haggis has been in touch to spread *doooom-and-gloooom* in your heart?' Tilly's fake Scottish accent was nearly as bad as Jamie's Irish one, and for a moment, Alice wondered why they bothered, before realising they had a common goal – to cheer her up and make her smile.

'Am I that predictable?' Alice asked wryly.

'Nope. But your mother is,' laughed Tilly. She froze, turning quickly to face the other way and dragging Alice with her. 'Quick. Pretend you're talking to me!'

'I *am* talking to you,' said Alice slowly, as though addressing a rather dim-witted child.

'No, I mean, properly – look all intense, or cry or something,' Tilly whispered forcefully.

Truth be told, thought Alice, neither of those were too much of a reach from her current emotional state, but she was still none the wiser until . . .

'Hi, Tilly,' said lovely Matthew Giles shyly, his neck mottled pink with the gumption it must have taken him to walk over and interrupt them, pushing his delightful mother Molly in her wheelchair.

'Hi,' managed Tilly begrudgingly, avoiding eye-contact like a truculent teenager.

Oh dear God, thought Alice, if this was how Tilly behaved with all her romantic conquests in Larkford, no wonder there were ripples of ill-feeling and concern.

'Well, aren't you two a picture! Girls' day out, is it?' said Molly brightly, her words slurring slightly but the light still very much in her eyes. Such a cruel condition – young-onset Parkinson's – robbing her of so much time and independence. Thank goodness for her gorgeous and capable son. He really was an inspiration to all of them – and he certainly didn't deserve the Campbell Cold-shoulder.

'Well, we thought we'd make the most of this glorious sunshine, didn't we, Tilly?' Alice said, when Tilly remained resolutely silent. 'Poor Tilly is keeping me company, having to listen to me moan on about missing Jamie. I think I may be starting to sound like a broken record.'

Molly reached out and took her hand, the tremor making it hard to maintain her grasp, but the tentative pressure nevertheless making it clear she felt for Alice; Molly was nothing if not empathetic of her fellow Larkford souls, even as her own life quietly disintegrated day by day. 'He's a good lad, your Jamie. Stay the course, Dr Walker. The good ones are always worth waiting for.'

It was exactly what Alice needed to hear, but possibly the worst thing she could have said to encourage her son, his hopeful face still firmly turned towards Tilly like a sunflower seeking out the sun.

'How's the fund-raising going, Matthew?' Alice asked, her heart going out to him, his unrequited love like a banner of vulnerability. 'Did I hear you have big plans afoot?'

He turned to her gratefully, still shooting hurt glances in Tilly's direction every few moments. 'It's going really well, actually. I can't believe nobody thought of it before, but I'm getting such a positive response from local businesses – although they're yet to put their money where their mouth is. Having a drop-in centre for Young Carers is going to make such a world of difference locally – ultimately I'd love it if we could offer more than a little distraction and support to the kids. Maybe some respite care too? But that's all a long way in the future.'

'Something fabulous to aim for though, Matthew,' Alice agreed.

He nodded. 'And I had no idea how much of an over-lap there was between our Young Carers and the Invisible Disabilities Support Group that Dr Graham set up at The Practice. I spoke to the counsellor the other day and we reckon it's even harder for the kids who are de facto carers for parents with the less obvious conditions, you know? To the outside world, everything *looks* normal, doesn't it? So there's less support, less understanding. I haven't quite worked out the logistics yet, but there's the possibility of moving the support group to the drop-in centre once it's up and running.'

All the shyness and awkward body language had slowly melted away, as he spoke with such conviction and consideration. He literally transformed in front of Alice's eyes and she got a small taste of what might have attracted Tilly in the first place. And of course, because it was Tilly, the moment Matthew's attention had shifted and his passion redirected, her interest was piqued once more, her head slowly meerkat-ing from the chunky scarf swathed around her neck.

'Don't you dare,' whispered Alice urgently, predicting exactly where Tilly's thoughts were heading, as Matthew bent down to tuck the blanket around his mum's legs more firmly – it may be sunny, but a chill breeze whistled down the valley occasionally just to keep you on your toes.

Tilly shot her a filthy look, which thankfully Matthew missed.

'You girls have a lovely day. My handsome son is taking me for lunch. Aren't I lucky?' Molly said, effectively bringing the conversation to a close and the two women watched them walk away without a word.

'She is, you know, in so many ways,' Tilly said after a moment. 'I can't think of many young men who would be willing to turn their lives upside down for their parents.'

They looked at each other, knowing only too well that neither of them – ironically, given their 'caring profession' – would be quite so quick to do so. But then, thought Alice, perhaps that had more to do with the relationships they had with their respective parents.

'He loves her,' Alice said simply, with a wistful sigh.

Tilly frowned. 'I wonder what it's like, to have that kind of unconditional love?'

The market swayed and billowed around them, as Alice and Tilly stood side by side, lost in thought. Alice couldn't say for certain where Tilly's head was taking her, but she knew clearly enough where her own thoughts led without hesitation. She already had two such loves in her life, she realised. And it was a timely reminder that giving Jamie the freedom to pursue his altruistic leanings was part and parcel of loving him. Coco, on the other hand, was always there, always loving, unconditionally by her side. She sniffed, hoping that Tilly hadn't noticed this over-welling of emotion.

'You should get a dog,' Alice blurted. 'I mean, if you're serious about staying in Larkford?'

Tilly looked around her, seeming to notice for the first time that almost every couple, every family, came complete with a canine companion. The Reverend Taylor was even bartering with The Cheese Man for tasty morsels to tempt Dibley's appetite; the Major and Marion sharing their morning pastries with Grover as though he were their baby, which in a way, to them, he probably was. 'Maybe. But then what could I offer a dog? I work long hours and I'm hardly reliable . . .'

'Making good progress with those commitment issues, I see?' teased Alice gently.

Tilly stuck her tongue out. 'Don't judge, Walker. You know I'm a serious head-case when it comes to relationships. Always have been.'

'Not always,' Alice reminded her gently, aware that she was walking on eggshells, aware that they never really talked about that time. That time, before Tilly's understanding of intimacy and trust had been so rudely violated. It seemed cruel in the extreme that the entitlement and arrogance of one cocky student could still be causing ripples in her friend's love life all these years later, but . . .

'Don't go there, Alice. Not today.' Tilly's tone was firm and brooked no argument.

Whether Tilly could actually see how much the shadows of the past affected the decisions of her present was anyone's guess, thought Alice, wishing that she could find a way to get through to her lovely friend. Maybe then she wouldn't feel the need to control every aspect of her dating life – or indeed give herself quite so freely and without thought of her value or worth. Only her work seemed to give her the emotional reward that she clearly craved, no doubt explaining why she sought out war zones and humanitarian crises, where other girls, other women, were helpless in the face of their situation. As a recovery plan it had held merit – initially at least – but all these years later, Alice couldn't help but wonder whether she'd let her friend down by not facing the issue head on.

'Walker. Stop it. I can tell where your mind has wandered off to.' Tilly raised one eyebrow and gave her a stern look. 'It's my favourite weather – sunny and cold – and the forecast says it's not going to last. Plus, I don't have to watch you and Jamie play love's young dream, not to mention that nobody has dropped dead overnight to the best of my knowledge. That's three for three, so let's just enjoy the morning, okay?'

'Sure,' said Alice. 'But I do think we were on to something with the dog idea. Might make you more approachable, more country, if you had a dog trotting along at your heels. You know, rather than slightly terrifying and aloof?'

Tilly nodded. 'You probably have a point. I mean, even that chap from The Hive that you all get so giddy about, looks more down to earth with all those yappity dogs swinging on a lead. Although I would never have pegged him as a little yappy dog lover. Just goes to show. You have to pick the right breed.'

Alice glanced at her appraisingly. 'I reckon a retired greyhound would suit you down to the ground: you're both quite highly strung – don't deny it – you like a nice long run, and you'd both be a little bit needy without wanting to admit it.' Her face lit up. 'Come on – there's no time like the present. Let's go and see Aurelia and Ariadne Adams – you'll love them. Mad spinster sisters who run their own animal sanctuary. Proper characters, but you'll have to be careful: sometimes you don't come away with what you went for. They reckon they have the gift of pairing up their animals with people's personalities.' She frowned. 'That's how Pru Hartley ended up with a pair of chinchillas.'

Tilly snorted with laughter; it was only too easy to see how Pru's rather chubby cheeks and unfortunate overbite might have been somewhat suggestive in that pairing. 'I'll think about it,' she temporised. 'And anyway, if I was going to get a dog, I always quite fancied a springer spaniel.'

Alice considered it for a moment, her gaze catching on poor Matthew Giles across the Market Place, his eyes still adoringly following Tilly's every move. 'Oh, I wouldn't get a spaniel,' she said, giving her friend a gentle nudge and nodding in Matthew's direction. 'It looks like you already have one of those.'

Chapter 14

Holly hovered uncertainly in the doorway to the kitchen, pretending to check the messages on her phone. She noticed with wry amusement that Elsie was pretending to read *Entertainment Weekly* on the sofa in the corner, having failed to turn the page for at least ten minutes.

Plum, however, was so focused on her new charges that she appeared to be oblivious to all surveillance; either that or she was pointedly, perhaps kindly, ignoring their clumsy attempts to keep tabs on her.

First days were tricky.

Not just for Plum, but for the rest of the family too.

She had arrived in their midst last night in a cloud of Rive Gauche and with a set of Louis Vuitton luggage that had even given Elsie pause. There was no doubting that Plum Castigliano was hardly the archetypal Cotswold nanny. On the other hand, in Holly's opinion, that was part of her innate appeal. Who needed a dour presence of conscientiousness in their home, when Holly's subliminal judgements of her own performance as a mother already had that covered?

'*Allora*,' said Plum, wiping the girls' sticky, post-breakfast faces with swift efficiency. 'It rains, but we go and explore the park today, yes? You can show me the . . . *scoiattoli*? How you say, skwizzels?'

'Squirrels,' smiled Holly, wandering into the kitchen as though she hadn't been lurking with intent. 'Are you heading out?'

'*Si*, yes, I mean. I am thinking in England that if we wait for a day without rain, then we are never going,' Plum said cheerfully, clearly unfazed by the prospect of some drizzle.

'I might come with you? Show you the sights, as it were?' Holly said, finding it harder to let go than she had imagined. This time round it was just different: yes, there were Ben and Tom to think about, not to mention their ever-depleting bank accounts, but this time, it felt like a choice to return to work, not a necessity. A small recalibration, it was true, but a world of difference in how Holly felt about the whole thing.

She watched as Plum set off upstairs to get the girls ready for their outing, efficient, affectionate and fun. Holly could only hope she didn't turn out to be too good to be true.

Standing alone in her kitchen for the first time in what felt like for ever, Holly breathed out slowly. How long, she wondered, would it take before she felt like herself again? It wasn't just a question of her body-image, of feeling at home in her own skin, although she often wondered whether it would have been more efficient to have simply been fitted with a zip! Four babies through the same sunroof? Okay, they were in two batches but still . . . Her stomach would never, ever be the same again, no matter how many Pilates classes she went to.

No, Holly's deeper concerns lay with how to balance her personal and professional selves – they had to fit together or she'd go quietly crazy. Likewise, the lines of demarcation in her marriage had been abruptly redrawn and she wasn't convinced she liked it: Taffy was at work, and she was holding the fort at home; there was never any question as to who would deal with the domestic side of their life anymore. It was like living in the 1970s. She eyed Taffy's breakfast dishes abandoned on the kitchen table with disdain. He would never have dreamed of just automatically leaving these chores to her last year. Last year, they were a well-oiled two-career, two-children machine. True, his reputation as the worst present buyer in Larkford had been repeatedly confirmed, but she could always, always reassure herself that the *thought* was there. This Christmas, that thoughtfulness seemed a more important litmus test than ever.

'Surprise,' said Taffy, bursting into the kitchen slightly out of puff. 'Boys are fine, don't worry,' he said, in response to the surprised expression on her face. 'I just popped back before work because I forgot to give you this.'

Holly's entire demeanour softened; it was a long-running joke between the two of them, for when they were rushed off their feet and hadn't had time for a proper goodbye. She stepped forward with a smile, ready to step into his arms for a proper kiss. Now this, she could get used to.

'Here you go,' said Taffy, tapping her lightly on the bottom with one hand as he passed her his dry-cleaning collection ticket with the other. 'Since you've got, and I quote "The world's best nanny" on hand, I thought you might be at a loose end and—'

He stopped, frowning in confusion at the expression on his wife's previously smiling face. 'What? I've got to work.'

Holly took a deep breath. 'And I'm helping Plum settle in, getting the car serviced, cleaning up after your break-fast – apparently – not to mention jumping through endless bureaucratic hoops with Patronising Patricia so that I too, can get back to work.'

If the tone of her 'apparently' hadn't tipped off Taffy that he was on thin ice, then there was really no helping him, Holly decided. Lizzie had a point: it wasn't the big stuff that wore you down, it was the gradual erosion of affection with 1001 mindless tasks that made up running a family and a household. Of course, she could pick up his dry-cleaning. But that was hardly the point, now was it?

Taffy blundered on, oblivious, it seemed. 'Well, there's no rush, is there? I thought Plum was here on trial? Take some time, enjoy the break. Isn't that the point of having her?'

All Holly's good intentions flew out of the window in her frustration at not being heard. 'Actually,' she said tightly, 'I thought finding someone lovely to take care of *our* children, so that I can return to my job – a job I happen to excel at – was the point.'

She walked out of the kitchen, not trusting herself to say more.

'I'll just leave the ticket here, then, shall I?' Taffy called after her.

It was the first time in Holly's life that she'd seen the point in taking GCSE Geography. An understanding of erosion suddenly seemed a lot more pertinent to adult life than she'd ever realised.

And maybe all that stuff about Darwin had been fairly spot-on too; she genuinely felt as though her life were a case of 'adapt or die' these days. If only, she thought, she could be a little more adaptable, without a whole heap of resentment creeping in.

Half an hour later, deep breaths taken, it was still taking every ounce of strength for her to stand by as Plum persuaded the girls into their onesie-suits and affixed the rain shield to the pram. Passing on little tricks and foibles she'd adopted over the last few months would doubtless make life easier for Plum, but would also stop Plum finding her own way, forming her own relationship with the girls that was separate from Holly's. It was a tricky line to walk.

Her reserve failed her. 'Oh, Plum, I should have said, Olivia hates the rain cover, so it's easier not to close it fully until you're outside.'

'Of course,' replied Plum, easily, completely unfazed. 'Also, Holly, I noticed Lottie wasn't so keen on her breakfast this morning. Does she have a different appetite to her sister perhaps?'

Holly smiled, and then spent the next ten minutes and the entire soggy walk through the Market Place filling Plum in on their individual likes and dislikes, all thoughts of taking a step back forgotten in the joy of sharing these tiny nuances with an attentive audience.

As the icy rain ratcheted up a notch, Holly gestured towards the warmth and comfort of The Deli. Both girls were asleep in the pram and it seemed like too good an opportunity to miss to get to know Plum a little better. 'Coffee?' she suggested.

Plum leaned against her shoulder fleetingly and smiled. 'You read my mind.'

Inside, the windows were steamed up and the contrast from the crisp, bright sunshine over the weekend could not have been more obvious. Autumn had clearly packed her bags. Holly savoured the aroma of espresso beans and warming pastries as she took off her coat, intrigued to see how everyone in her life was going to react to Plum. Certainly if her own husband's response was anything to go by, there would always be some measure of abject disbelief that Holly had knowingly, deliberately invited this goddess into their midst. Hattie, reliably, was the first to come and say hello.

'Hi, I'm Hattie. You must be Plum,' she said in a flurry of embarrassed words, attempting not to stare blatantly at this Nigella Lawson-style goddess in their midst.

Plum smiled. 'Your coffee smells amazing, Hattie. It's wonderful to meet you.' They shook hands and once again, Holly noticed how tactile Plum was – nothing handsy, or over-stated, just an easy familiarity and comfort in her own skin that Holly rather admired. Was it simply being Italian, Holly wondered, in which case there was little hope for her. Hattie gave Holly a grin and scooted off to make their coffees.

Plum reached over and swept Holly's damp ponytail from her collar. 'You are giving yourself a chill, Holly. Here, take my scarf until you dry out.' She folded her soft cashmere square and looped it around Holly's neck, before turning to concertina the rain shield back against itself so the girls could slumber peacefully in the coffee-scented respite of The Deli.

'So,' Plum said, after a few moments, waiting until Hattie had placed two steaming espressos in front of them. 'What are you going to do today, Holly? I am thinking a little treat is in order, no? A massage perhaps, or just a siesta? You are to be making the most of me now I am here. Soon enough you will be with your patients, but these few days are as much for you to *acclimatare*, as for me.'

'Acclimatise?' Holly suggested, with a smile, sipping at her coffee and feeling her shoulders drop fractionally lower with every moment in Plum's company. Somehow Plum making the same suggestion as Taffy was entirely more palatable, hypocrite that she was.

'*Si, certo*,' smiled Plum, closing her eyes and breathing in the softly scented aroma of cinnamon in the air. She paused and glanced over at Holly, leaning forward in her chair. 'I am wanting to be happy here in Larkford, Holly. So I am asking, please, for you to be telling me what *you* would like. I am here to help with your family, your way. I see you holding back a little this morning, not wanting to tell me my job and it is not necessary. They are your children, Holly. Only mine to borrow for a little while. I am wanting to be a part of *your* team.' She reached across and squeezed Holly's hand, never once dropping her gaze.

Holly swallowed. There was no doubt that she liked everything she was hearing, it was just that – well, how entirely comfortable would she feel if it were Taffy on the receiving end of Plum's intense contemplation?

Her own insecurities seemed to be blooming whether she liked them or not. Elsie – normally a font of all wisdom and interference had gone AWOL – no doubt back at Sarandon Hall fleecing everyone at poker, or perhaps romancing the noisy bastard with the sledgehammer next door, since he'd apparently taken a sabbatical from assaulting their eardrums.

She exhaled sharply, annoyed with herself for sounding more and more like a grumpy old git. She seriously needed to get back to work.

'Dr Graham? Do you have a moment?'

It took a second or two for Holly to recalibrate. Daphne Porter's worried face swam into focus, bending down beside her.

'I'm truly sorry to interrupt your coffee, but I would so welcome a few minutes of your time.'

With the girls fast asleep and Plum happily flicking through Hattie's menu, Holly felt comfortable slipping away, dare she say it, even a little relieved to feel needed. After all, she told herself, she was only at the next table.

The relief on Daphne's face told Holly this was not something she asked lightly. 'I've just come from The Practice

actually, and please, please don't think I'm being ungrateful –
after all, they fitted me in for an emergency appointment . . .
I'm just not sure that Dr Campbell actually heard what I was
saying, you know, really understood the issue.'

Holly nodded, realising she was navigating tricky waters.
'I'm sure Dr Campbell was thorough, but there's never any
harm in talking these things through. If you don't mind telling me? Unofficially?'

Daphne nodded. 'It's not me, you see, it's my daughter,
Hannah. She's at the Sixth Form College now.'

'My goodness, she's doing her A-levels already,' Holly realised. You turned your back for five minutes, it seemed, and
your patients turned into mini-adults overnight.

'She's not well, Dr Graham. She's just—' Daphne swallowed hard. 'It's not that she's not happy; she's withdrawn,
though. Different. Like I can't reach her and, I know it sounds
a little lame, but there has to be something to a mother's intuition, doesn't there? And I really thought that when she started
that acne treatment, she'd feel better, you know? No more
tears, looking in the mirror at least? But . . .' She shrugged
and held up her hands helplessly.

Holly nodded. 'I think you have to trust your gut. Just
because Hannah isn't sharing her worries, doesn't mean she
doesn't have any. Does she have a best friend, someone she
can confide in?'

'That's what I'm saying, Dr Graham. She's withdrawn
from everyone, not just me. She's on her own all the time at
college, I'm told, and she shuts herself away in her bedroom
at home. I think she's online a lot, but it's like a shutter has
come down and Hannah's not there anymore.' She sniffed.
'Her beautiful eyes, Dr Graham – it's like nobody's home.'

Holly put her arm around Daphne's shoulders and allowed

her to sob against her shoulder, wondering how Tilly could have let Daphne go home without a plan of action but unwilling to undermine her colleague in absentia. Problems with Hannah aside, it was obvious that Daphne wasn't coping. She thought about the wonderful relationship that Daphne and Hannah had always shared, friends as well as family. Something was obviously seriously awry and blaming it on 'typical teenage behaviour' wasn't helping anyone.

'Daphne, what's Hannah taking for her acne?' Holly wondered aloud, as she ran scenarios in her mind.

Daphne looked up. 'It's a special formulation, I think. Potent stuff. But then, her poor skin was so bad ...' She paused, her brow furrowed in concentration. 'I can check the name and let you know?'

Holly nodded. 'That would be helpful. I just want to cover all bases, you know? Now, in the meantime, can I make some suggestions about a few things that might help?'

Watching Daphne leave twenty minutes later, with a sense of purpose, if not a smile, Holly couldn't help feeling grateful that she'd found herself in The Deli that morning. It almost felt as though she were more use to her patients as their friend than their GP sometimes. A little answer to her prayer to be both mother and doctor. And at least this way she could give them a hug and a little more time. Although it worried her no end, that someone younger, someone less familiar with the nuances of mental health issues might simply have fobbed Daphne off. She wasn't pointing fingers at Tilly exactly, just making a note to herself that this was something that needed to change.

She looked up as Hattie greeted another gaggle of sodden customers, relieved that the twins were slumbering peacefully on and giving her a little chance just to chat with Plum – no interview questions, just easy conversation, and yet giving her so much more insight into their new team-member. And there was something about Plum's sudden politeness when she spoke of her previous employer that somehow felt off.

There was no doubt that the references had been faultless, but still – Holly couldn't help the frown that shadowed her face as her mind ran through the possibilities. She didn't dare think that maybe this was one of those cases where the references were too good to be true, just to facilitate an employee to move on. Should she have been trying to read between the lines when Signora Bellaconte had declared Plum to be 'loving and caring' or indeed, 'comfortable with the intimacy and sensitivity required from a live-in nanny'? Should she actually have been getting a reference from Signor Bellaconte as well? Perhaps *his* definition of intimacy might be a little different?

'Holly? Holly?' Plum said again, leaning forward and laying a beautifully manicured hand gently on her arm. 'Are you okay?'

Holly managed a smile. Plum had done nothing to deserve this suspicion. She'd been utterly focused on the children, and on Holly for that matter. She'd been polite when she met Taffy, but nothing more – no lingering handshakes or coquettish smiles.

Holly had to admit that there was every possibility that all these concerns might well be her own defence mechanism kicking into play. It wasn't lost on her that on this, her first day in months with childcare in place, she was sitting in a café with the nanny! Lizzie would blow a fuse if she knew that these were the 'plans' that had prevented the spa day she'd suggested. She didn't plan to tell Taffy at all.

'I thought that was you, Dr Graham,' interrupted a deep, gravelly voice behind them.

Holly turned in her chair, offering Plum an apologetic

smile. 'Oh. It's Mike, isn't it?' She craned her neck upwards, the chap from Bath Rugby monolithic in such confined quarters. Only the two toddlers swinging around his legs lent a softness to his otherwise imposing bulk.

'This is Ruby and Jim,' he offered. 'I made the rookie mistake of letting them sample The Deli's hot chocolate on Bonfire Night. I fear we're now regular customers.' His chest seemed to vibrate with the timbre of his laughter. 'And I have to confess, I was quietly hoping we'd bump into you too. I'm not sure how well I actually pitched the job among all the chaos at the weekend. But I've spoken with the Board and we'd really like you to come in for a chat.' He pulled up a chair without being asked, making sure that his children were equipped with colouring crayons as they awaited their hot chocolates. He was clearly no part-time dad, anticipating their every need with the ease born of regular practice.

'Well, it's a lovely offer, but—' began Holly.

'Don't say no until you've heard what we've got to say?' Mike cut in. 'If childcare is an issue, I did mention there's a crèche on site, didn't I?'

Holly shook her head. 'Actually, Mike, I'm sorry, how rude of me – this is Plum, our new nanny.'

Mike leaned over and shook Plum's hand. 'Lovely to meet you, Plum.'

Holly watched their interaction carefully, feeling guilty even as she did so. A guilt that only intensified when Plum was just the right side of polite and respectful, before returning to poring over Hattie's menu, very much casting herself as 'help' rather than 'friend'.

'There's no harm in having a conversation, is there, Dr Graham?' Mike persisted, a warm smile on his face that actually reached his eyes. 'I have to tell you that we've been keeping our eyes open for the perfect candidate for a while. The only applicants we seem to get are middle-aged blokes and frustrated rugby players.' He laughed at his own joke. 'And I don't see you falling into either category, to be honest. We need someone with a cool head in a drama, and in all honesty, my boys are never averse to a little maternal care.'

Holly couldn't help smiling too; he was so disarmingly charming and had somehow known exactly what to say to give her an out with Taffy and, apparently, Dan – as always, any news that affected her husband being up for immediate debate with his best friend. Of course, she didn't have a leg to stand on, since Lizzie had been her go-to confidante for as long as she could remember, but still, it would occasionally be nice if they kept *some* issues just to themselves. She was still mortified to know that Dan had heard all about her seasonal snoring.

She looked up to see Mike watching Plum appraisingly. She didn't blame him in the least; it was a bit like having a supermodel in their midst. Even she'd have been tempted to stare at Plum's natural and uninhibited beauty if she didn't know her. It was oddly reassuring that Plum seemed almost oddly disinterested in his attention.

Mike looked momentarily embarrassed, as he tore his gaze away from Plum sipping coffee and noticed Holly's amused smile. 'So, any thoughts on joining us, Dr Graham?'

'My husband—' she began, before catching herself and rephrasing what she wanted to say. 'To be frank, it's been suggested to me that having a female doctor on staff at the Club might fall under the same PR umbrella as the crèche? I mean, I'd be delighted if I thought that wasn't the case, but—' She paused, remembering Taffy's scathing reaction only too clearly. His dismissive comment about 'positive discrimination' still stung a little, if she was honest.

Mike shook his head. 'You need to come and see how we work, Dr Graham. Our crèche is a valuable asset and often fully booked, filled with not just the physio's children, but our players' children too. And yes, we're looking for a female doctor, or a male doctor with a comforting bedside manner, who won't be distracted by what's happening on the pitch. Backwards logic, I know, but effective. Some of our new signings are very young, away from home for the first time – they have enough people telling them they're wonderful; we feel a more nurturing approach is what's needed.' He slid a folded piece of paper across the table.

Holly opened it and her eyes widened in disbelief.

'And, I should mention, that's your basic salary on five mornings a week.'

'Oh,' said Holly eloquently.

'And then there's bonuses, overtime, match pay. So you can probably more or less double that.'

'Stop saying numbers,' said Holly weakly, her resolve not even to take the meeting crumbling in the face of such financial largesse.

'And there's plenty more where that came from,' said Mike. 'Come and meet the team. Where's the harm in that?'

Just then, in that moment, Holly honestly couldn't come up with a rational answer. Her boys were happy at school, her girls were in the care of an amazing nanny, and her husband? Well, her husband didn't seem to get why she wasn't prepared to shelve the last two decades of hard work, in order to play with plastic bricks and pick up his dry-cleaning.

'Name a date,' she said, swallowing hard to dislodge the ball of guilt that wedged in her throat. Where the hell was Elsie when she needed her?

Chapter 15

With Mike's numbers scrolling through her mind like the credits at the end of a movie, Holly found herself agreeing to Plum's suggestion that she should take the twins home for their lunch and give Holly a little time to herself. Watching Plum walk away with the pram gave Holly a most confusing jolt of discomfort; being away from her girls was obviously easier to justify in theory than in practice.

The downpour refused to pass and Holly wandered through the Market Place, attempting to reposition her umbrella to avoid the occasional dart of icy water down the back of her neck. It wasn't hard to imagine that winter was only just around the corner and with it the girls' Christening.

A lone magpie alighted on the church wall ahead and Holly obediently greeted him and his absent wife, becoming increasingly superstitious the more time she spent with Elsie. But truth be told, she felt as though she could do with a sign about now; so many parts of her life had taken on their own momentum that she didn't really feel as though she were paddling her own canoe anymore. And, as she knew only too well, this was not a situation to be encouraged.

She slipped into Sally's fancy gift shop. When in doubt, apply stationery.

'Ooh, Holly, how lovely to see you,' said Sally with feeling, having noticed the absence of sticky fingers or pram in her wake.

Sally was a little too particular in her approach to ever make the mums of Larkford feel truly welcome in her emporium of gorgeous delights, even if the children's gift section at the back was one of the finest in the area.

'I was only thinking about you the other day. Rather missed your words of wisdom at The Practice. That new lass is rather abrupt in her bedside manner, if you ask me.' Sally looked properly put out and was clearly in the mood to share her displeasure. It was becoming a regular occurrence and Holly couldn't help but wonder whether she was the only one privy to Tilly's apparent unpopularity among the female patients.

Holly had never been more grateful to see Reverend Taylor's smiling face, as she emerged from behind the greeting cards display in the middle of the shop. 'Ah, good morning to you, Holly. No nippers with you today?'

Holly allowed herself to be pulled into one of Reverend Taylor's all-encompassing maternal hugs and felt herself unclench in the warmth of her friendliness.

'Only in my head,' admitted Holly as though she were a crazy person. 'First day with Plum, the new nanny, and I'm having a little trouble adjusting. How I'll cope with going back to work, I do not know. So far, I've spent my first day off having coffee with Plum and now I've been banished to have some "quality time".' Her disparaging tone made it perfectly clear what she thought of that idea.

Reverend Taylor just smiled. 'Right then, no more excuses. You can come back to The Rectory and we can get this Christening organised.' She dropped her voice to a whisper.

'I also have one of Pru's chocolate gateaux from the bakery that might need a little attention, if that floats your boat?'

Glancing up to see that Sally was still poised for a good moan, Holly wavered before hearing Elsie's voice in her head: she had asked for a sign, after all. The swift purchase of a new notebook and Reverend Taylor's pre-emptive refusal to take no for an answer and Holly's afternoon had sorted itself.

All she had to do now was confess to Reverend Taylor that, between them, she and Taffy may have been a little disorganised with the invitations to putative Godparents, although she'd had a few intriguing ideas on that front. Hesitation and procrastination had seemingly slipped into their every decision of late. Initially Holly had put it down to baby-exhaustion, but now there was a certain latent ambivalence towards any decision beyond the basic. The more time Taffy spent at work and the more time she was alone at home with the girls, the wider the gap in their ability to function as a team. His reaction to her job offer was a case in point. She turned to Reverend Taylor and took a deep breath. 'Reverend, have you got time for a chat? Not about the Christening. I just need a friendly ear to talk through some decisions in my future and I really need someone who doesn't have a vested interest.'

Two (rather large) slices of chocolate cake later and both Holly and Reverend Taylor had settled into a post-cocoa stupor on the sofa in The Rectory. Dibley the terrier had curled up beside Holly and she stroked his fur on autopilot. 'So?' she said after a pause. 'What do you think I should do?'

'What do you *want* to do?' countered the Reverend easily. Nothing seemed to faze her and she was seemingly open to any and all seeking counsel or company. Of course, technically she was Church of England through and through, but still counted plenty of agnostics, atheists and various other denominations among her regular visitors. There was something of the therapist about the way she gently reflected their questions, guiding her visitors towards their own conclusions and she was no easier on Holly. 'If you had a blank canvas to design your life, where would you start painting? Seriously. Close your eyes and talk me through it.'

Holly did as she was bid, and not only because the warmth and comfort in the room was so incredibly soporific after such an early start. 'Well,' she began, 'the first part is easy – although I'm not much of an artist.' She mentally lined up a series of stick men – well, technically, one stick man, two stick boys, two stick babies and a stick lady. 'It all starts with family. Taffy and the kids, and Elsie.'

'Interesting,' said Reverend Taylor. 'What about you?'

'Me?'

'I can't help noticing that the only person who doesn't feature in this line-up is you,' Reverend Taylor said smoothly. 'I imagine Elsie would have something to say about that?'

'Oh God, yes,' replied Holly vehemently. 'Sorry, Reverend.' She furrowed her brow. 'Which means the next things I was going to paint are off base too – The Practice, the patients ... I mean, I'm a mum first, then a doctor, yes?'

'And a wife, a friend, a daughter ...' cut in Reverend Taylor. 'But I actually asked about *you*.'

'Well, I guess I just define myself by who I am to other people.' Holly shrugged. 'Lots of doctors do it,' she said defensively. 'That's not so very awful, is it?'

'Not awful at all; you're a very lovely mum, wife, doctor, friend, et cetera, et cetera. But you came to me and asked for my help. I'm giving it to you. And ironically I've heard you give the same advice to other people so many times: you can't pour from an empty cup. But why do you think it doesn't apply to you, Holly? Why do you expect so much of yourself?'

'Oh, it's never easy, is it? And now I'm judging myself for that too!' Holly fell back against the sofa cushions, startling Dibley from his nap in the process. 'I just can't quite distil what it is that *I* want, moving forward. I thought I wanted to go back to work, but leaving the girls with Plum, no matter how wonderful and capable she is, has been so much harder than I imagined. And it's only been a few hours.'

'Holly, would you allow me to be the devil's advocate for a moment?' Reverend Taylor asked.

'Is that even allowed?' Holly whispered with a smile, her eyes automatically glancing upwards.

'I think He'll indulge me in this. My question is simple – if it had been easy to walk away from your girls this morning, without a backwards glance, how would you have felt about that?'

'Oh,' said Holly quietly. 'Oh, I see what you mean.'

'Do you, though? Do you see the impossible standards you're setting for yourself? Damned either way. If there was one message I so wish I could share with your generation, it would be this: there is no *one* way to live, except *your* way.'

Holly nodded. 'And I'm assuming you and Elsie didn't confer or anything?'

Reverend Taylor shook her head gently. 'Sometimes we need to hear the same advice over and over until it takes. It's like the Christian who prayed and prayed to win the Lottery, until even Our Lord himself was forced to intervene and tell him to buy a bloody ticket!' She chortled happily at her joke. 'Authenticity is a tricky beast to conquer, Holly. So, let me ask you again: this blank canvas of yours, what does it look like?'

'I need time with my babies,' Holly said simply. 'For me, just as much as for them. After all, they grow up fast enough as it is. I think ...' She paused, blinking hard, surprised by her own thoughts as they tumbled into clarity. 'I think that I actually *need* to work to feel at peace with myself, knowing that I'm out there helping. But maybe that doesn't have to be at The Practice?'

Reverend Taylor simply nodded, unwilling to disturb Holly's tentative train of thought.

'And,' Holly continued to feel her way, 'I would never have even considered private practice, until everyone was so disparaging about that job offer. Now, it's like I'm just being contrary, because suddenly it feels, well, intriguing.'

'Because you want to prove the men wrong?' Reverend Taylor pushed softly.

'Because frankly the money's so good, I could work part-time and still contribute my fair share. I mean, I am the majority shareholder in our brood and it's not really fair that Taffy should pay.'

'Really? And do you think Taffy himself would agree with that statement?'

Holly frowned and shook her head. 'He'd be furious. But, somehow, it's my guilt. If that makes sense?'

'What about your patients here in Larkford? Would you miss them?' Reverend Taylor asked, intrigued despite herself.

Holly's laugh was a little hollow. 'I see more of them now than I did when I was working. I certainly get to hear about their lives more!' She paused. 'Actually, I say that like it's a bad thing, but it's not. Is it?'

'Are you asking me or telling me?'

'Err, both?' Holly chanced, still hoping on some level that somebody else might have all the answers for her.

'My theology professor at Cambridge always said the same thing to me, Holly, every time I saw him: nobody else can do the work but you. But he didn't mean essays and coursework, he meant looking in here,' she tapped her chest firmly, 'and finding our own truth.'

'Wise old bugger,' muttered Holly touchily.

'Indeed. People who are right do tend to be annoying, I've found.'

'So my "work" would be?' Holly made air quotes with her fingers.

'Finding out what would feed your soul. Or, in layman's terms, find out what your goal is and make a plan that gets you there.'

'You know what Elsie would say to that?' Holly asked.

'A goal without a plan is just a wish!' they both said in unison and Holly laughed, as the Reverend just shook her head and smiled.

'Goal first, then you can start plotting.'

'It's daunting though, even thinking about making these changes. Kind of knowing that I might ruffle a few feathers if I do – at home, as well as at work. Scary, really.'

'Well, maybe you need to want it more than you're scared of it. That's always the catalyst for me, anyway. I imagine a big set of scales in my head and wait for the balance to tip into action.'

Holly stared down at Dibley's sleeping body beside her, her voice cracking slightly, even as she attempted to voice her fears. 'But what if Taffy doesn't, I mean, what if he . . . ?' She swallowed hard, unable to formulate the fear that had shadowed her decision-making without her even being aware of it until this moment.

She'd been knowingly riled by his dismissal of the job

offer, of course. Little had she realised that her subconscious had taken his teasing so much to heart.

'Taffy isn't Milo,' Reverend Taylor said, going straight to the crux of the issue. 'Has he ever done anything, with his actions or deeds, that would make you doubt his commitment to you? He may not understand your choices right away, or indeed your priorities, but then I would say that's a communication problem, not a support problem, wouldn't you?'

Holly frowned, feeling disloyal to her lovely new husband for even entertaining these doubts and yet . . .

'Holly,' said Reverend Taylor, 'you wouldn't be human if you walked away from Milo without a few dents in the paintwork. Acknowledge them, if you can. It really is the only way to move on.'

'But why now?' asked Holly, a plaintive yearning for answers evident in the tremor of her voice. 'I've remarried. I've had two more children since Milo and I divorced. It hasn't bothered me before; why's it starting again now?'

'Because you're facing change again. Choices. Potentially life-changing choices. Your subconscious is trying to protect you because I don't think you've ever properly told it that the battle is over. The siege has passed, but on some lonely level you're still poised for a reprise.'

'And now I have to do the work? To make a plan?' Holly said.

'Yup. No shortcuts, I'm afraid. If you don't deal with this now, it'll just pop up again later on when you least expect it.'

'Baggage,' muttered Holly, shaking her head. The irony wasn't lost on her that she'd spent the last few months following Alice's excellent example by decluttering and editing her possessions, when all the time it was her thoughts and preconceptions that needed the most attention.

'Lots to think about, certainly,' Reverend Taylor agreed. 'Take it steady though, there's no rush.'

'But there is one thing that's a little overdue,' Holly said with a new sense of purpose. 'This isn't just my decision to make. It directly affects too many people. So maybe it's time I started exploring my options properly instead of talking in the abstract.'

'Just remember,' said Reverend Taylor, as she cleaved another hefty chunk from the chocolate gateau, 'that a plan without a goal can be just as tricky.'

But Holly's thoughts had already moved on, mentally filling out columns of pros and cons in her fancy new notebook, completely oblivious to the look of concern on Reverend Taylor's face.

Chapter 16

Connor sipped his pint of Guinness with deliberate slowness; there was, after all, no hurry to be home, nobody waiting for him, eager to share news of their day. He'd grown tired of social media and its ability to pick him up and smash him down in the space of a few short tweets.

Never read your own reviews, they'd said, right back when he'd started out in the music business.

Obviously, he'd done what all his bandmates did: nod sagely, completely agree and then go home and log on to Instagram, or Twitter, or whatever the site-du-jour seemed to be.

No matter what time of day or night, somewhere in the world, The Hive's fans were awake and ready to talk. Sometimes it had been exactly what he needed, especially in the wake of Rachel and the baby's deaths. But not always.

He couldn't quite put his finger on when the tide had turned against him: was it his increasingly political stance about healthcare – air ambulance provision in particular, of course, or his move to the countryside? Could it simply be that The Hive had outstayed their welcome in the public consciousness, only to be suited and rebooted for a come-back tour at some point in the future, doubtless because one of the band (Orlando – it was always going to be Orlando) had snorted their profits up their nose and needed to make a few quick bucks for alimony?

He sighed and glanced around the pub, eager for company but actually wishing he wasn't. He'd somehow lost the ability to be alone with his thoughts and staying with Lizzie and Will for all those months had meant he didn't even need to address the issue: silence was in limited supply in the Parsons household. A non-issue, with three kids, Lizzie and Will all happy to chat for hours.

He'd regretted signing the lease on the mews house last month, almost before his cheque had cleared. But he'd begun to feel as though his constant presence in Lizzie and Will's life was causing tension. They never said a thing, and Lizzie for one always seemed delighted to have his company, but Will was another matter. And their friendship meant too much to him to abuse their hospitality any longer. He'd persuaded himself it was time for a fresh start: who wouldn't want a townhouse in Bath to call home?

Well, as it turned out — him.

The longing for his own country estate had never waned, he just couldn't bring himself to return to Dorset — to the perfection he'd had, however briefly. Nor could he bring himself to sell up. And so the Dorset estate sat there, squat in the corner of his mind, a spectre at every feast, never far from his thoughts.

He glanced up as the door swung open and Holly and Taffy walked in, deep in conversation and almost oblivious to the world around them. Probably not the best time to blurt out his news.

On the other hand, he did have Holly to thank, did he not, for opening his eyes to the possibilities in Larkford and his own priorities?

'Holly? Taffy? Over here!' He waved to Teddy behind the bar. 'A bottle of your finest bubbles, Teds, please.' He turned and pulled Holly into a rib-crushing hug. 'There is much to celebrate!'

He felt a moment's disquiet that he'd misread the situation so completely. Sensors apparently still switched to off. Holly to her credit rose to the occasion like a pro – indeed, if he hadn't seen the momentary flicker of tension between them, he honestly wouldn't have realised that he'd stumbled into a marital dispute.

'I love good news,' Holly reassured Connor, pulling up a bar stool, even as Taffy hovered uncomfortably beside her.

'So what are we celebrating?' managed Taffy, when it became obvious that whatever topic they had been discussing so animatedly was now firmly closed, tucked away for later.

'Well, thanks to your adorable wife, you can sign me up as an official resident of Larkford!' Connor couldn't hide the excitement, or was it relief, in his voice. In his mind, his recovery had stalled until he could find a place to truly call home. 'The ink is barely dry, but I've signed on the dotted line and the money has left my account, so I think it's safe to raise a glass without jinxing it.' He didn't let on just how seriously he'd taken the concept of a jinx; it had taken all his efforts to bring Lizzie and Dan into the loop earlier.

Superstitious didn't come close.

Or was that neurosis?

'Seriously? Mate, that is just the best news!' Taffy exclaimed with feeling, all awkwardness instantly forgotten.

'Then this bottle should surely be on the house?' suggested Teddy, his natural eavesdropping as their local publican simply an accepted part of life.

'Nah, I think a round *for* the house should be on me, don't you?' Connor parried easily, quite accustomed to his wallet smoothing the way, where his slightly awkward social skills might not. It was something he was working on, along with a slightly less 'dark' sense of humour – after all, wealth and fame could only get you so far in life, as he'd discovered to his cost.

'Less booze talk, more house talk!' protested Holly. 'Tell us everything.'

Connor grinned widely, touched by her enthusiasm.

It was true, only moments before, he'd been allowing himself a brief wallow that his momentous news might go unshared, but now? His mercurial moods were seemingly part of life that he would have to learn to accept.

He held up his hands as though to encompass the whole pub. 'As you know, I have taken your advice, Holly. Wise, wise woman that you are. You are talking to the proud new owner of Peal Hall. And . . .' He paused to keep them guessing for a second to two, amazed that Lizzie and Dan hadn't already spilled the beans and stolen his thunder, 'and also the new tenant farmer at Blackleigh Farm. It's the perfect small-holding – gorgeous house in the heart of the town, and acres of rolling farmland only a short stroll away.'

'Perfect for a gentleman farmer, I'm guessing?' Taffy suggested, obviously doubting Connor's desire to get his hands dirty, or indeed to park his immaculate Range Rover anywhere muddy like, for example, a farmyard.

'Hardly a gentleman!' scoffed Connor, making sure that his round encompassed the regulars tucked away in their booths by the fireside. Generous to a fault, he did tend to gather friends like Sellotape, even if some of those 'friends' might not be so keen to socialise if they were ever expected to contribute to the tab. 'I've already asked Clive to give

me some pointers, haven't I, Clive?' He raised his glass
towards Clive Shawe, one of Larkford's most outspoken
organic farmers.

True, his organic salad produce was fêted by all the posh
supermarkets and he was certainly worth a bob or two, but
to look at him, with his sketchy dentistry and overalls, he
screamed old-school farmer, six generations in.

'Aye,' said Clive with a nod, before returning to his pint.

'And did he tell you that only gentleman farmers drive
round in fancy Range Rovers and you'll need to get
yourself a knackered old Subaru if you want to fit in?'
Taffy teased.

Connor coloured. 'He did not. But I take your point.' He
made a mental note to look into this, no longer feeling quite
so proud of his shiny new toy.

Clive harrumphed into his pint, only a hint of a smile
giving away his amusement.

'I've got so many plans for this place,' carried on Connor,
working hard to keep his enthusiasm afloat, slightly annoyed
that even such a tiny setback had dented his mood. He was
determined to enjoy every moment of his new project.
Determined. 'I'm going to have a herd of goats, really gorgeous Jersey ones with big brown eyes and that beautiful
russet colour?'

Clive just shook his head and carried on drinking. 'Ugly
goats make money too, you know.'

Connor watched Holly and Taffy trade amused glances,
suddenly feeling rather protective of his plans. 'I'm going to
have a dairy for making goat's cheese. All organic, you know.
And then I'll have my own honey, of course.'

'Of course,' said Taffy nodding. 'To go with the goat's cheese.'

'Right,' said Connor, unsure whether he was being teased

or not. 'Because they're the perfect pairing. And since I already have the bees—'

'Sorry, what?' interrupted Holly. 'You already have pet bees?'

'They're not pets, Holly,' Connor replied seriously. 'I have a few hives down in Dorset, but Clive assures me they'll be okay to move, as long as we do it at night. Apparently it resets their GPS, isn't that right, Clive?'

'Aye,' said Clive again monosyllabically.

'So I'll have my honeybees and the goats just to get me started. And did you know there's even the remains of a stone circle up on the hillside? Seriously. So, I have the best idea to—'

'So, it's kind of a hobby farm?' interrupted Taffy, clearly used to farming on a larger scale and with more of a focus on profits.

Connor let out a bellow of laughter, even as Holly clearly flinched at her husband's tactless response. 'Of course it is, Taffs. I'm hardly in it for the cash, now am I?' He shrugged. 'It'll make me happy just to potter for a while, keep me busy, plus now I have The Big House, it all dovetails rather nicely, don't you think?'

'Sort of boutique organic?' offered Holly.

'Ooh I like that,' Connor said nodding, scribbling it down on a paper napkin. 'Let's face it, I have nobody to please but myself and there is something truly grounding about tinkering about, without pressure or expectation. I don't have to worry about profit margins, so why not pour my time and energy into something I enjoy?'

Taffy looked duly chastened. 'Sorry, Conn. I wasn't being judgemental. Well, okay, maybe I was just a little bit. Stone circles are a bit two a penny around here, we're just spoiled I guess, and when you said you wanted a farm, I just imagined more, well, more sheep or something.'

'Not all farmers are sheep farmers, Dr Jones,' said Clive in a surprising burst of chattiness. 'We're not in Wales now.' He guffawed away to himself happily.

'So,' said Holly, ever the peacemaker, 'goats and bees, eh?'

'Yup,' said Connor. 'Honey and cheese. Maybe yoghurt too? It's a little biblical, but it appeals to me. You know, back to basics? Maybe a fig tree or two.'

'Never had a farm plan based on the Bible before,' grumbled Clive, a twinkle in his eye showing he meant nothing by it.

'First for everything,' Holly said, seemingly rather moved by Clive's commitment to help Connor get started. God only knew, Clive could be a cantankerous old bugger when he wanted to be, but there was more to his friendship with Connor than met the eye and it was obvious to Connor that Holly had clocked it. Losing a spouse, losing a child, it was something the two men had in common – decades apart and in all likelihood the only experience they did share, but nevertheless it had brought them together and for that, Holly was grateful. 'Although with all this biblical produce, you might need to make an offering to your pagan stones,' she teased.

'Did I hear that correctly?' interrupted Cassie Holland, barging into their conversation, only too happy to have taken her drink on Connor's tab, but clearly with something to get off her ample chest. 'Are you really so thoughtless as to introduce *bees* to Larkford?'

Connor shrugged, still unused to Cassie's bulldozer approach to life. 'Well, I don't think I can take full credit for that; they've been around here for thousands of years. Life wouldn't be the same without them.'

He noticed both Holly and Taffy wince at his jocular, teasing tone and knew immediately that he'd misplayed it.

Cassie drew herself up to her full height. At barely five foot four, it shouldn't have been that imposing, yet somehow Connor felt himself quail a little under her stern scrutiny.

'My son, Tarquin, is allergic to bees,' she said, over-enunciating every syllable as though he were simple. 'I'll fight you on this, don't think I won't.' She stormed out of the pub, puffed up with her own righteous indignation.

'Blimey,' said Connor as the door swung closed in her wake. 'I had no idea a few bees would get people so het up.' He looked crestfallen, all his good intentions feeling wobbly and uncertain.

Perhaps he was kidding himself?

Perhaps this was just another false start on the road to feeling like himself again? His stomach lurched at the very possibility. He wasn't sure how much gumption he had left in him to formulate another plan. He'd bet everything on black with this Larkford plan.

Not that he'd admit that to anyone.

Holly was quick to comfort him. 'Oh, Conn, you can't do anything around here without ruffling a few feathers. There's no way you can please all of the people, all of the time.'

He nodded, a pall now firmly cast over his celebrations. He took a deep breath, knowing how fragile his bonhomie could be these days and trying not to let one outspoken militant douse his good spirits. To anyone but Holly he might have laughed it off, but somehow she invited his confidences. 'I just wanted to do something a little special, make a name for myself outside the world of music. Do something tangible, you know? I really want to put Larkford on the organic map. With Clive's fresh produce and my goat's cheese and honey and I've other plans too, so I'll need to get everyone onside . . .'

'Well,' said Clive, cutting him off with a chuckle, 'at least if you put Larkford on this map of yours, then the satnav will stop sending everyone to a field on Lark Hill.'

'Oh, I don't know,' said Taffy, 'I quite like knowing we're off the beaten track a little.'

'You didn't say that when your cheese subscription kept being returned to sender because they couldn't find our house,' Holly reminded him.

Connor breathed out slowly, allowing himself to relax into their banter and slightly relieved to see that the earlier tension between Holly and Taffy had dissipated. Maybe Lizzie had a point: how much time did they actually get to spend together these days, with all of their various commitments and offspring? He swallowed the thought that, by rights, he too should have been exhausted from running around after a toddler about now. There was no point in constantly revisiting what might have been. It didn't stop him trying though, trying to imagine a future with Rachel and his baby still in it.

If nothing else, he would have loved to see Rachel's face when he told her the other plans for the land at Blackleigh Farm. The plans that would hopefully secure his entrée into the Larkford community and allow him to really make his mark on this sleepy Cotswold town. The plans that kept him sane at 3 a.m. when his mind refused to let him sleep.

It was all part of the same mental picture he'd conjured – the Connor that lived here in Larkford would be happy, settled, popular . . . And as long as he continued to believe that, to live that, then surely one day soon it would be so.

He paused, Cassie's wrath still echoing in his thoughts. 'Maybe you could give me some pointers about how to win people round? I can't imagine I'll be everyone's favourite nominee to take over The Big House?'

Holly nodded; it was no secret that 'new money' took quite a bashing from the locals, especially since none of them could ever afford the legacy properties they so coveted, and which Connor had bought as a cash purchase. 'Well, to be honest, I think your bees may be your friends with this one. I mean, you've been a resident for less than a day and you've already pissed off Cassie Holland, so I'd say that's generally a step in the right direction.'

Connor blinked, slow to compute, not quite getting the joke. 'Well, okay then,' he said, summoning another round of drinks and wondering, not for the first time, when exactly the disconcerting feeling of standing on quicksand might finally leave him.

Chapter 17

'Don't let that dog near me,' said the Major in a clumsy attempt at humour the next morning, as Alice showed him through to her consulting rooms.

Alice just smiled; she was only too aware that Coco's prowess at cancer detection made some of their patients a little nervous in her presence. She wasn't entirely comfortable with how some of them chose to communicate that, but still, this was a learning curve for all of them.

'And how are you, Major? Did that steroid injection in your hip give you any relief?' Alice asked, making sure he was seated before she started any conversation. It was one of Holly's top tips that Alice had gratefully taken on board: people in pain struggle to multi-task, so don't make them try.

The Major harrumphed a little as he got settled. 'Well, I've been doing lots of walking with Jess and Charlotte, getting the little horses used to their new home, you know, and I don't think I could have done that a month ago. My Grover can't believe his luck.' It was rare to have any conversation with the Major that didn't involve his beloved terrier in some way.

'Great,' said Alice, mentally checking the boxes for improvement, mood and social interaction. 'And how are the horses? I have to tell you that I think I'm in love with the little yellow one.'

The Major's smile lit up his face, the years and tension dropping away, almost as though talking about a beloved grandchild; although being Peregrine Waverly, he was unlikely to be so enthusiastic about something with less than four legs. 'Takes me right back, it does, caring for these little chaps. So much easier though in miniature. It used to take me hours, back in the day, to keep on top of all the grooming – you do everything yourself in the mounted regiments, you know, even the officers. But little Banana is an absolute joy.' He glanced down at the peacefully slumbering dog at Alice's feet. 'He'll be giving your little dog a run for her money on the assistance front too, if Charlotte and I have anything to do with it. You should see the improvement in young Jess's confidence since she's been working with Banana.'

Alice smiled, Jess Hearst clearly not the only one to have been given a boost by the little palomino. 'So what can I do for you today?'

'Well,' the Major stumbled over his words, still casting worried looks in Coco's direction, that in itself telling Alice what the Major's uppermost concern was. 'I seem to be having trouble with my plumbing. To be precise, Dr Walker, I feel as though I need to pee, while I'm still peeing. There's no respite. I've given up all the things I love: coffee, Guinness, even my afternoon cup of tea. My Marion is all about not irritating my bladder; doesn't seem to matter how much she's irritating me with all her advice—' He broke off, suddenly aware that he'd gone off on a tangent.

'And you're worried it might be cancer?' Alice suggested gently.

'Well, if you Google it . . .'

'Oh, Major,' Alice cut in, 'if you Google almost anything these days it will lead you to cancer one way or another. How about we do this the old-fashioned way? You can tell me about your symptoms and I'll use my cunning medical degree to work out what's troubling you?'

The Major nodded, seemingly comforted to have the responsibility taken out of his hands.

'So, how long has this been going on?' Alice asked, fully expecting him to say months, if not years; the Major's track record on avoiding medical attention preceded him.

'Oh, about a week, now,' said the Major. 'And it hurts, you know? To pee. Awful backache too.'

'And Marion insisted you came?' Alice checked.

'Oh no, Dr Walker, even I know something's amiss when there's blood in your wee.'

Alice let out a sigh of relief; even she had been concerned for a moment about the likelihood of prostate cancer, after all, he did fit the profile in terms of age and sex, not to mention his fondness for bacon. 'Let's get a urine sample for testing,' she said, handing him a small plastic container. 'But my feeling is that we're talking about a UTI, a urinary tract infection, and that a course of antibiotics will have you sorted in no time.'

'No cancer?' the Major clarified.

'Well,' Alice hedged, 'since you're here it's probably a good idea to check your prostate.'

The Major shook his head and stood up abruptly, his apparent reprieve making him skittish again. 'Let's try the antibiotics first, eh? I'll come back in for that exam once I'm feeling a bit brighter.' He eyed the box of latex gloves on her shelf with unease and made for the door, giving Alice little opportunity to protest.

'Sure you will,' she muttered sceptically as the door swung closed behind him. She felt like she was banging her head against a brick wall with some of the older residents of Larkford; when would they begin to realise that prevention was so much easier than cure?

If only there was a way to find some balance, she thought, as she checked her patient list for the morning and noticed yet another twenty-something with Google-itis. What was the cross-over age, she wondered, between the Worried Well and the Elderly Ostriches with their heads in the proverbial sand?

Wandering into the doctors' lounge for elevenses, Alice was miles away, wondering whether they had in fact got the focus of their Health in the Community programme completely wrong. If the last three hours had proven anything, it was that their over-sixties were almost as clueless as the teenagers in Larkford when it came to their own health and well-being. Sure, they weren't taking ecstasy or the morning-after pill, but that didn't mean they weren't flagrantly disregarding the instructions that came with their medication or indulging in 'one last fling'. Maybe Big Bertha should be doing the rounds of the old people's homes, as well as the schools, as the next part of their health initiative?

'Come on, come on, Alice. We need one more player,' called Dan from the table where it seemed half the team were congregated, money changing hands and banter already flying. 'Place your bets, ladies and gents, you've got to be in it to win it.'

Alice pulled a ten-pound note from her wallet and slapped it down on the table. She rather enjoyed the various silly jokes and bets for ever on the go, and never missed a chance to join in the fun. 'What's today's bet?' she asked.

Dan stepped back to reveal a box-fresh game of Operation laid out on the table. 'Well, Taffy here reckons he has what it takes to be an army surgeon. So we thought we'd put him to the test.' He waved a hand at a selection of whistles, horns and percussion instruments. 'It's not exactly falling mortars but I reckon we can distract him fairly comprehensively from the job in hand, don't you?'

Taffy's bravado was clearly waning a little in the face of Dan's absolute belief that he couldn't maintain a steady hand under pressure, not to mention the fact that everyone's money seemed to be piling up against him.

'A tenner says he can do it,' offered Alice supportively. 'But I need to make it clear that this is Coco's Bonio money, Taffy, so you'd better not let her down.'

'Oh dear God,' said Taffy in a strangled voice, 'I'm not sure I can live with that level of expectation.' He looked up and grinned. 'Luckily for me, Coco won't mind if I slip her a digestive biscuit instead.'

'Whose daft idea was this anyway?' asked Grace with a smile, sitting on the worktop and swinging her legs, watching closely but not joining in.

Everyone turned to look at her in surprise. 'Whose do you think?' said Jason with feeling, his not-so-secret hero worship of Dan bordering on the embarrassing at times. It took the nurse/doctor crush to a whole new level of political correctness.

'Shhh!' commanded Dan, winding the kitchen timer to two minutes, poised for the off. 'One, two, go!'

The nurses and Dan obviously took the concept of distraction incredibly seriously if the instant cacophony was anything to go by and Taffy soon had small beads of sweat on his brow as he attempted to wrangle miniature plastic body parts from their recesses, his gaze regularly flickering over to the nose. When Dan began to sing the song from the *Countdown* clock even Alice felt her pulse ratchet up a notch.

Ever the strategist, Taffy had worked his way down, even acing the notoriously pesky 'butterflies in stomach' that were inexplicably making their presence felt for Alice as she watched. She couldn't deny that her own stress levels seemed to be rising by the day, increasingly thrown into a role she didn't feel fully equipped for. And, as lovely as her male colleagues undoubtedly were, she was missing Holly's experience and guidance more than she could possibly have foreseen. Even having Tilly here had somehow become an extra responsibility on her shoulders.

Not that Tilly wasn't capable, she corrected herself; it just turned out that having a social conscience and a willingness to leap into any international fray did not necessarily translate into being an empathetic and nurturing GP. This wasn't siege medicine, after all; this was cradle-to-grave and everything in between. Watching Taffy struggle under pressure only served to highlight that the best family physicians didn't necessarily make the best army surgeons or Médecins Sans Frontières medics. Maybe she and Taffy were just cut from different cloth?

She pushed a mental image of her mother waving the family tartan around to the back of her mind and leaned against the worktop beside Grace. 'How's tricks?' she asked.

Grace smiled, her gaze firmly riveted on the game in play. 'I can't believe I feel so emotionally invested in the outcome, can you? Maybe we all just need to get out more?' She nibbled on a Gingernut and managed not to blink as the clock counted down and Taffy's cursing became more vocal.

'What the hell is a "Charlie horse"?' Taffy wailed. 'I've

been a doctor for more than a decade and never once had a
patient present with a tiny horse on his bloody thigh! And this
sudden obsession with miniature horses everywhere I look?'
He tossed the pincers aside as the kitchen timer went off and
pushed the hair off his forehead in frustration, looking wiped.
'Sorry, Coco. No Bonios for you. Just as well my feet are too
flat to let me in the army corps, eh, Dan?'

Dan shrugged. 'Well, now you're warmed up at least. Shall
we have another go? I'll put the batteries in this time.'

Taffy's aghast expression was priceless, as was Dan's when
he realised that Taffy leaping to his feet and chasing him from
the room was only partly in jest.

'Come back here, you little—' Taffy's furious words were
cut off by the door slamming closed behind him, to a chorus
of cheers from the nursing staff who had clearly been in
on the joke.

'They're just big kids, aren't they, really?' said Alice fondly.

Grace nodded. 'I'm not sure that Dan realises how much of
that would have to go, once he has a kid of his own though.'

Alice was silent for a moment, knowing that this was no
idle comment. 'Do you think it's possible he has no idea? I
mean, technically Taffy is a father of four and it doesn't seem
to have dented his joie de vivre too much, does it?'

Grace nodded. 'But then Taffy isn't at home doing the hard
work, is he? Holly is.'

'Oh,' said Alice, her own nascent thoughts that she might
yet be prepared to give motherhood a go firmly quashed.
'I see what you mean. But,' she hesitated, unwilling to
sound gauche but intrigued nonetheless, 'don't they have a
nanny now?'

'Oh, my darling girl,' said Grace, sounding every single
one of her forty-two years, 'having a nanny doesn't mean

you stop being a mother. You just have yet another soul in the house to handle. But what do I know? I never had one when the boys were small. I just stayed at home going quietly out of my mind and shaping my fears in Play-Doh.' She looked defensive for a moment. 'A lot of women do that, you know.' Grace paused, perhaps realising that she was verging on over-sharing, in danger of breaking the unspoken pact whereby mothers kept the next generation largely in the dark about the joys that awaited them, for fear of scaring them shitless.

'But I didn't have a career to return to, the way you will,' Grace said after a moment's hesitation, only serving to confirm Alice's suspicions.

'And you and Dan?' Alice asked quietly. 'Have you decided what to do?'

Grace shook her head, smiling sadly as she watched the two men dart past the window, slipping, sliding and hollering, their race of reprisals having branched out into the icy car park. 'I don't know,' she said simply. 'We seem to have reached a stalemate. I'm happy to adopt. I actually rather like the idea of starting over and raising a child here. But I can't pretend that the idea of a pregnancy at my age doesn't leave me cold. I know, I know, lots of women are having babies in their forties, but I already did that. Two whole decades ago.'

Alice looped an arm around her shoulders, realising just how deeply divisive this issue was becoming. She didn't need Grace to spell it out, that it might yet become a deal-breaker for her friend's relationship with Dan.

'Had you considered a surrogate?' she asked, her mind running through options, just as she would with any patient posing this quandary.

'Why? Are you offering?' Grace laughed.

'God, no!' Alice clapped her hand over her mouth. 'I mean, what I meant to say was—'

'God, no?' Grace suggested simply. 'Don't worry, Alice. I would never ask that of anyone. I could never ask a woman to give up her child, even if technically it's not really hers.' She shrugged. 'And that's the thing with adoption too. I think I could only justify it to myself if there was no mother in the picture.'

'So a pregnant teenager . . . ?'

'Might live to regret her decision,' Grace said firmly.

Alice sighed. There was only one person she knew who could really answer that. And there was no way on earth that Alice would ever ask her how she felt about it now, seven years later. But it was fair to say that, from where she was standing, Grace certainly had a point.

Chapter 18

Holly felt a moment's disquiet as she parked her car, badly, in the car park at the Rugby Club in Bath that same morning. It was easier to focus on her parallel-parking ineptitude, despite Elsie's masterclasses, than the fact that she had slipped away this morning without telling Taffy where she was going.

In fact, worse than that, she'd somehow misled him into thinking she was going shopping in Bath and hence the early start, in order to find a parking space big enough for the ridiculous Volvo she was now expected to drive as a mother of four. She switched off the ignition, not even caring that she was almost diagonally taking up two spaces, her heart thumping heavily in her chest.

What was she doing?

Even considering another job felt duplicitous, almost adulterous.

Keeping this meeting a secret made it even more so.

She blinked hard to block out Elsie's voice in her head; her shrewd questions, having overheard Holly on the phone making arrangements, had been spot on the money. 'What's your motivation here, Holly? Are you willing to abandon your principles out of sheer contrariness?'

Apparently she was.

In fact, the more Taffy and Dan had laughed at the notion of her joining the Rugby Club team over the last few days, the more determined she had become to make a point, apparently, no matter how skewed the logic.

It hadn't helped that Taffy had arrived home the night before bearing her favourite profiteroles from The Deli, before sweeping her out to the pub for a drink. Rather unprecedented on a school night of late, but then perhaps he was aware that he had overstepped the mark with her? He had been sweet and funny and attentive — she hadn't dared mention her plans for fear of disrupting their tentative détente. It had been just heavenly to relax in his company, helping Connor celebrate and, just for once, not trading job lists and grievances.

She took a breath and tugged down the hem of her smartest work jacket, which now gripped uncomfortably at her upper arms, reminding her with every movement that, whether she was prepared to admit it or not, she was still softened by motherhood in every sense of the word.

'Looking can't hurt,' she muttered to herself as she stepped out of the car, rows of Georgian buildings marking out the limits of the Rugby Club's territory. It was an inspiring sight. 'I'm just dipping a toe in the water,' she told herself, ignoring the flicker of guilt that persisted.

'You can't deny it's a first-rate facility,' said Mike with an expansive smile, as he showed her around the Rugby Club half an hour later. His determination in persuading Holly was almost admirable; apparently he was a man who knew what he wanted and was prepared to go out on a limb to get it.

Certainly greeting her with a platter of Danish pastries and the most divine Italian coffee had put a spring in Holly's step and distracted her from her moral quandary.

'But, Mike, you do realise that sports medicine is just not my speciality and I hardly know one end of a rugby pitch from the other.' Holly felt obliged to tell it like it was – there was little point in continuing the tour if he was under some illusion about her skillset. 'I'm a GP. A family doctor.'

'I know,' he said, perching on the edge of the ice bath in the Physio Suite. 'But as I keep telling you, we have zero interest in having an avid fan with one eye on the score. We want our club to feel like a family, and for players' families to have access to the best healthcare as well.' He looked around and dropped his voice. 'Look, a distracted player is not a successful player and we learned that the hard way last season. If our players need peace of mind about their children's health, or their spouses', it's a relatively cost-effective fix.'

'You mean I'm cheap at half the price?' Holly said wryly.

'Holly, you'd be cheap at twice the price.' He paused. 'I know you don't like it when I keep saying numbers, but does the same apply if I write them down?'

Holly shook her head. 'It's an amazing offer, Mike, either way. I'm just not sure how it fits into my life.' She held up her hand as he went to speak. 'And I know about the crèche, and thank you for the offer, but this is something I need to think about.'

He nodded. 'Of course. I'd expect nothing less. But still, let me show you a little of how we work.'

She followed him from room to room: from the extensive Physio Suite, via the sauna, the steam room, the therapy room with its plush sofas and soothing blue paintwork and upholstery. It was as though they had thought of everything.

'We're finding really positive results from looking at our players and their lives holistically. It makes sense though, right? If you're going through a divorce, your head isn't in the game. If you're in pain, you'll always be holding back a little. Well, our players have families and health issues and our next step is to bring their care in-house. At the moment, they're scattered all over the city and it's like a postcode lottery whether they can even get an appointment the same week, let alone the same day. So yet again—'

'Their head's not in the game,' finished Holly, nodding. It made an awful lot of sense. And if they were lucky enough to have the funding, let alone the facilities to make that happen, then she guessed she would be advising a similar approach. Imagine having access to that kind of care – every treatment plan tailored individually and supported with the appropriate care on-site. It was the kind of set-up that GPs dreamed of.

It was not a plan without pitfalls though.

'And how are the costs for the nursing staff, lab access and insurance looking?' Holly asked out of interest.

Mike paused, the first flicker of doubt crossing his face. 'We have comprehensive insurance for the Club already in place and surely we won't need a nurse as well?' He frowned. 'I guess I hadn't really thought about lab work.'

Holly couldn't help the way her eyebrows shot up in surprise; it was an automatic response. For a man who'd seemingly thought of every detail, this was a glaring oversight.

'Well, Professional Indemnity Insurance is a separate beast, I'm afraid. It's certainly worth discussing who would bear the cost. And nursing staff would be essential in any well-run practice – not to mention top-notch access to testing facilities and the like. There's quite a range of blood tests that are essential for a GP, diagnostically. You don't want to be over-referring to consultants all the time because you haven't got a full picture. It could very quickly become an expensive enterprise,' she said gently. She wasn't trying to rain on his parade, or indeed do herself out of a job, but it seemed to her that it was better to be frank upfront.

She walked thoughtfully around the players' lounge, noting with interest that there wasn't a single item left unbranded – without a logo or the trademark blue, black and white. She was all for holistic treatment of a patient – looking at the full picture of their well-being – but she couldn't help wonder whether, in some ways, having their entire life curated and choreographed on-site might actually be detrimental to their players' sense of individuality and, indeed, privacy. Most people didn't want their bosses to know about every little medical foible, and she couldn't imagine that rugby players were any different.

Even with all the reassurances in the world, she wondered whether there might even be a question mark over confidentiality, if her services were bought and paid for by management. Would she, indeed, be under pressure to disclose any issue that might affect future reliability as a player when contracts came to be renewed?

'Mike? Can you leave this with me for a few days? Not necessarily to think about whether I want the job, but just to see if there's a better way of getting you what you need for your players. There's just something niggling at me – the little worm of experience – that makes me think that, while you're definitely on to something with the holistic approach, there might yet be a better way of making it happen?'

Mike nodded. 'I have to say, Holly, that all that talk of Medical Liability Cover has got me wondering too. I can't believe it wasn't on my radar. I guess I just assumed that with all the other medics we have here on staff, it would be in place already.'

'And it might well be,' said Holly. 'But I think, to be honest, that we both need to do a little more due diligence before we go any further.'

She paused for a moment, taking in the polish and luxury of the facilities around her and frowned. 'Had you considered a private contract – a job share of sorts?'

Mike frowned and shook his head. 'Not really. We just assumed we'd have one more dedicated member of staff. How might that work?'

Holly ran her hand over the plush folded towels, the aroma of Deep Heat already dulling as her nose acclimatised to her surroundings. She shrugged. 'I don't know. It was just a thought, really. I love the idea of working here, and to be honest the extra money would come in handy, but even with all the wrinkles ironed out, I'm just not sure I'm ready to leave my patients at The Practice behind. And, if it helps, I know Dan Carter is terribly keen to talk to you.'

Mike nodded. 'Rugby fan, is he?'

'Blue and black through and through,' she replied with a smile. 'But I don't think it would be a bad thing to have a male doctor on the payroll too ... Alternate days or something. Choice is always good.'

All of Holly's research on the topic, and she had to confess there'd been a lot in the wee small hours, told her the same thing – private patients expected time, attention and choice. And since the law forbade GPs offering private appointments to anyone on their existing patient list, whatever solution they found, it would need to be a separate arrangement. The law, on the other hand, did not prevent them offering longer appointments for their NHS patients, as long as they could make the numbers add up. It seemed to Holly that there was an answer in her mind somewhere, if only she could stop the whirlwind long enough to grasp it.

Driving away from the Rugby Club, Holly checked her watch. With the boys at school, and Plum so competently taking care of the twins, she found herself increasingly adrift. It was all very well considering becoming a part-time doctor, but having a full-time nanny already had the power to make her feel superfluous in her own life – even if this was only the first week!

'First World problems, eh?' she said to herself, as she wound down the windows, both shocked and delighted by the blast of cold air that greeted her. Controversially, Holly believed that Larkford was at her finest at this time of year; the very last of the golden leaves clinging stubbornly to their branches as the winter swept in, bringing glorious sunny days and an invigorating bite of cold. In between the swathes of rainy grey, of course. Which, to Holly, made moments like this all the more precious, as though the town was putting on a show just for her benefit. A light frost dusted the trees and hedgerows, and the river sparkled in the valley below. Did she really want to leave this behind every morning, to make the schlepp through the traffic into Bath?

Holly was under no illusion that her current confusion was a symptom of too much choice – too many options. The chance to start again with a fresh sheet after her maternity leave was tempting in the extreme – the little voice in her head shouting out that she was more than just a mother and wanting to prove herself – but at what cost? Would it really be so awful to be the part-time mummy, part-time GP and PTA member? On the other hand, was she really happy to be an occasional team member, not fully included or, she rather suspected, fully appreciated?

Elsie's words echoed in her head: 'Motherhood can be the kiss of death for professional ambition, unless you're very strict with yourself.'

She had a valid point.

But surely, true liberation meant that she could also opt out of the rat race, should she so choose?

She slammed on the brakes suddenly, her heart lurching in her throat, as she barely avoided rounding the bend into Connor walking his rag-tag pack of dogs in the narrow lane. Connor ambled along beside them, his overnight transformation to eccentric rock-star-farmer seemingly almost complete.

Leather trousers tucked into battered wellies, traditional Cotswold gilet over a sloganed hoody from The Hive's twenty-one-country tour and talking loudly into the latest iPhone, Connor shepherded his assorted canines across to the lush, riverside pastureland for a romp. Canines that looked decidedly like the hotch-potch selection that Agatha Peal had been acquiring at The Big House for years; too soft ever to turn away a muttley in need, they were hardly a cohesive group, but nevertheless they stuck together with an obvious affection. It was certainly a good sign that Connor was putting down roots, Holly realised. He needed to be part of a pack. Without the imposed form of life with The Hive, he'd been dangerously adrift.

She wondered whether anyone else saw through him the way she did. The constant, almost frenetic activity? The forced bonhomie in the pub, as though it were a shield he'd erected to deflect sympathy or questions? She couldn't help thinking that his almost single-minded approach was a risky endeavour, making so many big changes all at once.

Spotting Holly at the wheel, Connor spoke briefly into the phone and walked over towards her, the dogs milling around his ankles and subsequently Holly's car. 'Hello!' she said, her arm resting on the open window ledge. 'You nearly gave me a heart attack!'

Connor grinned goofily. 'Sorry, got distracted by a call. I was so chuffed to have mobile phone signal, I forgot we were on a proper road.' He glanced up and down the single-track lane doubtfully, where the hedgerows had begun to claim even a share of that. 'This *is* a proper road, right?'

Holly nodded. 'It's not on the satnav, but you'll find a lot of the locals use it as a shortcut if they're going into Bath. Be careful, won't you?'

He glanced at her sideways, obviously realising that her simple request had more layers than a mille-feuille. Holly blushed. It wasn't her place to interfere, was it? But then, when had that ever stopped her?

'Lots going on for you at the moment, Conn. Take it steady?'

Connor shook his head. 'No chance. Gotta keep on swimming.'

He may have been smiling, Holly thought, but it didn't reach his eyes. In fact, every time she looked at Connor of late, the same word popped into her head: dysthymia. High-functioning depression.

His shark analogy wasn't lost on her either – keep swimming or drown was the subtext of his words.

But Taffy, and Lizzie for that matter, didn't agree. They thought she was looking for problems. When they looked at Connor they saw someone making positive changes after an horrific event, taking steps towards balance and a fresh start.

And God knows, the notion of a fresh start must be incredibly appealing for him.

She could empathise.

But she didn't quite buy into the hype. 'I'm coming over for a cuppa and a snoop soon,' Holly informed him. 'Anything I can do to ease the transition just say, won't you?'

Connor nodded. 'Of course.' It was clear from the tightening around his eyes that he had absolutely no intention of doing so.

Holly decided to bide her time, but that didn't mean for a moment that she wasn't convinced of her assessment. 'Are you walking every dog in Larkford today, or just Agatha's?' she asked with a smile, changing the subject and trying to count the number of wagging tails beating against her car door.

Connor waggled his eyebrows and grinned, relieved to be on safer ground. 'Just following doctor's orders, ma'am. Pick'n'mix you advised, wasn't it?' He gave her a wave and continued on his way, tooting a shrill whistle to bring his pack to heel.

Holly watched them go in her rear-view mirror, wondering whether at any point Connor could be tempted to confide in her. And if not her, then whom? She didn't like to think of him censoring himself with his friends to meet perceived expectations. Even his own.

She put the car into gear and it stalled almost immediately, as Holly banged on the steering wheel, struck by a moment of clarity. Pick'n'mix! That was the answer. Not just for Connor, but for her current situation too.

Pulling slowly away, she allowed herself a quiet whoop of delight. Somehow focusing on Connor meant her subconscious had been doing all the heavy lifting behind the scenes. She just needed to get to a notepad before life intervened and muddied the waters.

Chapter 19

Plum placed a tiny cup and saucer at Holly's elbow, the steam from the thick espresso carrying the most exquisite aroma into the kitchen. Using her own vintage stove-top espresso maker was her own small protest against the 'filthy, commercial dregs' that the British were apparently happy to settle for. Holly was not complaining – if coffee snobbery was Plum's only flaw, it was one she could happily live with.

Holly smiled her thanks, her skittering gaze returning to the array of Post-its and notes that covered the table and wishing that ideas that seemed so simple in one's head, driving through the Larkford lanes, weren't quite so slippery and evasive when you tried to pin them down on paper. It had been a long day, her visit to Lizzie notwithstanding. Far from being the tonic of friendship she had hoped for, Lizzie had been in a cantankerous mood.

'So your friend Lizzie, she is mending though, yes?' checked Plum, Lottie balanced easily on her hip, as she replenished snacks and nappies and various toddler accoutrements in her Louis Vuitton handbag, having already declared Holly's ducky nappy bag a *crimine contro la moda* – a sentiment that Holly had initially taken as a compliment until she'd Googled it.

Holly held Olivia against her chest so that she could sneakily breathe in the heady scent of her daughter's baby shampoo. 'I think so, yes. It's probably a good sign that she's getting bored.'

'Well, she's hardly making life easy for the people around her,' Elsie said, coming into the kitchen and snaffling Holly's coffee. 'You'd think that, with three children, she'd be delighted to have a little enforced recuperation.'

Nineteen pressed his snout against the French doors and grunted pathetically in greeting, still disgruntled at being banished to the garden.

'Maybe a little bit of meddling on her doorstep will give her something else to think about,' Holly mused, thinking of Connor and the vast house he had taken on. Planning the décor for a house like that could keep Lizzie busy for weeks if she could persuade Connor to give Lizzie free rein. And, from where she was standing, they could both use a little company and moral support.

'Well, meddling always cheers *me* up,' Elsie said seriously. 'Walk with me to The Deli, Holly? It'll do you good to stop staring at those Post-its and muttering to yourself like a crazy person. And besides, I have a hankering for cheesecake,' Elsie said, as she slipped into her quilted jacket, its delicate vintage shades making no secret of its designer heritage.

Holly brushed a little chalky residue from the sleeve. 'Where have you been, to have chalk dust all over you?' she asked, without really thinking. It was only Elsie's blustering response that actually caught Holly's attention. 'J'accuse!' she said. 'So you *do* know the new neighbours! *And* you've been round there snooping at their refurb.' Holly narrowed her eyes. 'You told me Connor had it all wrong.'

Elsie shrugged. 'Ooops.' She didn't elaborate and Holly

waited, poised for some nugget of information, some juicy titbit. Discretion had never before been Elsie's forte.

'Well?' Holly demanded after a moment. 'Aren't you going to tell me anything at all?' Her frustration bubbled over into her words, aggrieved that the clarity of thought she'd found earlier had seemingly deserted her the moment she walked through the front door. 'Are you having a torrid affair with some married man? A secret poker game? Give me something!'

Elsie was still stubbornly refusing to give so much as a hint as to the mysterious new neighbour's identity, but at least they'd had the diplomacy to start limiting the noisier jobs to the working week. Whether Elsie had been instrumental in passing along the neighbours' displeasure was anyone's guess. But she refused to be drawn.

'You'll have to come clean at some point, you know,' said Holly. 'You can't keep a secret in Larkford for long.'

'*You* might not be able to, darling girl, but *I* have been doing it for years,' Elsie said smugly, the affection in her eyes more of an embrace than a challenge.

Holly blew her fringe from her eyes and tucked her arm through Elsie's. 'We'll see,' she said confidently.

In a flurry of kisses and goodbyes, Holly and Elsie stepped outside, the Market Place peaceful for once under an increasingly leaden sky, in the lull between afternoon and evening. Elsie pulled up short and placed a hand on Holly's arm to quieten her.

On the bench opposite their house, young Jess Hearst was having what was clearly a deep and meaningful conversation. With a miniature horse. But the sharing and mutual adoration was no less expressive for being inter-species.

Jess leaned forward and buried her face into the tiny palomino's mane, murmuring words that Holly couldn't hear, even as the little chap whickered into Jess's shoulder. Not even three feet high and perfectly proportioned, Banana's palomino coat shone with health, much care and attention clearly having been lavished on his grooming.

So much for not intruding, thought Holly, as Elsie barrelled over to say hello. 'Well, aren't you delightful?' Elsie said, plonking herself down on the bench beside Jess and holding out a hand for Banana to snuffle. 'I've heard all about these chaps but I haven't had the honour. Jess, will you introduce us?'

Jess giggled, as ever sweet, charming and a little in awe of Elsie Townsend. It was so wonderful to see her young face relaxed and happy, thought Holly. She'd been through so much, and coping with her mother Lavinia's neuroses couldn't make for an easy home life at the best of times.

'Hi, Jess,' Holly said. 'How's the training going?'

Jess's face lit up. 'He's *so* clever, Dr Graham. He's completely house trained and he walks to heel, even without his lead rein. And yesterday he lay down when I asked him to.' Even though one side of her face was still oddly immobile following her accident, there was an animation there now, in her eyes, that Holly hadn't seen in a long time.

'He's just adorable, Jess,' said Holly, submitting to a thorough snuffling from Banana. 'He's the perfect size, isn't he? The ultimate in portable ponies; you could take him anywhere.'

A shadow crossed Jess's face. 'Well, not *anywhere*. The stupid school Mum's organised for me won't let him come too. If he was an eventer or a show pony then no problem. It's why I was going to go there to begin with . . .' She paused. 'They just can't see that he's more useful than any competition horse and I can't be tutored at home for ever. I'll go mad.'

'Can't you just say he's your emotional support horse?' Elsie chimed in, half-joking.

'I've tried that,' said Jess. 'I even made a video diary for the Headmistress so she could see how much he helps me, but she said it would be the "start of a slippery slope" or something. Stupid woman, stupid school.'

There was a hint of her mother's petulance in Jess's tone, but Holly could actually see her point. 'Maybe we should ask Alice or Jamie what to do. I mean, if anyone in Larkford knows about support animals, it would be them, yes? Maybe there's some rule we can exploit?' She couldn't honestly say why she felt so strongly about this, after all, it was a bit of a reach, wasn't it? Taking a miniature horse to school? And in all honesty, if she hadn't seen the enormous stress and turmoil Jess had been through over the last year and the huge strides she'd made in the last few weeks, then she probably wouldn't have believed it herself – Banana should really be available on the NHS. He certainly deserved a little status.

Elsie rummaged in her pocket and pulled out a packet of Polo mints. 'Is he allowed one?' she asked Jess.

Jess nodded. 'But he has to earn it. Here, let me show you.' She took one of the mints and knelt down beside Banana. 'Hug,' she said, and to Holly and Elsie's absolute amazement, he turned his head and cradled Jess's fragile body against his shoulder with his neck.

Even as he held her, his whiskers snuffled into her hand for the mint.

Even after his treat though, he stayed put, nickering gently and affectionately.

Holly felt the tears well up in her eyes and noticed Elsie was in the same predicament.

Elsie, of course, was not one for hiding her feelings. 'Oh, for the love of God, you can't go to any school that won't allow him to go with you!'

'Elsie!' admonished Holly. 'That's not really helpful,' she whispered forcefully.

'Well, it's true,' said Elsie bluntly. 'And why do you need to go away to boarding school anyway, when there's a perfectly good one in Larkford?' Elsie said, only serving to throw oil on the flames of Jess's brewing rebellion. 'Holly seems to have Mr French's ear, Jess, why don't we ask him if he'll allow an emotional support horse in *his* classroom?'

Jess's eyes grew huge with possibility. 'Do you think he'd listen to you, Dr Graham? Even a year would be enough to let Banana prove himself before we went anywhere to board.'

Holly breathed out, so uncertain of her role these days. Was she advising as a friend, a neighbour, a doctor? And was she actually prepared to risk Lavinia's wrath by wading into the debate uninvited?

'I tell you what, Jess,' Holly said after a moment, 'why don't I have a chat with Charlotte and Jamie about how one might go about making Banana's role official. I'm not sure your mum would like you basing your choice of school on this, but it doesn't hurt to ask a few questions, does it?'

The hope in Jess's eyes stayed with Holly long after she had left them, walking through the Market Place with her horse trotting neatly beside her, one hand on his withers and chatting away to him, nineteen to the dozen.

'Lavinia is not going to be happy,' said Elsie gleefully, her penchant for winding up the yummy mummies of Larkford well established. 'But I have to say that it's got to be worth it, just to see that young lass looking so happy again.'

Holly didn't comment, knowing exactly who would bear the brunt of Lavinia's displeasure. But maybe if she was intent on picking her battles, actually making a difference, then there was no better place to start than with Banana? Tiny horses and stroppy, social-climbing mothers first, secretive pensioners second. And then, only then, Holly decided, would she have the mental bandwidth in place to tackle her own dilemmas of duality.

'What's with this habit in Larkford of making everything miniature?' Connor said, as he ambled towards them with a smile. 'I'm supposed to be buying some goats, and they're all tiny as well. Beginner goats, according to the lady vet I spoke to on the phone. She seemed pretty sceptical about me coping with anything bigger.' He paused, looking a little crestfallen for a moment. 'She was kind of bossy and outspoken about it actually.'

Holly tried not to stare, her medical acuity still on high alert after their conversation earlier. 'That's just Kitty's way,' she said reassuringly. 'She's just great, actually, although I'm absolutely convinced she prefers animals to people.'

Connor gave her a sideways look. 'Don't we all?' he said drily.

'Oh well, if that's the case, you should take Nineteen back to the farm with you,' Elsie said, glancing disdainfully at the blooming stain on her cream suede pumps. 'He's rather outgrown his welcome as a house guest.'

Holly was about to protest. After all, Nineteen was her pig, not Elsie's, until she saw the logic in the situation: a happy home for her overgrown porker and the perfect excuse to check in on Connor once in a while. 'Seriously?' said Holly. 'Would you have him to stay? I can't give him to you because Taffy would never forgive me – they've bonded, apparently. But Nineteen's desperate for a little room to roam.'

Connor shrugged, unfazed. 'He can live in the orchard — apples and pears as far as his little porky eye can see.'

'Could he really?' Holly asked, rather touched by his instant acquiescence. 'He'd seriously love that; he adores fruit and it would appease my guilty conscience as well. One minute he's on the sofa by the Aga and the next he's out on his ear.'

Connor just shrugged again. 'It's fine. Really.'

'Oh, but you'll need a pig licence,' Holly remembered with a frown.

'Already got one,' said Connor, surprising her. 'I seem to have gained a reputation as a soft touch. Every Tom, Dick and Harry has been turning up at the farmyard with their ill-advised pets hoping I'll add them to my menagerie. I've already gained three Vietnamese pot-bellied pigs from the Wynters. Hence the licence.' He gave a tired smile. 'Nineteen will fit right in.'

As he walked away, Holly had to restrain herself from running after him and giving him a hug. All the animals in Larkford weren't going to fill the hole in Connor's life, and she couldn't help but feel that any enthusiasm for his new farming venture was simply a veneer applied for their benefit. Or possibly for his own? At this point it was difficult to tell.

'All the fresh air in the world, but he's still drowning, isn't he?' said Elsie quietly, tucking her arm through Holly's as his slight figure grew smaller in the distance.

Chapter 20

'Come on, seriously, settle down now. We have an awful lot to discuss and a full clinic after this.' Dan banged his hand on the table in the doctors' lounge, in yet another futile attempt to bring their weekly meeting to order. 'And if the forecast is anything to go by, we might need to implement a few emergency cover shifts too. Guys?'

Taffy stuffed two fingers in his mouth and whistled and the room fell instantly silent. Dan wasn't quite sure whether to be impressed or annoyed. Obviously his authority had taken quite the dent of late and now, seemingly, his unofficial role as Senior Partner gave him no guarantee of his team's undivided attention.

'Okay then,' he said, projecting his voice and adjusting his posture, calling on all his army training to get his troops back in line. 'Let's start with the basics, shall we, before we all get distracted by the promise of a few inches of snow? Can I remind you all that there's to be no fraternising with the patients – Jason, that includes you.'

Jason just looked innocently at him. 'It doesn't count as fraternising if it's same-sex friendships, does it?'

'It does if we're still putting you down as "undecided" on that front,' Taffy cut in apologetically, earning himself a stern look from Dan.

'What about Tilly, then?' said Jason grumpily. 'She's allowed to "counsel" all these students in Big Bertha and we're all supposed to pretend that they aren't completely in lurve with her?'

'Ah, but I'm not sleeping with them all, now am I?' Tilly fought back.

'Not all of them,' Jason agreed, giving her a wink.

Tilly shrugged. 'Obviously I'm not sleeping with *any* of them, but I can't help it if they happen to have excellent taste.'

The two of them together seemed to be dead-set on bringing The Practice into disrepute and their libidos were in danger of being itemised on their professional insurance docket.

'Give it a rest, Tilly,' said Dan tiredly, feeling the stress tighten his face and wondering how Alice's seemingly bright, educated friend could be quite so dim when it came to diplomacy.

'Well, to be fair,' said Jade, 'it's harder for the nurses than the doctors. Most of you are all coupled up, or don't want to be. We still have our lives to lead and Larkford isn't exactly a big gene pool, if you know what I mean?'

'You've just run out of fresh meat,' countered Jason with a grin, receiving a custard cream to the forehead in retaliation. Jade's aim was almost impressive.

Dan banged his hand so hard on the table that all their glasses and mugs leapt into the air. 'Does this sound like the kind of conversation that's appropriate at a Practice Meeting to you?' He glared around the table at the culprits.

'Let's take a look at the agenda,' said Grace into the uncomfortable silence that fell. 'Dan?'

Dan nodded, taking a deep breath and wondering when their team had begun taking such liberties. 'Item one,' he began.

*

'There you are,' said Grace, pushing open the door to the car park and stepping out beside him, a cup of tea in her hand. 'Do you want to talk about it?'

Dan shook his head but accepted the warm drink gratefully. That was the thing about storming out of a meeting, especially one where you were supposed to be in control; there wasn't really time to sort out jumpers and warm drinks. 'When did it get so . . . ?' Dan asked helplessly. 'It's like feeding time at the zoo in there. The left hand doesn't know what the right hand's doing and the chain of command is just falling apart.'

Grace nodded. 'Don't let's kid ourselves that this is new, though. It's been building for months.'

Dan frowned. 'Is this where you give me a lecture about being in denial again?'

'If you like,' said Grace with a shrug. 'But we both know you won't listen.'

Dan sipped the tea to buy himself a moment to think, the steam rising and bathing his face in warmth. 'And you still think this is because we're not leading from the front, Taffy and I?'

'Pretty much,' said Grace quietly, shuffling her feet and shivering. 'I know it's not easy, but if you two want any authority around here, then you might need to cut back on playing silly buggers at work. They're a young team and they don't necessarily know how to change gears — one minute you're all betting and playing Operation and hooning around the car park, the next you're being their boss, expecting their instant respect, and telling them what to do.'

'But that was never a factor before,' Dan protested, almost half-hearted in his dissent now, Grace's point having been so firmly illustrated by that disastrous meeting.

'It wasn't just you and Taffy running the show before.

Like it or not, Holly brought balance. Even when you two were arsing about, she was the voice of reason. I can't be that, because I'm the Practice Manager. I'm not a partner.'

Dan nodded. 'And I suppose Alice is still too young herself to have any authority?'

'And she's not a partner,' Grace repeated patiently.

Dan sighed. 'Between you and me, I do wonder what we're doing having Tilly on staff. It's so perfectly obvious she doesn't want to be here. I mean, she's a decent doctor, but she's clearly bored by the day-to-day. I see her struggling to find empathy with her patients, while her screen saver is still that landmine campaign. It's almost as though she's sending the patients a message that their issues don't really count.'

'What are you suggesting?' Grace asked.

'I honestly don't know. She's Holly's hire, Alice's best friend. I'm not really sure it's my call to make,' Dan said.

'Well, it is, actually. You're a partner; you can start the conversation at the very least.'

Dan balanced his mug on the wall beside the half dozen others that had accrued of late. 'Come here, you,' he said, pulling her into a hug. 'Where would I be without you?'

Grace didn't reply, merely folding herself into his arms. He knew, though, that she had plenty to say; she just sometimes chose to let him work things out by himself. Right now, that equation seemed to suggest that fun and responsibility at work ran in inverse proportion.

'I wish Holly would come back,' he said after a moment, already trying to find a way to wriggle out of the difficult choices in his future.

'Ask her,' said Grace against his chest.

'Oh no, I couldn't. It would be too much pressure. Taffy's been pretty clear about that,' Dan replied.

'And since when is Taffy Holly's gatekeeper?' Grace huffed, pushing herself out of his embrace and looking thoroughly peeved. 'She's a professional. She's a mother, yes, but she knows her own mind and from where I'm standing, she's putting all the wheels in motion to return to work. All the forms are in from the CCG, and their new nanny has already started. Did you think that was just so Holly could go out for lunch more often?' she asked incredulously, shoving her hands angrily into her pockets.

'You seem to feel pretty strongly about this,' Dan said, furrowing his brow and wondering where his comfort zone lay. Maybe that would explain why he was dithering so uncharacteristically. 'I just can't see how to move forward without ruffling somebody's feathers along the way,' he explained.

'Well,' exhaled Grace. 'You can't run a business properly if you spend all your time worrying about offending people. And you can't be a role model, if you're still behaving like a teenager yourself.'

Dan paused, trying not to take offence at Grace's outburst. After all, wasn't she supposed to be on *his* side, instead of shooting him down? 'Is this about having kids?' he asked tentatively.

'You defeat me,' Grace said tiredly, shaking her head. 'Not every conversation we have is about having kids. Not every thought *I* have is about having kids. That's your filter, Dan.' She shoved him angrily away.

'But you can see why I might think that? I mean, it's obvious you don't want a baby, so now you're criticising me for being too immature to be a dad!' Dan replied tightly.

'You're a moron,' said Grace, throwing up her hands in despair. 'You're pushing against an open door, but part of

parenting is compromise. You want to have a baby together?
You know I'm in. I just think that there is more than one way
to become a parent and it would be nice if we could consider
options that I'm comfortable with too.'

'What about me? What about what I feel comfortable
with?' Dan protested.

Grace paused. 'Do you know, maybe you were right just
now. I wasn't talking about kids, but I may as well have been.
If you want to be a dad, then grow up, and start acting like
one. Because for the record, the parenting doesn't just start
on the day the baby's born. So yes, be a grown-up. Be a
partner – not just at work, but at home with me too. Talk to
the women in your life and stop assuming that you and Taffy
Jones can work out what exactly is "good for us" over a pint
at the pub. Nothing in life that is ever worth having comes
easily, Dan. So find out what you really want and come back
to me. How's that for advice?'

Dan watched as Grace stormed back into the building and
felt a wave of nausea hit the back of his throat. What the hell
was he doing? Was this what self-sabotage looked like?

Of all the things in his life that truly mattered, surely his
work and his relationship with Grace should take priority?
But somehow, they were both throwing up obstacles that he
didn't have the reserves to handle right now.

Arsing about with his mate was easier.

It wasn't constructive, or sensible half the time, but it was
definitely less of a challenge.

Dan slipped back into the building and deliberately avoided
the doctors' lounge. He wasn't in the mood for any more con-
frontation today and if he saw Tilly Campbell in his current
frame of mind, he couldn't trust himself not to fire her on

the spot. If she wanted to be off saving the world, then maybe that's what she should do. Dan was more interested in saving this particular section of it.

He pushed open the door to his consulting room and stopped dead.

'Tilly,' he said warily. 'Can I help you with something?'

She nodded. 'It's one of my patients, actually. But I also wanted to apologise. I know I haven't exactly been the perfect employee recently, but I want you to know that I'm working on it.'

'Okay,' said Dan simply, not entirely believing the spiel, but willing to give her the benefit of the doubt one last time. Again, the path of least resistance.

'So,' Tilly said, tugging down her miniskirt to cover her thighs as she perched on the chair beside his desk, 'I went over to the Pickwick Estate the other day for some home visit Alice gave me. I suspect she had an ulterior motive actually, but that's another story. The point is, when I got there, well . . .' She looked uncomfortable, twisting her mouth to bite at her bottom lip. 'I wasn't being deliberately nosey. I just had a little look around.'

Dan waited, knowing only too well there was no point prompting this disclosure.

Tilly leaned across and typed May Fowler's name into his computer and the patient file opened automatically on the screen.

Dan quickly scanned the notes. 'I'm not all that familiar with her case. Holly handed her over to Alice.' He scrolled down the screen, the various entries painting a picture of ill health going back decades. Often help never sought until extreme measures were required. He looked up. 'Is she okay?'

'No,' said Tilly simply. 'And I spoke to Alice about it, but we both decided this needed wiser minds than ours.' She glanced at her watch. 'Actually Alice was supposed to be here with me to do this, but she got held up with Cassie Holland in reception.'

'And when you say "this" – what do you mean?' asked Dan. 'Is it time to think about residential care, do you think?' His glance flickered to May's list of prescribed medication and the frequency of the refills. 'If she's needing this much pain relief, then there are better ways to manage her discomfort if she's in the right place.'

A tentative knock at the door and Alice slipped inside in time to catch the end of his sentence. 'That's what we thought too, but then you have to consider May's granddaughter, Louise. Her mum – May's daughter – Keira, is still in hospital and, speaking to her oncologist, is looking at a move towards palliative care. We can't get May the help she needs, without leaving Louise without a guardian.'

Dan clicked through page after page, the computer system making it cumbersome to link up family members. 'Louise is three?' he checked. 'How on earth has May been taking care of a tot all this time without Social Services stepping in?'

Tilly glanced at Alice. 'Well, I think it's because she's an adoring grandmother who is very, very convincing at telling people what they want to hear. When I got there, she was expecting me, and everything seemed fine. But about half an hour after I'd left, I realised I'd left my phone there, so I went back.'

Dan sat back in his chair, realising in that moment how tempting it might be for someone to close their eyes and ears to this situation. To turn away from anything that might force a hideous decision. 'And?' he prompted.

'And they were both crying,' said Tilly, choked up even saying the words. 'Not snivelling or anything, I mean May was actually on the floor sobbing and the little girl was screaming blue murder from her playpen. Her nappy had fallen off and there was . . . Look I know, all parents have bad days too, but this wasn't that. This wasn't, I don't know, normal.'

'She's not coping,' Alice cut in. 'I went back again this morning just to be sure. Unannounced. Louise hadn't been fed, hadn't been changed. May could barely open the door, her hands were so swollen, and she was still in last night's clothes. The lift's still out. They haven't left the flat in weeks, according to the neighbour that buzzed me in.'

'Shit,' said Dan, breathing out slowly. 'As if that family hasn't got enough to deal with. And there's nobody else, no other relatives? What about the dad? Is he in the picture?'

'Never has been apparently. I checked with Records. Unknown,' Alice said. 'I'm not saying this lightly, but I think we need to make the call.'

Dan nodded. 'I'll pop round first. If we're going to be the instigators in pulling this little family apart, then I need to see this for myself.'

'Steel yourself,' said Tilly. 'I've seen some awful crap in my time, but that little girl just looks heartbroken. She has a mother and grandmother who love her to bits, but somehow, she's still all alone.'

'Come with me,' said Dan, all thoughts of firing Tilly forgotten. 'We can go together.'

Chapter 21

Connor took a deep breath, knowing he was running indecently late, and jabbed repeatedly at the mobile phone on
his dashboard, as he wondered just exactly how long the
vet would wait before she gave up on him as a timewaster.
'Popping out to buy pig feed' had turned into a ridiculous
farce of missed junctions and three-point turns.

No signal.

Not even a single bar. The urbanite in him howled in
despair, but a small part of his brain registered that this kind
of seclusion was exactly what he'd been searching for: no
constant Twitter updates, no calls from his manager, or his
PR firm – just living.

If he could even call it that.

Keeping busy was one thing; this frenetic activity of
late was another. He knew, on some level, that Holly had
rumbled him – had even been poised to throw himself on
her mercy and tell her the pathetic truth of the matter.
He'd felt sure that she would understand, could possibly
even help, but then his stupid pride had prevailed and he'd
walked away.

Alone in a crowd.

There was probably a song in there somewhere, if he could

muster the enthusiasm to pick up his guitar, he thought to himself with a wry smile

He put the Range Rover back into gear and pulled away, trying to ignore the metaphor that presented itself, lyrics forming in his reluctant subconscious, even as he attempted to navigate the network of tiny lanes that all looked uncannily similar to his untrained eye. The story of his life these days, or so it seemed: trying to find his way home.

Taking a tiny left-hand turn beneath the shadow of some ancient horse chestnut trees, light flurries of snow already dusting the bare, sweeping branches, Connor gave a start of surprise when he recognised how close he'd been to Larkford all along.

Metaphors, confirmed his subconscious smugly. Everywhere.

He blinked hard, as he parked the car, wondering whether meeting somebody new today was actually a good idea while he felt so fractured and disorientated. Making conversation, being polite, even when talking about building his herd of goats for the farm, somehow felt like a reach this evening.

A reach too far, perhaps?

Striding towards the pub, he stopped dead in his path. A rush of adrenalin spiking his pulse, thudding away at the base of his throat in a way he had almost forgotten.

It winded him for a moment, and he paused in the doorway, unwilling for this to be the first impression he made on the girl who sat inside waiting for him, her face tipped towards the fire instinctively, coltish legs folded under the pub table and an oversized Aran jumper swamping her delicate frame.

She turned, as though alerted by his gaze. 'Hi,' she said simply, with a smile. 'I'm Kitty.'

'Connor,' he managed, stepping forward and holding out his hand, finding himself unwilling to let go.

She gave him a curious smile. 'You're so not what I was expecting. I mean, putting aside the diva timekeeping ...' She gently let go of his hand and pushed a half of local cider towards him across the table, conversation in the pub garden merely adding a blurring backdrop to her words.

Connor gave himself a little shake as he sat down opposite her, suddenly feeling like a gauche adolescent in her company. She was everything he never looked for in a woman and yet ... He couldn't stop staring at the slightly crazy-looking bundle of hair on the top of her head, which fell gently to frame her face with natural, blonde-streaked tendrils. She certainly didn't meet the somewhat, dare he say it, heftier mental picture of the bossy lady vet he'd been prepared for and he found himself both chagrined and immediately off balance. Not to mention completely out of his depth.

Women like Kitty Clarke didn't cross his path that often. If ever.

As the pub filled around them, and the soft blanket of snow silently deepened outside, their conversation flowed easily and hours later, Connor couldn't exactly recall what they'd even talked about. Goats, certainly. Larkford, of course. But it was more a sense of having found, against all odds, that single, meaningful connection that had been so markedly missing in his life. She didn't seem to mind his notable lack of witty repartee or hopeless lack of interest in current affairs; she wasn't obviously enthralled by his looks or wealth either. She just, well, listened to him as though she truly heard what he was trying to say. It was awfully intoxicating.

Kitty ripped open a bag of crisps, shrugging as he refused her offer to share. He was quietly impressed, he realised, by a girl who was unfazed by a Pickled Onion Monster Munch.

And who knew that was even a factor in how you felt about somebody? Kitty's natural ease of movement and confidence was seemingly born from a complete disregard for appearances or status. It was something he himself could only aspire to.

'So, do you have a plan?' she asked, breaking into his thoughts. 'Beyond the goats and the bees?' She gave him a wicked smile. 'Everyone here has heard all about your bees!' She nodded her head over to where Cassie Holland was holding court at another table.

Connor shook his head. 'She'll be the death of me, that woman.'

'Ah, she's all talk and no trousers. Mostly,' Kitty reassured him. 'She just likes to get on her high horse about some things. Obviously, you seem to have piqued her interest, though. Sorry about that.'

'Not the best start to my plans,' he agreed. 'Although, hopefully she won't object to the goats you've found for me. I mean, they're pretty tiny and inoffensive, right?'

Kitty grinned. 'Well, you're going to be the one getting up close and personal with them. So I guess we'll wait and see. Perry's herd are kind of adorable, as well as high-yielding, so you're probably safe.'

'Well, obviously, it was adorable I was aiming for,' Connor said, even as he wanted to kick himself at the clumsy, slightly teasing tone that had crept into his voice.

She just shook her head and smiled. 'You're okay, you know? I was all braced for a wanker in leather trousers mansplaining animal husbandry to me, but you're all right.' She clinked her glass against his. 'You just need a little confidence in your plans if you're to see off the Cassie Hollands of this world. Stop apologising for every decision you make.' She reached across the table and squeezed his hand supportively. 'Your farm, your choices.'

Connor nodded, wondering whether he could extrapolate that advice across the board. Own his decisions a little more assuredly and stop the doubts creeping in.

'Let me run something past you . . .' he began.

It didn't make any sense whatsoever, to be spilling all the details of his closely guarded secret to a woman he'd only just met, but then, nothing about this evening made any sense at all. True, the heady feeling of making a connection was undermined at every step by an insistent thud of guilt for dropping his guard and allowing himself to enjoy a little company, but somehow that wasn't enough of an incentive to walk away.

'So, in my mind's eye, it's a Winter Solstice celebration, a family festival,' he explained to Kitty, his voice low and confiding, as he reached into his back pocket and pulled out a brightly coloured flyer: hippy-dippy artwork and bubble writing loud and clear on a glossy page of A4. 'This is just a draft copy, but I want it to be something really special – music, books, food, glamping – the works. I want to really put Larkford on the map.'

He stopped, waiting for her reaction, hesitating when none was forthcoming. 'What do you think?'

She nodded, taking her time to read the flyer, before looking up with a smile. 'I think it's ambitious. I think you're slightly mad to take on so much at once. But . . .' She smiled warmly. 'I think if anyone can do it, you can.'

He felt the give of tension releasing in his shoulders. Quite why he hadn't confided in Lizzie or Holly he couldn't say, but having Kitty Clarke's approval suddenly felt crucial to the entire endeavour.

He knew it was a little gung-ho – festivals happened in the summer months, everyone knew that – but he just didn't have it in him to wait until next year. This winter was his brand-new, fresh start – a new house, a new business and, now, a new way to be in show-biz that didn't require endless touring and hotel rooms with his band. 'At Home with The Hive' was too good an idea to ignore. And once he'd stumbled across the remains of the tiny stone circle at the peak of Blackleigh Farm, its ancient presence had seemed like a sign. A sign he couldn't ignore.

'I know it's a lot to take on, what with moving house and setting up the farm,' he said, 'but I've already got some head-lining bands teed up, and it will be the perfect opportunity to launch my new honey and cheese brands. I've even got a commercial sponsor lined up – "Bee-you-tiful"? You've probably heard of them?' He paused. 'I've thought this through, Kitty – it isn't a whim,' he added for good measure, as much to convince himself.

She shook her head. 'I wouldn't judge you if it was. But don't underestimate how much time and energy goes into setting up a new business, especially where livestock are involved.'

Connor nodded, knowing she had a point, but also accepting that nobody in Larkford really knew him yet. They knew him as a widower, a theoretical rock star and as Will and Lizzie's friend. They hadn't met Connor Danes in his professional and driven persona – they had no idea what he was capable of achieving when he put his mind to it. You didn't top the Billboard charts on three continents simultaneously without having a certain drive and determination, after all.

He just needed to find a way to harness that again.

To find his way back without losing the plot entirely.

He was out of practice on so many levels, he realised, watching Kitty as she carefully folded her empty crisp packet into a perfect, tiny triangle.

How did one even begin to ask a girl out these days?

Always supposing that was a good idea in the first place.

He opened his mouth and closed it again, suddenly assailed by a raging gamut of emotions. He gripped his empty cider glass so tightly it was in danger of imploding, breathing out gently but surely to release the panic. 'I ought to be going,' he said abruptly.

The flicker of disappointment on her face reassured him more than any words.

'I'll pop over tomorrow when Perry delivers the goats to Blackleigh Farm,' she said, switching back to the professional with an almost audible sigh. 'You're going to love them, Connor. He's named them all after the Larkford matriarchs, and to be honest, it's kind of fitting. You'll have to show them who's boss right from the start, or they'll run rings around you, okay?' She stood up, passing him back the flyer. 'Maybe the same applies to your festival plans too, eh? Own it?'

Connor just nodded, words eluding him momentarily, feeling conflicted and confused. 'I've had a really lovely evening,' he managed after a moment. The first in a very long time; but she didn't need to know that. Stepping outside together, the sweeping reality of Larkford under snow somehow made their evening feel all the more surreal and he instinctively reached out to take her hand. The wrought-iron street lamps cast pools of light amongst the whitened shadows and every sound was dulled by the layers of whispering snow that continued to fall.

'I'm glad the two of you have hit it off,' interrupted Clive Shawe gruffly, stomping over to them and making them jump, just as Connor was considering whether a kiss on the cheek was inappropriate, professionally speaking. 'You'll be seeing lots of each other, no doubt, with all the waifs and strays that this one is gathering for his homestead.' Clive chortled, his role as Connor's 'agricultural adviser' having given him free rein with an opinion of late.

Connor smiled weakly, only cheered by the notion that Clive might indeed be right, glancing at Clive's companion as though his life had in fact taken a turn for the surreal, or that second pint of cider had been a mistake.

'This is Nigel,' said Clive, by way of introduction.

'Hi, Nigel,' said Connor automatically, a little shocked to receive a breathy kiss for his trouble.

'You'll be needing Nigel on your bit of land, if you want to keep those goats in check,' said Clive.

Connor squinted at the rather tufty donkey critically. 'Is this another one of your wind-ups?' He held out a hand towards Nigel, who planted his velvety muzzle in Connor's palm and snuffled affectionately.

Clive merely offered him the lead rein. 'He's been feeling a little lonely since his missus passed over, so keeping a herd of goats in check should keep him happy. Not to mention the roof on his stable isn't up to this.' He waved a hand vaguely at the snow, as though it were a perfectly logical reason to bring your donkey to the pub of an evening.

'Right,' said Connor, still poised for the punchline, glancing at Kitty for reassurance.

'Good plan,' said Kitty easily, nodding. 'And look at him – what a sweetheart.' She buried her face in Nigel's furry coat, crooning adoringly into his neck. 'You lucky, lucky boy,' she said over and over, before emerging with dust on her forehead and her hair even more dishevelled.

Connor looked from one to the other, a flicker of doubt that he was being had still nudging his subconscious. After all, hadn't Lizzie warned him about potential hazing from the local farmers as they struggled to accept Connor's 'boutique outfit' as a going concern?

In that moment, though, he decided he didn't really care. He and Nigel clearly had a lot in common. And by the looks of it, Kitty was already a fan of his ridiculous overbite and floppy ears.

'Kitty's vetted the goats for me this afternoon,' Connor told Clive, suddenly feeling the responsibility to carry the conversation, even though Nigel's arrival had completely thrown him. 'So we're all sorted for tomorrow.'

Clive just nodded, thrusting Nigel's lead rein into his hand. 'Weather permitting,' he said, before turning abruptly and walking away.

There was an awkward pause.

'I'll come over with you now and help get him settled, if you like?' Kitty suggested. She smiled and scruffed Nigel's ears affectionately. 'I'd quite like to meet the bees too, if I may?'

Connor stilled, wondering how she seemed to instinctively know that the honeybees were his Achilles heel. Their hives were now dotted among the fruit trees in the orchard at Blackleigh Farm and their soothing buzzing was the one thing that made him feel at peace these days. The idea of them now, huddled together around their queen, perhaps shivering slightly and taking it in turns to feel the chill on the outside of their little apian family, made him feel quite emotional. It seemed a little unfair that penguins got all the good PR on this heroic team effort to keep warm. But then, when it came to his bees, he was a little biased.

The only question was whether he was ready to share that

part of his life just yet. 'They're not really settled since the move from Dorset,' he prevaricated.

'Okay,' she said, taking the hint, reaching up to kiss him lightly on the cheek. 'I'll leave you boys to it. Stay warm.'

Connor caught himself from leaning in, the soft vanilla smell of her hair alluring and anxiety-inducing in equal measure.

'But I'll see you tomorrow,' he said. He held her gaze for a moment, willing her to understand how he was feeling, wondering how he could even begin to communicate that, when he didn't yet understand it himself. Hoping she had somehow heard the unspoken.

Chapter 22

Holly hummed along to the radio as she prepared a platter of supper snacks for the kids, mindlessly popping a miniature breadstick into her mouth, before remembering that she had fully intended to give them up. Oops.

Platter in hand, Holly leaned back against the open play-room door and took a short moment to savour the small, yet significant changes Plum had brought into their lives. Tom and Ben were engrossed at the large craft table that Plum had found at the Red Cross shop, busily making seasonal collages with flour-and-water glue from heaps of magazines appropriated from Elsie's stash of glossies as part of their evening entertainment.

Tom's brow was furrowed in intense concentration and, Holly couldn't help but notice, he hadn't thumped his brother even once in the last half hour, even amongst the borderline hysterical excitement at the first snow flurries banking up in the garden and promising a snow day of sledging and snow-balls tomorrow. Olivia and Lottie shuffled around happily on their play-mat, with Eric wedged firmly alongside as blocker. They really needed to savour every moment before the stop-start spurts of running took over and nobody ever sat down again, thought Holly with an indulgent smile. Even Olivia's determined cruising was enough to get her across the room, hence Eric's sudden interest in joining in the fun, well that and the large quantity of well-chewed rusks that could be relied upon as a handy snack.

There was homemade (from scratch) minestrone soup bubbling away on the hob and the distant rumble of the washing machine, dishwasher and tumble dryer sounded like the finest trio Holly had heard in a long time.

Not only that, but she'd actually washed and blow-dried her hair just now, simply because she could. Even overlapping with Plum during this transition period still gave Holly more time than she'd had to herself in years.

And yet.

And yet, still she felt this overwhelming need to have a purpose outside the home. She adored spending time with her babies and sons, revelling in their glorious preciousness and affection, but that couldn't be the beginning and end of it all. Not when the doctor in her mind suggested all the ways she could be helping other people as well. Jess and Connor and Hannah for starters ... Anything less would surely be selfish folly, it told her, repeatedly and with feeling. The novelty of lunch out, or a spa day would last about a fortnight in Holly's approximation.

So maybe that's what she should do?

She could take every moment of the next few weeks, helping Plum settle in and her children to adapt, and also catch up with friends, make a start on the Christmas shopping perhaps. Who knew, maybe she'd even have time for a massage or a manicure without it being a complete waste of time and money? And then, she decided resolutely, she was going back to work.

And if the team at The Practice were coping so bloody

well in her absence, then maybe it was okay to explore other avenues. After all, it wasn't exactly as though Dan, Taffy and Alice made it seem as though they even needed her. Mike, on the other hand? Mike just kept naming numbers that seemed to climb every time they spoke, in his quest to win her over to the dark side. He was nothing if not persuasive.

'You hiding away with your babies?' said Taffy, surprising her. 'I thought it would be nice to be home for bath-time for a change, in case you needed some moral support.'

'How very lovely,' said Holly with feeling, this small gesture so typically Taffy that it came with a sense of relief that perhaps they weren't really so off-piste with one another. A few more hours in the day, a little more time together, and maybe they'd be back on track in no time. Maybe it was just taking them a while to adjust – two babies, twice as much upheaval, perhaps?

Reassured, she leaned back against his chest. 'You can help me watch how fabulous our children are,' she smiled, knowing that nobody else could possibly be as biased as the pair of them together.

'Another tricky day for you obviously,' Taffy joked, wrapping his arms around her waist. He didn't even seem to notice how much his 'jokes' were bothering his wife these days, to the point that she'd given up pointing it out, merely ignoring him and hoping he'd take the hint. Lizzie, of course, was keen that she employ positive reinforcement, just as Jamie the dog trainer had taught her. And Holly had been trying, she really had; there just hadn't been much to reward in his erratic behaviour of late. Coming home to help with bath-time was definitely a step in the right direction though, she reckoned, deciding to make the most of it and not bite at his tactless remark.

Plum came towards them, a stack of neatly folded babygros in her arms. 'Holly? Your mobile was ringing a moment ago, but I was in the laundry. I wasn't sure if you answered or maybe there's a message.'

'Thanks, Plum,' said Holly, impressed as ever by Plum's seeming ability to walk the tightrope between efficiency and intrusion.

'Leave it,' urged Taffy. 'Come and have a drink with me for a bit. Just at the kitchen table. Nothing fancy. Plum's here now.'

'Sounds great,' said Holly, recognising an olive branch when she saw one, handing over the proverbial reins to Plum with a grateful smile, and heading for the kitchen, a lightness to her step. It was so unusual for Taffy to be home this early that she couldn't help but hope the partners had seen sense at their meeting. She wasn't a fool; she knew that Taffy shot down all of Grace's suggestions about Holly coming back to work. But maybe this was the time to have a proper conversation about how life with four children, two careers, a labradoodle and a hormonal pig might actually work. For all of them.

Holly surreptitiously turned over her mobile in a moment of doubt, as she poured out two small glasses of Plum's delicious mulled wine at the kitchen table, just checking it wasn't something urgent. Just Dan. No message. She tipped the rest of the breadsticks from The Deli onto a plate for them to graze on. It would be hours until their supper but the cooking smells emanating from the Aga were making her stomach rumble.

Taffy stirred Plum's soup appreciatively, flourishing the ladle so a small splatter of tomato flicked across the worktop. He made no move to wipe it up, instead leaving the splatters to congeal. 'Right then, Wifey, sit yourself down. We have much to discuss and we don't have long if I'm going to be Captain Bubblebath tonight.' He reached across and snaffled a handful of grissini. 'And it looks like we'll be up at dawn to make snowmen at this rate, so we should probably aim for an early night.'

'Okay,' said Holly, trying to be concise and efficient with what she wanted to say. 'I've been wanting to talk all this through properly for ages so this is perfect. Did you read the website?'

'The website?' queried Taffy. 'My mum hasn't got a website.' He frowned in confusion. 'She's just feeling a little sidelined since young Plum arrived, that's all. And I promised her I'd talk to you about Christmas. I know it's weeks away but apparently she's phoned a couple of times and you haven't called her back. She's feeling pretty disposable, to be honest.'

Holly carefully put her drink back on the table, untouched. 'And did she happen to mention when she phones? Hmm? Every single sodding day at bath-time, that's when. I know I have another pair of hands now, but have you ever tried bathing four children and talking on the phone at the same time, have you? Because I did, the first gazillion times. And every single time, I explained. But she doesn't listen.'

'That's a bit harsh. Maybe it's just a good time for her to chat, you know, while Dad's out doing the feeds on the farm,' Taffy suggested.

Holly breathed out slowly. Arguing about his mother's inability to read a clock wasn't going to get them anywhere. 'So I'll phone her. At a time that works for us.'

He shrugged, seemingly losing interest in the conversation and having obviously said what he came to say.

'It's lovely that you're here, actually,' persisted Holly,

'because Mike has been pressuring me for an answer and I'm still not sure what to say. I can't help thinking there's something to be gained by offering a—'

'Mike? Rugby Club Mike? I thought we'd already agreed it was a non-starter?' Taffy interrupted.

'No,' said Holly firmly, her hackles immediately rising. 'We agreed it might be tricky logistically at first, getting in and out of Bath every day, but that the extra money would be nice. Covering a full-time nanny on a part-time wage was always going to be a juggle.' She enunciated each word slowly and clearly, taking care not to sound accusatory or downright fucking furious.

Taffy just sighed and shook his head. 'You know it's not a real job, Holls. Come on, you need more from your work than just pandering to a bunch of over-privileged rugby players. And, you know, it's private practice, isn't it? Of course the money's good. It has to be for you to sell your soul.' He laughed at his own joke.

Holly blinked hard, a wave of nausea giving her pause. This was not the advice he'd given Dan when it sounded as though the job might be open to offers. When exactly had Taffy decided that his husbandly persona should be so closely modelled on her ex?

'It is a real job, with a real salary. And since none of my other "partners" seem to miss me at The Practice, maybe it's not so very daft to consider negotiations with the nice man with the big cheque book.' She drew the line at quoting Elsie's line about going where she was celebrated, not where she was tolerated, but she felt she'd made her point, if only by the shocked expression on her husband's face.

She missed him.

She truly did.

She just had no idea right now where her Taffy had gone.

Surely if anyone was going to flip out over the extra off-spring in their lives, it should be her?

A hammering at the front door jolted her from her self-righteous reflections and Holly got to her feet automatically.

'If it's one of your lame ducks or lost souls, can they come back tomorrow?' Taffy quipped, the accompanying smile not quite meeting his eyes.

Holly just ignored him. Picking her battles was a strategy that got her through the day without punching anyone, on the whole.

'Dan?' she said in surprise. 'Is this a team outing?' She stepped back to allow Alice and Tilly to follow him inside, trailing clumps of snow into the hallway, a small blonde girl clinging tightly to Tilly like a koala, her hair matted to her scalp and her clothes on the wrong side of tired. 'And who's this?'

'Can we get her some tea, Holls?' asked Alice, clearly deflecting any questions until they were safely established inside the warmth of the house.

'Of course,' said Holly. 'What do you fancy, my love?' She was about to offer a bowl of soup when her professional reason asserted itself. Who knew when this little tot had last eaten a proper meal, or indeed what she was used to. Start small, start easy. She mentally scanned the contents of the fridge. 'How about a little macaroni cheese? I'm Holly, by the way.'

The girl said nothing, utterly mute, shivering slightly, eyes wide.

'This is Louise,' said Tilly, cradling the featherweight toddler on her hip.

'I'm so sorry to just turn up like this,' whispered Dan as Tilly walked on ahead. 'We didn't know where else to go. The last few hours have been ... Well, let's just say we couldn't let her be taken into care, not until we've spoken to her mum.'

'Where is her mum?' asked Holly, her voice so low that Dan had to lean closer to hear her.

'She's Keira Fowler's little girl. And May's been admitted now too. I just don't think that poor family can cope with Social Services running amok at the moment,' Dan replied, obviously still in shock.

'We found May unconscious,' Alice whispered. 'We think she may have accidentally taken too many painkillers. We did what we could and the paramedics have taken her to Bath. But that still leaves Louise ...'

Holly nodded, mentally recalibrating. They didn't need to ask. She knew perfectly well why her team had landed on her doorstep. She had the space, she had the time and more importantly, after years of caring for the Fowler family, she had the motivation. 'She can stay here for a bit until we work out what to do. But we need to let Keira know, so it's official and above board. To give her peace of mind that she's safe, if nothing else.'

'Let me make a few calls,' said Dan, heading back into the dining room where he couldn't be overheard.

Taffy poked his head into the hallway where Holly was quickly thinking through all the steps she needed to take. 'It's like a busman's holiday out here. What's going on?'

Holly took a deep breath, for some reason doubting that Taffy might react the way she needed him to. He hadn't been himself of late, but right now, she needed him to step up – to be the man she fell in love with. 'We need to help out for a few days,' she said, as she guided him back towards the kitchen and briefly explained the situation.

'Okay then,' he said simply. 'Tell me what I can do.'

Holly's heart seemed to bounce with relief, the compassionate look on Taffy's face enough to repudiate any doubts she'd been nurturing.

Plum was at the stove, reheating the macaroni, Tilly leaning back against the worktop beside her, Louise still clamped firmly to her waist. It was a side of Tilly that Holly hadn't seen before; clearly Louise's plight had touched her in a way she could somehow relate to. Even the filth on Louise's skin didn't seem to faze her.

Plum looked up. 'Your friend Alice is in the playroom with the girls and her Coco. I hope this is okay?'

Holly nodded. 'Taffs, can you go and give Alice a hand? I'll get a bath running for this little one. How do you feel about bubbles, Louise?'

Louise gave a barely perceptible nod, but it was enough to give Holly hope. She knew only too well what a difference a full tummy and some clean clothes could make to a child in distress. Who knew what she'd really seen that day, but the clean rivulets on her face spoke of far too many tears.

She held back for a moment, fascinated by the unspoken teamwork between Plum and Tilly to comfort this traumatised child without overwhelming her. Sometimes hanging back a little resulted in more progress than leaping in with both feet. Neither of them were mothers, but both were equally impressive in their instinctive nurturing. Holly felt a bubble of emotion in her chest that she could only describe as pride.

'Okay then, Lou,' said Holly, pulling up a chair at the table. 'Are we going with ketchup or without?' She flourished the enormous plastic tomato that Ben and Tom adored so much, despite Elsie's shudder of distaste every time it came out of the larder.

Louise said nothing, but her hand reached out in longing.

'With ketchup it is, then,' said Holly, as Louise lunged towards her, Tilly manfully managing not to drop her, until she had safely landed on Holly's lap. 'Steady, steady, Lou,' said Holly, as the ravenous little girl began to shovel pasta into her mouth with a spoon. 'Slowly, my darling, or you'll have tummy ache.'

'Thank God you were here,' said Dan quietly from the doorway, his voice a little choked with relief.

'Give yourselves more credit,' said Holly, as she wiped a smear of ketchup off the little girl's face on autopilot. 'You guys had this covered. I just happen to have more kit than you. Thank you, Plum, and you, Tilly.'

The pair of them exchanged a smile, still like bookends by the Aga, the promise of a nascent friendship hovering in the air between them.

Dan pulled up a chair. 'It's all sorted for a few days' respite care here, if you're sure?'

Holly nodded. 'Of course. We'll make it work.' She glanced outside, at the swirls of white framed by the window. 'It doesn't look like we'll be going far for the next few days anyway, so what's one more child in the mix, right?'

She gave him a reassuring smile, only to find that she had completely lost his attention. His gaze rested firmly on Louise. 'Poor little mite,' he murmured. 'Do you think she'll remember all this?'

Holly shrugged, deep in thought. 'I guess that depends on what happens next.'

Chapter 23

Holly sat back on the sofa and watched the five pink-cheeked children in her care. Plum was beside her and they both cradled well-earned cups of coffee in their hands.

What a difference a day made.

Louise, or Lulu, as Ben and Tom had instantly renamed her, had yet to utter a sound, but she now pottered happily around the playroom, picking up bricks that had tumbled from the boys' tower and handing them over dutifully. She wore a fresh, soft knitted dress and a pair of stripy tights, after a mercy mission to Lizzie's that morning to raid Lily's wardrobe. Her blonde hair fell in clean, silky curls and her eyes were bright after a decent night's sleep.

'It's amazing how well she's adapting, don't you think?' Holly asked Plum quietly, acknowledging to herself recently that while she may be a mother, it was actually Plum who had more experience on the childcare front.

Plum nodded. 'She is a brave little one. I think truly she's just happier for a little security and routine. Have you noticed how she copies everything Ben does? That's her way of saying "you look happy, I'll do what you're doing".' She paused, instinctively lowering her voice. 'Is there any more news from the hospital?'

Holly shook her head; that morning's updates had not been good for Keira or May, both sequestered away on their different wards. 'There's lots of reasons for wishing them well, but mainly our focus has to be giving this little one a few days of normality, a little family life, before the next bombshell.'

Almost as though the very word had summoned her, Elsie arrived in the front hall with a flourish, clearly rather tipsy, letting the front door slam loudly in her wake. She tossed her Mulberry handbag and fur-trimmed parka to the floor and sat down beside Holly with a whoosh. 'Lovely man, that Teddy Kingsley. He gave me lovely bubbles with my lovely lunch.' She sighed contentedly. 'I love snow days.'

Holly and Plum exchanged amused smiles, it took quite a lot of 'lovely bubbles' to get Elsie this sloshed. 'And why would he do a thing like that?' Holly asked, intrigued. 'And please tell me you ate more than a salad?' She passed Elsie the platter of breadsticks and was amazed to see Elsie, the habitual epitome of elegance, dive in with both hands.

Plum giggled beside her, not quite sure what to make of this uncharacteristic behaviour.

'I'm schel-ee-brating, you see?' said Elsie once she'd inhaled every last breadstick on the plate. 'It's been soooo long and now ...' She threw out her arms and hiccuped. 'I can tell you my lovely, lovely, lovely secret.'

Holly paused, waiting, almost holding her breath, her eyes instinctively checking out the third finger of Elsie's left hand.

Empty.

'And?' Holly prompted after a moment, when it looked as though Elsie was on the verge of nodding off mid-sentence.

'And what?' asked Elsie, all innocence. 'Do you want to know my lovely secret too, Holly-Bolly-Polly?' She smiled and clasped Holly's hand tightly to her chest. 'I love you,' she sighed.

'And I love you too,' said Holly, just the tiniest hint of frustration colouring the sentiment.

'So,' Elsie said, 'I decided I didn't want to be away from all this, you see.' She looked Holly straight in the eye. 'I was missing you all too much.'

Holly softened instantly. 'We've been missing you too. That's why it's been so heavenly having you back these last few weeks. I know it's not the same, and you're willy-nilly back and forth to Sarandon Hall, but—'

'Oooh, no!' said Elsie with feeling. 'Ghastly place. Too much money, not enough class. Got chucked out of there months ago. Not a minute too soon either.' She hiccuped again. 'And don't go looking so shocked. It had to be done.'

'You mean, you got chucked out – on purpose?' Holly checked.

Elsie gave a secretive chuckle. 'Only way, darling. Couldn't wait to give me my money back. Hush-hush, you know? Because of the scandal.'

'The scandal?' managed Holly weakly.

'Tha's right,' confirmed Elsie with a nod. 'But don't you worry, my darling. I have been working on a very clever, very secret plan of my own. Which is why,' she said, jabbing her finger in Holly's direction, 'we're schel-ebrating.'

Holly didn't even bother asking what exactly they were celebrating at that point, simply waiting for the dramatist in Elsie to have her moment.

'You, my darling, are looking at your new next-door neighbour.' Elsie pulled a set of keys on a Tiffany key-ring from her pocket and twirled them around her fingers, until they went flying off under the sofa. 'Oops. And yes, it was me all along with the noisy builders! I was in such a hurry,

you see, to get it all beautiful and sorted and perfect and just
everything I have ever wanted in a house all for myself.' Her
words tumbled over one another in their haste to be free. 'Not
a single compromise have I made.' She smiled beatifically. 'I
wanted it to be perfect, so you wouldn't worry, my darling.
So you wouldn't think you were going to be lumbered with
me when you found out the truth about Sharadoo, I mean,
Sharada – oh blast – that god-awful, nouveau-riche, socially
climbing, waiting-for-God, hell hole.'

'So,' said Holly, with a smile that lit up her entire face,
'you're coming home then? Just one door over and with your
favourite people right next door?'

'Exactly,' said Elsie emphatically, wrapping her arms
around herself in delight. 'Right. Next. Door,' she said and
promptly fell asleep.

'Only me!' called Dan from the hallway, letting himself in
without hesitation, stamping the snow from his boots. 'I've
come to give Louise her check-up?' He barely even acknowledged the slumbering pensioner in their midst, so intent was
he on getting an update. 'How's she doing today? Taffy said
she slept okay? Any progress?'

Holly nodded, still completely astounded by Elsie's well-
lubricated confession. She couldn't help but wonder how
much of it Elsie had actually intended to share . . .

'Earth to Holly?' Dan said, after a moment, when no
answer was forthcoming. 'Have I come at a bad time?'

'Sorry, just a lot going on today.' She blinked and tried to
recalibrate, Dan looking at her strangely. 'So, right – yes, all
good actually. I think she was just exhausted, to be honest. If
we're going to have issues, my money's on tonight. Although
you'd think she'd be worn out from making snow angels all

morning. She's got a fearsome appetite for one so small. She seems seriously underweight to me, though.'

'I thought so too,' said Dan with a frown. 'At least she's here now.'

'Exactly,' said Holly, 'but it's hardly a long-term solution, is it?'

'Nope,' said Dan. 'But Keira's much happier about her staying with you, informally as a friend, while they make a plan. Better than going into the foster system. Grace managed to have a frank conversation with the oncology team this morning. Only the next few weeks will tell if we're looking at palliative care options, or if there's still a chance.'

Holly sighed, still somehow hoping that she'd been wrong in her original assessment. She could only be grateful that Keira had called in to The Practice last year, after months of being given the run-around. IBS, her own GP had maintained, unsympathetic to her tiredness, pain and bloating. The notion of ovarian cancer was still overlooked far too often. It was small comfort that they'd bought another year for Keira – too little, too late. 'And there's no other family?' Holly asked.

'None,' said Dan.

He really was a sight for sore eyes, Holly decided moments later, his fringe flopping into his face as he attempted to cross his long legs, sitting on the floor, so the kids could crowd around him. Ben and Tom, of course, were only too familiar with Uncle Dan, but even Lulu was tempted over. Holly glanced up with a smile, half expecting Plum to be as captivated by the sight as she was, but other than an easy smile of greeting, Plum had busied herself scooping the younger girls onto her lap, as their pudgy starfish hands reached out for the little bowls of cereal and quartered grapes that Holly had prepared earlier.

Dan and Holly worked together seamlessly to assess Lulu, in the hope that she wasn't even aware she was getting a check-up, just a chat and a game. Her legs were skinny and her belly a little bloated, but she could almost be mistaken for a different child to the one who had arrived there the day before. 'And she still hasn't said a word?' Dan clarified quietly.

Holly shook her head. 'She understands everything, though. In fact, she seems quite switched on, just a little withdrawn, you know?'

'Hardly surprising when you think what she's been through,' Dan agreed. 'And I know it's tricky with the weather and everything, but are you really okay to have an extra child for a while? And don't forget, if the power goes out, Teddy Kingsley's got his generator rigged up at the pub again this year, so we can all congregate there for some hot food.'

Holly nodded. 'We'll be fine. The Aga's on here and we've no shortage of logs for the wood burner. Plum and I are working as a team, so hopefully nothing too big will slip through the cracks.' She didn't dwell on the fact that a few things almost certainly had; she just couldn't quite put her finger on what they actually were. 'Besides, I'm not sure anyone's being terribly efficient today, are they?' Certainly the Market Place had been filled with delighted school children hurling snowballs earlier, not to mention their equally chilled parents enjoying an unscheduled day off work. No doubt some of them would actually welcome a lock-in with Teddy at the pub should the power go out later.

Holly sat down on the sofa and relieved Plum of the girls. 'Plum, can you rug up the boys and pop them outside for a bit while the sun's still out? They can wear off a little more steam before it gets too cold.' Elsie slumbered on regardless, every now and again giving a very genteel snore that made everyone giggle. 'Lulu?' said Holly. 'Can you stay here with me and Dan? We'd like you to do some lovely pictures?'

It was some testament to Dan's patience that he managed to coax anything out of Lulu at all, even as the boys' shrieks and laughter could be heard from the back garden. Her eyes seemed to flit about, searching for a constant, and it took quite a while to settle her down with a few crayons and a sheet of paper. Neither of them were particularly surprised when she picked up a red crayon and began to scribble minute marks in the corner of the page. It was all too telling of a frightened, shy child, presumably outside of her comfort zone – assuming she even had one.

As Dan picked up blues and greens and yellows and began to doodle silly faces, Lulu put down her own crayon and snuggled in beside him, clapping her hand over her mouth should a laugh dare to escape. Her eyes followed his every move. After five minutes or so, she reached out and took the green crayon, slowly and carefully making marks in an attempt to imitate Dan's. She looked up at him trustingly and then down at the page. 'Mine,' she said clearly.

Holly wasn't the only one in the room to shed a tear.

Even as Dan ignored call after call on his mobile, no doubt summoning him back to work, Holly didn't have the heart to show him the door, to risk severing the tentative bond that was blooming in her playroom.

'Mine' had been swiftly followed by 'doggy', 'oink-oink' and 'cake'. It was very clear what had impressed itself most upon Lulu's mind since she'd arrived at Holly's house.

Dan leaned in and gave Lulu another rendition of his frog-on-a-log song that soon had the little girl's eyes dancing with mischief. Not a laugh exactly, but so very nearly there.

'Right, young Miss Lulu,' said Dan, as he ignored yet another call. 'I have to go to work now and make some people better.'

'No,' said Lulu firmly.

'Maybe I can visit again tomorrow?' Dan asked, as though it were entirely dependent upon her inviting him.

Lulu just shrugged, seemingly shrinking before their eyes. She waited until Dan was halfway out of the playroom door. 'Bye,' she said and returned to the crayons.

Plum's endless efficiency meant the boys were now dried off, flushed with happiness and exhausted, having earned their time in front of the TV, and she stepped in to help with the three girls.

Holly walked Dan to the front door. 'I'm so glad you popped round,' she said with feeling. It wasn't only Elsie's news and Lulu's progress that had made her day; watching Dan connect with that little girl had been almost wondrous. If only Grace had been here to see it, Holly couldn't help but think it would have given her hope too. After all, for a man who had decried the concept of ever being able to take in someone else's child, he'd done a pretty good job of nurturing that little soul this afternoon.

She pulled open the front door to let him out and almost walked straight into Mike Urquhart.

'Sorry I'm a bit early,' he said, shaking Holly's hand warmly. 'Matthew and I got things organised in record time. He's a wonder, that boy.'

Holly managed a polite hello, the niggling sense of having forgotten something important finally resolving itself.

'Dan Carter,' Dan said, holding out his own hand. 'Mike, isn't it? From the Rugby Club?'

'Nice to meet you, Dan,' Mike said. 'You work with Holly

at The Practice, I gather? Young Matthew speaks very highly about the whole team.'

Dan nodded. 'Well, it's lovely to see him finding his own groove around here. Thanks for helping him out with the sponsorship. Is that what you're here for, because I could stay? I mean, it's lovely of Holly to keep doing all the liaison, but she is technically on maternity leave and we're all wary of putting on her. Hands full, children everywhere and all that.' He laughed uncomfortably at the stony reception his humour had received.

'We're good; you get back to work. Hands full, patients everywhere and all that,' Holly said tightly, annoyed that both Dan and Taffy seemed to have slotted her into a box marked 'New mother – do not disturb'. Unless they wanted childcare, of course, she thought irritably, before stamping down hard on her annoyance. She knew that bringing Lulu here had been the right thing to do; she just couldn't quite correlate her own identity anymore, and Dan standing on her doorstep like a Viking protector wasn't exactly helping.

'No wonder you were so distracted when I arrived,' Dan whispered intently with a meaningful look as he kissed her briefly on the cheek to say goodbye. Holly didn't know how to tell him; he truly didn't know the half of it. She still couldn't quite believe that she'd comprehensively forgotten Mike was even coming over.

She tried not to read more into that than she should.

And promptly failed.

'Come on in,' she said warmly. 'I've an inebriated pensioner asleep on the sofa, five children on the rampage – one of whom is in emergency foster care – and a sulking hormonal Gloucester Old Spot in the back garden, pining for his youth. Cup of tea? Or something stronger?'

Mike followed her through to the kitchen, shrugging off his Bath-Rugby-branded ski jacket, not even missing a beat when she instantly abandoned him to check that Plum had the kids – and Elsie – under control.

'One of those days, huh?' he said as she returned, noticing that he'd already filled the kettle and popped it on the Aga to boil.

'Something like that,' Holly said with a smile. 'Although they seem to be happening with increasing regularity.'

'It sounds like you'd actually be coming to work for a rest,' he said jovially, unflinching at the chaos on the kitchen table, even as Holly deftly tidied away her scribbled plans and Post-its.

She didn't feel it was prudent to confess that, with everything going on here for the last twenty-four hours, she hadn't even given a thought as to how the job on offer would fit into her life and she felt instantly lousy. He'd vouched for her with the board, pushed for a tempting package to win her over, and she hadn't spared him a moment's thought since Lulu arrived.

Seriously, Holly, she chastised herself, how hard would it have been to call and postpone and save him the journey, a journey that could have hardly been straightforward, today of all days. Harder to do, of course, if your mind conveniently erased the appointment altogether.

'Look, there's no pressure from me,' Mike laughed. 'You've clearly got your hands full this week, but I guess I'd just like to get a feel for where you're at.' His words were in complete contradiction to his demeanour, leaning forward, keen as mustard.

All plans are made to be changed, Holly thought to herself. In all her consideration of goals and plans, not once had she stopped to build in the contingency that real life required.

Money was nice, a sense of being courted for a prestigious job even nicer, but would it actually tick the box in her soul where she got to make a difference?

'I'm so sorry, Mike—' she began.

He held up a hand, persistent in the face of Holly's imminent refusal. 'Don't say no just yet. At least let the dust settle? Or the snow melt?' His smile couldn't disguise his genuine disappointment. 'We have the budget,' he said, for maybe the sixth time since they'd been discussing the project, as though the money were burning a hole in his pocket.

'Well,' said Holly with a tentative smile, 'I've been giving that some thought, actually, and to wildly misquote *Pretty Woman*: I can help you spend it, sir.'

Chapter 24

Connor couldn't help but wonder what his bandmates would think of his new life in Larkford. Whereas they, for the most part, still skulked around London in dark glasses and grimy t-shirts, being shuttled from glamorous hotels to fancy parties and nightclubs, being fêted for their achievements, he himself now counted an amiable, shaggy donkey as his confidant and companion, Nigel seemingly proving a salve to the roiling anxiety that hovered in his peripheral vision every moment of every day.

Together, they'd just had the most blissful day with Kitty getting the dwarf goats settled into their cosy new home, watching as they gambolled endearingly in the tythe barn, leaping from straw bale to bale with exuberant delight, each one disconcertingly named after the dowagers of Larkford. Although he'd had to draw the line at adding 'Elsie' to his herd.

Rural life, he decided, was definitely softer on the soul. He hadn't even missed a beat when Holly had suggested he might like to add the attention-seeking Nineteen to his ever-growing menagerie, setting up residence in the orchard — come summer there would be apples and pears as far as his little porky eye could see. The more the merrier, as far as he was concerned; Blackleigh Farm was fast becoming a refuge for the lost and adrift in their animal community. An anchor of reality for Connor when he needed it the most; animals needed constant care and attention, limiting the time available for introspection and anxiety.

Nigel, it seemed, took his new responsibilities seriously, refusing to be left behind when a trip to the pub had been mooted, now contentedly sauntering along beside Connor and Kitty through the Market Place. Almost unrecognisable under the drifts of snow, the scene was like something from one of those hefty coffee table picture books, albeit with the residents of Larkford taking full advantage of their snow day; certainly the row of anatomically correct snowmen was probably more Instagram-appropriate.

Even the snow was different in the countryside, Connor decided. Swathes of sparkling white drifts covered the fields and, in the Market Place, it was melting into pools of crystal rather than the greying slush he was used to on Ken' High Street. Cars had been abandoned under their individual igloos and the snow seemingly embraced by one and all (once the livestock were safely tucked up obviously) as an excuse to spend the day together letting off steam. He wondered if it could possibly last: a few more inches of snow tonight and the valley would be cut off completely. Would they still be so enthusiastic then?

The icy shell forming on the snow crackled with each step and Connor flinched for a second, as his hand brushed against Kitty's, a flicker of electricity passing between them. Even as Kitty reached out and gently took his hand, gave a fleeting squeeze and let go, Connor felt his thoughts begin to somersault in that disconcerting way that meant he had lost control of his equilibrium.

He never knew what the trigger might be; sometimes just a simple thought was enough.

And the thoughts he was having about Kitty Clarke were anything but simple. 'Kitty—' he began, his voice cracking.

'What the hell do you call this?' shouted Cassie Holland stridently, making both Connor and Kitty jump and chasing whatever words he'd managed to formulate from his mind in an instant.

Cassie stood before them, flushed and furiously waving one of the draft flyers for the putative festival in her hand.

He automatically checked his back pocket for the flyer he carried everywhere, as a talisman of sorts. Empty. Not exactly the way he was planning on pitching Phase Three to the town.

'I think you've got a bloody nerve, coming here with all your money and your self-importance and your *bees*!' Cassie spat the last word in distaste at the very notion.

It was only a matter of moments before half the town had emerged from their shop fronts, or abandoned their snowmen to earwig on this latest showdown. It seemed that Cassie's dislike for Connor even eclipsed her vocal condemnation of poor Alec French at the school. When Cassie 'took against' someone, she didn't need to have rhyme or reason on her side and she wasn't one for changing her mind.

Kitty took hold of Nigel's lead rein and placed her hand warningly on Connor's arm.

But Connor was well used to hecklers and caustic reviews.

He knew perfectly well how to brazen it out in public, to make sure that nobody ever saw the pain or vulnerability he actually experienced on the wrong end of a vitriolic attack, even in his current fragile state.

'Oh, thanks, Cassie. I wondered where I'd dropped that.'

He squared his shoulders and took four fast paces towards her, plucking the flyer from her fingers before she could react, folding it neatly and sliding it back into his pocket. He couldn't ignore the idea that, with jeans this tight, it was highly unlikely that the flyer could have fallen out without a little 'help'.

Cassie rounded furiously, turning to include their new-found audience in her tirade. 'He's going to overrun the town with musicians and their groupies, and their drugs, and their sex, and their—'

'Oooh,' said Lucy, the receptionist from The Practice who'd been out to stock up on HobNobs, 'are you having a concert?'

'This is a disgrace,' said Malcolm Bodley, their ineffectual local councillor, at the same time. 'I shall be having words.'

'Actually,' said Connor, raising his voice but keeping his cool, even as his heart hammered furiously and his fingers tingled ominously, 'I'm organising a festival to celebrate the Winter Solstice. With music and food and books ... And I'm hoping that it will bring lots of people to Larkford who might never have experienced the community and the beauty that I have been lucky enough to enjoy with you. I hope they spend money in your shops and your restaurants, stay in your hotels and B&Bs, and generally put Larkford on the map as the Capital of the Cool Cotswolds.' He shrugged, his friable energy suddenly flagging. 'I was actually hoping you'd be excited.'

Nigel broke into a perfectly timed yodel of braying that drowned out everyone else's words.

'I think Nigel speaks for most of us,' said Kitty firmly. 'It's a wonderful idea and an excellent way to promote our town, for business and tourism.' She spoke so firmly that it was almost as though she were reminding everyone clustered around them of their manners and there was a hushed lull once she and Nigel had finished saying their piece.

But it was only a momentary respite, before the huddle of residents seemed to divide in two: both sides equally vocal and equally unswerving.

'Crikey,' said Connor, his words only audible to Kitty right beside him, in the swell of outspoken argument. 'Who knew the idea of one little festival could rile up quite so many people, quite so quickly?'

Kitty gave him a sympathetic smile. 'Anyone who lives here, actually.'

'Oh,' said Connor, deflating still further, floored a little that his own desire to make a difference, to contribute something positive to his new home town, should have triggered such a reaction.

'Give it time,' said Kitty gently. 'And maybe find a way to communicate what you were trying to achieve before the nay-sayers gain any traction. We're only a small community, but there's a lot of big personalities. And some of them do love something to oppose.' She grinned. 'It doesn't always seem to matter *what* they're opposing; they just love a good argument.'

Connor blinked at the scene of acrimony he had unwittingly created. It was just as well that his purchase of The Big House and his tenancy of Blackleigh Farm were both signed and sealed, or he got the impression that half the town might be driving him out of Larkford with pitchforks.

'Give them time,' said Kitty easily, leaning her head briefly against his shoulder by way of moral support, her warm breath misting in the cold air. 'Rome wasn't built in a day.'

'I wasn't aiming for a new civilisation,' said Connor, longing for more than fleeting contact, and yet shying away at the same time. 'I just thought it might be a bit special, you know, to have a fabulous festival right here that everyone could enjoy. To celebrate the history of this place if nothing else.'

'We'll find a way to make this work,' she promised, earning herself a watery smile.

'Well, if nothing else,' said Connor with a sigh, 'then at least Nigel here believes in me,' he said, scruffing the donkey's mane between his ears.

Kitty leaned forward apologetically, teasing out the remains of the flyer from Nigel's mouth. 'Oh, Nigel,' she said in disappointment, as the donkey hung his head and Connor's face dropped.

'Et tu, Brute?' he said.

Connor braved the Market Place later that same evening, lights illuminating each and every window, feeling as though he might always be on the outside, looking in. There were some people in Larkford apparently who objected so strongly to his festival plans that they were prepared to deface his stupid bloody Range Rover before he could even sell the thing.

It was an absolute kick in the guts, he couldn't deny it, but they didn't seem to realise he was as stubborn as Nigel the donkey when backed into a corner. If anything, their very dissonance only spurred his ambition forward, even as his brittle mood took yet another battering.

'I see I'm not the only one walking the lonely streets at dark,' said Elsie, emerging from Holly's front door in a faux fur coat that reached her ankles, looking almost shifty.

'Crowded head, empty heart?' Connor replied, earning himself a winsome smile for recognising the line of poetry to which Elsie eluded.

'Something like that. Or perhaps the opposite – difficult to be sure at my age.' She paused. 'You look a little glum, darling,' Elsie said. 'Dare I ask about your festival-thingummy?'

Connor shrugged. 'I had Docie Lynn on the phone just now,' he said, casually name-dropping the chart-topping sweetheart of the moment. 'Heard about the festival and wanted to know if she could perform. Her manager's coming down for a meeting. Apparently Docie's into all things organic and "Cotswoldy" – I have no idea what to tell her; yes, you can come, but you might get egged by the locals?'

'Ah, but at least they'd be organic eggs,' Elsie said with a twinkle, her humour nevertheless missing the mark.

'Tell you what,' said Elsie, tucking her arm firmly through his as she slipped a little on the icy pavement, 'since you're clearly in need of a little indulgence, a little A-list pick-me-up, I'm going to show you something that not many people in Larkford have seen.'

She walked up to the door of Number 44 and slipped a shiny new key in the lock. 'Are you ready?'

Connor simply nodded, bemused, wondering for a second whether this feisty octogenarian was actually coming on to him. As he stepped inside though, he couldn't help but gasp. 'Oh my God – whose house *is* this?'

'Mine,' said Elsie simply, with a pride and possessiveness that made him instantly smile.

Convention be damned: Elsie had decorated this house to her own tastes, rather than those of the traditional Georgian oeuvre. There were no Wedgwood blues, or sage greens in sight. In fact the hallway was a triumph in cool lilac and grey – still warm and inviting due to the multitude of vintage magazine articles framed and hanging hotch-potch all over the walls, fitting together like a carefully curated mosaic.

'I decided I'm too old to be modest about my achievements. There's nothing worse than being underestimated, I'm finding. So this little project – this house that belongs to nobody

but me – comes with no memories of heartbreak, or disappointment. So it's going to be my epitaph. Good idea, no?'

'Amazing idea,' said Connor, utterly entranced, and wondering why he himself hadn't done something similar at The
Big House – a fresh start, of course, but with all his greatest
achievements and loves on display for everyday celebration
and reminders. 'You are my Yoda,' he said with a smile.

Elsie chortled. 'And you haven't even seen the drinks fridge
yet.' She waggled her fingers for him to follow her as they
walked from room to room. Her taste and style still prevalent,
even though it was clear that the intention was to shock and
engage, rather than soothe and welcome her guests.

'And what does Holly think about all this? It's quite a
departure from your usual style?'

'Ah, well, who wants to be ordinary? And, to be honest,
I'm slightly bottling it about showing her. It turns out, hers
is the only opinion – after my own – that truly matters to
me,' Elsie confessed.

'I can see that,' Connor said, deftly twisting the champagne
bottle until the cork eased free and pouring out two delicate
coupes of vintage fizz. No flutes for Elsie – old school glamour, all the way. 'But, I have to say, Elsie, that if Holly loves
you half as much as I think she does, she's simply going to
be thrilled that you've a home and a project that you love.'

'Ah, love,' toasted Elsie, raising her glass to his before
taking a sip. 'Never a straightforward one, is it? I mean, look
at you – pining away for your lovely wife, denying all those
nascent feelings towards our gorgeous vet I gather—'

'Bloody hell,' said Connor, choking on his champagne.
'You really don't miss a trick, do you?'

'Not if I can help it,' Elsie smiled. 'But if I may, as one
who has been both divorced and widowed, can I offer a little

advice?' She didn't pause; the question was purely rhetorical. 'It's not very often in life that you truly connect with someone. Celebrate your time with Rachel, as a love that was lost. Seize the moment with Kitty, and allow your heart to heal.'

When she said it, thought Connor, it sounded so simple.

Elsie smiled. 'Easier said than done though, yes?'

'Something like that,' agreed Connor, topping up her glass and sitting back into one of the plush velvet armchairs, whose vivid pink colour and petal-shaped cushions gave the disarming illusion of reclining among upholstered labia.

'I'm so glad you like my fanny chairs,' said Elsie bluntly. 'I did have a moment's pause when I bought them, that some chaps might find them, well, a little overwhelming.'

'They're lovely,' croaked Connor, unwilling to admit there was a chance he might be one of them, as he took another sip of champagne.

An hour later, and slightly the worse for wear, Connor stepped out into the Market Place, popping the empty champagne bottle in the recycling bucket as instructed. The wrought-iron streetlights cast curlicues of light and shadow across the otherwise deserted space.

Deserted that is, apart from the very person he wanted most to see. Or possibly to avoid.

Lit only by the sodium glow, Kitty was attempting to gently lift Mrs Hudson's ancient wolfhound into the back of her knackered Subaru with some difficulty. He bounded across the Market Place, skidding and sliding, just in time to catch Jamieson's hind-quarters as they slipped out of her grasp. 'Crikey. He's no lightweight is he?'

Kitty sniffed miserably and fondled his rather shaggy ears, gently cupping them to make sure he couldn't hear her. 'Mrs

Hudson can't cope with him anymore. She's not in the best of health and neither is poor Jamieson. Dodgy hips, dodgy back, dodgy knees. It's just too much for her.' She gave herself a little shake. 'He's had another funny turn tonight and she called me out in a panic. I'm supposed to take him to the clinic and do the deed.'

'No!' gasped Connor, himself an increasingly soft touch whenever it came to animals. He'd lost count of the number of times Clive had chastised him for it – apparently farmers were simply supposed to harden their hearts. His success as a farmer was in grave doubt if that really were a prerequisite.

Between them they lifted Jamieson into the boot, into a nest of Puffa jackets and Vet-pad. He looked soulful in his demise.

'Is there really nothing to be done for him?' Connor said, putting his arm around a tearful Kitty and blinking hard, even as a tiny part of his subconscious registered their momentary intimacy.

'Well, if he was my dog—' Kitty broke off and sighed. 'It doesn't matter.'

'Yes, it does,' said Connor. 'If he was your dog . . . ?'

'Well,' said Kitty, perching on the edge of the boot and cradling Jamieson's enormous head in her lap, seemingly oblivious to the light flurries of snow that slowly began to whirl in the chill breeze. 'Big dogs don't live very long. Their hearts can't cope, you see. But he's only eight. If he had more regular exercise, some hydrotherapy or something, and a decent daily painkiller he could easily have another two years of quality life left in him. But it's expensive, you know, and Mrs Hudson's insurance policy won't cover it. I guess she thinks it's the right decision.' She looked up at Connor and his heart thudded deeply in his chest at the very expression on her face. 'The Rescue Home won't take him.'

'Then I will,' blurted Connor suddenly, before his brain could even engage with what he was saying out loud, or indeed question his motivation. 'I can afford his drugs, I've got plenty of space at home and there has to be somewhere local I can take the old chap swimming? What's one more dog among the chaos of Agatha's pack?' He shrugged, buying into his own argument without hesitation as he saw the light in Kitty's eyes at the very suggestion. 'And it is my favourite Irish whiskey too. Maybe it's a sign?'

'Or maybe you're just a big softie and a very lovely man?' Kitty stood up and kissed Connor lightly on the cheek. 'Thank you.'

His heart pounded erratically in his chest and he felt the all-too-familiar forewarning spackles in his vision, but this – this moment – was too important to sully with his angst. 'You'll help me, though, yes?' he managed, wondering if she understood that he wasn't just talking about the dog.

'Of course,' she promised with a gentle smile.

Had he really just adopted a geriatric wolfhound just to see that look upon her face, he wondered. The sight of Jamieson's trusting expression told him the truth of the matter – he and Jamieson needed to stick together. He'd have adopted him no matter what.

And the fact that Kitty would help him settle in? Well, that was both a blessing and a curse – because as quickly as he'd recognised his true feelings towards her, so the unbearable punch of guilt inevitably followed – the one that made an appearance every time he forgot about Rachel and dared to be happy, even for a moment.

Yes, Kitty was his kind of girl. But she could be his friend.

Friends was okay.

Elsie was wrong; friends was enough.

Chapter 25

'Morning. You're up bright and early,' said Holly, whispering into her mobile phone as the rest of the household negotiated its fragile passage from sleep to breakfast.

'Early, yes. Bright? Not so much.' Alice took a breath and swallowed hard. 'I've been up all night being sick. And there's no way I can get into work. I've checked the schedule and everyone else is fully booked all day—'

Holly felt a momentary frisson of annoyance: they didn't seem to want her back at work, until they were in a pickle and then, apparently, it was okay? Or was this simply because the Larkford tom-toms had been beating since Mike's doorstep encounter with Dan?

'Holly? Are you still there?' Alice asked plaintively. 'I'd be so grateful. And I know it's short notice, but maybe it could count as one of those "Keeping in Touch" days that Patricia was banging on about. Hang on . . .'

Holly flinched; there was obviously nothing bogus about Alice's illness. She gave herself a mental shake: wasn't a day of normality what she'd been dreaming of lately? A day to be Dr Holly Graham and actually talk to her patients in an official capacity rather than tiptoeing around the issue in the park, playground, or deli? Not to mention ticking another one of Patricia's tiresome boxes?

Plum poked her head around the door. 'I make pancakes for the little ones. You would like?'

'Oh, I really would like,' said Holly with feeling, unconsciously adopting Plum's slightly pidgin English. She paused, one hand over the mouthpiece of the phone. 'I may need to pop into work for a while today. Will you be okay with quite so many children in the house?'

'Of course,' Plum said, looking almost affronted by the question. 'It's like with a puppy, yes. First we feed, then we walk, then we rest and repeat.'

Holly smiled, Plum's innocent competence rather beguiling. 'Sounds perfect,' she said. Whether Elsie would be quite so easy to manage, once she finally surfaced with another hangover from hell would be another story. Perhaps it would be kinder anyway, to let her recover before peppering her with the multitude of questions that Holly was simply dying to ask? Starting with the house, or Connor, or the house . . .

Holly returned to her phone call with a lighter sense of purpose. First her kids, then her patients. Breathe and repeat, she thought to herself with a smile.

Holly felt her shoulders lift just a little as she walked through the Market Place, her feet squashed into heeled boots and her favourite work dress gripping rather more tightly than she'd remembered. The snow clouds had blown through overnight and a gradual thaw had already begun, Larkford literally sparkling in her early morning beauty, but it was the way Taffy's hand had automatically sought hers as they left the house that had made her spirits soar.

'I've missed this,' he said easily, swinging her hand, and

conveniently forgetting that he was the main culprit for putting up barriers and delaying this very moment. In a funny way, it was almost better to have a spontaneous return like this – no time for Holly to worry about the kids or stress about compliance. No time for Taffy to overthink the whole situation and start listing obstacles.

It was certainly a side to him that she could never have foreseen. Since becoming a dad, he'd seemingly shed his laissez-faire approach to life and spent more time worrying and planning than was surely healthy. Even with the arrival of Plum, the most conscientious and solicitous nanny that Holly had ever encountered, Taffy's grip on the tiller of their household was still white-knuckled and tense. It would be interesting to see if that extended to his professional demeanour too these days.

She gave his hand a loving squeeze. 'I've missed this too, just taking a breath together before the next part of the day.' She leaned into his side affectionately. 'I'm quite excited about seeing everyone again.'

Taffy turned to her, bemused. 'But you see everyone all the time?'

Holly shrugged. 'It's not the same though, is it? I've been a civilian for months. Now I'm part of the team again.' She paused. 'If you'll have me?'

Taffy shot her a queer look. 'Is that what this whole back-and-forth with the Rugby Club has been about then? Were you trying to make a point? Of course, we want you back. Just, there's no rush, is there? And anyway, the timing is yours to choose now, you know that, once the twelve-month mark ticked over.' He paused, frowning, as though worried he was putting ideas into her head by quoting the partnership agreement, as though prioritising anything other than their children would be a mistake. 'But we're managing fine if you need longer.'

He was trying to be considerate, her logical brain could understand that much. It was just that, in the process, she came away feeling, well, a bit disposable. At some point, the boundary between considerate and patronising had apparently become impossibly blurry.

If she'd had any concern about being welcomed back with open arms, the effusive greeting she received from Grace and Lucy should really have put her mind at rest.

'Holly! Now, are you a sight for sore eyes!' said Grace, pulling her into a rib-crushing hug as though they hadn't seen each other only last night. 'God we've missed you. And you're ready to come back? Not being strong-armed by puking Alice?' Grace shot a worried glance in Taffy's direction that was obviously not meant to be spotted.

Holly took a moment, wanting to start as she meant to go on. 'Oh yes, poor Alice. But hopefully a few quiet days and she'll be right as rain, and it's the perfect excuse for me to get back to work.' She too glanced at Taffy. 'I've been poised for the off for ages, but it's good to make a staggered return, don't you think? And, honestly, finding a decent nanny has made it so much easier.'

Taffy hesitated, seemingly braced for his beloved to throw him under the proverbial bus, smiling at Holly weakly when she said nothing.

'Speaking of nannies, though, Holls, if I pop home mid-morning, can you go home for lunch?' Taffy said, obviously not sharing her confidence in Plum's abilities. 'We're not checking up on her if we happen to swing by unannounced, are we?'

Holly shook her head. 'She's really capable, Taffs. I was going home for lunch, anyway, but really? Mid-morning drive-by?'

'I'll go,' volunteered Tilly, wandering through reception with a vast takeaway coffee in her hand. 'Plum's a sweetie and I'd love an excuse for a coffee break. Plus, you know, it's less obvious than Dithery Dad here turning up.'

'Dithery Dad?' Taffy turned and scowled at her.

Tilly just shrugged with a laugh. 'Ah, but the truth hurts. Besides, Lulu's on my list of follow-ups for today. So, there you go, problem solved.'

The two of them left the room, still bickering, and Holly breathed out slowly. 'Maybe I'm not the one who's been most worried about finding the perfect nanny, but I have to tell you, Plum is a wonder.'

Grace smiled. 'Well, whatever it takes, it's truly lovely to see you. It really hasn't been the same around here.' She gave a nervous laugh. 'I have to confess I was a bit worried when Dan said you might be considering a move to private practice.'

Holly shook her head. 'I like it here,' she said simply, seeing no reason to share her convoluted reasoning process. Besides, as far as she was concerned, the timing of being back here couldn't be better – the perfect way to discreetly dip a tentative toe in the practical waters with her thus-far, theoretical plans.

'How's little Lulu settling in?' Grace asked, following her lead. 'I've a call booked in with Keira's consultant later this morning, if you'd like to take it?'

'That would be really good actually. I need to know whether she's up to a visit, or whether it would just be too distressing for them both. I gather they haven't actually seen each other in weeks and I can't help thinking . . .' She paused. 'Well, obviously it's not my decision to make. She really is a very sweet little girl though; Dan was amazing with her, by the way. So patient.'

Grace nodded with a smile of recognition. 'He's just a pussycat really.' Another phone line began ringing out on her desk, Lucy still welded to the first, juggling call after call. 'Now, spit spot, you've patients back to back I'm afraid. A few sledging injuries and chesty coughs fitted in for good measure. I hope that's okay.'

It was more than okay, as far as Holly was concerned. It was ideal.

Any opportunity for hesitation or doubt would be eclipsed by the steady ebb and flow of patients. Ten-minute slots, constantly changing personalities and parameters: it was the perfect way to ease herself back into medicine, she decided.

In at the deep end.

She pushed open the door to the waiting room, hurriedly annotated list in hand. She looked up and the sense of serendipity that had flickered in her periphery all morning announced its presence with a flourish. 'Daphne? Hannah? Why don't you both come on through?'

She hesitated for a moment, unsure for a second where she should actually be this morning. Was her consulting room still actually *hers*, or was that where Tilly had set up shop?

'Coffee's on your desk, lovely to see you, Holly,' called Maggie as she let herself into the pharmacy with the thumb scanner clicking open the lock.

'Come on in then,' said Holly, taking a breath and pushing open her door, memories assailing her as she took in the all-too-familiar smells, groaning radiator and morning sunlight. 'How great to see you both today. You're my very first post-baby patients,' she said with a smile, determined to put Hannah at ease.

The teenager was almost a caricature of angst and discomfort, long sleeves tugged down over her hands and hair hanging over her face. A face, Holly couldn't help but notice, that was visibly less acned than usual, but at what price?

'So,' she said, 'what can I do for you?' She saw no need to let on that Daphne had already given her a pretty good insight into how things were going when they'd spoken at The Deli.

Hannah refused to look up, her shoulders hunched and abject misery in her every movement.

There was an awkward pause before Daphne could restrain herself no longer. 'Oh, Dr Graham, I'm so glad it's you. I know you'll understand.' She reached over and gently pulled back one of Hannah's sleeves.

'Oh my darling,' said Holly automatically, struggling to reclaim her professional vocabulary. She took Hannah's hand and held it gently, waiting for the young girl to look up, taking her time; ten minutes be damned.

'Tell me,' she said quietly after a moment, when Hannah's troubled gaze had drifted up to Holly's face, even through the heavy filter of her fringe.

Hannah shook her head, tears welling. 'I just feel so . . .' Words failed her, but it wasn't the first time that Holly had seen this look of total, utter desolation on a patient's face. It *was* the first time that she'd seen it on a seventeen-year-old girl however, and she felt her newly vulnerable heart break a little.

'You are not alone, Hannah. This is a temporary feeling that *will* pass. I promise you. This is not for ever.' It seemed urgently vital that, if Hannah left here today understanding only one thing, it was this.

Hannah nodded. 'Mum said the same. But that doesn't mean I can live like this.' She dropped her head into her hands and the bleak keening that came from her cut through Holly as surely as the razor this poor girl had taken to her own arms.

It was as close to a cry for help as Holly had ever heard. She rested one hand on Hannah's shoulder as she scrolled through her notes on the computer, trying not to completely lose her temper when she saw that Hannah had already been in a few days ago, just after she and Daphne had spoken, and yet her acne medication remained unchanged. Whatever might be the underlying cause of her depression, continuing to give her a drug that listed suicidal ideation as a possible side-effect was nothing short of negligent.

'Hannah?' Holly said gently, blatantly ignoring the flashing red light on her phone that was no doubt Grace chivvying her along. 'Hannah? Will you let me help you? I want you to listen if you can, okay? Daphne, it's important that you hear this too. I need you to stop taking your acne medication. It's important. And it will take a couple of days to clear your system, so we need to make sure that you feel safe and supported during that time.'

Hannah looked up, aghast. 'But my skin?'

The poor girl didn't seem able to compute that her skin was actually the least of her worries at the moment, the depression clouding her judgement on almost every level. In so much pain, she was cutting herself to find relief, but terrified of her complexion returning to its previously blighted state. Holly watched Hannah rip at her dry and flaking lips with her teeth, unable to see that this could hardly be considered a preferable outcome.

'Hannah, I think it would be a really good idea for you to talk to a lovely team in Bath, who see this all the time, and hopefully you can stay a few days with them, just while your thoughts settle down. They can help you feel better and there are people there who are specially trained to guide you through your feelings.' She glanced across at Daphne, hoping that she understood, hoping there was no need to articulate the words 'suicide watch'.

All she had to do now was persuade the already over-burdened system that Hannah Porter was worthy of a bed. Daphne was a single mum and was already fraying at the edges; in Holly's opinion sending them home with the emergency phone number for when feelings turned to plans was just too big a risk to take.

'Daphne, can you and Hannah take a seat in the waiting room for a moment while I make a few calls? Don't go home, just wait for me, okay? Hannah, okay?'

They left the room, hands clasped together, and Holly breathed out slowly. Talk about a baptism of fire!

She picked up the phone, trying to arrange her thoughts into the most persuasive argument for a hospital bed that she could muster. The number for the Crisis Resolution Team was embedded in her memory and this time she wouldn't be so easily fobbed off. This time, there would be no wait and see. She swallowed hard and dialled the number.

Chapter 26

By lunchtime, Holly was reeling and she was fully prepared to admit that pedantic Patricia, her return-to-work liaison, may have made a valid point or two. This wasn't just about finding the perfect childcare, or fitting back into her work clothes; there had been a fundamental shift in how she viewed the world, how emotionally invested she became, and how vulnerable she herself felt trying to tackle her patients' problems.

She'd been kidding herself, she realised, if she thought that car park consultations and coffee shop 'off the record' chats had kept her eye in. One appointment after another, after another, was like a deluge of suffering and she was like a giant sponge soaking it all in.

'Teflon not Velcro, Teflon not Velcro,' she murmured to herself as she showed her final patient of the morning to the door. She'd been delicate after having Ben and Tom, but something about the financial necessity of that situation had toughened up her exposed vulnerabilities quickly. This time, with Olivia and Lottie being a little bit older, and with so much more support in place, she had assumed the transition would be painless.

She'd been wrong.

She pressed her hand over her mouth to stifle the sob that

was building in her chest, shutting herself in her room so that none of her colleagues could bear witness to her losing the plot quite so comprehensively. Was it possible that Taffy, unburdened as he was by hormones and working-mother's-guilt, actually had a more realistic take on their situation than she did, she wondered, ready to forgive all his over-protectiveness in the light of this new information.

She pushed her shoulders back, ignoring the hollow ache in her chest. All she had to manage was the short walk through the building and then she was heading home. She'd never been more grateful to Taffy for insisting that half a day was enough to start with, however much she had resented his patriarchal bossiness at the time.

She walked out of the door and straight into Dan.

'Whoa,' he said laughing, 'someone's in a hurry to get home. Are you sick of us already?'

Holly shook her head. 'Of course not,' she lied.

Dan shrugged. 'I find it hard getting back into the swing of things after a fortnight on the beach. I can't imagine what it's like for you.'

The feminist in Holly wanted to stamp her feet in protest at his assumptions, but in reality there was more than a grain of truth in his words. She settled for the middle ground, a half-truth. 'I guess I'd just got used to having all the time in the world to chat to people, you know, out in the wild. Being their friend as well as their doctor. Ten-minute-medicine requires a different bandwidth, maybe?'

Dan's expression tightened. 'Well, you wouldn't need that in private practice. I didn't realise you were still in discussions with Mike Urquhart?'

Holly frowned. 'I didn't approach him, Dan. And yes, we're talking, but mainly because the club has disposable funds and I'm keen to help him spend them.' She paused, not wanting to show her hand too soon. 'Their sponsorship of Matthew Giles's Young Carers Group has been invaluable,' she reminded him.

'So you're not taking the job?' Dan pushed.

Holly shrugged, a little thrown by the intensity of his questioning. 'Are you asking because you're worried about losing me, or because you fancy being a Rugby Club GP yourself?' she teased, unwilling to let him off the hook too soon after his arsey questioning, laughing a little to alleviate the tension.

Dan just shook his head. 'Let's not fall out over this,' he said ambiguously.

'Deal,' said Holly. It was easy to agree, with no personal agenda of her own to accommodate. 'Well, I need to head home, although I was hoping to see Tilly. She popped in to give Lulu her check-up earlier.'

Dan's entire demeanour changed at the mention of Lulu's name and Holly couldn't suppress her smile. 'Maybe you could swing by again later? Lulu really seemed to relax around you. Maybe she can recognise the big kid in you? It had to come in useful at some point.'

Dan gave her a nudge. 'Oi. Less of the mocking please.' He paused. 'She is an absolute sweetheart, isn't she? I can't get over the difference in her already. You'd hardly recognise that poor neglected little tyke we found at May's flat now, would you?'

Holly found herself conflicted: to her mind, neglect had an element of intent. May had just been overwhelmed and incapable. Was that really the same thing? Thinking about the hungry, dirty child that had been carried into her kitchen barely three days ago, she was aggrieved to find that her own assumptions might be in need of reassessment.

'She slept right through last night,' Holly said. 'I think

she's settling, but she was really weird around Elsie. Maybe
on some level, her grandmother has left more of a scar than
we'd realised.'

Dan frowned. 'Old people upset her?'

'Maybe? Luckily Elsie's been too distracted to notice the
last few days. She's busy causing mischief elsewhere.' She
stopped, not quite sure of whether Elsie's secret was truly out.
When she'd phoned home earlier, Elsie had still been in bed,
sleeping off her evening with Connor.

'It could just be that five children is beyond her tolerance,'
Dan suggested. 'We need to make a plan. Lulu can't stay with
you for ever and it doesn't look like she's going home any time
soon,' he continued, all his animosity about the job having
completely dissolved into empathy and affection. 'I'll make
a few calls later and get an idea of options for her, shall I?'

Holly nodded, resting a hand on his arm. 'But, Dan, don't
rush this. She's happy at ours and Keira's happy knowing
where she is.'

'And what about you? And Taffy?'

'We're fine. Honestly. What's a little more chaos? See you
later, maybe?' Holly checked her watch and left Dan standing
in the corridor, thoughtfully distracted. To Holly's mind, it
was a toss-up whether he was thinking about Lulu Fowler or
Bath Rugby, but either way, she wondered whether Grace
deserved a heads up that big changes were on their horizon.

Only two hours later and Holly finally felt the tension in
her shoulders give. She sat next to Plum on a bench in the
parkland behind the church, bundled up in her down-filled
coat, one hand automatically rocking the double pram, where
Olivia and Lottie slumbered peacefully through their siesta.
Ben and Tom ran loop after loop in between the ancient horse

chestnut trees, making tracks and hurling snowballs, and Lulu, ensconced in a padded 'Eskimo' snowsuit, had plonked herself down in the snow, working her arms and legs to make smudgy snow angels and chortling with delight. Every now and then she'd thrust pudgy fistfuls of snow towards her open mouth and Holly or Plum would need to leap forward to intervene. She was so content in her game, though, that only a gentle distraction was required. To Holly's mind, this little girl had probably had a lifetime of upset already; Holly and Plum had already agreed that loving guidance was the only way forward from here, warm baths and hot chocolate on the horizon to deal with any chill.

Holly was actually a little grateful that Lizzie was in a self-imposed purdah-of-grump today. She really didn't have the emotional reserves to cope with Lizzie's post-operative boredom and mood-swings, no matter how selfish a friend that made her feel. And Plum was surprisingly easy and enjoyable company, as though she instinctively knew when to speak up and when just to be still, in the moment.

Holly tilted her head back and let the sunshine warm her face – another thing she had come to take for granted, she realised. Her fresh-air addiction being not quite so welcome at The Practice, her patients quite rightly objecting to her windows being thrown open wide at every opportunity.

Holly looked around in surprise as a gentle whinny echoed around the parkland. She couldn't help but smile at the sight that greeted her: Charlotte, the Major and Jess walked towards them, Banana the miniature horse rugged up and trotting happily at Jess's side.

'Afternoon, ladies,' said the Major, bending at the waist and doffing his flat cap, as was his wont.

Jess bounded over to say hello to Lulu, sitting down

cross-legged in the snow beside her. 'Hello, I'm Jess. Do you want to make a little snow dog with me?'

That in itself was remarkable enough, Jess's introversion since the accident having been of almost clinical concern not that long ago. But what took Holly's breath away was Lulu's reaction to Banana – or was it vice versa? Clearly the tiny palomino had more empathy than most humans Lulu had encountered in her short life. Banana wormed his way between Jess and Lulu, snuffling their hands gently and whickering as they balled up snow, patting it into shape to create their sculpture, occasionally nudging Jess for attention, before laying his tufty head on Lulu's shoulder. Her eyes went wide for a moment in surprise, before the most beautiful volley of giggles erupted and she buried her tiny hands glee-fully in Banana's mane.

Holly swallowed hard, tears that had been far too close to the surface all morning making themselves known. She glanced over at Plum, Charlotte and the Major, reassured that she wasn't alone.

'Would you look at that,' said Charlotte. 'Isn't he a charmer?'

Holly nodded. Charming, of course, but more than that, Banana appeared to have some kind of healing energy that brought out the very best in those who had been traumatised.

'Any progress on finding a school for Jess?' Holly asked, her eyes now firmly fixed on the adorable equine tableau in front of her, any thoughts of snow dogs forgotten as the girls made a willing Banana the focus of their game.

Charlotte sat down on the bench beside her. 'Not so far. Lavinia's holding out for a boarding school place, apparently.' There was a wealth of feeling in those last four syllables.

Lavinia didn't work, they had a live-in housekeeper, and space wasn't an issue, yet she was still determined to send her only child away to school. She was somehow convinced that it was the only way for Jess to have a decent education, or indeed 'friends worth having'. Her snobbery was in danger of damaging her daughter's long-term recovery from her traumatic brain injury, but nobody had been able to get through to her. Least of all Jess.

'I can't bear to think of them being separated,' whispered Charlotte, 'not when Banana seems to help in so many ways. Did you know she hasn't had a single panic attack since they've been together?'

'I didn't, no,' said Holly, finding it only too easy to believe. The bond between Jess and Banana was almost tangible in its strength. The way Jess was now plaiting his tousled mane was just adorable, as was the clumsy ham-fisted way that Lulu attempted to copy her every move. 'Any luck talking to Mr French?'

Charlotte shook her head. 'There's not a lot he can do, if Lavinia won't put Jess down on the state school placement register. He seemed open to the concept at least, but even he would have to jump through all sorts of health and safety hoops.'

Holly nodded. 'If you want my honest opinion, the best thing we can possibly do is get Banana officially registered as a support animal. At that point, at least, there are legal precedents to follow.' She frowned. 'I don't suppose you know whether Lavinia had a change of heart about applying for Jess's disability status, do you?'

The Major harrumphed angrily at the very question. 'Daft woman says it would be too demeaning and they don't need the money. Doesn't seem to realise that it's about more than cash; it's about getting Jess access to the support she needs. She could give the bloody money back if it irked her so, but at least Jess could access some of the services she's going to need.' Peregrine Waverly was the biggest surprise to Holly of late; his emotional investment in Jess's recovery may have started from a position of guilt, but he now treated her like the granddaughter he'd never had. His time in the armed forces clearly gave him a good idea about what was ahead for Jess, as she struggled to find her new normal with her diminished capacities.

'I'll give Jamie Yardley a ring later, although he's coming over for the Christening next week. We can quiz him some more then,' Holly said. 'Let's find out how we make Mr Banana official?'

Banana looked up at the very mention of his name and a cascade of snow crystals fell from his forelock. Holly slowly breathed out, enjoying the fact that she could still apparently help her patients and spend time with her own children at the same time. It took her a moment to realise she had inadvertently included Lulu in that moniker without a second thought.

Holly stood in the doorway later that afternoon, watching Elsie, Ben, Tom and Lulu engrossed in a Pixar movie and wondered if she were having a midlife crisis. Her in-at-the-deep-end return to work had somehow succeeded (where all manner of soul-searching had failed) when it came to pinpointing the very essence of what had attracted her to the notion of private practice – the opportunity to practise medicine the way she instinctively wanted to: without an enormous ten-minute hourglass hovering over her head throughout every appointment.

She'd also considered the possibility of fostering Lulu full-time and the effect on their family dynamic if Lulu happened to have her own Banana-equivalent support animal to aid her recovery and transition.

In one of her patients, she would have put this erratic behaviour down to an over-burdened mind and a subconscious cry for help. But right now, it all seemed perfectly logical to her.

Something, somewhere would have to give, for her to be the doctor she wanted to be, the doctor her newly vulnerable state *demanded* she be.

Elsie looked over and smiled warmly, and Holly was touched to see her making an effort to build a rapport with Lulu, even if a small part of her suspected that Elsie was conveniently delaying the conversational elephant in the room. Holly was dying to have a nosey next door, but in all honesty, not quite as much as she was to hear all about the self-managed scandal that had dictated its necessity.

Holly looked up as the front door opened, Taffy tiredly managing a smile. 'We have company,' he said.

Grace and Dan hovered on the doorstep behind him. 'I hope we're not intruding?' Dan asked, his hand clasping Grace's tightly.

'No, no, come in. I'll get the kettle on,' Holly said easily, as Taffy leaned in to give her a kiss in greeting.

'I know you said you were missing the team, but there doesn't actually seem to be much opportunity to *really* miss them, does there?' He pulled her into a hug. 'Now, how did it all go this morning? Are we seriously putting the kettle on, or is this the perfect excuse to sample my special cider?'

Dan shrugged off his jacket and hung it on the staircase finial. 'Did someone say cider?'

Holly smiled. 'Come and see this. It will lift your spirits far more than Taffy's dodgy homebrew.'

'Hey, I was merely making sure that all the apples in Larkford didn't go to waste. Nobody else was picking them—'

'Shh,' said Holly, beckoning him over to join them in the doorway.

Tom, Ben and Lulu were all schlumpfed together in a pile of arms and legs, their heads leaning against one another as they watched *Toy Story*, transfixed.

'Oh,' said Grace. 'Oh, but she is just beautiful.' Further words seemed to elude her but the look on Dan's face was all too telling. As was the way Dan and Grace's hands were entwined, a conversation taking place in the touch of their fingers.

Holly had to swallow hard, her emotions altogether too close to the surface these days. Was this what her rambling subconscious had been trying to tell her? To keep Lulu in their lives, did she necessarily have to live at Number 42?

'Has she spoken again?' Dan asked quietly, but Holly shook her head.

'We have had giggles though. Apparently Banana the miniature horse just *has* it.'

Lulu blinked as she watched the movie and then slowly her gaze rose to the adults clustered in the doorway. Her face split into the widest smile and her little arms shot out in longing. 'Dan!' she said.

He was across the room in two strides, sweeping her around in his arms. 'Hello, trouble. Did you see the tiny pony today?'

'Dan!' she said again happily, wrapping her arms around him like a koala.

Dan's eyes filled with tears and he turned to Grace. 'Come and say hello to Lulu, Gracie? Lulu, I want you to meet someone *really* special.'

'Hi,' said Grace shyly, as Lulu regarded her suspiciously from under her ridiculously long eyelashes, her clasp on Dan ever tighter.

'Hi,' Lulu said in the end, after a pause that made Holly's heart loop-the-loop in anticipation. Lulu tilted her head to one side, appraising this newcomer to her world. 'Hug?' she offered.

Chapter 27

Alice wrapped the blanket around her shoulders a little tighter and tried not to feel rattled. Her day was really not going to plan: not only had she essentially press-ganged Holly into returning to work, she was also missing out on a lovely evening of wine and nibbles and plotting. There wasn't long now until the girls' Christening and Alice had been over the moon when Holly had first asked her to be Olivia's god-mother, but right now she suspected all the plans were being finalised around Holly's kitchen table without her.

And, if she were honest, planning the Christening was much more in her comfort zone than offering spiritual guid-ance to a baby!

She swallowed another wave of nausea and wondered which of her patients had passed along this little bug. Or indeed whether picking up a prawn sandwich from the motorway café had been such a clever idea. It was a remnant of her upbringing that Alice sought to quash: any time any-thing goes wrong, apportion blame. Likely as not, she was just run down from overdoing it, but still . . .

She hesitated before picking up the phone to call her mother. Jamie was doing some night work with one of his clients and the prospect of a long evening with no company stretched ahead of her. She still couldn't quite begin to process how much she missed him; she'd been a self-contained, independent adult for so long, that this longing, this ghastly neediness, was a double-edged sword. On the one hand it served to confirm the strength of her feelings for him; on the other, it made her feel vulnerable in a way that was uncomfortable in the extreme. Next weekend couldn't come quickly enough, and she was grateful that Jamie was to be one of Lottie's godfathers; it gave them a bond, a preliminary perhaps to them making some kind of commitment to each other? Not marriage – she wasn't ready for that. But something?

She shook the thought away, regretting it instantly as the room swivelled unbidden around her. Seeing Jamie, standing here in front of her, would be the only real way to know – was she pining for him, or the idea of him?

She paused before dialling Orkney; crikey, she must be feeling low if she was banking on comfort from her mum. A lecture on returning home to Orkney? Yes. A blunt conversation about men who won't commit? Absolutely. Supportive, loving compassion? Don't hold your breath.

Her mum genuinely didn't seem to understand that her daughter had no wish to be married, no wish to move home and only a desire to savour every moment of her new-found happiness with Jamie and Coco. Stomach bugs and geography permitting.

'Only me!' called Tilly, as she let herself in. Decked out in a surgical face mask, bright yellow Marigold gloves and a paper smock, she looked like an extra from the movie *Outbreak*. 'Is it safe to come in? I come bearing Dettol in industrial quantities and chicken soup from The Deli. Oh, and Hattie sends her love.' She posed theatrically for maximum effect. 'I hope you appreciate me taking my life in my hands to keep you company?'

Alice hung up the phone mid-dial without a second thought. 'I truly, truly do,' she said with feeling.

'Are you feeling any better?' asked Tilly sympathetically, perching on the far end of the sofa, placing as much distance between herself and Alice as was humanly possible in the compact and bijou sitting room.

'I am, actually. Just a bit grumpy, you know, about missing out.'

Tilly laughed and her surgical mask inflated with warm air. 'Ooh yes, it's been a festival of delights at work today. I can see why you'd feel hard done by!' As she went on to describe the litany of maladies she'd handled that day, Alice held up her hand to make her stop, as her stomach lurched uncomfortably at the very thought of Billy Frank's verruca harvest.

'So you see, kicking back with *Gilmore Girls* and a bucket's not so very awful.' Tilly smiled. She hesitated for a moment, uncharacteristically tentative. 'Are you feeling really rough, or could you manage a little advice?'

Alice's smile slipped straight off her face, almost mirroring Tilly's removal of her surgical mask. 'Are you okay?' she asked. Problems that required advice, where Tilly was concerned, tended to be of the life-changing, continent-swapping variety and scale.

Tilly nodded, biting her lip and looking increasingly uncomfortable. 'I am, I mean, I'm fine. I think. I just—' She cleared her throat determinedly and that was when Alice went straight to Defcon One.

'Oh God, and I can't even give you a hug, in case I give you the plague! Coco? Go hug Aunty Tilly,' Alice said, possible scenarios running in her mind on a loop.

Coco gave her mistress a sideways look, but did as she was bidden. And even though Tilly wasn't really a dog person (and Coco knew it), she still buried her face in the little dog's fur to disguise her stricken expression. 'I really did come over to give you soup,' she mumbled through Coco's ears.

'And I'm sure it will be lovely soup,' said Alice, 'but is there any chance we could talk about why you're dripping all over my dog?'

Tilly snorted, a laugh subsumed by a sob. 'Don't be too sympathetic, will you?'

'Hard to be,' said Alice, aiming for nonchalance, 'when I have zero clue what's going on.'

Tilly took a visible breath and pulled herself together, as Coco gratefully escaped back to the warmth and comfort of Alice's blanket. 'I was going to leave,' she said bluntly. 'I was just waiting for Holly to come back, you know? I mean, I was drafted in for maternity cover, anyway. So, once Holly came back, I was going to leave.' She looked up at Alice to gauge her reaction. 'But then Holly came back today . . .'

Alice was working hard to maintain a composed front. She'd known Tilly for long enough to realise that this was just the opening salvo.

'And now?' she said.

Tilly shrugged. 'Now, I don't know what to do. It's taken me by surprise a little. Holly coming back, even for a day, means I'm nearly done here, doesn't it? And, in all honesty, I'd been counting the days – part of me feels like I've been in one place for too long. As long as it's temporary, I can justify a few quirks, can't I? Maybe the odd inappropriate relationship? Maintain my air of mystery?' she said, aiming for humour. 'But then you went and showed me the Pickwick Estate and

I can't get those people out of my head. I mean, it was easier to think about moving on and leaving all these privileged Cotswold families behind, go back to South America or something, but now I know—'

'Now you know what it's really like. It's not just Range Rovers and Hunter welly-boots,' said Alice gently.

'And now I don't want to go anywhere.' She sighed dramatically. 'And I'm blaming you for this,' said Tilly clearly.

'I can live with that,' said Alice, perfectly happy to have Tilly's reawakening on her conscience.

Tilly threw a cushion at her. 'You're not taking this seriously!'

'I am,' replied Alice. 'I'm just trying to keep a little perspective. One of us needs to, if you're going to lose the plot.'

Tilly looked up and smiled, genuinely amused to hear her own words – words that she had been saying to Alice for years now – quoted back at her. 'Oh, how the worm has turned,' she said.

Alice chucked the cushion back at her. 'Or has the student become the master?'

Tilly shrugged. 'You know, I think it may be a case of the blind leading the blind with us, actually. Have you ever noticed that we're never sorted and settled at the same time?'

'Have you ever noticed that neither of us are exactly sorted and settled? At least, not according to the gospel of Orkney,' Alice countered.

'Your mum still on at you to go back?' Tilly said.

'You could say that. She's gone up a gear though since Dr Sjorgen confirmed a retirement date. She's still holding out for a batch of mini McWalkers and some island kudos from being "the doctor's mum". It's not really a sustainable scenario, but that's my mother for you.'

Tilly smiled. 'Well, at least she cares enough to pester you, annoy you and generally piss you off. I mean, that's nice to know, isn't it? Holly's mum doesn't seem to give a rat's arse about her new twins, or her earlier set, come to think of it. That's got to sting.'

'She's not even coming to the Christening, if you can believe that. She's sending Premium Bonds instead,' Alice confirmed.

'Ah well, if in doubt, send cash. It worked for my Aunt Ophelia for years and we were always pleased to hear from her,' Tilly said, unimpressed.

'So,' said Alice, not to be distracted by Tilly's obvious ploy to change the subject. 'Are we staying or going?'

Tilly frowned. 'The thing is – and don't shout – it's become rather obvious that I am a rubbish GP. I mean it. I really struggle with going the extra mile for the moaners and the whiners and the First World problems. Don't get me wrong: I listen and I treat them. I just don't seem to *care* as much as you and Holly do.'

'Ah,' said Alice. 'And here was me about to suggest a course or something. I'm not even sure you *can* teach empathy, though, Tills.'

Tilly shook her head. 'How can I be so emotionally invested in some patients on the other side of the planet, and not in my actual neighbours?' She sighed. 'I don't really know how to be a GP, but it occurs to me that if I want to keep being one, I think that should change.'

'Probably a good idea,' said Alice with a smile, watching her friend's mental machinations.

'And you jest, but I've found a course – a three-day one about connecting with patients blah, blah, blah . . .' Tilly said earnestly.

Alice laughed. 'I have to tell you that may not be the most encouraging attitude to start off with though ... Is it just a disconnect after years of working in the Third World, do you think? Maybe your parameters need recalibrating?'

'Well,' huffed Tilly, 'I haven't worked out how to turn myself off and back on again. I'm not a fucking iPhone.'

'Nooo,' agreed Alice, 'you're definitely still running on Android ...' earning herself yet another cushion lob.

'You're not being very helpful,' Tilly said quietly, as though Alice should automatically have all the answers.

'And you did not come here just to bring soup,' Alice said matter-of-factly. 'Now, in all honesty there's only one question you need to ask yourself: do you even want to stay? Because if your heart is in the Sudan, or Ethiopia, all the courses in the world aren't going to change that, but if you want to stay ...'

Tilly nodded. 'I'd like to. I mean, I didn't really give this my best shot. I was just here to take a breath, spend some time with you, have a little fun ... It wasn't a calculated decision, but now, suddenly, I find I want to try. Seeing little Lulu makes me want to try.'

'So stay,' said Alice as if it were the most obvious thing in the world. 'And go on that course. And what about a mentor? Someone to actually guide you through becoming a GP, rather than just throw you in at the deep end? If I'm honest, I'm not sure we gave you the best start here either. It was all a bit chaotic and you seemed so capable ...'

'Well, I am *very* capable,' protested Tilly, 'when it comes to hard medicine. It's the soft issues that leave me flailing. It's not easy to admit, but I think on some level, when I arrived, I had the misconception that depression and infertility and things like that were issues of the privileged – everyone else in the world is busy getting on with the business of staying alive.' She paused, clearly uncomfortable in her confession. 'I don't feel like that anymore.'

'Well, that's progress, I suppose.' Alice paused. 'I guess a lot of things must feel like that when you're used to dealing with famine and epidemics. But it doesn't make it less of an issue for the patient suffering through it.'

'Do you think this is what maturity feels like?' Tilly wondered, ever the Peter Pan of their med school cohort.

'Seems unlikely, while you're still having dodgy flings left, right and centre, to be honest. Actually,' Alice paused, 'we should probably talk about that too, because if you are going to stay, then something needs to change.'

'Empathy *and* chastity?' challenged Tilly.

'I was aiming for discernment,' Alice said quietly. 'Aiming for balance rather than extremes. A relationship rather than a one-night stand. Isn't there anyone you've met here that's intrigued you enough to want more?'

Colour flooded Tilly's face, taking Alice a little by surprise. In all the years she'd known Tilly there had been no one with the ability to produce such a reaction in her best friend, who was clearly calibrated into the love-them-and-leave-them school of thought. It was hardly surprising, given her history, but still . . . Maybe it wasn't such a shock that it was little Lulu Fowler, heading into the foster system, that had provoked this about-turn in her friend's behaviour.

Tilly was unable to meet her gaze, it seemed, as she became suddenly fascinated with the warp and weft weave of the sofa throw. 'Well, it's nothing really. But, I mean, well—' She paused and cleared her throat. 'There's only one person I've felt a proper connection with since I've been here. You know, that instant connection? That feeling that they just *get* you?'

Alice nodded, trying not to be put out that she herself didn't apparently tick that particular box, before realising that they weren't talking friendship here; Tilly really was opening up to the possibility of Someone Special. 'And?' she prompted.

Tilly shook her head. 'It can't go anywhere. And maybe I'm the only one who feels that way – we haven't discussed it. Not to mention, that it feels a little too close to home. First rule of camping applies to relationships too, you know: don't poop where you eat.'

Alice mentally flipped through the Rolodex of likely candidates and frowned as the thought occurred to her. 'Honey, technically, I think that ship has sailed. You've already been shagging half the under-twenty-fives in town – most of whom are registered at The Practice. You've already crossed the Rubicon.'

A smile flickered across Tilly's face. 'It didn't matter so much when I was planning on leaving.'

Alice nodded, taking Tilly's words as a decision to stay. 'Well, then, let's get you settled, get you properly supported at work and who knows what might be in your future? Or who?' She may have been fishing for a name, but Tilly ignored the question.

She stood up and hugged Alice tightly, seemingly happy to risk catching her plague for the sake of a little solidarity. 'Who knows?' she whispered into Alice's hair with a smile, allowing a little hope to brighten her voice and her mood.

Chapter 28

'And who, might I ask, are we staring into the distance and pining for?' interrupted a voice into Connor's reverie, his early morning amble with Jamieson hardly a cardio workout, but nevertheless giving him time to think, time to breathe and reflect. A dangerous combination, as it turned out, if the embryonic lyrics drifting through his mind were anything to go by.

He turned and saw Elsie appraising him, with her head tilted slightly to one side, her breath leaving visible puffs in the cold air. 'Hello, trouble,' he said, bending down low to kiss her pink, powdery cheek. 'You look like you're on a mission?'

'Always, dear boy. Always. Can't let a little snow slow you down.' She grinned, her hi-tech Salomon hiking boots somewhat at odds with her full-length faux fur, and he could almost see the cogs turning in her mind. 'I was thinking that you looked like a man in need of a life raft actually. A little adrift – lonely in a crowd and all that?'

Connor shrugged disconsolately. There was no denying that Elsie was spot on the money as always. 'Some days are easier than others,' he prevaricated. 'Some days involve journalists . . .'

She nodded astutely, in no need of elaboration. In many

ways, Connor realised, she would be the perfect confidante, understanding only too well the downfalls of a life lived in the public eye.

There was a disconnect inside him and he had no idea how to fix it, for any solution would surely require him to lay his soul bare, to allow a level of honesty, vulnerability and intimacy that he couldn't quite bring himself to acquire. Was this the alternative though? Shallow friendships, a gaping hole in his heart where mutual support and understanding could be?

It wasn't as though he could blame his new friends, though, he realised. Railing against them for not being there for him when he needed them – for on one level they had been.

Superficially.

But how could they help, after all, if they didn't even know the extent of his problems, deceived by his own fraudulent façade? And the longer it persisted, the more he continued to shatter into tiny pieces, no use to anyone, even himself.

'I had a phone call late last night from some scuzzy journo,' he blurted out suddenly, 'asking if my Solstice festival was a "memorial" to Rachel and the baby. And honestly? I just wanted to punch him. Over a year since they died, Elsie, and I'm still like this. It just doesn't seem to get any easier.'

He held out his hands helplessly, unshaven and scruffy, his ailing Irish wolfhound propped against his leg – unclear who was supporting whom – vulnerable in a way that he could never have foreseen a few months ago, as though the effort of maintaining the pretence had simply left him in a moment. 'And the only way I can keep going – keep getting up in the morning and going through the motions of living – is by keeping busy, fielding meetings, wooing managers. And look how that's turning out: I try to do something nice for my new home town and suddenly I'm a social pariah.'

Elsie said nothing, just nodded, almost as though she were unwilling to break the spell of his confessional.

'I'm beginning to wonder if I did the right thing in leaving Dorset, to be honest,' he confided tentatively, unused to sharing his private feelings, but somehow intuiting that Elsie could identify. She was a safe pair of hands. 'At least there was no expectation on me to be anything other than the "grieving rock star" there. I could have quietly drunk my way through this feeling, binged on boxsets, and be back on tour by now.'

'Do you really think so?' Elsie asked, intrigued, leaning against the Cotswold-stone wall beside him, brushing the snow crystals aside and following his gaze along the frost-gilded water meadows. 'If we're being honest, I've never found that grief responds terribly well to drugs and alcohol. Although, to be fair, I never tried the boxsets ...'

He looked over at her then, at the tenderness and affection in her voice. 'See. This is what I have to contend with, living here ...' His voice broke. 'How can I be angry and self-destructive when there are so many people around me who seem to bloody care? Even though they have no idea. Even though I don't understand why; I'm a selfish son-of-a-bitch most of the time.'

'Well, yes, I can see that,' Elsie said scathingly. 'You've been rubbish at helping Lizzie through her recovery; you haven't supported any local businesses in setting up your new enterprises; and your festival plans are frankly self-serving and narcissistic.' Elsie gave him a gentle punch on the arm, which actually hurt more than he cared to admit, fragile on every level this morning, it seemed.

'You can put yourself down as much as you like,' Elsie continued, gathering momentum, 'but you need to remember that, to most of us here in Larkford, you're just that chap

Connor, who sadly lost his family in horrible circumstances. Why wouldn't we want to support you?'

'Nobody wants to support the festival though, do they? The only fecking thing keeping me going, moving forward, venturing out into the world again.' Connor sighed. 'I mean, it was nice to think I could exist in a world of cheese and honey, but we both know I might need a little bit more.'

'Do we, though?' Elsie challenged him. 'If you had a fulfilling personal life and your own boutique business? Is that a belief that bears scrutiny?'

Connor scruffed the tufts of fur on Jamieson's head, and the first hint of calm crossed his face. 'You're not impressed by my credentials at all, are you, Elsie?'

'Should I be? Are they making you happy? They've made you rich and famous, of course.' Elsie waved a hand dismissively as though that were a given of no importance. 'But you moved here to make a fresh start and to be a little gentler on yourself at a pretty hideous time. You're not the first and you won't be the last.'

'Cheering,' he said drily, unsure whether he was supposed to be comforted by the notion of other people feeling just as bereft, just as broken. Jamieson licked his hand reassuringly and Connor steeled himself to ask the one question that had been haunting him for weeks now. 'When do you know, Elsie? When do you know whether it's just grief, or whether there's a real problem,' he tapped his forehead, 'up there?'

Elsie considered for a moment. 'Firstly, I don't think you could ever say "just" grief – it's a process, isn't it? It's not linear and it's different for everyone.' She paused again, caught up by her own memories. 'I still have days when I wake up literally winded by the realisation that my boy Ginger is gone and that's four decades later. But most days? Most days it's barely a shadow in the back of my mind. I've filled my life with friends and love and laughter. Deliberately, actually.'

Connor blinked, pushing away traitorous thoughts of Kitty that he had no business thinking. 'So more time-down-the-pub, less trip-to-the-funny-farm, you reckon?' Connor clarified, able to pinpoint even in that moment that it didn't feel like quite enough. Anywhere near enough, actually, as he teetered on this precarious precipice. He hadn't realised until recently that it was possible to feel this lonely, this hollow, while surrounded by people and animals every day. And he'd been on tour with The Hive for months on end before now, so that was saying something.

'Well,' Elsie mused, twisting her wrist to check the chunky Cartier timepiece that rotated under its own weight as she did so, 'if you're convinced that this festival of yours is going to keep you sane and focused, we could always attempt a little social rehabilitation? If you're not too busy for the next hour or so?'

'Say what now?' Connor looked worried and well he might where Elsie was concerned. Sometimes, he wondered if her advice was always quite on point. Sometimes, it felt as though the force of her personality stepped in where common sense might reasonably have otherwise prevailed.

'Darling boy,' Elsie said firmly, seemingly stepping back onto firmer ground, judging by the renewed confidence in her voice, 'this festival idea of yours is obviously getting more than a few backs up around here. And that Cassie Holland seems even more het up than usual recently. Heaven knows what's flown up her organic skirts, but why not have your say? Come on, I'm live on Radio Larkford in ten. You can be my esteemed celebrity guest and tell all the listeners about your vision. You know, the way you described it to me originally?'

'But I ...' Connor held up his hands. 'I've nothing prepared.'

'That's the beauty,' Elsie said assuredly. 'You'll speak from the heart rather than a press release. Let Larkford get to know the man behind the brand. To most of them you're still Connor Danes from The Hive – they have no idea you're just as flawed and befoibled as the rest of us. Tell them about your gratitude to the town for welcoming you at a "difficult time", if nothing else.' She paused. 'If this festival is what you say you need, then let's make it happen.'

It was the work of moments, but Elsie was seemingly unused to hearing the word 'no', possibly because her highly selective hearing simply edited it out. Once she had an idea in her head, she ran with it. Apparently.

Either way, when the light bulb above the studio door at Radio Larkford flickered on a short while later, Connor found himself sitting in the hot seat – headphones on and the smell of haddock from downstairs assailing his nostrils. The weight on his chest was still there, but the blur of frenetic activity had driven all other, more self-destructive, thoughts from his head. Maybe Elsie's crackpot scheme had merit after all, he thought.

Bright, breezy, upbeat.

He was a professional.

He could do that. Hopefully.

'And here on the show today, we have Larkford's favourite new resident, Connor Danes, and while some of you might recognise that name from the Hit Parade, or whatever you call it these days, there is so much more to the man than foxy guitar riffs. Stay tuned and find out more, after hearing him in devastating style on this worldwide hit from The Hive.' Elsie moved the sliders on the console in front of her and Connor's distinctive guitar stylings filled the studio.

'Okay?' said Elsie, with a twinkle in her eye. 'Lizzie is going to be so peeved that I nabbed you as my guest. Serves her right for taking so long to recover.' She smiled impishly. 'Now, steer away from anything too vanilla, darling, won't you? We want the listeners to get to know the real you.'

Connor swallowed a sudden wave of nausea at the very idea. Even he couldn't cope with the reality of that right now.

'So,' Elsie continued, totally missing his discomfort in her drive to get the show on the road, 'do you want to talk about the festival first or shall we dive straight in and talk about your rebirth as a gentleman farmer, get the ladies' pulses racing with thoughts of you in a pair of ripped jeans and Hunter wellies?'

It had been going so well, thought Connor, having almost relaxed into the easy banter that Elsie so excelled at, whether on the airwaves, around the kitchen table, or propping up the bar at The Kingsley Arms.

They'd had a laugh, played a few of his favourite music picks and he felt good about how he'd described his idea for the festival. He'd wanted to be clear that this was something organic in every sense of the word – not a highly funded event run by professionals with zero-interest in their community.

They should have quit while they were ahead, hindsight offering twenty-twenty vision, of course.

If he had to pinpoint the moment the interview went south it would have to be when Elsie announced a phone-in.

No warning, no preamble – and the switchboard lit up.

It was always nice to talk to fans on the radio, there being none of that discomfort from having your personal space invaded, as it always, always was. No folded slips of paper bearing phone numbers, or occasionally scraps of lacy lingerie wrapped around a hotel room-key. Radio gave him a little bit of distance, so even when he recognised the second caller's voice, he hadn't felt so much as a flicker of alarm.

That hadn't lasted long.

'I think,' said the new caller, her tone dripping with disdain, 'that you have a bloody nerve, turning up in our community, taking over the houses and farmland of respected citizens – no doubt bribed by your filthy lucre – and now this? Do we need your celebrities and your fancy authors and your hot-shot chefs swanning around our town looking down their noses at us? No, frankly, we do not.'

'Well, hello, caller,' laughed Elsie easily, still somehow oblivious to the car crash slowly unfolding on her watch. 'Why don't you introduce yourself to our listeners?'

'As you know perfectly well, I'm Cassie Holland. I'm the only person with the balls to stand up and say that we don't want your filthy festival and debauched crowd in our town.'

People were used to Cassie climbing on her soapbox and mouthing off, but there was an edge of hysteria to her voice, slicing across the airwaves that suggested she wasn't entirely in control of herself today. Connor glanced across at Elsie in alarm.

She held up a soothing hand, a gesture to allay his concerns, before dropping it sharply as Cassie continued.

'And don't think I'm going to sit idly by and watch you drag Larkford's reputation through the mud either. I have some rather interesting photos of some of your friends and what they've been doing, while they've been here in Larkford – you can see them under the hashtag "spottedinlarkford" – and I have to say your sponsor was pretty interested when I sent them over.'

'Oh, Cassie,' began Elsie, her blink-rate indicating some level of the panic she was at last beginning to feel. 'And with that, it's time for another—'

'They've pulled your sponsorship, you know, now that they've seen exactly what kind of a druggy—'

'And here's a little Eric Clapton – another one with definite flair on a fretboard,' Elsie almost shouted into her mic, cutting the phone-line and ramping up the volume of the CD only to gasp in horror at the unfortunate parallel as Eric blasted out the opening verse of 'Cocaine'.

Connor's phone jiggled silently on the console in front of him and he picked it up, the screen lighting up with tweet after tweet, message after message.

'Well, you can't say she isn't committed to her cause. Bee-you-tiful have pulled their support – biggest lifestyle blog in Europe now thinks we're tainted and seedy apparently. Too contentious. So that's nice.' Connor nodded his head, like one of those jiggling toys on the parcel shelves of Ford Escorts everywhere, something in the movement appeasing his jangling nerves.

'Maybe I should just admit defeat and scratch the whole thing,' he murmured, half to himself. The resistance to the very idea of his festival seemed to be dividing the town in two – and those who were against it seemingly had no filter when it came to sharing their reasons why. Whether those reasons happened to be true or not.

Even as Eric Clapton assured him that cocaine did not lie, he knew for a fact that Cassie Holland did. Loudly and unapologetically, if it stood between her and getting her way. Surely his friends weren't crass enough to be using drugs in public places, except Docie's manager, of course – but then, insulin injections hardly counted as drug use, did they?

He pulled off the headphones abruptly, swallowing down a cloying wave of panic and claustrophobia. Whatever rock bottom felt like, it couldn't be worse than this tsunami of overwhelming emotions. Too much. On every level. Elsie held out her hand to him, apology in her eyes, for once lost for words.

But then, what could she possibly have said to offset the damage from appearing on her show? Not just to the festival, but to Connor's fragile hold on his new reality.

It seemed like the cruellest irony of all, that, when he'd finally risked opening up and sharing his vulnerability, had needed support the most, he found himself ill-equipped to ask for it; the vocabulary simply eluding him.

'I think I'll be heading off now,' said Connor, his tone disjointed and jerky, as he leaned forward to kiss Elsie's cheek, taking a moment to squeeze her hand – in search of comfort, but finding none – before striding out of the room and letting the door swing closed behind him.

Chapter 29

'Feel better,' said Holly as she hung up the phone the next morning, trying not to embrace the embarrassing *schadenfreude* that had enveloped her at the thought of covering another sick day for Alice. There had been an inkling of a plan in the back of her mind since about 4 a.m. and this, she felt, was the perfect opportunity to put a little meat on its bones.

'What are you looking so smug about?' asked Elsie with interest, as she limbered up in her disconcertingly bright leotard and leg warmers. The only thing silver that Elsie was contributing to the Silver Swans ballet class was her hair.

Holly grinned. 'Well, very sadly poor Alice is still under the weather.'

'Yes, I can see that you're devastated,' Elsie said with her trademark raised eyebrow.

'I have to cover her morning surgery again, that's all. And Plum is coping so brilliantly here that it seems too good an opportunity to miss. It's okay with you, Plum, yes?'

'But of course,' said Plum easily as she sliced bananas onto five small plates with incredible dexterity and speed.

Holly turned to Elsie and dropped her voice a little furtively, unwilling to share her plotting with Taffy until she'd done a little more research. 'I just want to explore whether there's any way for me to have the best of both worlds: more time with my patients, yet still be at The Practice.'

'Private healthcare for the great unwashed?' Elsie queried.

'Not private, just better,' Holly said with a frown, holding her finger to her lips as Taffy strolled into the kitchen.

'Morning!' he said breezily, all the brighter for having managed an unprecedented block of six hours' sleep. 'Any lovely plans afoot?' He took in Elsie stretching over the back of a chair. 'Obviously Elsie's on a mission to snap as many ligaments as she can in a single day!'

Elsie, Holly and Plum looked at each other and shook their heads, almost in sync, laughing at Taffy's panicked reaction at being outnumbered in his own kitchen.

'I'm coming with you, actually,' said Holly, handing him the pancake spatula, as she bounded up the stairs to get dressed. 'Wait for me,' she called down the stairwell.

'Crikey, somebody's back on the full-fat coffee this morning!' said Taffy, a little thrown by Holly's early morning energy burst.

Elsie's head spun around like an eagle owl, slowly but no less menacing. 'Are you telling me that this,' she lifted her coffee mug from the table and waved it alarmingly in the air, 'is *not* full-fat?'

Taffy blinked, knowing that Holly would kill him if he let on about her cunning decaffeination plan.

'It is a special Italian blend, that is all,' interrupted Plum, earning herself a grateful smile from Taffy and a suspicious glare from Elsie. 'I find it very tasty.'

'Ready!' called Holly, barrelling into the kitchen with her boots in one hand and applying lip balm with the other; if there was one thing that parenting taught you, it was how to get dressed in a hurry. 'And after work, you, Elsie Townsend, owe me one guided tour of Number 44. Deal? Don't think

I didn't notice that Connor Danes getting the priority treatment.' She teased, delighted to see Elsie blush furiously. Holly shook her head. 'I don't know, these celebrities . . .' She kissed Elsie lovingly on both cheeks and smiled. 'When you're ready to share, I'm here and excited to jump on board, deal?'

'Deal,' said Elsie gratefully, as Taffy cleared his throat and muttered repeatedly about the time.

With a flurry of hugs and kisses among the children and promises of a fun outing to see the 'tiny horses' that afternoon, Holly and Taffy made it to the front door and stepped out into the Market Place with that heady combination of freedom and guilt that all working parents experience.

Taffy checked his watch. 'Coffee on the way?'

'God, yes!' said Holly with feeling, wanting to ride the adrenalin rush of her hurried change of plan for as long as possible, and slightly relieved to see that Taffy hadn't become some punctuality fiend as she'd feared. He'd just wanted to stop and tank up. 'This decaf thing is killing me,' she told him.

'And Elsie suspects,' Taffy said, as though his own faux-pas had nothing to do with that.

'Tomorrow's problem,' said Holly firmly, her skill at compartmentalising getting a little more developed every day. 'Today, I shall be mainly focusing on patients and Matthew's funding application and, if I'm really, really lucky, I have big plans for going to the loo all by myself.'

'Well!' said Taffy with a grin. 'That's just reckless.' He paused, his brain obviously not quite as perky as his wife. 'What funding?'

'You know Mike Urquhart from the Rugby Club? Well, he's going to put a suggestion to their board that Matthew's Young Carers group have a regular provision so that they can plan ahead a little, rather than living quarter to quarter.

Matthew's talking about setting up a permanent drop-in centre somewhere and Mike seemed really keen to help. It's a question of investment really, rather than seasonal sponsorship? It was a slightly mad suggestion, I know, but Mike seems to be going for it.'

'You seem to be talking to Mike an awful lot these days,' said Taffy, somewhat missing the point of the conversation. 'Is he still pestering you to take that stupid job?'

'It's not a stupid job,' Holly protested, before realising how defensive that sounded. 'And I'm not taking it, you know that. My priorities are here, but that doesn't mean I can't explore a few options – you know, you scratch my back et cetera, et cetera.'

Taffy nodded. 'Okay. Sorry. I don't know why I get all het up when I think about you leaving The Practice. It just doesn't sit very comfortably with me, that's all.'

Holly frowned. 'Always supposing I can come back properly, not just as sick cover when you're stuck.' Even as the words came out of her mouth, she could have bitten them back. The whole tone of their conversation shifted.

Taffy shook his head. 'You're a partner, Holly. You can come back whenever you bloody well choose – always assuming that's what you actually want? Maybe you need to think about where your loyalties lie? All this talk of Bath Rugby Club hasn't gone away, has it?'

Holly sighed, their lovely, jokey, romantic walk through Larkford sullied yet again by sulking and logistics. 'Well, maybe you should say the same to your friend Dan, because he's biting at my heels to get the Bath gig too,' she retorted peevishly.

She knew that revelation would sting, but somehow the filter on her words had slipped the moment they'd both jumped on the offensive. 'Look, nobody's taking any jobs anywhere else, okay? Nobody has committed to anything, and everybody – and I do mean everybody – has their priorities straight. Kids first, yes? As we agreed. And if we could actually have a conversation that lasts more than five minutes without an interruption or a misunderstanding then I reckon you would see that.'

'Oh,' said Taffy, sounding eerily like Ben and Tom after a telling-off.

'Exactly,' said Holly. 'Now, do you still want to get this coffee, or are you champing at the bit to run off and ask Dan what his plans are?' she asked him easily, knowing all too well where his mind would be fixated.

He dithered. 'Maybe we should all sit down together again and talk this through?'

'You think?' teased Holly. 'Look, we all know that a proper Partners' Meeting is way overdue, so let's just put one in the diary and then breathe, okay? You can save up all your issues and grievances, and I can have a better idea of a few plans I'd like to implement.'

'What plans?'

'Now that would be telling,' said Holly, pausing for a moment, 'but I think you'll like them. I've just been thinking, ever since I've been at The Practice, we've always been on a mission to rescue something, or change something – isn't it time we took a step back and tried to *build* something instead – something we can be proud of?'

'In all our free time?' Taffy said drily, unintentionally raining on her parade. He shrugged. 'Have you noticed how we're all just juggling so much that we're not really communicating – at home, or at work?'

Holly nodded, quietly delighted to hear him acknowledge it, accepting that she might need to pick her moments a little more carefully before talking about change. 'But it won't last for ever. That's parenthood for you. And if it helps, I'm told it's just the first eighteen years or so that are the hardest.'

Holly sat back in the doctors' lounge three hours later and smiled. She knew without a shadow of a doubt that every single one of her appointments this morning would have been more measured, more effective and less stressful for her patients had it been just five minutes longer.

She'd Googled the stats in the wee small hours, when the idea buzzed round her brain and refused to let her sleep. No longer were GPs legally required to offer ten-minute appointments; it was at the discretion of each practice and each GP. Obviously there were cost and care considerations. Either a longer working day to see the same number of patients, or fewer patients seen ... Compromises either way. But what Holly needed to consider was whether the benefits outweighed the obstacles.

Having seen young Carly Bartlett this morning, and spent nearly twenty minutes unravelling and reapplying the dressings required for her inflamed psoriasis, maybe it was just something to consider for chronic conditions that were less than straightforward?

Ah, but then, whichever way you looked at it, you'd be creating a tiered system; who's to say that one patient might feel hard done by, if he'd only got ten minutes for his throat infection?

If only she had the time and the information to think things through more clearly. Simply booking people in for double appointment slots just didn't really address the issues.

'Holly?' Tilly stood beside her, fidgeting from foot to foot and clearly loath to interrupt.

'Everything okay?' Holly asked, sitting forward on autopilot, always assuming the worst when a junior doctor looked this nervous. The time Alice had got the ear syringing kit stuck in Gladys Jones's ear was a notable example.

'Have you got a moment? To chat? I'd just love to ask you something.'

Well, thought Holly, obviously that answer being 'no, no, hell no'. But of course, she smiled, and scooched over on the sofa. 'Sure,' she replied, kissing goodbye to her five minutes' peace, but trying to be a good egg about it.

Tilly sat down and folded the fabric of her culottes into pleats in her nervousness. 'Well Alice and I were talking. And I confessed to her that I'm, well, not a very good GP.' Tilly glanced up to gauge Holly's reaction.

Holly just nodded. 'Okay.' She didn't honestly feel that she could contradict her, having heard how she'd handled the Hannah Porter case quite so clumsily. Something she'd intended to address, but, she reminded herself, they all had to start somewhere.

Tilly blinked, all braced to bat aside Holly's reassurances and a little off balance when none materialised. 'So, the thing is, I was talking about moving on—'

'Oh no, that's not the answer,' Holly cut in. 'You can't just run away if things are difficult. The only way around this is to go through. To get better.' She wasn't proud that her immediate thought was that one less doctor on staff would essentially scupper all her plans for reorganisation.

Tilly nodded. 'That's what Alice said. In fact, Alice went one further.' She paused, culottes fully concertinaed. 'She thought that having a mentor, someone with more life experience in a family setting, maybe, might be a good way for me to learn. I mean, I know all the medicine inside out and back to front; it's just the empathy that seems to elude me.'

Holly laughed; she didn't mean to, but it was like talking to a young Julia Channing and she couldn't help but draw comparisons with her ex-colleague. On the other hand, what if Julia had asked for help earlier in her career? 'Oh, I'm so sorry, Tilly. It's not that your situation is funny. It was just a déjà vu thing for a moment.'

Tilly shrugged. 'I don't really get it.'

Holly laid her hand on Tilly's arm and smiled. 'You're not really supposed to. So, do you want me to talk to Taffy for you? See if he's up for a little mentoring? Or maybe Dan, actually, as he has a little more time on his hands.'

Tilly said nothing, almost as though she were hopeful that Holly might cotton on by herself.

'Oh,' said Holly after a moment. 'You weren't thinking . . . ?'

Tilly nodded. 'I would be so honoured if you would mentor me. All the patients talk about you so highly, and the team here too. The number of times they've pointed out how *you* would have done things over the last year . . . It's like your way is the Gold Standard around here.'

'Are you just blowing smoke up my arse, young lady?' Holly said shortly.

'No!' Tilly smiled. 'Well I suppose I could have just not mentioned it.'

'That might have been better,' Holly said firmly, determined not to be a pushover, but secretly delighted to hear that 'her way' was widely considered the right way. It boded particularly well for making changes, on the basis of 'what was best for the patients'.

She frowned. 'Well, Tilly, I'm really touched that you asked. But you do know I'm not really back yet – not to mention the four, well, five, children that I have at home . . .'

'Don't say no,' said Tilly, suddenly animated. 'What about a trade? I mean, with all that stuff on your plate, I get that mentoring me is not really viable. But, well, it has to be you.'

Holly shook her head. 'Flattery is a risky ploy, you know. Give me reasons. I mean, be blunt. Tell me what you need to learn.'

Tilly started counting off reasons on her fingers, all well considered, eloquently phrased and alarmingly Holly-specific.

'And really, it comes down to having some understanding of becoming a mother, raising a child and all the inherent concerns that are part of the package. We're all really good doctors here, Holly, but you're the only mum. We need to learn what makes the difference between a functional appointment and one where the patient goes away feeling fully heard and understood.'

'Bugger,' said Holly simply.

Tilly's face broke into a smile. 'So you'll do it? You'll be my mentor?'

'You'll need to walk the dog with me first thing every morning. Early. Sometimes the pig comes too. We can talk through your day ahead and evaluate the day before. It's literally the only time I have free.'

'Great,' said Tilly, not batting an eyelid at the bizarre arrangement. 'I've been meaning to get fit.'

'And then we might double-up on some appointments, the trickier ones, so you can see how it evolves.' Holly paused. 'I think it's really important to evaluate these as well. We both know the Hannah Porter situation was less than ideal.' Tilly opened her mouth to speak, but Holly held up a hand. 'No recriminations, Tilly, it's just a learning curve. I had a similar situation with a patient when I first started out that didn't end so well. It's not something you ever forget.'

Tilly nodded earnestly and Holly decided just to jump in

with both feet. 'And in return, you are going to become my secret research assistant.'

'Secret assistant, or secret research?' clarified Tilly.

'Both,' said Holly firmly. 'I'm going to need some data to make a few planning decisions and you're going to help me collect it. Quietly.' She appraised Tilly's sparkling eyes, now filled with excitement and promise rather than nerves. 'Can you do that?'

Tilly held out her hand. 'Deal,' she said, flopping back into the sofa cushions with a sigh of relief.

'Am I really so terrifying?' Holly asked, intrigued.

'Not terrifying. I just knew that you had your hands full already, so it was a bit of a long shot, and I really wanted you to say yes. I don't know how you do it.'

'Neither do I,' said Holly frankly. 'I just have really good help and lovely friends, I think.' She was only too aware that without Plum, Lizzie and Elsie, there was no way she could even entertain a return to work, let alone her madcap plotting.

'And how is Plum settling in?' asked Tilly. 'She seems really fun, really focused.'

'The kids adore her,' said Holly simply, not wishing to talk out of school.

'I thought I might invite her to the pub one night so she can meet a few people in town? When I first moved here, I only knew Alice, but that was hard enough.'

'That's a really lovely idea,' said Holly, touched that Tilly also bought into the paying-it-forward philosophy that she herself espoused. 'She only works three nights a week, so it shouldn't be too hard to arrange.'

'Brilliant,' said Tilly simply, looking pleased, and Holly began to wonder whether the young girl beside her had ever really settled in Larkford, and whether they should, in fact, have had this conversation months ago. 'Now, while you're feeling benevolent, how are your gingerbread-making skills? I was hoping to make some with the kids for the Christening but we only seem to end up eating the dough.' She paused. 'It does not bode well for the Bake Sale either.'

Chapter 30

The weekend was upon them before they knew it and Holly watched Lulu standing in front of the mirror, twirling this way and that in the primrose tulle skirt. Taking her shopping had been a delight and an education.

'Pretty,' said Lulu, pointing at her own reflection.

'Beautiful,' agreed Holly.

Although Lulu remained a child of few words, she had a natural charm that seemed to be growing by the day as her confidence flourished. Today would certainly be a challenge for her, but Holly had no worries on that front; she had a few ideas up her sleeve to keep things running smoothly.

Ben and Tom charged into her bedroom, striking superhero poses back to back – Batman and Darth Vader unlikely allies for the day. Holly couldn't help but smile at their determination. 'And what happened to your smart trousers for the Christening?' she asked.

'Didn't fit,' said Ben, flashing a complicit glance at his twin.

'We must have grown,' added Tom, ever the more adept with a fib.

She knew full well that the proper thing to do was insist upon a change of attire; she knew also that some of their friends might struggle to accept how casual they were being about the girls' Christening, but Holly saw no need to tie herself in knots pleasing other people.

It was quite remarkable how quickly her pendulum had swung from people-pleasing to authenticity over the last few months; perhaps parenting quite so many children might have that effect on anyone? Equally, in bringing Plum into her home and family, she felt a responsibility to lead from the front, to demonstrate with her actions the kind of family she was trying to build – one of inclusion, acceptance and peace. Picking her battles was both a necessary by-product of having too much on her plate, and a timely reminder that not everything actually mattered.

If her boys were happy and comfortable in their chosen outfits, wasn't that more important than the aspirational family photo traditional on these occasions?

Lulu twirled once again in front of the mirror, her two superheroes flanking her in the reflection. Holly blinked, trying to capture the moment in her mind's eye to revisit time and time again – a perfect moment of family life, a mental photograph to be treasured.

'How are we doing, Wifey?' asked Taffy from the doorway, one of his soft, slow smiles lighting up his face at the scene.

'All good,' replied Holly, grateful that Taffy seemed to be fully present this morning, rather than the distracted plonker he had so often been of late. 'Plum's just giving the girls some food and then we're good to go. Once we've wrangled them into their Christening gowns, anyway.'

Taffy watched the boys and Lulu twirling and laughing and a shadow of guilt passed over his face. 'I know Mum's been a bit OTT about those bloody gowns, but it's important to her.'

Holly nodded. 'I know. I do.'

She didn't.

She couldn't understand why Patty had this obsession with frilly, lacy Christening gowns for the girls. This wasn't 1922. In a world of cotton and stretch fabric, it actually seemed a little cruel to bend and fold her babies into these starchy, itchy dresses.

Taffy perched on the edge of the bed beside her, apparently able to read her like a book. 'You have to remember, Holls, that she missed out on all the girly stuff with us. I was the size of a decent turkey when I hatched and my brothers were bigger still. She didn't get the chance to dress us up and fuss over us.'

Holly nodded. 'But surely all her granddaughters can't be subjected to this deluge of frilliness?' She paused. 'Don't you think it's funny that all of you have had daughters? It's like the Universe is trying to balance out the Jones DNA or something.'

Taffy grinned. 'Wouldn't be at all surprised. Four Jones boys is enough for anyone.' He picked up the Christening gowns from the bed beside them, wincing at the prickly lace that snagged on his fingers. He looked at the dresses, then up at her face and Holly could almost see the cogs turning in his mind, as he attempted to please both mother and wife.

She took his hand. 'Look, if this is what you need, then this is what we'll do. But to be clear, once they're old enough and looking at the photos, I am laying full responsibility at your door.' She grinned. 'There's no way they're blaming me for those monstrosities.'

Taffy looked up, watching the boys at ease, having fun. 'This isn't a you-versus-Mum problem, though, is it? The priority is the girls.' He smiled ruefully. 'They have a right to enjoy their big day too.'

Internally, Holly cheered. If there was one thing she'd

learned about married life with Taffy, it was that he liked to make his own decisions. She could lead him there, lay out the options, but ultimately, lurking in his subconscious, was a man who needed to feel that his say was important. He would never admit it – it certainly wasn't a part of the enlightened man he strived to be, but nevertheless . . .

She reached under the bed and pulled out a box, leaves of tissue paper rustling. 'How do you think your mum would feel about these, as a compromise?'

Taffy unfolded the two dresses, identically soft cotton lawn in the lightest shade of lemon, the tiny cream tights and bootees tumbling out onto the bed. Feminine, fresh, soft and comfortable. He glanced up and saw Lulu's eyes widen in excitement. 'Like me!' she cried, holding out the layers of her primrose skirt.

Taffy's eyes crinkled into the smile that Holly loved so much, as the penny dropped with what Holly was trying to achieve, with such a simple gesture, to show Lulu that she was part of something bigger than herself.

'Just like you,' he said, standing up and twirling her around in his arms, Holly's heart lifting as Lulu's shrieks of laughter grew with each spin.

There was no doubt in Holly's mind that Larkford's idea of 'wetting the babies' heads' was a little extreme. The ceremony had been tasteful and considered – even if Dan had jokingly insisted on making the Reverend specifically invite him into the church, just in case he was harbouring the devil – and the godparents had, on the whole, behaved beautifully. Holly smiled to herself that it was the godparents' behaviour rather than that of her children that had given her most cause for concern.

Seeing Alice's face light up as Jamie made the ceremony by the skin of his teeth, courtesy of an airline delay, only served to confirm that they had made the right choice by keeping it local. The girls' godparents really were their extended family, the people who would surround them as they grew up. A little incestuous, possibly. But equally reassuring.

And now, The Kingsley Arms was the focal point of the proceedings, with champagne flowing and canapés circulating and Holly having the secret suspicion that a more absorbent food choice might have been advisable.

Plum walked over to where Holly was quietly feeding the girls, Ben, Tom and Lulu looping around her legs with each step. 'And so now we have time for the chicken. Hop up.' She gestured for the three older children to sit around the table, Lizzie's children running over to join them, with Coco and Eric in hot pursuit, nudging in between them for a prime 'chicken' location.

Obviously Holly wasn't the only one hoping for more substantial sustenance, as Dan soon joined them, pinching chips from the children's plates and making them squeal. He sat down beside Lulu and began telling a joke about bogeys that had all of the children in fits of giggles and Lulu's eyes wide – no adult in her usual orbit being perhaps quite so irreverent and silly. The expression on Dan's face as Lulu laughed told a thousand stories and Holly looked around automatically for Grace.

Several metres away, but watching their interaction with a heartfelt intensity, Grace was leaning against the bar, ostensibly listening to one of the Major's amusing anecdotes. She noticed Holly's attention and smiled, a wistful hint of emotion reflected in her eyes. If only, thought Holly ... If only Grace and Dan were able to have the conversation they clearly needed to have to make sure their tracks ran together, parallel and true, rather than criss-crossing needlessly as they both struggled to agree on a destination.

Tilly sat down beside Holly, scooping Olivia onto her lap for a cuddle. Holly flexed her newly liberated arm and smiled her thanks; there was nothing like carting around growing twins to improve one's upper body strength, but sometimes it was nice to have a little break. 'You're looking incredibly stylish today,' Holly said, taking in Tilly's unusual polish and panache. 'You're very sweet to get so dolled up for these little urchins. I'd like to say they appreciate it, but . . .' She gestured helplessly towards the yoghurt stain on the skirt of her dress.

Tilly shrugged, apparently easy either way. 'Alice helped me out. I just needed a little lift. You know what it's like — it turns out there can be too much of a good thing when it comes to comfy clothes.'

Holly nodded. 'It's one of the perks of coming back to work actually. I have to actually get out of my dungarees. Far too comfy.'

'Maybe we should all just wear scrubs and then we wouldn't have to give it any thought,' Tilly suggested. She dropped her voice. 'I just wanted to say thank you actually. I hadn't realised how much I'd been stressing about my role here until I talked to you. Thinking about leaving . . . I guess I just wasn't sure how useful my particular skillset actually was around here.' As she spoke, her eyes followed Plum as she darted around the table, helping the children cut up their food, refilling drinks and mopping up spills.

In the face of Plum's remarkable efficiency, Holly was half tempted to say the same about herself. 'Well, I for one would be really sad if you left. I think Larkford has a lot to offer, and I believe you do too.' She paused. 'I've been thinking a lot about our mentoring plan actually. Not to mention our little research project. How about you promise to stay for six months and then we'll review?'

'Only if you promise the same,' Tilly said. 'I heard a rumour you were thinking of private practice.'

Holly flushed a little. 'You really shouldn't believe everything that you hear; there's always rumours in Larkford.'

'Hmm,' said Tilly, not so easily fobbed off. Her eyes were still following Plum around the table, but the cogs in her mind were clearly whirring. 'That's one of the things I can't seem to get used to, actually.'

Elsie appeared at Holly's elbow, looking decidedly sheepish and uncharacteristically keeping a low profile. 'Hello, my darlings, room for a small one?' she asked, without waiting for a reply, as she squeezed into the gap between them on the upholstered bench.

Holly glanced over towards the door, uncertain what had prompted Elsie's sudden desire to join the children's table, when indisputably the better part of this party was happening at the bar. A geriatric cohort in red trousers or pearls hovered in the entrance, weighing up whether they would be welcome at what was clearly a private party. They had Sarandon Hall written all over them, and yet Elsie pressed herself against Holly's shoulders in an unusual display of physical affection.

As Teddy Kingsley apologised and waved them on their way, Elsie visibly relaxed. 'Do you know,' said Holly, 'that's the third time you've been incredibly cagey around your cronies. I'm beginning to think there's more to your departure from Sarandon Hall than you've been telling me. Like what kind of scandal got you booted out of a swanky retirement community with a cheque in your hand!'

Elsie sat up a little taller, her familiar flippancy already reasserting itself. 'You know me, darling, I couldn't keep a secret if my life depended on it.' She stood up and returned to the bar with a relieved smile, only serving to convince Holly that her favourite pensioner did indeed have something up her sleeve. As if buying and renovating an entire townhouse right next door wasn't enough . . .

As Plum took charge of Lottie, leaving Dan on duty as children's entertainer extraordinaire, Holly stood up and stretched. It had been a huge mistake to squeeze into this dress, no matter how lovely it looked, or indeed how flattering the photos might be. She glanced down at the girls in their peachy-soft lawn dresses and considered when she might start taking her own advice. She surreptitiously tugged at the constrictive underwear making this dress even a possibility and swallowed hard, indigestion her almost constant companion today.

And that's when she realised.

In fact, there was a small part of her that wanted to rush across the bar and share her light-bulb moment with her patient right there and then. The very cause of Pru Hartley's ongoing battle with chronic acid reflux had been right in front of her eyes – well, under Pru's clothes to be more precise. Years of failed dieting had meant that Pru's Pantz had become an everyday staple in her wardrobe, as she refused to give in gracefully and accept the role of portly baker. If only they'd looked beyond the medical and into the sartorial, they might have found a solution that didn't involve endless prescriptions and restrictive diets.

Tilly was right, of course, a stylish ensemble could give you a lift, but there was a darker side to fashion that was best avoided at all costs. To Holly's mind, it was yet another endorsement of her lifestyle-litmus that if she couldn't run after a toddler, lift a baby, or enjoy a meal, then any trend was best ignored.

Holly grinned, enjoying that feeling of solving a puzzle, of helping a patient and, let's face it, of knowing that even allowing for her maternity leave, she was still a community GP at heart – her patients never far from her thoughts. She wondered how many private doctors could honestly say the same.

Chapter 31

Grace tentatively sipped her ginger and rhubarb Bellini, Teddy Kingsley's cocktails being notorious for unseating the uninitiated. As the hit of alcohol made her blink, the fresh, sweet and sour taste of the local rhubarb liqueur made her smile and she nodded her approval to Teddy, who was hovering behind the bar awaiting her verdict. It was to be his gift to Holly and Taffy – the perfect cocktail with which to wet the babies' heads.

'Just gorgeous,' she said, 'but maybe limit them to one per person or you'll have Pru Hartley attempting to Riverdance again, and nobody wants that, what with her dicky hip.'

Spoken partly in jest, Grace knew only too well that a little alcoholic lubrication went a long way in Larkford – their over-familiarity with one another's lives left little by way of reserves, and anything that tipped the scales to further loosen tongues and inhibitions was, in general, to be avoided.

For the sake of the peace.

For the sake of continued friendships, tolerances and neighbourly relations.

After all, you didn't necessarily have to love thy neighbour, but outright acrimony in a community this small tended to burn hot and fast. It was, in short, unsustainable.

She only had to glance at Cassie Holland to illustrate her point: the way she aggressively avoided the new headmaster, hectored every parent in town with her green agenda and, of late, went out of her way to gird Connor Danes's festival plans with ill feeling and acrimony.

Sadly, on this last, she was not alone. Everywhere Grace turned this past week, there had been huddles of discussion and distrust about Connor's festival. Grace sighed and slipped another canapé down to Noodle and Doodle at her feet, relieved that Holly's definition of friends-and-family at this event extended to the four-legged variety as well.

Even the thought of Connor pulled her up short. She squinted through the groups of friends chatting, laughing, celebrating and realised with a dull thud that Connor was not among them. Connor, whose moods of late had been mercurial at best. Connor, who had phoned only yesterday to try and get an appointment with Alice, only to mutter 'not to worry' despondently on hearing she had no availability, and turning down the offer of an appointment with Taffy 'because he wouldn't understand' before abruptly hanging up.

Grace felt the Bellini churn in her stomach, an acidic bile suddenly choking her, as a cold wave of prescience swept over her. Could it be, had she actually turned away a patient in urgent need? Because from Grace's perspective, mental health issues like depression were often more worrying than the physical. But then Connor wasn't depressed, was he? All that energy being funnelled into his new ventures? He surely wouldn't be able to pull all that together, if he was struggling to get out of bed in the morning.

She crossed the room in four strides, catching hold of Kitty Clarke's arm, tugging her away from her bovine conversation with Rupert and Mims. The vets of Larkford, it seemed, were equally as committed to their patients as the GPs, even on high days and holidays.

'Have you seen Connor today?' Grace asked, aiming for casual enquiry and falling well wide of the mark.

Kitty shook her head. 'I haven't actually, but I wasn't sure he'd be here anyway though, you know? I mean, he loves Holly and Taffy, don't get me wrong – I just thought that, well, it being a Christening and all that . . . ?'

She didn't need to explain further; her awkward skirting of the issue was really explanation enough.

Grace nodded, momentarily appeased, disbelieving that she hadn't considered it. 'How do you think he's doing?' she asked Kitty. 'Really?'

Kitty shrugged. 'He's a bit of an enigma really, isn't he? I feel for him, actually. Can't be easy being him some days, can it? Everyone seems to have an opinion, sometimes before they've even met him.' She cast a filthy look in Cassie's direction, her outspoken judgements carrying across the room. 'And some people just seem to take against him on principle, as though it's a natural price to pay for being successful. Professionally, I mean.'

They both stilled for a moment; nobody could ever accuse Connor of having a successful personal life, after all.

Grace sighed. 'You know, I genuinely believed that trying things The Larkford Way, would make all the difference for him. Being in a community, all pulling together, but he just seems so—'

'Lost?' finished Kitty, nodding, a slight flush colouring her neck. The genuine concern and affection for him were all too clear to Grace, even if it was obvious that Kitty herself was still in denial. 'He took on Mrs Hudson's Irish wolfhound without a second thought, you know? And with all the other animals that seem to have been foisted upon him of late . . .'

'He's not great at saying no to anyone, is he?' Grace agreed. 'Or maybe he can just recognise a lonely soul?'

'Who's a lonely soul?' interrupted Alice, still pale and wan, sipping at sparkling water, but determined not to miss out. Especially as Jamie had flown in for the weekend and was circling the room, happily in his element, a drink in his hand and a smile on his face.

'Connor,' said both Grace and Kitty at the same time.

Grace felt that same flicker of alarm as she watched the expression falter on Alice's face. She never got to know what was said inside the consulting rooms at The Practice, of course, but Alice clearly knew more than she was letting on.

'Where is he?' Alice asked, looking around, although generally it was never hard to spot Connor in a crowd – his height, his charisma and his habitual crowd of hangers-on normally marked out his presence whether he liked it or not. 'I'm sure Holly said she'd invited him.' Her brow furrowed as the same train of thought clearly passed through her mind as Kitty's. 'Still, maybe it's not his cup of tea? He's probably wining and dining Docie Lynn in some posh Cotswold eaterie, saved only for those in the know.'

Alice didn't sound convinced, but Grace didn't miss the tightening of Kitty's expression at the very suggestion.

'I need to look in on Jamieson later anyway,' said Kitty. 'I'll get all the scandal for you then.' She managed a smile and Alice nudged her sympathetically, catching Grace unawares. Normally so attuned to those around her, she had somehow missed the flourishing friendship between these two. It was obvious, now she came to think about it – both utterly obsessed with animals, both young, committed professionals without families to rush home to. She smiled at the thought that they had each other for moral support, even as she felt superfluous for a moment. All her attention of late had been so caught up with Dan and their plans for the future that she knew she'd neglected her friendship with Alice; she just hadn't realised that Kitty had stepped so smoothly into the breach.

As she watched the easy banter back and forth between them, she realised how far out of the loop she had fallen, especially when Jamie ambled over, tousling Kitty's hair with easy affection and familiarity. The decade between them suddenly felt like a lifetime.

Grace slipped away, almost unnoticed, as Kitty began filling Jamie and Alice in on the progress of each individual goat to join Connor's venture, obviously already invested in the enterprise. Whether that was professionally or personally remained to be seen, but Grace couldn't help thinking that Kitty would be the perfect antidote to many of the stresses and dramas in Connor Danes's life.

'Heard you talking about Docie Lynn just now,' said Pru Hartley with an acerbic tone, as Grace wandered over to the table where all the Christening goodies were laid out as a buffet. 'You'll get tarred with the same brush, you know, if you get involved in that Connor's plans and schemes. He's a troublemaker, no doubt. He's going to drag this town's good name through the mud, you wait and see. So long "prettiest market town" and hello "drug-ridden festival hell hole" – you mark my words.' Pru rubbed at her sternum irritably, her acid reflux obviously acting up, the more she worked herself up.

'Surely not,' said Grace easily, refusing to bite – except into one of Pru's deliciously moist brownies. 'It's really not that kind of festival. You should talk to him about it, honestly.'

Pru looked at her darkly. 'As if there's any other kind of festival. You Google Glastonbury and see what I mean.'

'Talk to him, Pru. He's one of the good ones.'

Pru gave her a scathing look. 'You'll note that he's not here, is he? Supporting the very people who made him welcome?' She tutted. 'Cassie's right: I don't think rock stars are known for their community spirit, Grace. Don't be swayed; dead wife or not, that one's nothing but trouble.' She paused, making an abrupt conversational turn. 'Now tell me — what do you think of them brownies? They're gluten-free, you know. I've been experimenting a bit because I reckon there's a chance I'm celeriac.'

'You're what?' Grace managed, spraying crumbs everywhere.

'On account of my stomach problems — cutting out the gluten might be the answer, according to Dr Graham. You know, celeriac?'

As accustomed as they all were to Pru's constant malapropisms, it still took Grace a moment to realise she meant coeliac, by which time, Pru had turned away to offer more cake to the Reverend, her sudden Christian politeness in direct contrast to her comments about Connor, leaving Grace disquieted by both Pru's vehement outburst and her casual disregard for the English language.

True, there was only a handful of people who knew the reality of Connor's situation — and Grace was beginning to doubt that even they saw the full picture — but was Pru actually typical of how the other Larkford residents viewed him? If so, he might actually be up for more opposition to his plans than he realised, or she'd acknowledged.

She abandoned her delicious brownie on principle, her

empty stomach protesting loudly, seeking out Dan among the crush of bodies for a second, sane opinion. Were lots of her friends and neighbours rather more two-faced than she'd realised?

She marched across the room, upset at how disappointed that thought made her feel, even though the slight was surely Connor's not her own. Seeing Dan still happily ensconced at the children's table, she ground to a halt, abruptly changing gear, as her breath caught in her throat and all annoyances dissipated in a single moment.

As Dan pulled out Lulu's chosen playing card with a dramatic flourish and the little girl gasped in delight at his apparent magic, Grace only had eyes for Dan – for his adoring gaze, his unerring focus and his absolute attentiveness to one small exuberant child.

'They're gorgeous together, aren't they?' said Holly quietly, coming to stand beside her. 'Do you think he sees it yet?'

Grace had to swallow very hard before she was capable of answering. 'I don't know. I daren't hope. He never – I mean, he always said that—'

'The theory of adoption is very different to the reality, don't you think?' Holly suggested gently. 'Maybe for Dan, it would have felt like an arranged marriage, whereas this is clearly—'

'Love at first sight?' said Grace, an emotional wobble to her voice.

'I think so,' said Holly, tucking her arm through Grace's as much in affection as support. 'Maybe it's worth having the conversation again. Time might be of the essence, if you're serious about Lulu.' She sighed. 'I can't bear the thought of her being shuttled from pillar to post. I even suggested to Taffy that she just stay with us – she's happy, she's settled. Losing her mum and her grandma will be hard enough.'

'And what did Taffy say?' asked Grace, her heart in her mouth, as she waited for the answer.

'He said that she was happy with us because of the sense of family and belonging at home; that there was only really one person she'd truly bonded with . . .'

'Dan?' managed Grace, tears filling her eyes as Holly nodded. 'And do you think he—?'

'I think he loves her, whether he knows it yet or not. I think he loves her far more than any of these other hare-brained schemes he's been cooking up to keep himself busy,' Holly said.

Grace's focus returned unerringly to the tableau in the corner, as Ben, Tom and Lulu bested each other in a rambunctious game of Snap and Dan watched on contentedly, no apparent interest in heading to the bar or talking to his friends.

Still waters ran deep with Dan Carter, as Grace knew only too well, but perhaps there was more going on behind those hypnotising brown eyes than even she had realised? Were their choices really so disparate if she maintained her stance on pregnancy? She sighed, no answers immediately forth-coming and no idea how even to begin the conversation with Dan. It hardly boded well for their future as potential parents, if they were still stumbling over the basics.

If nothing else, Grace realised, today had been a timely reminder about the dangers of putting all of one's eggs in a single basket, not to mention the fleeting nature of happiness and security. A gentle nudge from the Universe, perhaps, that actions spoke louder than words ever could?

Chapter 32

Holly smiled, finally able to relax – the deed was done, the troops were fed and watered and nobody had fallen out, even when Tilly's gingerbread men had taken out one of the Major's fillings. It was the very definition of success, by any measure of the recent Christenings in Larkford. What's more, it had provided the perfect excuse to get Alice and Jamie in the same country, nay, the same room and it was immensely cheering to see that their instinctive chemistry was still very much in evidence.

If only there was a logical way to bring him home for good – a solution that didn't require Alice to lose her dignity and beg, ideally, although Holly could see that she was sorely tempted.

But then, look at him. Jamie Yardley was a wonderful man. Not that dissimilar to Taffy in many ways – always wanting to do the right thing, even when that meant occasionally short-changing their loved ones into the bargain. Seeing Taffy and Jamie side by side, exchanging stories, really highlighted the thought in her head.

She clearly wasn't the only one.

'Now, in a cinema near you – *Two Good Men*!' said Lizzie, in her best bonkers-American-movie-trailer voice. 'You want the truth? You can't handle the truth.' Lizzie grinned, disproportionately pleased with herself. 'Maybe you should warn Alice what she's getting into. Being with a "good man" is not for the faint-hearted.' She threw an arm around Holly's shoulders and squeezed, dropping her voice to a whisper. 'As well you know.'

Holly smiled weakly. 'You'd never imagine that "doing the right thing" could ever be considered a character flaw, would you?'

Lizzie just nodded and then kissed Holly firmly on the cheek. 'Not something that will ever trouble my darling Will,' she said, glancing over and catching him checking the rugby scores on his iPhone and propping up the bar. 'Do you think I should intervene or leave the poor bastard in peace? He should really get a medal just for not upping and leaving me recently. Apparently, I am not an easy patient,' she said, shrugging as though the claim eluded her.

'Am I to understand that you've replaced me, Holly?' Elsie's imperious voice beside her made Holly jump, cutting through the conversation around them like crystal and prompting Lizzie to make a swift exit. Elsie after a few glasses of fizz was always a little unpredictable, but there was an edge of friction in her voice that worried Holly more.

'I hardly think that's even possible,' she replied with a smile.

'Oh really,' said Elsie, thawing not even the slightest. 'Then perhaps you could tell me why Reverend Taylor over there is oh-so-delighted that you've taken her advice – *her* advice, Holly – about your quandary.' Her brow furrowed and she leaned forward, dropping her voice to a stage whisper. 'And I didn't even know you *had* one!'

Holly felt a little blindsided, somehow having assumed that her conversation with Reverend Taylor might have fallen under the privacy of a confessional, despite neither of them being Catholic, or indeed any confessions having been shared. 'Erm—'

Elsie took her hand and squeezed it. 'Not that I mind you asking a Higher Power for a little input, my darling, but I never feel you're getting the full picture, if you discount the sins of the flesh.' She gave a slightly tipsy wink and stumbled against Holly's side. 'If I'd known you were having "marital difficulties" I'd have been only too happy to offer a little wisdom of my own.'

Elsie's version of discretion meant dropping her voice a scant decibel and exaggeratedly mouthing her words. There couldn't be a single soul in a three-metre radius that hadn't heard every single word.

'It's not marriage stuff; it's been work stuff,' Holly protested unconvincingly, knowing as well as Elsie did, that the boundaries between the two were rather blurry in this particular situation.

'And . . . ?' queried Elsie, her pique seeming to thaw a little in the light of Holly's obvious discomfort, conveniently disregarding the fact that she'd hardly been forthcoming herself of late.

Holly glanced around, knowing she'd made a mistake in putting off the inevitable. There was no pulling the wool over Elsie's eyes, and now they were having this conversation in the middle of a Christening party! 'And, I've been trying to reassess my priorities. You know: mum, wife, doctor, friend, et cetera . . .'

Elsie shook her head. 'There's no point trying to make a linear decision – you're all of those things – and they all overlap. At best what you have there is a Venn diagram. Yes, that's right, I was paying attention when Tom showed me his maths book.' She waved her hands around in the air, as though to illustrate the intersecting circles, and sloshed champagne all over her wrist. 'You'll end up going bonkers if you try and tease your tangled web apart, you know,' she proclaimed.

'Too late,' replied Holly with a strangled laugh. She paused. 'Do you ever feel like there must be a Secret Option Number 23 in life, that you just don't know about yet?'

'All the time,' said Elsie seriously. 'But you know, I think sometimes the best way has to be *your* way – because you're the one who has to live with the consequences, you know. So,' she finally dropped her voice to a discreet level, 'if there's a deal-breaker – something that you know you just cannot accept, then you have to give that priority, don't you? Because everything else is just a question of degree.' She glanced around the pub for an example. 'Take young Tilly, for example – so busy striving, questing for the Greater Good, she's been ignoring her deal-breaker.'

'Which is?' Holly asked, intrigued.

Elsie shook her head with a smile. 'I can hardly tell *you*, before she's figured it out herself, now can I? Don't worry, it won't affect her work, but I think somebody ought to tell darling Matthew that he's barking up the wrong tree.'

'Whereas I'm surrounded by a veritable arboretum of trees – an embarrassment of riches – and I still can't make up my mind what to do for the best. First World problems, eh?' said Holly, before visibly giving herself a shake. 'But we've plenty of time to sort me out. Today is about the girls.'

They turned to look at Olivia and Lottie, out cold in their pram, blankets askew and sticky fingers shoved in their mouths.

'Obviously they're savouring every moment of it,' said Elsie drily, but at last, finally, with a warmth and humour in her voice that had been noticeably missing. 'And look who else is enjoying their day in a party frock.'

Holly slowly exhaled, unaware she'd even been holding her breath on this one, as she took in the scene around the table. Dan, Grace and Lulu, all oblivious to the room around them, deeply involved in a game of Snap that had Lulu shrieking with laughter every time somebody won a round. Her cheeks were flushed a healthy pink and her eyes were bright, clean bouncing hair tumbling from her smart ponytail and traces of chocolate on her dress from her special sundae – she was literally unrecognisable from the pale waif that had arrived in their lives.

'Oh, that one will be a heartbreaker one day,' said Elsie shrewdly.

Holly could only hope that Elsie didn't mean any time soon. From where she was standing, the possibilities for heartbreak were only too obvious.

Any thoughts of love, life and Venn diagrams were quickly put firmly on hold half an hour later, as a wave of discontented voices erupted in the bar. Holly looked up sharply, unwilling for any local dramas to disrupt the day. Her heart sank a little as she saw Taffy at the very heart of the dispute. Excusing herself from Elsie's side and making sure that all of her children were still safely under Plum's watchful eye, Holly walked towards him.

'It's just short-sighted and stubborn,' Taffy was saying. 'Almost as if you're against the idea on principle, just because of who he is.'

'And maybe you only like the idea *because* of who he is,' cut back Cassie Holland, her face red and her fists tightly curled in anger. 'You and your incestuous little clique – oh so supportive of each other, but do you ever stop to think about the rest of us?'

Holly blinked hard, a little thrown by the vociferousness of Cassie's ire. 'What's going on?' she asked. 'This is a Christening after all, not a town meeting.'

The group around her quieted instantly, some of them, like Pru Hartley, looking a little ashamed of themselves, almost as though they'd forgotten why they were drinking mulled wine and eating miniature sandwiches at three o'clock in the afternoon.

'Connor's a good guy,' Taffy said, as he stood up from his bar stool and made to walk away. 'His intentions are good.'

'The road to hell is paved with good intentions,' shot back Cassie, brazenly determined to have the last word.

'Well, you would know,' said Taffy over his shoulder, with uncharacteristic bite.

Holly caught his arm as he strode by. 'Are you okay?'

He shook his head. 'You know how some days it's amazing living in such a tight-knit community, where all our lives overlap? Well, today isn't one of those days.' He sighed. 'This is supposed to be our day, but instead it's just another melting pot of arsy neighbours and intrusive opinions.'

'True,' said Holly. 'But were you honestly expecting anything different? And for every Cassie Holland, there's a Grace Allen, or a Tilly Campbell — it's all about balance. Look.' She turned and gestured towards the children's table where Dan had now initiated a slightly boisterous game of 'Who am I?'.

Grace, Tilly and Plum were all dotted around the table with various children on their laps and sticky fingers on their winter finery, faces alight with the easy joy of letting go and embracing their own inner child.

'Do I like muddy puddles?' asked Tilly with enthusiasm.

'Or have a brother called George?' She made little oinking noises, as she tickled Tom beside her.

Holly cast a glance over her shoulder back towards the bar where tensions were still running high. 'It's all about where you choose to focus.'

'And not just this afternoon, eh, Holls?' Taffy said, looping his arm around her waist. 'I think sometimes it's just easier to see the things I'm looking for.'

Enigmatic wasn't normally a word she would have applied to her lovely husband, as a rule, and Holly looked up at him in concern, trying to read his expression. 'And what are you looking for, Taff?'

He shrugged. 'I don't know. If I'm honest, I haven't known for a while now.'

Holly stilled beside him; old habits died hard and she couldn't deny that, even second time around, married life wasn't quite the plain sailing she'd been hoping for. She said nothing, waiting for him to elaborate.

'I just feel ...' He paused and his hand tightened on her waist. 'I just feel as though I'm not doing anything properly these days, as though everything is a compromise. I'm hardly around for the kids, so by extension I'm not really winning awards as Father of the Year. And then you go and get this offer from Bath that knocks any financial contribution from me into the shade ... Dad says—' He stopped mid-flow, clearly editing himself.

'Well,' said Holly, intrigued, 'what does your dad say?'

'It's not important,' Taffy mumbled, pulling away slightly to glance back into the bar.

'It's important to me,' Holly countered, 'especially if it's making you feel like this.'

Taffy turned to face her, his eyes filled with a

disappointment and sadness that took her breath away. 'I'm failing,' he said, his voice cracking with each word. 'I'm not being the husband or the father I wanted to be and I'm letting you down.'

'Says who?' Holly said, her indignation getting the better of her restraint. 'Your dad?'

Taffy shrugged again, his gaze now firmly focused on the spectacle of Dan being an apparently feisty unicorn. 'I know Dad wants me to be the breadwinner, the man of the house, the kind of dad that keeps all the financial balls in the air so you can focus on the children. And I know that's how it should be. It's just, well, it doesn't feel right to me.'

Holly wove her fingers through his own, until it was impossible to tell where his hands ended and hers began. 'That wouldn't feel right to me, either,' she said gently. 'And since when do we live in the 1970s anyway? I mean, I love your parents, I do – but have we ever made our life choices according to their beliefs, Taffs? I mean, *ever*?'

Taffy blinked hard. 'But I—'

'But nothing,' Holly said firmly. 'We need to build a family that works for us and advice is lovely, but I'm not your mum and you're not your dad. This is our marriage and our children we're talking about. I'd much rather hear about the kind of dad *you* want to be . . .'

Taffy turned away, pulling her with him, ducking out through the door into the pub garden, before any of their guests could see the tears welling up in his eyes. 'What's the matter with me, Holls? I never used to turn on the waterworks whenever I felt all over the place?'

'Ah, well, you can blame Lottie and Olivia for that. Welcome to parenthood. You'll be crying at the John Lewis Christmas advert this year too, just so you know.'

He sniffed and managed a watery smile. 'I don't think I'm cut out to be a seventies dad. Or a husband.'

'Thank Christ for that,' Holly laughed, kissing him lightly and tucking herself into his side for both comfort and warmth. 'Now stop trying to be someone you're not, or whoever it is you think you *should* be and answer the bloody question – what kind of dad do *you* want to be?'

'I want to be at home with the kids more,' he blurted. 'I want to not feel so utterly jealous that you are. I want to be there when they take their first steps, not handing out antibiotics and painkillers. This is just too important to miss. But then,' he paused and dared to glance down at her face to gauge her reaction, 'we can't both be at home with our babies and you do kind of take precedence, you know, as the manufacturer.'

Holly nodded as she took in his emotive words, not to mention his unwillingness to burden her with his worries, and wondered just how long this had been eating away at him. It certainly explained a lot about his moods and behaviour of late. And their relationship: trading logistics instead of endearments had become their new normal.

'And I guess when you come home and I tell you about how difficult my day has been . . . ?' she ventured, shivering slightly with both cold and apprehension.

'Well, that just makes it worse,' he confirmed.

'Oh, Taffs,' said Holly with feeling, 'what am I going to do with you? We seriously need to talk to each other more. I've been finding it so hard, resenting you almost, for getting to be with our patients every day. For managing to keep your professional identity and still become a parent.'

His look of complete bewilderment told Holly enough

to reassure her that he had been genuinely oblivious to her concerns, rather than thoughtless or arrogant. In her mind, oblivious was a lot easier to fix.

'So you wouldn't mind if I took a little paternity leave and we swapped for a bit?'

'Mind?' said Holly. 'I think it's brilliant. I think you'd love it. And I venture that you might even appreciate your days at work a little more too.'

He grinned, shrugging out of his jacket and draping it around her shoulders. 'And you might moan less about your days at home!'

'I don't *moan* . . .'

'Yeah, right, so you don't give me a rundown on how many feeds, how many nappies, how little time you've had to yourself all day, the moment I walk through the door?' he teased her gently, rubbing her arms to ease the chill.

Holly paused. 'I do do that, don't I? But not because I'm complaining — it's more that I want you to understand that it's hardly a picnic. You and the other partners keep going on about "enjoying my time off" — I've never been so exhausted or brain-numb in my entire life.'

'Worse than when you were a junior doctor?' Taffy said, momentarily blindsided.

'Much, much worse,' Holly reassured him with a smile. 'And now you get to join in too . . .' she grinned.

'Will people think it's a bit, you know, wet – being all New Man about this?' he wondered out loud. 'I have no idea what my dad will think of it.'

'Do you actually care?' asked Holly gently. 'If you're happy and I'm happy and the kids get to build a proper relationship with their dad, does it honestly matter what anybody else thinks? If we actually talk to each other, rather than resent each other, aren't we in a better position to judge what's right for our little family?'

'Not so little,' laughed Taffy, the relief evident in the crinkle around his eyes.

'True, but I suspect Miss Lulu might be moving on sooner than you think,' Holly agreed. She paused, wondering how frank to be. 'Taffs, I have to tell you, I'm a little relieved. I was worried we were in trouble, you know, you and me?'

'Me too,' he whispered. 'But I don't want to be. And I feel kind of stupid now, for not talking to you sooner. I was just so busy trying to be the perfect dad, the perfect husband . . .'

'That you ended up being neither, and miserable to boot?' Holly suggested. 'Maybe we should limit your dad's sphere of influence to woodwork and craft beer?'

'And sheep,' Taffy said, nodding. 'He knows an awful lot about sheep.' He frowned. 'You know, it's just that my parents have always been so happy, and I loved growing up with them, I thought they'd got it right.'

'There's more than one way to peel an orange. So, we learn from our mistakes and we make a new plan,' Holly said, with more confidence than she actually felt.

'Repeat as necessary?' Taffy smiled and Holly could only nod, as she breathed easily for the first time in what felt like a very long time.

Chapter 33

'So you don't need me anymore?' said Plum, her hands automatically settling on her hips à la pissed-off-Italian-mama, as she attempted to make sense of what Holly had explained to her over breakfast the next day.

'Oh no, Plum, that's not what I said at all,' Holly replied, somewhat panicked at the thought of losing their very lovely, if somewhat quirky, Italian nanny. 'Of course we still need you. And we want you to stay. It's just that Taffy and I will be taking turns to work half-days.' She paused, formulating her words with care. 'Although to be honest we haven't quite worked out the details yet. But, Plum, with five children under five, we can't do this without you.'

'This is true,' acknowledged Plum with a relieved smile. 'I mean, no disrespect to your husband, Holly, but see this?' She lifted up Lottie's t-shirt dress to show that Taffy had also dressed her for the day in a backwards nappy and pyjama trousers. 'He can learn, though, if he is wanting to. Change is good.'

'I quite agree,' said Holly with feeling. 'And we'll make it a smooth transition, just as soon as we've worked out how.'

'Sometimes just knowing is enough. Once you get your light-switch moment, you start to feel more relaxed and in control.' Plum nodded.

'Light-bulb moment,' Holly corrected after a moment to work out what she meant.

'*Si*,' agreed Plum. 'Like when you meet someone special and everything else begins to make sense.'

Holly put down her coffee and turned her undivided attention to the nanny. 'Do tell,' she said with a grin. 'Is it Teddy? Or Matthew?' She wracked her brains to think who she'd seen Plum chatting with at the Christening.

'Oh, Holly, always so funny,' laughed Plum, as though the teasing required no actual answer, and that she hadn't quite grasped Holly's penchant for matchmaking. She stood up with a dozing Lottie in her arms. 'I think somebody is ready for a nap.'

Holly nodded and yawned for a moment, before she realised that Plum wasn't actually referring to her. As Plum sashayed across the room, effortlessly balancing Lottie on one hip, there was a fresh brightness to her step. Holly couldn't help wondering who had put it there.

An ignoble thought popped into Holly's head: surely it couldn't be the prospect of more quality time with Taffy? Please God she was reading that wrong. If anything, Plum was always far more attentive to Holly and her friends than to Taffy and Dan and their noisy rugby rabble. Unless that was the cunning of it, said Lizzie's sceptical voice in her head.

Holly shook her head, as if to dislodge the disloyal thoughts – Plum had been nothing but sweet, diligent and attentive. Just because she looked the way she did, didn't mean she was angling to become 'the other woman'.

'And you're quite sure about this?' Taffy asked, as they walked across the Market Place together, their occasional silences no longer filled with unspoken resentment, their gloved hands clasped together. 'I'll do a half-day today and you stay on for evening surgery. Then tomorrow we'll swap?' He looked daunted and excited at the same time, the extra bounce in his step purely charged by a nervous energy akin to his first day at a new job. Which in a way, of course, was exactly what it was.

After all, his father's advice had come straight from the '1970s Dad' school of parenting and for all Holly's hopes and her perfectly logical assumptions that Taffy would be a fully new-age-hands-on father, she'd been sorely disappointed so far.

If only she'd known he was holding himself back, deliberately letting her take the lead ... Well, she'd have been cursing him less behind his back, for one thing!

'It's going to be a learning curve for both of us,' Holly said. 'But I have to say, I'm mainly just thrilled that we're talking about this, you know, rather than letting it fester.'

'Fester, fester, rot, rot, rot,' teased Taffy, giving away his secret chick-flick appreciation.

Holly smiled, so much common ground between them that had never gone away – even though she hadn't always been able to see it for the last few months. 'I'm just saying, once more and for the record, it's no picnic being at home. It's not just the kids and their homework, it's the house and getting ready for Christmas.' She frowned. 'And I'm always convinced there'll be someone or something I'll forget ...'

Taffy shot her a sideways glance. 'Sure. But, I mean, Plum's there too. How hard can it be?'

Holly stopped dead on the pavement, unsure if he was teasing her or not, poised to wallop him either way. He turned to smile at her and caught both her hands in his before she could act on the instinctive thought.

'Look, it's going to be an adjustment for both of us and

we're finding our feet this week. So all I'm saying is – let's do just that. Let's save any big decisions until we're on a more balanced footing. Both of us. I'll wager you've forgotten how draining a full week of healing the sick and placating the whiney can be.'

'Maybe,' gave Holly graciously. 'But there are a few other things that I wanted to implement. I really don't want to miss out on this Funding Application for the Young Carers either and—'

'One step at a time,' cut in Taffy. 'Big picture, remember?'

Holly frowned. 'But maybe I could just—'

'We might miss out on all sorts of things, if we don't take a moment to breathe.' He paused and a flicker of doubt and discomfort shadowed his eyes. 'Holly, I feel like we've been given a fresh start. And I've been so worried about us – you and me – and the kids . . . It just hasn't felt "right" for a while, you know? And now, we're talking, actually communicating again and I know that we'll be okay . . . But I can't do anything that might jeopardise that again, even if it is what's best for The Practice. Do you understand? You and our children are everything to me.'

Holly felt a little winded by his emotional transparency – so out of character as to be almost worrying. And yet, he made a valid point. If their emotional investments flowed outwards, who would be keeping the home fires burning?

She dashed the image of a smiling Plum from her mind, obviously more unsettled than she'd realised by their earlier conversation. She had nothing to worry about on that front, if the expression of love on Taffy's face was any measure at all.

'I'm sorry,' she said simply. 'There's been a lot to adapt to, to get used to and I've had to do so much of that alone . . .' She swallowed hard. 'I suppose all my plotting and planning with the twins and how my working life would fit around them reflects that – I was thinking about me as a "me" not an "us".'

'My fault,' said Taffy gruffly, a little overcome perhaps by his part in her emotional withdrawal. 'Maybe we should get the Team Taffy t-shirts out again?'

'How about we make some new ones? Squad 42 hoodies?' Holly suggested lightly, hoping that he might get the message that, at this point in their lives, he may not be the primary stakeholder. 'And you know, I'm all for taking things slowly, but I really feel that it's time to consider whether The Practice needs to adapt a little too. If we're making changes, my inclination is go big, or go home.

'I mean, if I'm going to leave my kids every day and come to work – frankly just to pay the nanny – then I'd like it to be work I'm proud of, you know? No half measures. I want to make the biggest difference I – we – can by whatever means necessary.'

Taffy frowned in thought. 'Do you think we should warn the others that you're on a mission again? If you're going full Ninja, it seems only fair. I mean, Dan seemed really happy about the new plan last night, but—'

Holly shook her head. 'Don't you dare say a word until I'm ready to share. If there's one thing I've learned recently, it's that a change of perspective makes all the difference. I'm coming back with objectivity. It's kind of disconcerting actually. A bit like when I got my reading glasses. You realise you've been muddling on for years, making do, squinting and then – *boom* – clarity.'

'And I'm guessing you've switched the coffee back to full-caffeine?' Taffy asked after a short pause, earning himself a disparaging look from his wife. He smiled. 'Am I not allowed to tease you yet? Is that part of this new arrangement?'

Holly slipped her hand into his and rested her head against his shoulder. 'You can tease me all you like, as long as you take me seriously too. I mean, what's the point of putting my career on hold and taking a step back, if I can't capitalise on the lessons I've learned and the clarity I've found – I want to move forward, but mindfully, not reacting to whatever crisis is brewing next.'

'And there's the whole raising-our-babies thing too,' he said gently.

'That too,' Holly agreed. Certainly, she never thought she'd be taking such advantage of all the benefits her partnership agreement at The Practice had to offer. This flexibility certainly knocked any of Patronising Patricia's return to work schemes into a cocked hat and she was inordinately grateful for Julia Channing's rampantly feminist approach to drafting their individual agreements. Even if it had taken Holly a while to make the most of her partnership status, impeded more by a desire to always, always do the right thing. Maybe she wasn't quite so different to her husband after all?

'Morning!' called Alec French as their route took them past the school gates, where he was manfully tacking up a sign about the latest after-school bake sale; a sign that was smothered in a tasteless array of tinsel and glitter, yet another reminder for Holly that Christmas was looming and demanding her attention.

Holly smiled in greeting. Not too much, just a little: enough to be polite and without giving her hormones notice. After all, she reasoned, since she was no longer furious with her husband and he happened to be standing right beside her being loving and supportive, any illicit thoughts about the lovely Mr French must be firmly quashed.

Mr French, for his part, was helping this along nicely with his stern expression. 'Please don't say *you've* forgotten to bring in your bakes as well!' He shook his head in disappointment. 'I've never had to cancel a bake sale before but we've had so little by way of donations ... And we've no extra funding for the pantomime trip ... I'd truly hate to have to cancel that too.'

He looked truly bothered and Holly's go-to motherly-guilt was quick to flare. 'You won't really cancel, will you? I'm so sorry – I had remembered, but then with the Christening, it completely slipped my mind.'

'You and the rest of the parents,' he said grumpily. 'I even made a point of saying they didn't have to be homemade offerings – I know lots of parents are pushed for time. But that may have been a mistake: I've got three boxes of Mr Kipling, a hemp-seed cake and three fivers.'

'A fiver cake?' Taffy queried, somewhat missing the burden of his cry.

'A five-pound note, on the basis that's what they would have spent buying a cake, so let's cut out the middleman. But in this case, the middleman is teaching the children how to raise money rather than just asking for a handout.' He shrugged. 'And to be honest the hemp-seed cake looks just awful.'

'Two guesses who donated that,' Holly said with a smile, distractedly checking her watch. 'Look, how about I pop home and get Plum on the case with a couple of big tray-bakes? You could cut them into squares and sell them individually?'

Alec French's face lit up, his smile illuminating his eyes, until their very blueness seemed to twinkle. 'You could do that?'

'I could and I will, but I'll have to get moving.' Holly

turned away, trying to ignore the flutter of pleasure she felt, choosing to believe it came from the warm glow of benevolence.

As she slipped and slewed back across the icy Market Place, checking her watch once more, she realised that it was all very well having a fresh start with Taffy and with work but that, just as it would take a little while to rebuild their bridges, the same might be said for surrendering the few buoyancy aids she'd been using to keep herself afloat, her flirty Headmaster fantasy among them.

She pushed open the front door, already out of puff, perspiring in her heavy down coat and wondering whether volunteering Plum's services was quite the done thing.

She froze in the doorway.

Obviously what counted for the 'done thing' in Italy was slightly different. She cleared her throat loudly, but the couple wrapped around each other in the drawing room made no move to draw apart.

To be fair, Holly thought, with an unwelcome flash of envy for their uninhibited passion, they seemed pretty much oblivious to everything around them, so intent were they on exploring each other's bodies.

'Erm, guys . . .' she attempted again, almost transfixed as she watched their hands slip into each other's hair. Shocked, winded almost by the passionate scene she'd encountered. By the fact that she herself had been oblivious to the growing attraction that now seemed so obvious in hindsight. 'Knock knock?'

She hesitated, unsure of the protocol for confronting her colleague and her nanny, caught canoodling during the working day. She was actually astonished to find that it was this salient point that rattled her the most. Who was she to say, after all, where the attraction may lie — even if she was a little blindsided — but surely taking care of her children had to be the nanny's priority, not nailing the nearest dishy doctor?

'Plum?' she tried again. 'I'm ho-ome!' she called loudly, opening the front door again to allow it to slam heavily into place.

The two sprang instantly apart, hair tousled, eyes wide, pupils dilated.

'Morning, Tilly,' said Holly gently, her voice soft.

'It's not what you—' began Tilly anxiously, tucking in her blouse with jerky flustered movements, oblivious to the tight look of hurt that flashed across Plum's face at her immediate evasiveness.

'It's not a problem, Tilly, and please don't leave on my account,' Holly said in her best, most soothing, reassuring voice. 'I guess I should have seen this one coming,' she added with a smile. 'You two make a lovely couple.'

It took very little to sum up the budding relationship she'd walked in on: Plum showing only concern that her boss had effectively caught her *in flagrante*, but with no embarrassment or shame; Tilly on the other hand, was clearly new to the notion of a same-sex liaison, almost hiccuping in her distress at being outed so summarily.

'Please, Holly, you won't say anything?' Tilly managed.

'It's not my place to say a word,' Holly said. 'But maybe that's something you two should talk about. After work.' She paused. 'Although Larkford isn't the easiest place to keep secrets, I have to wonder why you would want to? Everyone here will be pleased that you've found each other.'

'Everyone?' said Tilly disbelievingly.

'Everyone who matters,' said Holly firmly.

'And you don't think—?' Tilly began, before Holly interrupted her.

'My only concern is that Plum's focus should really be on her charges during the working day. What, or who, you do in your free time is entirely up to you.' She smiled. 'Seriously, if I wasn't pissed off that you're snogging when you should be taking care of my kids, I'd be popping open the champagne. You're both far too lovely to be alone, when you could be so happy together.'

There was a tiny part of Holly's mind, she had to concede – although only to herself – that was relieved. There had been no ploy in Plum's indifference to the male attention she inevitably attracted, no cunning wiles in play. And maybe Tilly's determined bed-hopping might yet come to an end, if she was prepared to admit her true feelings and inclinations, even if only in private for now.

The hardest part of all this would be keeping the news to herself, she realised. Oh and possibly mentoring Tilly had taken on a trickier, more personal, dimension.

She took in their dishevelled and awkward appearances, Plum clearly aggrieved at Tilly's embarrassment. 'Right, I need to talk to Plum about tray-bakes. And, Tilly, you can walk to work with me in a minute and give me the skinny on this lovely new relationship on the way.'

Start as she meant to go on, she decided. Open and unflappable.

She paused. 'But seriously, girls, if you're on duty with the kids, you're on duty, okay?' she said firmly.

'Okay,' they both mumbled like teenagers and Holly had to turn away to disguise her smile.

Chapter 34

After a hectic morning surgery, somewhat compounded by her late start, yet another homing-call from her mother, and a succession of apologies to each subsequent patient, Alice was more than ready to run to the pub to meet Jamie at lunchtime, even though Coco's deep brown eyes pleaded with her for another walk in the park. The little chocolate-coloured cocker took enormous delight in gambolling through the last of the snow drifts, until the clumps of snow in her fur were like golf balls hanging from each leg. Not for either of them complaints about the cold; indeed compared to an Orkney winter it barely counted as a tad brisk. Nevertheless, Alice felt fragile, craving company and hot chocolate and someone to fuss over her that she would catch her death without an Aran jumper spot-welded to her very person.

And for that, she needed Tilly, not Jamie.

She needed Tilly to confirm that she wasn't the kind of girl who dropped her friends the moment her boyfriend came to visit. And that, should the worst ever happen in her own life, she wouldn't be drowning her sorrows alone in liquor and prescription meds.

'Coo-eee. Only me,' she said, poking her head around the door of Tilly's new consulting room, hastily snaffled from

Phlebotomy for her use since Holly's return. 'Pub? It'll have to be quick, but rumour has it Teddy's making those lush sausage rolls again.'

She broke off, confusion shadowing her face. Tilly could always be relied upon to rally at the prospect of skiving, or pubs, or indeed flakey pastry ... And yet, nothing. No reaction at all.

'Tills?' Alice ventured, concern escalating at the sight of the pregnancy test on her desk and her reddened eyes. 'Bloody hell – did you have any idea at all? I mean, how on earth are you going to cope?' It wasn't a considered reaction to the prospect of her friend having a baby, she had to admit, but even so she was staggered by the almost ferocious reaction it apparently provoked.

'Jesus, Alice – I wouldn't have pegged you for a bigot!' Tilly dashed away a fresh onslaught of tears.

'There's nothing bigoted about wondering how the hell you'll raise a baby on your own!' Alice retorted, their friendship as always quick to heated words. She could only hope that, on such a sensitive topic, they might also follow their usual pattern and be quick to find common ground and absolution for their outburst.

'What?' Tilly said, wiping her eyes on the sleeve of her top and swivelling her chair to face Alice dead on. 'What are you going on about?'

'The baby,' replied Alice, gesturing to the positive pregnancy test in the emesis bowl on her desk. 'Your baby. Why on earth would you take the test without me here, after last time?'

'Oh, for fuck's sake,' exclaimed Tilly, tipping the entire arrangement into the red-topped bin. 'That's not mine. Just my last patient. Are you going to have a go at me about keeping on top of my disposables now too?'

'Believe it or not,' Alice said, sinking down into the chair beside her, 'I didn't actually come in here to have a go at you about anything. I thought you might fancy a little break, some fresh air, to spend some time around healthy people rather than . . .' She gestured around the small dark room that boasted only a token gesture by way of a window and even that faced into the shadowed pathway that ran alongside the building – hardly optimal working conditions.

Alice paused, her brain taking a while to catch up. 'But if you're not up the duff, then why the tears? I mean, Tilly – in all the time I've known you I've only seen you cry maybe once and that was when Steely Dan the tortoise didn't make it through hibernation.'

'Steely Dan was the *best* tortoise, wasn't he, though?' Tilly said, setting off a fresh bout of sobbing. 'And how many tortoises can say they went to med school, eh? That tortoise was going places . . .'

'Tills, what's going on? And, also, can I ask – why did you call me a bigot?'

Tilly suddenly became fascinated by the tissue in her hands, shredding the layers apart with intense concentration. 'I thought you were talking about something else, someone else.'

'The someone else you're crying about?' Alice asked quietly.

Tilly nodded. 'We had a fight. I wanted to keep our relationship quiet while I worked out how I felt. It's all pretty new to me and I didn't know how people might react.'

'To you being in a relationship, rather than shagging random punters every Friday night? Surely everyone will be pleased for you . . . Unless, Tilly, please say he's not married?' Alice asked, uncertain why Tilly was playing her cards so close to her chest, or why she suddenly seemed to give a damn what anybody else thought.

Tilly sniffed and shook her head. 'It's Plum,' she said briefly. 'I'm in love with Plum.'

'Oh,' managed Alice, struggling to change mental gears and virtually speechless. Although, the more the thought percolated in her mind, the more everything about her friend made more sense. 'How on earth did I not know this about you? How did I miss this for a decade?'

Tilly gave a nervous laugh. 'You think it's weird that *you* didn't know – how fucking unbelievable is it that, until I laid eyes on Plum, *I* didn't have a clue.'

Alice shrugged with a smile. 'Well, if you're going to go that way, may I say *mazel tov*. Plum's just wonderful. And surely way out of your league?' It was staggering how quickly the two of them had returned to their usual repartee. Even a change in sexual orientation was seemingly not enough to knock them off their stride.

Tilly clasped Alice's hand in gratitude. 'I have no idea how people are going to react. Plum's so mellow about all this. She's been out for years and I think she must have forgotten how big a deal it is.'

'Is it, though?' Alice queried. 'I mean, after everything you've been through over the years, is it really so extraordinary that this is what makes you feel good? And besides, maybe it's just Plum that you love? Doesn't necessarily mean that any other woman out there would float your boat.' She paused. 'Should I just shut up now?'

Tilly laughed. 'Why change the habit of a lifetime now?'

'Well, you are,' Alice retorted. 'So, if I may be blunt, is this why you've been playing fast and loose on the dating scene?'

'Shagging anything that moves?' Tilly countered. 'Maybe? I don't know. It just felt like I was always looking for something – you know, to feel more? Something better? To feel in the moment? After all that hideousness at uni with that entitled prick, and then giving up the baby? Maybe in hindsight all the serial shagging should have been a red flag, but it's counter-intuitive, you know . . .'

'I do,' said Alice. 'But you need to promise me you won't lose Plum just because you're afraid. Go and find her, Tilly. Tell her what you told me. If she's half the woman I think she is, there really won't be an issue.'

'If she's half the woman I think she is, then I'm finished with men,' Tilly said awkwardly, gathering her things and pausing by the door. 'Thank you, Al. For understanding, I mean. Even if I don't just yet.'

As the door swung shut behind her, Alice realised that she'd only once before seen Tilly look so vulnerable and that even now, it was a wonder that Alice was the only person who knew about her child. About how that child had come about. She could only hope and pray that Larkford would live up to her expectations and provide the accepting home that Tilly so obviously needed.

'Stay in bed with me,' said Jamie, gently but deliberately sliding his hand over her waist. 'If I'm going to chuck a sickie to stay home with you, there's not much point if you're not here.'

Alice stretched in sated happiness, delighted with their impromptu liaison. Poor Teddy Kingsley's lunch menu hadn't stood a chance. 'Are you saying that last night wasn't worth it?' she teased him. 'Besides, I'll see you after work, and again at bedtime . . .' This time, it was her hands doing the teasing and Jamie groaned in surrender.

'Argh, you'll be the death of me, Walker. I have to fly back tonight and you know it. Even though I would do anything to spend every Sunday eating toast in bed with you, and every

Monday morning waking up beside you. It's just not possible at the moment,' Jamie said, with slightly less conviction than he had on his last visit home.

'We need a plan,' said Alice. 'Holly's always making plans and lists – maybe we should do that?'

'My list is pretty simple actually,' Jamie confessed. 'Find a replacement for me in Donegal so I can come home to my girl. Oh, and find a full-time job to come home to. That part-time offer from the training centre just isn't enough.'

Alice frowned. 'They sent you to Donegal on a temporary placement and then cut your hours for when you get back? That's pretty shitty by anyone's standards.'

Jamie looked fairly ambivalent about the prospect. 'There's been a change of management, and a change of funding. I rather suspect I'm better off elsewhere.' He paused. 'I'll be a dog walker if I have to. I just need to come home now.'

'Well,' said Alice, trying not to overwhelm him with her delight, 'I gather Connor has quite a few now . . .' She giggled, as he tickled her in reply.

'Argh, come on, woman, stop talking about other men when you're in bed with me.' He leaned forward to kiss her, stopping abruptly at the expression on her face. 'Al? I was only joking.'

Alice shook her head. 'Connor! Shit . . .' She sat up in bed and started to pull on her blouse. 'I was going to call in before afternoon surgery.' She hunted around for her shoes, feeling ridiculously guilty. 'I can't believe I forgot.'

'He'll understand,' Jamie said, confusion writ across his face. 'I can pop in this afternoon if you like, while you're at work?' He paused, obviously waiting for Alice to reply. 'Or is this a doctor thing? A mate thing? A date?' he ventured. 'Alice? Earth to Alice?'

'Hmm?' Alice looked up, distracted and flushed with remorse. 'I just need to check . . .'

Jamie pulled on a t-shirt and swung his legs over the edge of the bed. 'Is he okay, Al?'

Alice stopped, one shoe in her hand, hair swinging into her eyes. 'I honestly don't know,' she said, almost on the verge of tears that her professional responsibilities had been so easily ditched in favour of a nooner with her boyfriend. 'It might be nothing. Just a feeling really.'

Jamie knew better than to question one of Alice's intuitive feelings, even apparently realising that today was not a day to tease her as he usually would about whether there was the hint of Orkney witch in her ancestry.

'He's been struggling a bit lately,' Alice said after a moment, weighing up how much was in the public domain, and could reasonably be shared. Certainly her conversation with Holly only this morning about high-functioning depression was protected by privilege, no matter how much she might welcome Jamie's insight on the situation.

Jamie nodded. 'Tough call. I mean, as a doctor, you can't treat grief, right? But then, who's to say that's all it is?'

Alice glanced up sharply, wondering if she'd said too much, stunned as always by Jamie's instinctive ability to grasp a situation.

'I had a client once,' Jamie said quietly, slipping into his jeans. 'We thought he'd turned a corner, perked up, seemed brighter . . . But it was just because he'd made his decision.'

Alice roughly pulled her hair back away from her face. 'Fuck,' she said simply, running from the room.

'Wait, where are you going?' Jamie said, chasing after her in his bare feet.

'Connor's!' she shouted back over her shoulder, as she ran down the stairs, Coco at her heels.

Alice arrived at The Big House to find Kitty hammering on the front door to no avail. 'No sign of him?' she asked help-lessly, having somehow convinced herself of the worst possible outcome on the run over here. She had seen, in fact, in her mind's eye the defence she would have to make for her abject failure to spot the signs before it was too late. Jamie's com-ment had propelled a vague niggling concern into hyperdrive.

'But the dogs aren't barking either,' Kitty said gently, spot-ting Alice's face. 'So don't go there. He told me he was fine. I called him last night after the Christening no-show – I heard Cassie Holland bragging about that horrible radio phone-in, so I was worried. But he *promised* me he was fine.'

'But you obviously didn't believe him, or you wouldn't be hammering on his front door in your lunch break,' countered Alice astutely.

Kitty gave her a sideways glance, before setting off towards the back of the house. 'Come on then. We'll just break in.'

'What?'

Kitty shrugged. 'No big deal. I do it all the time if there's an animal in distress and the owners aren't around.' Alice was lost for words as Kitty rootled around among the plant pots and pebbles by the back door, coming up triumphant with a slightly rusty, but nevertheless effective key. 'Don't look too shocked,' Kitty said. 'Aggie Peal used to get me round when-ever she had hospital stuff going on.'

They walked into the kitchen together, the closed win-dows and total silence so unusual as to make them both pause. 'He's not here,' Alice said unnecessarily.

They looked at each other, the same thought clearly occurring to both of them, as they ran from the room, calling his name, checking the house from top to bottom. Breathlessly, Kitty leaned against the kitchen table and gave Alice an embarrassed look. 'Guess we might have overreacted,' she said. 'I mean, the dogs aren't here either. And neither is his ridiculous car.'

'Right, yes. Quite,' managed Alice, equally out of puff.

They both looked up expectantly as the back door flew open, only to be disappointed. 'Only me,' said Jamie. 'Any sign?'

The girls shook their heads, an uncomfortable feeling still hovering in the room. It hadn't *felt* like an overreaction, Alice realised. Worrying about Connor's well-being felt authentic, a little part of her subconscious mind now flagging up all the reasons she should, quite rightly, be worried about him. Even the pictures on the dresser were a stark reminder of just how different Connor looked these days to the happier times captured on film. The change so gradual, over the last year, that they could certainly be forgiven for missing the weight loss, but to have missed the hollowness in his eyes?

Just because he'd been functional, didn't mean he hadn't been struggling.

Alice glanced around, uncertain what to do next, as Kitty tried his mobile yet again.

'We should go to Dorset,' said Jamie into the silence.

'What? Why?' Alice said. 'Why do you say that?'

Jamie held up a bundle of paperwork that had been left spread all over the kitchen table. 'Because I'll wager that's where Connor's gone. Look – all these sale contracts, deeds of title . . .'

'He's selling the estate?' Alice checked.

'He's getting his affairs in order,' said Kitty at the same time and they looked at each other in confusion.

'I'll drive,' said Jamie, pulling his car keys from his pocket and heading for the door.

Chapter 35

Alice blew her fringe from her eyes and pulled over to the side of the road, if it could even be called that. 'And you're quite sure we're going the right way?' she asked Jamie in the seat beside her, a large-scale Ordnance Survey map flapping in the welcome breeze as she wound down the window allowing the stifling heat in the car to dissipate.

They'd taken shifts driving in the end, through the most awful conditions, never quite sure that the snowy lanes were heading in the right direction and the further south they drove, the less evidence they saw of the promised thaw. It was some testament to their concern that they had persevered, grateful to the sturdy four-wheel drive, that even so skidded occasionally and made their hearts race.

And now, poised near the top of yet another hill, Kitty leaned forward between the front seats, pointing to the tiny icon on the map that apparently represented the only dwelling for miles around, among the rolling hills and valleys of deepest Dorset: Connor's Dorset estate.

They all looked at each other for a moment, no doubt all thinking the same thing – was it any wonder that an ambulance had been unable to reach Connor's wife in time? As the crow – or helicopter – flew, civilisation was but a twenty-minute hop away, but following these winding single-track lanes, Alice had lost all sense of direction.

'Well, if he wanted to hide away, he chose the right place at least,' Jamie said quietly, squinting at the map and turning it this way and that to pinpoint their own location. He looked ahead doubtfully, as Alice put the car into gear on the steep slope and pulled away. 'According to this, it's just around the next bend, but I don't see how ...'

They crested the hill and words caught in their mouths; the view opening up before them was breathtaking, so remotely wild and unspoiled. A narrow driveway wound down to the valley below, branching away from the lane itself, flanked by frosted, pollarded beech trees, their very presence disturbing the occasional flurry of a bold pheasant making a break for it. At the bottom sat a whitened oasis of lawns surrounding a sprawling house, Connor's much-blighted and forlorn Range Rover the only sign of life.

'Are you ready for this?' Alice asked, glancing back over her shoulder as they approached, still unclear as to the exact nature of Connor and Kitty's friendship. Having spent the last three hours in the car together, Alice had an even deeper respect for their lovely vet, sharing the absolute commitment that Kitty brought to her work and her animals, not to mention her obvious affection for Coco.

From where Alice was sitting, it was entirely possible that Kitty's concern might be just as much for Jamieson as for Connor, and she couldn't help thinking that would be a missed opportunity. But this was no time for matchmaking. They genuinely had no idea what they were walking into and it was no coincidence that Alice had restocked her doctor's bag thoroughly before they left. One heard such awful things about rock stars hitting 'rock' bottom that she wanted to be prepared. Whether anything could prepare them for what lay ahead was anyone's guess and she squeezed Jamie's knee gratefully, thankful for the moral support.

Nobody, not even Connor's Estate Manager, had seen or heard from him since the radio show. Only Kitty had briefly spoken to him on the phone, and was now replaying the conversation in her head on repeat in case she'd missed something crucial. It had taken all of Alice's resolve to accept that not every story had a happy ending and there was a voice in the back of her head urging her to brace for the worst.

Isolation.

Depression.

Humiliation.

Never a winning combination.

A flurry of barking caught them all unawares, as they parked the car, a veritable pack of mismatched hounds hurtling around the corner of the house in greeting, their excited breath in hot puffs of misty air. Jamieson loped along behind Agatha Peal's excitable troop, targeting Kitty for his affection, his tongue lolling and his tail thwacking so hard against Kitty's thighs it would doubtless leave bruises.

'Morning,' said Connor quietly, appearing from the same archway, filthy wellington boots and a shabby Puffa waistcoat making him almost unrecognisable. Together with the beginnings of a beard and deep shadows under his eyes, it suggested that personal hygiene had not been high on his agenda but Alice couldn't have cared less. The wave of relief at seeing him alive, if not well, made her clasp the car door for support.

'You found me then.' His tone was ambivalent, as though he would have been unmoved either way.

'Of course we found you!' exclaimed Kitty, striding forward to pull him into a hug and ignoring his cat-like stiffening response. 'We were hardly going to let you fester down here for ever, were we?'

Connor glanced around, his glazed eyes following the stunning elevations and copses that marked out his territory, falling to the dogs milling affectionately at his side. 'I can think of worse ways to go, actually. Touring springs to mind.'

'Hmm,' said Alice noncommittally, still attempting to find her equilibrium. Even in this sweeping rural paradise, it was clear that Elsie's maxim held true: you can be miserable anywhere if you take yourself with you.

It was now their job to persuade Connor to come home to Larkford, where there was no doubt that a little love and support would help to get him back on the path to happiness.

Assuming he forgave them for letting him down.

Assuming he was prepared to give them another chance.

'Any chance of a cuppa?' said Jamie easily.

'Or something to eat? It's very nice down here, but have you any idea how long it's been since we passed a coffee place?' Alice urged herself to manage nonchalance. There had been enough drama already.

There was a flicker of amusement in Connor's eyes that buoyed Alice immediately. 'That's rather the point, though, don't you think?' Connor said, with a small gesture towards the heavily frosted woodland and snow-covered hillsides surrounding them. Agatha's dogs were clearly on message already, gambolling and haring around the sweeping lawns and shrubberies, knocking loose showers of snow and in Seventh Heaven at the freedom.

Filthy wet paw prints led the way into the kitchen – a jaw-dropping statement of cream-painted wood and granite, somewhat undermined by an array of half-empty baked bean cans, some with forks sticking out of the top, not to mention an entourage of empty wine bottles in varying shades and a flurry of annotated sheet music spilling all over the table.

'Taking good care of yourself then, I see,' said Kitty, giving Connor a sideways glance.

Jamie pulled open the fridge and gagged slightly at the whiff of curdled milk and God only knew what else. 'Okay, well, have you got any coffee at least? I'd settle for some beans if that's all you've got? I'm bloody starving.' His stomach rumbled a crescendo, endorsing his statement.

Connor hesitated, emotions flickering across his face, almost as though offering coffee or sustenance might in some way obligate him, an implied acceptance of the terms of their visit. He wasn't a stupid man and he could obviously tell that the three of them hadn't driven all this way on a social call.

He flicked on an impressive coffee machine, which gurgled and chuntered into the silence. 'Why did you come?' he asked.

Alice was ready, primed with a tactful answer, sticking to the plan.

She had not accounted for Kitty's emotional reaction at Connor's obvious decline. 'To bring you home,' Kitty said firmly, stepping forward and clasping both his hands. 'To bring you back to your friends, to the people who care about you. And to stop you doing anything you'll regret.'

Connor said nothing, merely pulled his hands away and busied himself with the complicated machine, flicking coffee grounds everywhere as he did so with trembling hands.

Kitty cast an anguished glance over at Alice, yet waded in again with both feet. 'What about Jamieson? He needs veterinary care.'

'There are *other* vets in the country, Kitty,' Connor said, his back turned and his words muffled. 'He and I are doing just fine. We're cut from the same cloth, the old boy and me.'

This taciturn, scathing Connor wasn't one that any of them recognised and Alice thought, yet again, that bringing Lizzie or Will might have been a better solution. After all, Connor barely knew the three people in this room, owed them nothing, not even an explanation – and yet . . .

Alice accepted the offered espresso with a smile, wandering around the kitchen, taking in the all-encompassing views from every window. Not another soul in sight. True isolation – both literal and metaphorical.

'We've come to say sorry,' she said simply.

With the benefit of hindsight, of course, it had been a mistake to bring Kitty. Perhaps it was the illusion of his old life and new life overlapping that seemed to make Connor flinch every time she spoke, or touched him. And it was obvious from the familiarity and frequency of her touch that theirs was a friendship that had prospects.

'Come and show me the grounds then,' Alice encouraged, as the sun finally broke through the cloud cover, and the coffee had long since been replaced by wine. Very good wine, as it happened. Clearly Connor's cellar had a lot to recommend it, nervous breakdowns aside.

Kitty was lying on the enormous sofa in the kitchen, Jamieson flaked out, snoring, half on top of her and the other dogs pressing themselves tightly around her. She wasn't going anywhere. Jamie sat back at the kitchen table, feet propped up. 'I'll stay here.' He gave Alice and Connor a brief nod, his presence benign but reassuring.

Connor needed no encouragement, only serving to convince Alice that her intuition was right. When worlds collide . . .

Stepping from the momentary brightness of the landscaped lawns into the cover of the trees, Alice felt the temperature drop still further. With each step, she and Coco kicked up the virgin snow, the first to break its crisp finish. 'I can see why you love it here,' she said to Connor. The rural isolation of Connor's Dorset estate made Larkford look positively cosmopolitan by comparison and the snow only compounded its rare beauty.

'It's very special,' he agreed, 'but hardly the reason you're making the longest house call in NHS history?'

'Oh, this isn't a house call,' Alice countered instantly. 'I'm not here as your doctor; I'm here as your friend. In fact, there was so much competition for the Find Connor Mission, that we all drew straws. Me, Lizzie, Will, Holly, Taffy, Elsie – even Clive was beginning to wonder where you'd scooted off to.'

Connor raised an eyebrow sceptically. 'And you got the short straw?'

'Exactly!' said Alice, blushing furiously as she stumbled into his trap. 'No! I mean, not the short— That is, I won.'

'I appreciate you coming, I do. But you're on a fool's errand. If there's one thing the last few weeks have taught me, it's that I can't run away from my problems.'

Alice's brow furrowed. 'But isn't that exactly what you *are* doing?'

They stepped out into a wide, open glade, which was crisscrossed by deer tracks, startling a pair of red kites, who swept up into the air with such grace and majesty that Alice found herself speechless. She glanced around and her gaze fell upon a single winter cherry tree, its nascent blossom incongruous against the snow, and it became clear that theirs had been no aimless ramble.

'I ran away *to* Larkford,' Connor corrected her. 'So there's no wonder it didn't work out. I needed to come back here. To deal with it properly. I guess I just realised that I can't live with one foot in the past, or it will always be calling to me . . .'

'So, selling the estate?' Alice ventured.

Connor shrugged. 'Time to say goodbye.' He saw her wince and a half-smile tugged briefly across his face. 'It's nothing dramatic. Why do people always assume that if you're creative, you're all about the drama? It's a question of practicality really. How can I commit to a life in Larkford, building a business there, if I've always got this place as a bolthole? It's just hard, you know, to let go? Let alone to start building a new life . . .'

He stepped over to the tiny cherry tree in the centre of the clearing, its very fragility showing its youth. 'Rachel and I planted this tree the same weekend we found out she was expecting.'

'Oh,' managed Alice quietly, imminent tears beginning to gather and a prescient tingle at the back of her neck.

'This was supposed to be our forever home. My grand-children were supposed to climb this tree and learn about its history. Our family history. How can I move on, Alice, and leave this tree behind?'

'Bloody hell,' gulped Alice, all professionalism long since having deserted her. 'I have no idea, Conn. Not a bloody clue.' She sniffed inelegantly. 'But I do think you're right and that living with the past is no way to build a future. And I think that Rachel would agree. I mean, I didn't know her – but you do. You know that she would want you to be happy again.'

Connor gave a wry smile. 'She used to tease me about the second Mrs Danes, you know? But it was only ever funny because we knew it wouldn't happen . . . It still won't.'

They stood in silence for a moment, Coco circling around them, contentedly drinking in the feast of new smells and delights. It was certainly tempting to think that this rural idyll might hold all the answers that Connor was obviously looking for, but Alice held firm. He needed people around him, specifically people who cared, as he made his next steps into the world.

She opened her mouth, about to tell him just that, when he spoke.

Not necessarily to her, or so it seemed. Perhaps *near* her was a more accurate assessment, as he quietly unburdened his soul.

'I didn't go looking for fame, you know? I was just this awkward, spotty, gangly teenager – I looked as though I'd got caught in the elevator doors. But I loved my music. And then I got to college and there were four of us. Just having fun, jamming together. It gave us something to focus on while everyone else was getting girlfriends . . .' He gave a small, tired laugh at the memory. 'And then, one day, there was Rachel. She saw something in me, I guess. She saw enough to make it worth her while to shack up with a music nerd, when she could have had her pick of any man in the Student Union.

'And she made me a better me. Even without all the fame and the success and the madness – I was still a nicer bloke when she was in the room.

'And now, without Rachel, it's like I've forgotten how to be "Connor Danes" – I've forgotten how to be anything other than that awkward kid.' He shrugged. 'Sitting with her in Hyde Park blowing bubbles at the pigeons is the last authentically "me" moment I remember before this whole crazy Hive thing began. I have no idea who to be now,' he finished despondently.

Alice reached out and wrapped one arm around his shivering shoulders, resting her head against him. 'Just be yourself, Conn.'

'I have no idea who that is. And how clichéd is that?' he replied earnestly. 'Middle-aged rocker trying to "find" himself by organising some mad music festival? You know, I think it's because we all missed the part where most people grow up – we got to carry on playing every day and got paid to do it . . . I'm just a teenager in an ageing body at this point.'

He shook his head as Alice made to contradict this assessment. 'Maybe I should have bought a Porsche instead of a farm and just embraced it?'

'A full on midlife crisis?' Alice said doubtfully.

'Or finally time to grow up, right?' He sighed. 'She'd like the irony I suppose. Rachel. Me quitting the band now, even though I couldn't do it when she asked me to.' He paused. 'She was worried I was going to be Peter Pan,' he explained, his fingers still grazing the delicate blossom of the cherry tree in front of them. 'She wasn't sure you could be in a band and still be a good dad.'

Alice certainly wasn't going to acknowledge that Rachel probably had a point. There was nothing to be gained by adding to the burden of Connor's guilt.

'So I've been thinking, while I've been here, that somehow, I owe it to Rachel to find something positive out of this whole ghastly mess.'

'Like the festival?' prompted Alice.

He shrugged. 'Maybe. But actually I was thinking more about other people's kids. The kids that don't know that eggs don't come in boxes or what a cow looks like, or what grass feels like walking barefoot . . .' He nodded to himself, as though a decision had been made.

'Like an outreach programme?' Alice said, trying to follow his train of thought.

'Well, it seems mad to me that a third of the kids in this

country don't know where milk comes from, you know? And who are they more likely to listen to, eh? "Connor Danes" or some crusty old farmer?'

Alice eyed him up. The stubble on his jawline, the filthy wellies and tattered muddy clothes, smiling at the look of peaceful determination that had settled on his face. 'A distinction without a difference, my friend,' she said, tucking her arm through his and feeling his laughter vibrate through her.

Baby steps, she thought, as they walked back towards the house, to Kitty, Jamie and the other dogs. At least he was thinking ahead, thinking of a future. All she had to do now was persuade him that his future was in Larkford, among friends.

Chapter 36

Back in Larkford, Dan and Taffy wound their way among friends, neighbours and patients to snag the last available table in the pub, both of them relieved to have finally heard from Alice. It seemed as though the whole team had been holding their breath for a while there.

No matter what came next, Dan thought, whatever Connor decided to do, at least he was safe and supported. At least the dialogue was open.

Laughter and the rustle of crisp packets punctuated every conversation around them, the recent snow days clearly having achieved more in the way of camaraderie and bonhomie than any number of medical interventions and Dan couldn't help thinking that it was exactly where Connor should be. Although . . .

'Who knew it would be so busy this afternoon,' grumbled Dan, as the pub's enormous wood burner belted out heat and he pulled off his jumper, tossing it onto the chair beside him, earning quite a few appreciative stares as his shirt rode up revealingly.

Even Taffy found himself staring a little at the impressive six-pack that Dan was sporting. 'Jesus, Dan, how in hell are you getting fitter with age when the rest of us are declining into spuds?'

Dan raised an eyebrow at Taffy's prurient interest in his stomach. 'Something you'd like to share with the group?'

Taffy scowled. 'Ignore me, I'm just jealous. I have to tell you that I knew having babies was a challenge for a woman's figure, I just hadn't realised what a toll it would take on mine.' He prodded at his own softening stomach in annoyance. 'The less sleep I get, the more crap I eat — and there's always, always snacks in the house for the kids.'

'Ah, the vicious circle of life,' said Dan, addling his idioms. 'Of course, some of us spend hours working out to distract ourselves from our deficiency in that department. So, you know, swings and roundabouts.' He sipped at his orange juice, eyeing Taffy's cola with longing.

'Dare I ask how things are progressing on that front?' Taffy asked, dropping his voice until only Dan could hear him.

'Well, I guess two steps forward, one step back is a fair approximation,' he said, not quite meeting Taffy's eye.

'Hang on,' Taffy counted on his fingers, 'that still means you're moving forwards though, right?'

Dan looked up, trying and failing to keep his voice level. 'Let's just say that my thoughts on adoption aren't exactly what they were. And that Grace and I seem to be singing from the same song sheet for once, but it's not straightforward.'

'Nothing in life that's worth having ever is,' said Taffy.

'You've been living with Elsie too long,' Dan countered.

'No such thing,' Taffy said with a grin. 'I can't pretend that peace and quiet is something we have a lot of at Number 42, but I couldn't be happier. The more the merrier as far as I'm concerned.'

A flicker of anxiety crossed Dan's face, however much he tried to hide it. 'I know we're supposed to be keeping it under our hats; but it seems weird not to share this with you. Can I tell you something, just between us?'

'Always.'

'Grace and I, well, we've been exploring a few options on the adoption front, or possibly even a legal guardianship, but really all our hopes are kind of focused on one child—'

'Lulu?' Taffy interrupted with a knowing smile.

'Lulu.' Dan nodded. 'I don't know what it is about that child, Taffs, but I've fallen completely in love with her. And Grace too – there's just a connection between us and her circumstances are so up in the air, but she's everything I could ever wish for in a daughter and more.'

'You're soulmates,' said Taffy simply, with slightly uncharacteristic insight. 'And it's obvious to anyone watching that she feels the same. She gravitates towards you, Dan, as though you're the only person in the room. And let's face it, her circumstances, as you put it, really don't have a happy ending in sight, do they?'

Dan shook his head. 'Grace and I talked to Keira yesterday, all above board – and offered our home for Lulu. She hasn't got long left, poor girl, but she's incredibly focused when it comes to her daughter. I get the impression, though, that she was hoping that Holly might decide to make the current arrangements more permanent.'

'Whoa,' said Taffy, breathing out in a whoosh. 'You mean, she wants Lulu to stay with me and Holly, like, officially join the family? I hadn't realised.'

Dan nodded, a half shrug doing little to conceal how invested he was in this conversation. 'I guess. I mean, you guys have form on the parenting front; I don't.'

'Yes, but Grace does. I know her kids are all grown-up and they're not exactly the most reliable of visitors, but they're good kids, yeah? Isn't one of them in the army now?'

Dan nodded. 'Freddie is in the Welsh Guards and Luke is a carpenter on the Duchy Estate in Cornwall. Nice lads. Bit crap at keeping in touch with their mum, but seem fairly genuine.'

'Is there anything you could do to convince Keira that you and Grace are the answer?' Taffy asked.

'I'm not sure I want to "convince" her – either she thinks we'll take care of Lulu or she doesn't, but it has to be her choice. Well, hers and May's – but I'm not sure May even knows what day of the week it is anymore. The clock is running out for both of them.'

'When did life get so complicated?' Taffy mused, obviously feeling the burden of expectation heavy on his shoulders.

'When we became grown-ups, I suppose,' Dan replied.

'What? When did this happen?' Taffy replied with a weary grin. 'This is fresh information!' He shrugged. 'Do you know what, though, I think Holly would agree with me, that even if Lulu was living with you, she'd still be a part of our family in every way that matters. Maybe Keira will see that too ... Or maybe she should actually talk to Holly about it. I mean, my wife is rubbish at saying no to people in need, but she's spread pretty thin these days. And she's being brilliant about me wanting time with the kids, and maybe even bringing the Rugby funding into the fold.'

'She's not still thinking of taking the job?' Dan's head shot up like a meerkat.

Taffy shook his head. 'Yes, but no, but ... You know I said how we were planning on restructuring our working lives so we both got a bit of what we needed? Well, Holly seems to have taken it one step further in her head – she's trying to tick that box for everyone at The Practice. Now, it might be a fool's errand, but—'

'When Holly sets her mind to something, never say never,' Dan interrupted thoughtfully. 'So we each get to do a day in Bath? Is that the plan?'

Taffy shrugged. 'I've given up trying to second-guess how her mind works. I've only just learned to actually tell her what I'm grizzling about rather than wait for her to guess. Communication works – who knew? Relationships are never easy, are they? In real life, I mean.'

Dan leaned forward and gave Taffy a nudge towards the window. 'And I imagine you're not the only one thinking that, right now.'

Taffy turned to see where Dan was looking and his mouth dropped open in surprise. 'Is that my nanny holding hands with our junior, while walking my kids?' he managed in staccato bursts.

'Looks like it,' Dan said with a grin. 'Life in Larkford is nothing but incestuous, is it? Go, Tilly. Look how sweet they are together.' Dan tried not to show his surprise; Taffy was looking stunned enough for both of them. It was some measure of the man he wanted to be that he swallowed all the one-liners that sprang immediately to mind.

'I can't believe our nanny is a lesbian,' Taffy stumbled after a moment. 'She never said. I mean, it explains why she never laughs at my jokes, but thinks Holly's are hysterical.'

'Does it, though?' Dan asked sympathetically. 'It could be that you're just not that funny these days.'

It was as though he had questioned Taffy's very reason for being, based on the filthy look he earned in reply.

'I suppose every town should have a lesbian,' Taffy said after a moment of consideration.

'Happy towns have two,' quipped Dan in reply, colouring with embarrassment at his lack of restraint.

Taffy just grinned. 'They do look happy though, don't they? I mean, if you ignore the slightly terrified glances Tilly keeps shooting our way.' He stood up and opened the window. 'Come and join us, I'm in need of a cuddle!' he called out. 'From the twins, I mean,' he clarified hastily.

Dan chortled to himself, relieved he wasn't the only one tripping over himself in a bid to be as supportively open-minded as possible.

'Grab a seat and I'll get some drinks in,' Dan said as Tilly and Plum came into the pub, weaving their way through the tables towards them. 'Looks like we have some good news to celebrate?' He smiled at them both. 'I love lesbians,' he blurted and then froze on the spot as Taffy wet himself laughing. 'I mean, I'm so pleased that you've found each other – that you're happy, being together, that is, and—'

'Me too,' ventured Tilly, shaking her head and trying not to laugh at his obvious distress, as he dug himself in deeper. 'Well, if we're being *strictly* accurate, it's only this one actually.'

Plum glanced over her shoulder and smiled at Tilly as she and Taffy liberated the twins from the pram to be passed around and admired as always.

'Good choice,' said Taffy, trying to avert his gaze from Plum's neckline as Olivia tugged at the fabric and gave everyone nearby an ample eyeful of cleavage.

'I hope this is okay, that I did not mention sooner?' Plum said, obviously aware that Taffy was in fact her boss.

'Sure,' said Taffy. 'I mean. Yeah. Our Tilly might even stop being a flight risk if you give her enough reasons to stay.' He settled back into his chair, a babe in each arm and with a wistful look at his pint.

Plum and Tilly smiled at each other in that knowing way that new couples do, as though they were the only people in the world who understood each other completely.

Dan returned with a trayful of drinks and snacks, having even thought to bring a long straw for Taffy. 'Bumped into Matthew Giles at the bar.' He gave Tilly a meaningful look and she glanced over his shoulder in alarm. 'He's all buoyed up by this new funding package and keen to celebrate.' His clumsy attempts at conveying his cryptic message were utterly wasted though.

'Ah, this Matteo – he is the one who is loving my Tilly, yes?' Plum said, completely unfazed, and blissfully unaware of how smutty her innocent words sounded with her Italian accent.

She paused and waited a moment for Matthew to turn around with his tray of drinks, glancing their way. Turning, she cupped Tilly's cheek in her hand and leaned in to kiss her thoroughly, passionately, leaving no doubt in anyone's minds as to the exact nature of their 'friendship'.

'And that,' Dan said drily, as every single table around them fell silent, 'is how you share news in Larkford.'

Plum pulled away, her eyes fixed on Tilly's. 'So, now we have no secrets and you don't have to tell a soul. *Non c'è problema.*'

Tilly pressed her hands to her lips and blinked. 'Well, when I said I didn't want to *tell* everyone, that's not *exactly* what I had in mind,' she whispered.

A slow but emphatic round of applause echoed round The Kingsley Arms, punctuated by occasional whoops and hollers. Larkford might at times be backwards in moving forwards, thought Dan, but the affection for Tilly was obvious in their reaction. Perhaps the team at The Practice hadn't been the only ones to watch in concern as she ricocheted from one disastrous hook-up to another?

'Well, I guess your way works too,' said Tilly, blushing to the very roots of her hair. 'Nothing left to say, is there really?'

'Oh, I think one or two people might have a few questions,' said Dan quietly, as he noticed the expression on Matthew's face, along with one or two others who had clearly shared Tilly's bed only recently.

'Not today, though,' said Taffy, attempting to wrangle his bendy straw into submission. 'I think today is about welcoming Plum properly to the fold.'

'The fold?' queried Plum. 'What am I folding?'

'He means the team,' whispered Tilly, not letting go of her hand. 'My team.' She paused and corrected herself: 'Our team.'

'Go, Team Taffy!' Taffy said with feeling. 'I still have t-shirts left if anyone's interested?'

Dan just shook his head. 'You're so behind the times, mate. It's Squad 42 all the way now – Holly sent out an email.'

'Of course she did,' said Taffy, shaking his head in amused defeat.

'So, lots of change on the horizon. Lots to celebrate,' said Dan. 'I think we may need a little continuity, just to keep us on the straight and narrow.' He froze. 'Not like straight, straight – but you know what I mean,' he blustered.

'What did you have in mind?' asked Tilly curiously, pointedly ignoring his verbal flailing.

Dan glanced around the group with affection. 'I'm thinking a league. Or a competition of some kind.' He paused as inspiration struck. 'We need a Championship Game-Off. Cluedo. Jenga. Monopoly. All the Classics.'

'Work hard; play hard,' Taffy said. 'But even I have to admit the dartboard was a mistake,' he said, glancing over at Maggie, their pharmacist, and the stunning black eye that was turning steadily ochre.

'Okay then. Winner to be announced at Connor's festival thingy,' Dan said firmly. 'Sounds perfectly sensible to me.'

'Sensible?' queried Tilly, knowing full well that the team would jump on this idea in a heartbeat.

'Well, I shall have you know that we are in fact professional grown-ups. As has only recently been brought to my attention. Of course we'll be sensible,' Dan countered.

'Although, to be completely honest, my mum doesn't let me play Monopoly anymore,' Taffy said quietly. 'Something to do with over-enthusiasm.'

'Hmmm,' said Dan. 'Well, in my league you can be as enthusiastic as you like!'

'*Madonna mia!*' murmured Plum under her breath. 'What have you started?'

Chapter 37

Holly pressed the heels of her hands into her eyes and breathed out slowly the next morning. The headaches in her life were both literal and metaphorical these days and she could see only too clearly how easy it would be to continually reach for the 'slightly stronger' painkillers; slightly stronger, in her professional experience, meaning opioids. Opioids meaning a slippery slope to addiction – even the over-the-counter, common or garden packs you could buy freely from any pharmacy. It was certainly food for thought, not only where her worsening headaches were concerned, but also some of her patients.

She'd had quite a shock, coming back so abruptly after her maternity leave, at how many of her patients were relying on these meds just to function in their lives. Yet another example, she felt, of how a longer conversation might be more helpful – and save money – in the long run, than simply writing a prescription. They would never dream of sticking a Band-Aid on a dirty cut, but when it came to the thorny, subjective issue of 'pain', it seemed as though that was exactly what they'd been doing. That alone was motivation enough to keep pursuing her plans, no matter how many obstacles were seemingly determined to fall in her path.

She took away her hands, blinking in the light and squinted at her phone screen.

So much for business as usual.

Any thoughts about focusing on her planned reshuffle at The Practice, or even her re-entry to the work place, shelved in light of a moment's indiscretion.

She was actually a little stunned at the emails tumbling into her inbox from some of their patients. From everything Taffy had told her, the reception to Tilly's new relationship status had been overwhelmingly positive at the pub, and yet . . .

She quickly tucked her phone away as Plum bustled into the kitchen, all five children suited and booted for the walk to school. 'So, I drop the boys and then take the girls to visit Banana, yes?'

'Yes, please,' Holly replied, this impromptu visit to Blackleigh Farm the most sure-fire way she could think of for giving them all a little breathing space to quash the rumours and narrow-mindedness that seemed to have gathered impetus overnight. 'The Major knows you're coming and that Lulu wants to meet the new little horses. I imagine the twins will sleep all morning, waking up so early.'

Plum nodded, her glance flickering to the large station clock that dominated one wall of the kitchen, not to mention their lives at times. There were never enough hours in the day.

'Holly,' she said quietly, 'I am not blind to what is happening, what people are saying in the town – sending emails to Tilly – and perhaps I should have been a little more *discreto*. Oh Holly – *mi dispiace, non è mai stata mia intenzione*—' Her words tumbled out, one on top of another, bursting with emotion that conveyed something of her meaning, even if Holly's schoolgirl translation was a little muddy.

'Stop, Plum. Stop. My Italian can't keep up with you,'

Holly said gently. 'Look, nobody's judging you here. Would a little more discretion have been a good idea? Well, probably, yes. But mainly because Tilly has a position of responsibility in this community and, maybe yes, Larkford is a little slow to move with the times.' She took a breath and reached out to squeeze Plum's hand reassuringly. 'We need to support Tilly now, okay? It's all very new for her, to feel the way she does, and her job means that she's probably going to find it harder than you to adapt. Okay?'

Plum nodded, looking discomfited and ill at ease with herself for the first time since she'd arrived in their lives. Holly sighed. The last thing she needed right now was to be holding the nanny's hand while she worked through her own personal and professional crises.

She had enough on her plate.

She remembered all too clearly Elsie's words of wisdom when they'd first considered the idea of a live-in nanny or au pair: 'So long as you realise you're gaining another child, as well as some help with the ones you've already got, then you won't be disillusioned.'

How very true.

Holly stood up and poured some coffee into a travel mug, pressing it into Plum's hands with a warm smile. 'Enjoy the fresh air, enjoy the countryside and leave Tilly's professional image to us, okay?'

'I have let her down,' said Plum tremulously. 'Oh, Holly, what did I do to her? This is her home, her job, her image and I just wanted everyone to know . . . I have been so shellfish!' she wailed. 'Only thinking about me and what I want.'

Holly couldn't help a small yelp of laughter, not just at Plum's malapropism, but also at the sheer ridiculousness of the situation. It hardly needed a boost of continental drama. It was surely Tilly who needed their compassion and support most. This was obviously not Plum's first rodeo and yet she seemed to have no concept that Tilly might need a gentler approach to a whole new world of same-sex relationships.

'Plum. Take the kids to school, keep the twins warm and let me talk to Tilly, okay?' she said firmly, the clock above the table forcing the issue.

Plum got as far as the door, before turning to face her with a tear-stained face. 'If you want me to leave, Holly, I would understand.'

'Don't be daft, Plum,' said Holly bluntly, making sure she kissed all of the children in turn on their way out.

Dear God, she thought tiredly, as the door closed behind them. Elsie had been right on the money. Unfortunately her own parenting experience to date had only prepared her for playground scuffles and supermarket meltdowns. She had never felt so ill-equipped.

Her phone rang beside her on the table – Patronising Patricia – well, thought Holly, let's see what she advises on this one.

'I'm so glad you called, Patricia,' she said. 'There's an adjustment issue at work I'd love your thoughts on.'

Holly walked into The Practice twenty minutes later, late and frazzled, to find Grace waiting for her in the hallway, a cup of coffee held out as an offering and an apology on her lips. 'I hope you had your Ready Brek this morning?' she said. 'I'm so sorry but your clinic is massively overbooked. Alice is en route back from Dorset, but until then I've had to share Tilly's patients out among you all.'

'Are you serious?' Holly checked, almost waiting for the

punchline. 'I can't believe people would actually boycott her clinic because she happens to like girls. Frankly, based on half the men in my acquaintance, so do I! It's bizarre.'

'Well, as insightful as that was,' said Grace with a twinkle, 'you've actually got the wrong end of the stick: it's Tilly who's refusing to see patients. Apparently she got a few judgey emails and is dying of mortification.' Grace shook her head. 'Poor girl, doesn't know whether she's coming or going. Yesterday she was all "out and proud" – snogging in the pub – and today she's—'

'Oh hang on,' interrupted Holly, 'that's hardly fair. From what I heard, she didn't really get much of a say before Plum landed a smacker on her.'

'Oh,' said Grace, clearly wrong-footed. 'Well, I'm all for a little bit of what you fancy doing you good, but it's not rocket science to see that a little careful handling might have made the transition easier. For everyone.'

Holly shrugged. 'They're young, they're in love. Common sense just goes out the window, doesn't it?' she said wistfully. 'Being a grown-up, considering all the options, weighing up the right strategy – well, it just doesn't have the same rosy hue, does it?'

'That was said with feeling,' Grace replied, tucking her arm through Holly's as they walked towards her consulting-room door. 'Tell you what, let's get through the sapphic shuffle and then we'll make a plan to do something spontaneous.'

Holly turned. 'You see! Did you hear that? You can't *plan* to be spontaneous. Let's face it – our days of snogging in the pub are long gone.'

'Speak for yourself,' Grace countered.

'Not to mention that, according to Patronising Patricia, I shouldn't try and mother everyone at work, just because I've

had a baby. I don't think she knows her advice is about five
years too late!'

Grace glanced at her watch. 'Speaking of which, I don't
suppose you could pop in and have a word with Tilly just to
reassure her – it would make the whole day go one hell of a
lot more smoothly with all hands on deck.'

Holly swigged the coffee and gave Grace back the mug.
'There'd better be Danish pastries in my future, Grace Allen,'
she said, striding towards Tilly's closed door, taking a deep
breath as she did so.

Pushing open the door, she could see immediately that
Grace hadn't been exaggerating. It was as though the über-
confident Tilly they all knew (and worried about) had
proverbially left the building. Instead, Holly took in her pale
anxious face and the sleeves dragged down over her hands,
her whole demeanour designed, presumably, to avoid attention or notice.

'Well,' said Holly, 'I hope Connor Danes knows what a
bloody good friend you are!'

'What?' said Tilly, intrigued despite herself. 'What's
Connor got to do with any of this?'

Holly perched on the treatment couch and shrugged.
'Well, nobody's talking about that awful radio phone-in, now,
are they?' She smiled. 'I think he should really say thank you
in person, don't you?'

Tilly frowned. 'You know I've seen you pull this routine
with Ben and Tom a hundred times? You can't just "jolly me
out" of this – obviously it was a huge mistake . . .'

'Why?' Holly countered. 'You like Plum; she likes you.
Just because it's a slight deviation from your usual love-'em-
and-leave-'em routine, doesn't mean it's a mistake. In fact,' she
paused, determined to make sure she had Tilly's undivided

attention, 'I might go so far as to say it's the first truly authentic decision you've made since you joined us.'

'Are you saying I've been living a lie?'

'Nope. It can't be a lie, if you didn't know either, right? And, from where I was sitting – admittedly grossly pregnant, and utterly hormonal – you've been questing for *something* from the moment you turned up at the auction all those months ago. Maybe, your Damascene moment isn't about your patients, and your causes and your charitable works. Maybe, it's about finding out what makes *you* tick?'

'I'm not a clock, Holly,' Tilly said sulkily, but it was obvious that the words were playing over in her mind. 'Do you mean all my volunteering was just a symptom of confusion?'

'Nope. Just that you were looking for validation, right? Trying to fill the hole in your chest, the longing to belong, that no amount of one-night stands could satisfy.'

Tilly chewed on her bottom lip. 'I don't feel like that with Plum. And I don't feel as though I need to charge off to the Andes to make a difference. When we're together it just feels normal, like I've always known her.'

'You see,' said Holly. 'Now, how can something that makes you feel so grounded and authentic possibly be a bad thing? Or something to be embarrassed about? I mean, if old Mrs Doo-Dah has a bee in her bonnet about girls who like girls, I would suggest that's her issue, not yours. And certainly not something to prevent you from doing the job that you happen to be getting rather good at.'

Holly breathed a sigh of relief at having made even the smallest of connections; she was navigating blind here. No matter what Patronising Patricia had said, the only way forward had to be instinctive, had to verge on the maternal. And based on Tilly's hands slowly emerging from her sleeves and the full-bodied sniff stopping tears in their tracks, something of what she'd said must have resonated.

'How on earth do you know all this stuff?' Tilly said, after a moment.

Holly shrugged. 'I watched an awful lot of Oprah on maternity leave?'

Tilly stood up and walked across the room. 'Now, if I give you a hug, I'm not coming on to you, okay? I'm just saying thank you.'

Holly laughed and squeezed back, a little overcome by how much this awkward, cagey girl had come to mean to her.

'And I should probably say the same to the indignant Mrs Doo-Dah and her wonky nipple. God forbid, I might take one look at her droopy old bosom and be unable to resist her.' Tilly huffed. 'It's okay to let Coco sniff that one out, right? If she can get past the smell of cabbage, I mean.' Tilly chortled as she released Holly from their hug, her entire demeanour now lighter and more like her usual self – just without the sharp corners.

Holly smiled broadly, choosing to ignore any disrespect to Mrs Grayson, who frankly had jettisoned the right when she wrote that hateful email.

Ah, youth, she thought, bowled over by Tilly's ability to bounce back and wondering when she herself had lost the knack.

Authenticity and resilience seemed to be transforming the young woman before her. And maybe the answer really was that simple and Billy Ocean was, in fact, a prophet before his time – when the going got tough, the answer was simply to get going.

Holly glanced around Tilly's boxy consulting room and frowned, all her plans for The Practice seemingly illuminated, yet hardly bearing in mind the lack of sunlight in this cupboard.

'Now, Tilly Campbell, as your mentor, I believe you need to see a few patients and then, you owe me some serious research. I've had a few more ideas ...'

'Well at least my nervous breakdown has been inspirational,' said Tilly with a cheeky grin.

'More than you could possibly know,' said Holly slowly, as the cogs in her brain slowly slotted together and began to turn.

Chapter 38

Holly drew a looping line to connect the circles on the diagram in front of her, before sitting back to sip her coffee with a smile.

Progress indeed.

She couldn't help but wonder how she'd soldiered on for all those months without these small moments of respite to regain her equilibrium, assuming perhaps that balance, much like her beloved skinny jeans, was simply another casualty of having twins. Twice.

But now, taking a break in The Deli in the hiatus between clinics, knowing that both Plum and Taffy would be taking care of her children and enjoying the feeling of seclusion from the steamed-up windows, she felt able to give a little more of herself without risking complete meltdown.

'Nice pebbles,' said Hattie, as she placed a plateful of goat cheese crostini beside her, already familiar with Holly's affinity with visual planning. 'Are you organising everyone in Larkford now?'

'No-o,' said Holly with a grin. 'Just my kids, my colleagues and their entire work-life balance.'

'Easy,' said Hattie smiling. 'I'm guessing you might want another coffee?'

'Make it a double?' Holly replied with feeling.

It had seemed such a simple concept in theory, to try and work out what each person's 'deal-breaker' was – to pinpoint the priority issue that would make the difference between a day being meh or rewarding. Not so much in practice, as it turned out.

One person's meat really did seem to be another person's poison: in this case, the concept of simplifying and diversifying their working lives to give them all a sense of both job satisfaction and professional accomplishment – without sacrificing their personal lives into the bargain.

Holly was beginning to understand why there was such a large motivational section in the bookshop now. It was almost as though she were late to a party she hadn't known she was even invited to.

She glanced up as the door swung open, heralding a draught of chilled air from outside and a sight for sore eyes. Connor gave her a self-conscious smile as he walked in, pushing his wayward hair back from his forehead, his newly acquired beard now trimmed into submission.

'You're back!' exclaimed Holly, leaping up and giving him an awkward hug, noticing how thin he felt in her arms and jolted by a sense of relief. 'Well, thank fuck for that!' she said, earning herself a smile at least for the profanity and enthusiasm. She dropped her voice. 'I've been so worried about you.'

He shrugged. 'I guess you weren't the only one.' He dipped his head towards the door. Outside, Alice was pacing the pavement, Coco following her every turn, as she talked intently into her mobile phone. 'I think they just thought if they outnumbered me, I'd have no choice but to come back.'

'Sounds about right,' Holly agreed with a gentle smile.

'But you were coming back anyway?' she checked. 'I hadn't completely misread the situation, had I?'

It was unprofessional and it was a little self-serving, but Holly's boundaries were increasingly blurred when it came to Connor – first his friend, never really his doctor, but yet somehow with the burden of responsibility had she missed the warning signs.

He paused. 'I guess so. For Hattie's coffee, at least.' He picked at the hem of his unravelling jumper as he placed his order, before turning back to Holly and dropping his voice. 'But maybe their half-cocked intervention wasn't such a bad idea – willing myself to feel better was kind of counter-productive, to be honest.'

Holly nodded. It was ever thus with this kind of depression: the more you pushed yourself to keep on going, the worse the symptoms could become. 'Well, I for one am glad to see you. If nothing else, Nineteen has been pining for you in your absence.'

Connor smiled, the first genuine flicker of positive emotion since he walked through the door. 'You know, for a porker, he's remarkably health-conscious. Loves a windfall apple, doesn't he? By the tonne! I think he rather likes living in the orchard. Even with all the honeybees humming away in their hives.' Connor flinched unwittingly, looking around and lowering his voice still further, clearly so fragile and easily unsettled. 'Holly, be blunt with me: Do *you* think I'm being selfish having an apiary at the farm, if there are children nearby with bee allergies?' he asked, Cassie's relentless criticism now apparently internalised and tormenting him.

'I might be wrong, but I think there were bees in Larkford before you came to town. Rest easy on this one, Conn,' she reassured him.

He nodded, clearly unconvinced, and obviously having reached that stage where believing the bad things was easier than accepting the good. 'They won't range far – even come summer – I've set up the hives in the orchard so they won't need to. So, unless young Tarquin decides to start scrumping, I reckon he's pretty safe,' Connor said, his brow furrowed. 'What's the bets that whoever gets stung next summer will come knocking on my door, though?'

'Let's cross that bridge when we come to it,' said Holly kindly, unwilling to buy into his catastrophising, trying to catch the right moment to make her own suggestion. 'In the meantime, maybe you and I should have a proper chat? Not here; at The Practice?'

Connor hesitated, glancing outside to Alice. 'Probably a good idea. I mean, Alice is lovely, but . . .' He shrugged.

Holly rested a hand briefly on his shoulder. 'We'll get you sorted,' she said. 'I promise. But no shortcuts, okay?' She thought back to Reverend Taylor's advice all those weeks ago. 'Nobody else can do the work but you, Conn, but we're all here to help. You won't be short of support. And if you'd rather see Dan or Taffy?'

He shook his head, his vulnerability flashing across his face for a moment. 'I gather you're the headshrinker of the team. But I can't promise you I'm going to be an easy patient. I just know that I can't go on feeling like this and pretending that's okay. It's getting harder and harder to keep up the façade, you know?'

Holly nodded. Connor's ability to 'switch on' his public face had not escaped her notice. If nothing else, she was convinced that the 'high-functioning' part of her diagnosis for Connor was spot on the money. How exhausting that alone must be, she thought.

'I'm *so* glad you're back,' said Holly once more, apropos of nothing, surprised by the lump of emotion in her throat.

Connor glanced up from his fraying cuff. 'Ah, you big softie, Holly. I bet you don't say that to all your patients.'

'No,' she said simply. 'I don't. But you're not just my patient, Conn, you're my friend and like it or not, there are lots of people in Larkford who care about you and want to help with your—'

He flinched again. 'Has it been that obvious then, that I'm losing the plot? Should I expect another flurry of journalists on my doorstep any day now quizzing me about my nervous breakdown?' He stopped mid-rant, looking embarrassed for a moment. 'But that's not what you meant, is it?'

'Nope,' said Holly easily. 'I meant the festival, really. But if you choose to let people in about your health too, then I would wager the same applies.'

Connor shrugged, clearly discomfited at the very thought. For someone who lived life in the public eye, he was a sur-prisingly private man. 'Yeah, about the festival . . .'

It was obvious from his tone that he'd made a decision; a decision that Holly couldn't and wouldn't endorse. 'You're not jacking it in,' she said firmly.

'Why not?' Connor replied. 'I've lost my sponsor. And it's not as though it's played out the way I'd hoped. I mean, I'd *hoped* to wow everyone with a stellar line-up and the prospect of a boost to local tourism, but it seems I misread the room.'

'Ah, the room,' said Holly kindly. 'Don't feel bad. The thing about the room, is that it can change in a heartbeat. It's part and parcel of living in a small town. Plus, you know, there are some pretty strong characters in Larkford who like to throw their weight around, but it doesn't mean they speak for everyone, even if they are shouting louder.'

They shared a loaded glance, knowing exactly whom they were talking about.

'Besides,' said Holly firmly, 'it's been proven time and time again that a clear sense of purpose is incredibly helpful in treating anxiety and depression. We can't have you wandering around aimlessly, adopting every waif and stray in town to populate your farm, can we?'

Connor shook his head. 'Are you saying that I'm under doctor's orders to go ahead?'

'If you like?' Holly said with a smile. 'In fact, I think we should organise a summit meeting. You can't do everything on your own, Conn, and if you want my honest opinion – although you didn't ask – you might find everything a little easier, a little less overwhelming, if you let some people in? Start with the festival, then the farm, you know? Just accept that sometimes it's good to have family around you and, I can promise you that in Larkford, we take the definition of family fairly loosely. It's more about the love than the legality.'

He gave her a sideways look. 'You're all a bunch of hippies, you know that?'

Holly grinned. 'Said the man organising a Winter Solstice festival!'

'And food!' Connor protested, despite himself. 'There's a whole vision thing going on. Food and music and the farm . . .'

'Hippy!' she accused with a grin.

Matthew Giles stood up from his table in the corner and walked over to the counter to get a coffee refill to go, smiling at their easy banter and laughter. 'You two look like trouble this morning,' he said by way of greeting.

'Always,' said Holly. She glanced across at Connor, wondering if what she was about to say was a step too far. 'Matt? Listen, we're putting together a working group to really get

Connor's festival off the ground. I don't suppose you'd be interested, would you? I had a few thoughts about getting Bath Rugby on board as a sponsor too, so we'd really appreciate your input?'

Connor simply nodded. 'Would love to hear your thoughts, mate. What you've achieved for the Young Carers is phenomenal. Hats off to you.'

Matthew's delighted smile at the recognition lit up the room. 'I'm so touched that you've noticed. Although, I have to say, the overlap with Dr Graham's Invisible Disabilities group is eye-opening. Especially when it comes to the mental health side of things – I mean, what could be more invisible than anxiety and depression? And yet that's what a lot of these kids are dealing with.'

Holly felt Connor stiffen beside her, relaxing only as he realised that Matthew wasn't making a personal dig, merely talking with dedication and enthusiasm about his work.

'The festival sounds amazing, by the way,' Matthew said to Connor. 'I'd be delighted to get involved. And not just because I'm a fan; I think it's exactly what this town needs, to be honest. I mean, living in the countryside is great when you're a grown-up, but how much stuff do we actually offer around here for our teens?'

He waved a hand around the room. 'I for one would be thrilled to see anything on the agenda that pulled them away from their phones.'

He wasn't wrong, Holly thought. Although, as a parent of younger children, it wasn't exactly on her radar; she realised it probably should be. Every person under twenty-five in The Deli, not to mention on the Market Place outside, seemed to be wedded to their phone.

Alice included, who waved insistently at Connor for him

to bring their coffees outside. Clearly any awe she felt for the rock star in their midst had long since evaporated. To Holly's amusement, he did as he was bid, thanking her and Matthew sincerely as he left, carefully balancing two takeaway espressos and a bagful of Danish pastries in one hand.

'Nice guy,' said Matthew easily.

'One of the best,' Holly replied, watching him with Alice through the window, sharing a *pain au chocolat*, no scruples or pride between them now after what they'd shared together the last few days. Even their conversation was seemingly supplemented by Alice's omnipresent iPhone though, as she showed him something that made Connor laugh in a way that gave Holly both comfort and hope for his long-term recovery.

'Tell me, on the phones?' Holly asked Matthew, intrigued. 'What are they all looking at?'

Matthew grinned. 'Instagram, Snapchat, Twitter, games . . . Where do you want to start? And sometimes it's a great support network — some of the young carers in my group keep in touch that way and it means they don't feel so alone. Sometimes, it's just fun being nosey, you know. Like #spottedinlarkford — you can waste *hours* just scrolling through that.'

'Spotted in what now?' Holly asked, even as Matthew tapped on his own phone and pulled up the screen on Twitter. 'Oh my God — how did I not know about this? It's genius. Ooh.' Holly flinched as she scrolled down and caught sight of a few choice tweets about Tilly. 'And a bit mean. I had no idea. Do people really read this?'

'Yup,' said Matthew, shaking his head in amusement at Holly's reaction. 'Everyone in town but you, apparently.'

'Isn't it a bit, I don't know, horrible? To be talking about people behind their backs?' Holly asked awkwardly.

Matthew gave her a sideways look and clicked on the photo of Tilly and Plum holding hands. 'Behind whose back?' he said, as the dialogue pinging around online included, apparently, plenty of vocal input from @BaliaToscana – The Tuscan Nanny. The same Tuscan Nanny who was proving to be a bit of a liability, in Holly's opinion.

No matter how amazing Plum was with the children, it seemed her personal life was steadily encroaching. Clearly a conversation needed to be had. And not online.

In person.

Sooner rather than later.

She paused, intrigued despite herself. 'Is there anything on here about Connor's festival?'

Matthew frowned. 'You're weird, Dr Graham. Everyone else I know – first thing they do is check to see if they get a mention. You? You go straight to the festival.'

'Well, it was uppermost in my mind,' she protested, even as her own logical brain agreed quietly with Matthew's assessment.

Matthew flicked across the screen and post after post seemed to be dedicated to slamming Connor's concept. 'It's such a shame really. Short-sighted too, business-wise. I mean the Solstice angle alone has to be a money-spinner in this part of the world, right? Not that we'll be troubling Stonehenge or Avebury any time soon.'

Holly nodded, wondering whether Connor himself had seen this particular thread. She was more convinced than ever, having talked to him, that having a singular sense of purpose was integral to his ability to move forward, to settle here, to essentially start over.

As Matthew took his leave, promising his commitment to their working group, Holly sat back in her chair, deep in thought. She wasn't sure why it hadn't occurred to her sooner, but suddenly all her doodling and plotting for The Practice seemed one-dimensional and shallow.

What applied to Connor applied equally across the board.

Everyone needed a sense of purpose, a goal that was uniquely theirs.

It was all very well Holly trying to work out what pushed everyone's buttons, but ultimately they needed to be the ones pushing them, to take responsibility for their own happiness and satisfaction.

She picked up her phone and typed in a message before she could have second thoughts:

Tilly, I'd like you to take over running the Health in the Community Scheme – and Big Bertha – your ideas, your plans, you're accountable – what do you think?

Barely a second elapsed before a string of emojis pinged up on Holly's screen – she wasn't sure what half of them were, but the overwhelming message of positivity was backed up by the second text that followed almost instantly.

Yes please!!! I cannot thank you enough, Ace Mentor. This is EXACTLY what I needed Tx

Holly smiled and deftly coloured in one pebble on her diagram, considering her working lunch at The Deli time well spent. All she had to do now was tackle the rest of the Christmas shopping. She sat back in her chair and sipped her coffee; you couldn't rush these things, she decided.

Chapter 39

'Is she saying anything?' asked Grace the next day, her back to the semi-frosted window of Keira's ward, as they waited in the 'family room'.

'I can't really see,' Dan replied, his voice twisting in timbre with frustration. 'Maybe Henry was wrong and we should just go in there and talk to her ourselves?'

Grace shook her head. 'Actually, I agree with Henry. And he is the big-bucks family-law man. What's the point in hiring him if we ignore his experience? Besides, he has a point – if we talk to her ourselves it might seem like coercion. Either way, it's all a little bit ghoulish.' Grace knew that her heart was ruling her head at this point, but the mother in her could barely begin to imagine the agonising decisions that poor Keira Fowler was trying to make right now.

No relatives.

No reliable friends.

And her mother at death's door too.

How terrified must she be of making the wrong call for her daughter's future? Possibly preferring to make no call at all, and let the chips fall where they may?

Nominating Holly as temporary guardian may have been a hurried gut-call, but it had been a good one.

And no matter what reservations Taffy had shared with Dan at the pub, Grace knew Holly only too well: there was no way she would turn Lulu out of her house unless there was a loving home awaiting her, ideally sanctioned by Lulu's mother. From where Grace was standing, it was all too realistic a prospect that Lulu might be staying exactly where she was.

Indefinitely.

She turned to Dan. 'Let Henry do his job. But if he and Keira's solicitor talk her through all the options, then it's her decision, isn't it? Her informed decision. And that has to be the priority here.'

It was easy to say the words, but part of her wanted to do just as Dan suggested; to sit down with Keira, and May if necessary, and tell them how much having Lulu in their lives, in their family, would mean to them – could mean to Lulu.

Perhaps if Keira saw Lulu and Dan together – ideally to see with her own eyes the almost tangible bond that had grown between them?

But these were hardly ideal circumstances; the softly-softly approach had only got them so far and now, thanks to a vicious bout of pneumonia, time was quickly running out for Keira.

Grace wound her hand into Dan's and rested her head on his shoulder.

'I love you,' she whispered softly.

'And I love you too,' said Dan with feeling. 'And for what it's worth, I'm so sorry I kept blocking the idea of adoption. If only I hadn't been so stubborn, we'd already be on the right path, had the right vetting, bought the right house ...' He sighed. 'We just don't look good on paper, Gracie.'

She genuinely thought her heart would break a little at the

despondent look on his face. 'No,' she said. 'I'm not doing regrets with this, Dan. Whether she comes home with us, or stays with Holly, Lulu's a gorgeous, lost soul who's now a part of our lives and I want to be grateful that so many lovely people are around to catch her if she falls. Isn't that the most important thing? And yes, I would consider it a privilege to be her guardian, but also her surrogate aunt, or her friend . . .' Her voice cracked. 'An absolute honour to be her parent.'

Dan nodded. 'I can't even bear to think about what would have happened if May had just kept on pretending to cope. All those pain meds just kicking around on the kitchen worktop with a toddler in the house?' He shuddered. 'So really any outcome that gets Lulu into a loving family environment is better than taking her chances in The System, isn't it?'

Grace angled her head to try and see how the meeting was going, but all she could make out were three fuzzy outlines and a conversation that sounded like Charlie Brown's teacher.

'Why do you think Henry wants us here?' Dan said. 'Do you think he knows something we don't?'

Grace shook her head. 'More likely the other way around, don't you think? If time is short, then surely better that we're on hand to answer any questions that come up?'

'I guess you're right. I mean, can we honestly hope to have conveyed how we feel in that stupid letter?' Dan said.

'It was not a stupid letter,' Grace countered. 'It was heart-felt. And informative. Not to mention, a necessary part of the process.'

'It hardly scratched the surface though, did it?' Dan said quietly.

Grace dashed a tear away from her eyes at the look of absolute love and commitment on his face. Never had she imagined that Dan falling in love with somebody else would bring them closer, strengthen their bond. But then never had she imagined a child like Lulu.

She glanced at her watch, practicalities as always keeping her sane. 'I should probably phone Alice and warn her you might be late – see if she can stay on for your evening clinic?'

'I'll do it,' Dan said. 'It's me asking the favour, after all, and she did seem pretty peeved earlier on. What was that about, do you think?'

Likewise, it was easier, Grace noticed, for Dan to shift his attention to the team at work, than to try and second-guess what was happening in the next room. As he talked about work, his entire posture changed, and she bit her lip, trying not to show how incredibly concerned she was. If he were so emotionally invested *now*, what would he do if Keira's decision didn't go their way?

'. . . and then she muttered something about her mother having a point about professional growth and left!' Dan said, shaking his head. 'God knows what she meant.'

Grace shrugged, a little guilty that she'd completely zoned out and missed what he was saying, just like every single time she attempted to watch a weather forecast. 'I think Alice and Tilly might be having a few adjustment issues, what with Holly coming back, and there being so much talk of change.'

'Well, I think Tilly's making enough changes in her personal life, don't you?' Dan said with an easy smile. 'Maybe we should have a word with Holly – slow things down a bit – I know she wants to make her mark and get back into the swing of things, but . . .'

'Don't you dare start with that patronising waffle,' Grace cautioned him. 'Who better to be looking at how effectively we work, than a partner with a few months' objectivity and five children to juggle. Not to mention Taffy. Surely

Holly deserves that we hear her out, before naysaying her suggestions?'

'Yes, boss,' said Dan, leaning forward to pull Grace into his arms. 'And I wasn't naysaying – whatever she's plotting will no doubt be well-considered, efficient and inspirational. It's just, well, I worry that there's only so many hours in the day.'

'So, let her decide what to do with hers! If she can take care of that houseful and still bring a little professional scrutiny to how we plan our practice, then I for one remain in awe, not apprehension.'

Dan held Grace tightly, kissing the top of her head, as she nestled deeper into his arms, craving security.

The door swinging open beside them startled them apart, both instantly trying to read the expression on Henry's face.

He paused a moment, almost as if for effect. 'Well, I have news. Whether it's good or bad rather depends on you.' He gestured to the chairs beside them and all three sat down, as if coordinated, Grace barely managing to perch on the edge of her seat.

'Keira likes you both,' Henry began. 'And she's open to the idea of Lulu coming to live with you.'

'Oh, thank God,' breathed out Dan tremulously, rather getting ahead of himself.

Henry held up a cautionary hand. 'But she has concerns. And, in my professional opinion, it would be wise to address them with some urgency.'

'Holly? It's Grace, can you talk?' The mobile phone shook in her hand as she attempted to make her voice sound as normal as possible. After the last hour of emotional conversation at Keira's bedside, and with her doctors, that was easier said than done.

'Err, hang on a sec?' Holly said in reply, sounding as though she were somehow in the middle of Piccadilly Circus during rush hour. Suddenly the cacophony went silent and Holly's voice could actually be heard. 'Okay – I've shut myself in the laundry room. I can hear you now.'

Grace laughed. 'It's a bit of a last-minute request actually. Do you have any plans later?'

'I'm around, if you want to pop by. But Plum's taken the evening off to get some quality Tilly-time.'

'Right,' said Grace. 'Well, the thing is, we need you and Taffy for an hour or so – just to help with a Lulu-related thing. Two things really. Do you think the kids would mind a spontaneous evening out?'

'I think the parents would *adore* an evening out, spontaneous or otherwise,' said Holly. 'And between us, I'm sure four adults can keep five small children in check.' She paused. 'Although, if I brought Elsie, we'd have a one-to-one ratio and maybe slightly better odds of finishing a sentence?'

'Bring Elsie,' said Grace firmly. 'And Holly? Don't tell anyone, will you?'

Grace hung up and missed Holly's perplexed reply: 'I couldn't if I wanted to.'

'Right,' said Grace, turning towards Dan with sparkling eyes, 'now it's your turn.' She passed him the phone and dashed away the tears that were quickly filling her eyes; it had been an afternoon of poignant turbulence, and the day wasn't even over yet.

Grace clasped Dan's hand tightly. Now that this was actually happening, knowing that Taffy and Holly and their marauding clan were on their way, the time for nerves had surely passed.

'No cold feet?' Dan asked gently.

'Toasty warm,' she replied. 'And, actually, I cannot think of a better reason to get married, can you?'

'Like generations before us,' he agreed. 'Even if our "baby" will be sitting in the congregation. And isn't actually ours.'

'Yet,' Grace reminded him. 'Three small things, remember? Three small reservations that we can so easily remedy to give Keira peace of mind.'

'And we'd be doing this one sooner or later though anyway, yes?' Dan clarified, concerned that he might be railroading his putative bride down the aisle.

'Well, I was rather hoping to live in sin for an unbelievably decadent amount of time, but this works too,' she teased him. 'And frankly it is about time we stopped procrastinating about where we're going to live. Renting Holly's old house was never meant to be a permanent solution.'

They paused then, fingers entwined, both obviously thinking back to the third 'small thing' that Keira had asked of them.

There was no doubt that getting married and building a steady home life would help with that too. When the time came.

Dan turned to Grace, his eyes filled with his love and admiration for the woman standing beside him. 'One step at a time, okay? And no steps that make us feel uncomfortable. Deal?'

'Deal,' replied Grace, kicking off her heels to prove her commitment to the cause. 'No uncomfortable steps.'

The ancient church doors swung open with a creak, silhouetting the gaggle of children and adults in the doorway.

'And I thought Holly and I had the monopoly on shotgun weddings around here!' called Taffy, his eyes creased up in a smile and striding forward to shake his best friend's hand.

'Thanks for coming,' Dan replied. 'We could hardly have done this without you here.'

'Oh, I don't know. I think it's more important that you and your barefoot bride show up,' he said, noticing Grace's lack of shoes and looking confused. 'Is this some clever wordplay on barefoot and pregnant that I'm missing?'

'Nope,' said Grace with a smile. 'It's all about comfort.'

'Oh well, in that case,' said Holly, slipping her own heels from her feet in solidarity.

Tom tugged at her sleeve impatiently. 'Mummy, Mummy – if it's a shotgun wedding, can Ben and I go home and get our Nerf guns?'

Grace swallowed a smile. 'Maybe later?' she offered.

'Now, are we ready, ladies and gentlemen?' asked Reverend Taylor, stepping out of the vestry in a crisp white cassock. 'Are we expecting anyone else?'

'No,' said Grace. 'Just our nearest and dearest for a little moral support.'

'Well, since you *obviously* all remember me reading the banns for this lovely couple,' Reverend Taylor gave her mini-congregation a complicit smile, 'I will waste no time in joining together two of my favourite people in Holy Matrimony.'

There was a loud creak as the door of the church was pushed open again, and Hattie, Will and Lizzie slipped inside, any attempts at discretion utterly failing. 'Sorry, sorry, don't mind us, we just couldn't bear to miss this,' said Lizzie in a stage whisper.

'Word's got out,' murmured Taffy, standing beside Dan as his Best Man.

'Welcome one, welcome all,' said Reverend Taylor. 'Now, as I was saying—'

'Are we too late? Did we miss it?' said the Major, as he and Marion pushed open the door a little wider, with much groaning of its ancient hinges. 'Only, there's a rumour in the pub—' He stopped dead, as a huge smile lit up his face. 'As you were, Reverend.'

'Quite, well, yes. Anyway. We are gathered here today to bring together this man and this— Oh, for the love of God, leave the bloody door open, otherwise we may never get to the good bit!' the Reverend burst out, with uncharacteristic frustration, as three of the nurses from The Practice peeked into the church, with Charlotte Lansing and Banana incongruously on their heels.

'Do you, Dan Milton Carter take this woman to be your wedded wife – in sickness and health . . .'

'I do,' he said simply, holding Grace's gaze with his own, his eyes filled with adoration.

'This is even better than the Royal Wedding,' sniffed Elsie tearfully in the front row, rootling around in her handbag for a handkerchief and momentarily letting go of Lulu's hand.

Grace paused, still trying not to laugh at the discovery of Dan's much-hated, and long-concealed, poetic middle name, trying to compose herself for her own 'I do'. She felt, more than saw, the tiny presence standing beside her and glanced down, losing any hope of composure as she saw Lulu's face smiling up at her.

'Me too?' she said adorably, reaching out her hands to take Grace's and Dan's, standing between them in her little yellow dress.

There was an outbreak of scuffling from the pews, as one and all took a few deep, calming breaths. Certainly from the back of the church it was a sight to behold.

Flickering candles from the Advent wreath reflected in the stained-glass windows, illuminating the couple at the front, joined together or so it seemed, by a tiny figure in primrose yellow.

'I do,' said Grace when her moment arrived, not a trace of nerves or reservation in her voice, not so much bringing together two soulmates, as three.

'You may now kiss the bride!' said Reverend Taylor, herself a little overcome.

'Me too!' cried Lulu again, hopping up and down excitedly, until the entire, ever-expanding congregation burst into spontaneous cheers and applause.

'That went well, Mrs Carter,' said Dan smiling, as he lovingly rested his forehead against Grace's.

'I could get used to this,' said Grace with feeling, unable to pinpoint whether she meant Dan's absolute focus and admiration, or the tiny hand woven into her own. From where she was standing, the two ideas were inseparable, as indeed family should be.

Chapter 40

'Oh, I do *love* a good wedding,' said Elsie, still emotionally fragile three hours later, as the impromptu reception continued apace in the kitchen at Number 42. 'Although a little advance notice around here to buy a hat on occasion would be nice.'

Hattie had nipped back to The Deli and returned bearing sufficient lasagnes to feed the five thousand and Teddy Kingsley had closed down the pub for the night and turned up with enough fizz to lubricate them all very nicely.

All the children had been duly bathed and pyjama-d, and were now mingling among the grown-ups, snaffling hugs, treats and attention as though by right.

'How're you feeling?' asked Holly, intrigued as she topped up Grace's glass, taking in her flushed cheeks.

'A bit shell-shocked, to be honest. And here was me, thinking I would never take the plunge again,' Grace said quietly. 'But actually, when we were taking our vows, it just felt right, you know?'

'I guess it depends on the motivation,' Holly replied.

'I think you might be right,' Grace agreed. 'Even though the whole situation is a little bittersweet. Poor Keira. I daren't think what she must be going through.'

'How about you focus on how much you're helping her?

Surely it's better for everyone if Lulu has a loving home to go to,' Holly said gently.

Grace nodded. 'And you're quite sure you don't mind? I know there was a chance that Lulu might have stayed with you, and she's settled here so well . . .'

'I'd like to think that Number 42 might be her home-away-from-home sometimes. I mean, if you ever need a babysitter? I'm sure Aunty Holly and Uncle Taffy could be relied upon?' Holly hoped she made it sound as though she were completely adjusted to the new plan, but she couldn't pretend she hadn't been a little taken aback.

Only last night, as Lulu had been having one of her night-mares and Holly held her in her arms, she'd decided that there would always be a home for her here, an extra stocking on the mantelpiece this Christmas. And Keira *had* all but asked her to step up.

Knowing that raising four children would be hard enough didn't seem to be the barrier it had once been. The more she got to know Lulu and her sweet little quirks, the less of an issue it became.

But now . . .

Now, two of her best friends were offering Lulu a home – a loving home. Choosing to adapt their lives to accommodate her, become a family. She really couldn't be happier, she told herself, taking another flute of champagne and drinking it down in one gulp.

'I have no idea how we're going to find a home so quickly, either,' Grace continued, almost oblivious to Holly's mental machinations. 'I mean, we've been looking for a doer-upper for months now. And nothing. But it means the world to Keira, apparently, that we're homeowners, not renters.'

'Maybe she's had one eviction too many in her own life and

doesn't want that for her daughter?' Holly suggested astutely. 'But be careful what you buy, if you're buying in a rush, won't you?'

'Of course,' said Grace. 'How are you getting on with your new neighbours? Have you even met them yet?'

'Ah, well, about that—' Holly began, before Elsie fixed her with a querulous glare.

'The whole place needed a complete gutting,' Grace blundered on. 'We went to look round it actually. We reckon the old chap who lived there before lived in absolute squalor. Lost out to sealed bids in the end,' Grace confided. 'There can't be a room in the place that they haven't gutted based on the workmen coming and going. My money says they won't even move in; they'll just gut it and flip it.'

'Have you been watching those property programmes again?' asked Elsie calmly, not rising to the bait.

'Oh I love those!' exclaimed Grace, obviously more tipsy than she'd realised, as she surprised even herself. 'But then it makes it all the more disappointing when you go house-hunting yourself and it's all vile. Expensive and vile!'

'What's the rush, though?' Elsie asked. 'Surely you need to acclimatise to married life, before you take on the stress of a building project? It's not easy, you know. Trust me.'

'I kno-ow,' agreed Grace. 'And normally I'd agree. But it's a question of what we can afford. A doer-upper is our best shot at creating a lovely family home.'

'But—' Elsie began, before Holly leaned in and tactfully updated her on Keira's second request: a family home of their own.

Elsie clasped her hand to her throat. 'Oh my Lord! You mean, you need to get everything sorted that quickly?'

Grace nodded. 'It's a shame about next door really, because it would have been lovely. And, Elsie, you're quite right, a building site would have been stressful, but that's why we could have afforded it. But you know what it's like with sealed bids. So, we missed out. *Que será, será* and all that.'

Elsie seemed to pale for a moment, almost spilling her champagne. Holly reached out to steady her. 'I think you might need a little something to eat,' she said, settling her onto one of the kitchen bar stools a little precariously, wondering why she was still so intent on keeping her property purchase a secret. Surely enough people knew by now?

'I'm fine, don't fuss,' snapped Elsie, rather uncharacteristically humourless. She distractedly sipped the water that Grace had the presence of mind to pour out, even if half of it had missed the glass entirely.

'So,' Holly asked, intrigued and recognising a prime opportunity to get Grace to spill the beans. 'Marriage, a home ... What else did Keira ask you to do?'

'Ah, well, that's the tricky one, actually. She doesn't want Keira to grow up as an only child. She doesn't want history repeating itself and for her to have no family to call on as she gets older. It makes sense. It does. It just opens rather a large can of worms.' She hiccuped slightly. 'I mean, I never thought Dan would agree to adoption in the first place ... Let alone twice.' She sighed. 'I guess that's why Keira thought of you, Holly. A ready-made family. Not a flat-pack quick assemble like me and Dan.' She'd reached that slightly maudlin stage of tipsiness now, and Holly felt a lurch of guilt that the same thought had even flickered on the edges of her own subconscious.

Surely, it actually meant more that Dan and Grace were prepared to go to such lengths to comply with Keira's last requests.

'I have a confession, Grace!' blurted Elsie suddenly, just loud enough for Grace and Holly to hear, even as the rest of the party ramped up around them. 'The thoughtless, noisy neighbour next door? It's been me.' She glanced up worriedly. 'I bought it for me. I certainly didn't mean to outbid anyone like you and Dan. I just wanted to be close to this little lot. In fact, I rather fancied knocking a little door through just there ...' She waved a hand towards the kitchen wall and looked incredibly sheepish. 'I had a plan, you see ...'

'Oh my God!' Grace laughed. 'All these weeks and you never said a word! But why?'

Elsie fidgeted so uncomfortably on the bar stool that she nearly went flying. 'Oh Lord, well it's all going to come out one day. I made a mistake, Grace – a cautionary tale of making a big decision in a hurry. Sarandon Hall was a bad fit right from the start. I may have rather misjudged how much I would enjoy it there. Awful people. The kind that cut the nose off the brie without a second thought.' She shuddered. 'Awful. So, well, I had to get thrown out.'

Elsie shrugged at Grace's shocked expression. 'It was rather fun actually, in the end. It's still quite shocking to me, what they were prepared to let me get away with before they gave me my marching orders.'

'What did you do?' breathed Grace, entranced.

'Oh, a lady never tells tales,' Elsie said primly, with a smile.

'I want to be like you, Elsie,' Grace slurred, wrapping her arm around Elsie's shoulders and making them both wobble. 'I want to just grab life with both hands and think "fuck it" – but I care too much what other people will think. Like now – I should be dancing with my new husband, but I've had a little teeny-tiny drink and I'm worried that he won't approve.'

Having 'a little drink' seemed to have opened up a side to Grace that Holly, for one, could never have predicted – because in Holly's eyes, Grace already was the together, motivated, confident person she was apparently aspiring to be.

'Do you know what, Grace? You should buy my house. I only bought it to be closer to this little lot without getting under their feet. And well, it was a little project of mine ...' She took a deep breath. 'The décor won't be to your taste at all but ...' She steadied herself on Holly's shoulder and Holly's concern was evident on her face.

Elsie took a breath and turned to face Holly. 'Darling, would you mind terribly if I grow generally geriatric back in my old room?'

'I'd be delighted,' said Holly. 'I've adored having you back these last few months. Even if it was under false pretences.' She dropped her voice to a whisper, 'But, Elsie, are you quite sure about this? What happened to it being your dream house? Your one chance to do something purely to your taste?'

'So,' said Elsie, swivelling to face Grace, her head lagging slightly, making her look like a Thunderbirds puppet for a moment, bluntly ignoring Holly's question. 'Would the new Dr and Mrs Carter like to set up residence at Number 44? I won't stiff you on the price, I promise. And – ooh now there's a thought – if you still knock that doorway through, then Lulu could come and go as she pleased, if she was in need of company. Siblings on demand, as it were. Just while you're waiting to fall in love with another little soul. That's the only way to build a family, really – it's not about blood ties, it's about the love. Every day.' She squeezed Holly's hand tightly, a wealth of emotions in her clasp.

'Speaking of which,' said Taffy, as he wandered past and caught the tail end of the conversation, 'I need to rally the bride. It's time for the speeches.'

Holly clasped hold of her side, as the laughter became almost painful, and wished she'd had the foresight to go for a wee.

Taffy's irreverent Best Man speech was somehow all the funnier and fresher for being completely off the cuff.

'And I think, at that moment, in a flop-house in Latvia, I knew that Dan and I would be friends for life,' he said to whoops and hollers. The groom was red-faced, but laughing too.

'And of course, we must all remember that Grace here, wasn't in fact the first love of Dan's life to reside in Larkford . . .' Taffy continued, even as his audience held their collective breath awkwardly. 'It behoves me, of course, to mention Gerald the Goose on this auspicious occasion. I for one, am glad that the noisy bastard wasn't invited, for there is no doubt that he would have stolen my thunder on the speech-front. Gerald, we toast your friendship and commitment, in your absence. To absent friends.'

The room as a whole cheered.

'But really, I have to tell you, that there is a special kind of magic that happens when your best mate falls in love with someone so utterly wonderful that you don't mind sharing them. Much.' He grinned and turned to Grace. 'Take care of him, Gracie. He's just a big softie at heart.

'It's also, I believe, tradition for the Best Man to thank the bridesmaids. And since this wedding was clearly planned on the back of a napkin, I raise a toast to Lulu for stepping up and being quite the prettiest spontaneous bridesmaid I have ever seen. To Lulu!' Taffy gave her a wink and Lulu blushed sweetly, hiding her face in Grace's skirts as everyone turned to look at her.

She was, Holly realised, completely unrecognisable as the wan, mute waif who had walked into their lives and stolen all their hearts. A warm glow of achievement eclipsed any possible reluctance about letting her go.

Taffy was on a roll now, his tongue surely loosened by

Teddy's fizz and the heightened emotions in the room. 'My own lovely wife – some of you may have met her—' There was a ripple of laughter in the room. 'Well, she's always telling me that it takes a village. And on this occasion, as on so many others, I believe that she is right. Holly and I, for one thing, could not do our work without Plum and Elsie holding the fort at home.'

Holly breathed a sigh of relief. Not only because she'd wondered where her loquacious husband had been heading for a moment, but also because she'd belatedly realised that it hadn't even occurred to her to run the Elsie situation past him before agreeing.

'We couldn't balance our work life, and the demands of parenthood, without Alice, and Tilly, and yes – even on occasion – Dan picking up the slack at The Practice. We are incredibly fortunate to live in such a place. It is some measure of my esteem for the lovely couple we're celebrating today, that I have no doubt that their family life here in Larkford will enjoy the same unconditional love, willingly given support and above all, our best and most heartfelt wishes for their very happy future together. Ladies and gentlemen, charge your glasses. I give you the new Dr and Mrs Carter.'

Taffy stepped down from the coffee table to whoops and cheers of celebration from some, relief from others. Taffy as a Best Man was an unknown quantity and at least some of their friends must have been worried about just how many tales were about to be told out of school.

Holly rushed forward to greet him, eyes shining. 'I couldn't have said any of that better myself.' She pulled him into a rib-crushing hug. 'It's nice to feel appreciated,' she murmured into his chest.

'Well, we do all right, don't we? You and me, muddling through,' Taffy said.

'Makes me think though,' said Holly, pulling back for a moment. 'I'm on the right track, aren't I, with the plans for The Practice? Everyone needs their own village – at home and at work. I guess the whole thing is just interconnected.'

'Incestuous, you mean?' Taffy countered. 'Some days our lives just feel like one of those domino rallies, you know? As if one small tip knocks the whole thing out of balance.'

'Then part of our remit has to be emergency domino support, doesn't it?' Holly offered.

Taffy frowned. 'Have you been at Teddy's elderflower liqueur?'

Holly shrugged. 'Was it in the champagne cocktails?'

Taffy shook his head and hugged his wife. 'Domino support it is. And maybe a little separation of Church and State?' he suggested hopefully.

Holly bit her lip guiltily. 'So now wouldn't be a good time to mention that Elsie's moving back in and that Dan, Grace and Lulu will be living next door?'

Taffy paused and Holly held her breath. If he agreed to this without complaint there was every chance that he'd be on board with her plans at The Practice come Monday morning.

'Next door?' he queried. 'Makes sense. And maybe they can tell *their* workmen to keep it down to a dull roar.' He paused and his gaze flickered over towards the party wall. 'You know, we could probably even knock a little doorway through, just in case Lulu wanted to pop by?'

Holly just nodded, seeing no reason to let on that the sledge-hammers were poised and at the ready. 'Sounds like a lovely idea,' she said, just before she kissed him.

Just because it wasn't *her* wedding reception, didn't mean she couldn't celebrate the magnificence of marriage, Holly decided with an elderflower hiccup.

Chapter 41

'Will we never learn?' groaned Holly, popping two para-cetamol from a foil strip and downing them with a double espresso. Her bag of jelly babies lay open on the table in front of her and her trilogy of hangover and migraine repair was complete.

And yet.

Had the lighting in the doctors' lounge always been so very bright, she wondered.

'I genuinely think a monkey may have crapped in my brain overnight,' said Alice eloquently, deftly guiding Coco's kibble kisses away from her face, as she swallowed a wave of nausea. 'I'm blaming you, Dan.'

Dan just grinned and glanced across to reception where his new wife was kicking arse and taking names — never cross a Practice Manager who's had three hours' sleep and no breakfast. 'I promise never to get married on a school night ever again. Okay?'

He deftly buttered a stack of toast, trimming off the crusts with care, and made his way through to reception. Holly blinked, always a little overemotional when tired.

'That's love, that is,' she said, as Grace's face lit up at the very sight.

Taffy, who had spent the last five minutes repeatedly opening every cupboard and the fridge in the hope of finding something comforting to eat, turned to watch. 'When Dan falls in love, he falls hard.' He picked up the buttery, crumbly, discarded crusts and chomped thoughtfully, worry creasing his forehead. 'They'd have got married eventually, right? Even without Keira's provisos? They'll be happy together?'

''Course,' replied Holly, hoping she was right. What did it matter now anyway? The deed was done. And, for now at least, the bride and groom both looked suitably content. 'And since they'll be living next door, I'm guessing we'll be the first to hear if they're not. Quite literally.'

She wasn't quite sure how she felt about Elsie's incredibly generous offer. On the one hand, hadn't she herself benefited from Elsie's selfless largesse? Wasn't it therefore hypocritical to be concerned about her offer to Grace and Dan?

But on the other?

Holly confessed that she rather liked the idea of Elsie being just next door, having her own space and her own social life and, one day, a downstairs bedroom if necessary. She adored the notion of Elsie having a space that was so uniquely, fabulously her very own for the first time in her life. No husband or children to pander to. From everything Connor had told her, the interior of Number 44 was like taking a walk through Elsie's inner mind, even though she herself had yet to have the privilege. Apparently, *she* had to wait until it was completely finished for the Big Reveal – they really had been watching too many property programmes on TV.

She couldn't deny that Elsie was generous to a fault, but that didn't stop Holly from wondering if she'd really thought this through – or whether she was blindly waving Dan and

Grace off in the very last lifeboat without a thought for herself. As indeed, she always had done.

But now?

Well, now, Holly couldn't help worry that Dan and Grace were simply taking on too much, too quickly. Even buying travel insurance gave you a fourteen-day cooling off period. The way they were going, Dan and Grace would have cobbled together 2.4 children, a marriage licence and a mortgage by the end of next week.

She frowned. She was all for ensuring that Lulu was welcomed into a loving family environment, but she couldn't help but feel that Keira was, perhaps quite rightly, sketching out a dream scenario, rather than what was actually realistic, or sustainable. It was all very well dictating terms, but Lulu wasn't a commodity to be bargained over – surely knowing how Dan and Grace felt about her, the life and security they could offer her, should be enough?

Holly smothered a yawn. Maybe she really had been living with Elsie too long, but the temptation to interfere was overwhelming. And it had nothing to do with how incredibly fond she was of the little girl who had slotted into her own family like a missing jigsaw piece. Or how she felt about giving her up.

Maybe she could visit Keira, ask her to relax the provisos she'd set out for Dan and Grace, the hoops she'd carefully dictated for them to jump through?

'Oi, earth to Holly. Calling Holly?' Taffy said, obviously not for the first time. 'Were you planning on seeing any patients today?'

She stood up and stretched. 'Lead the way. I am brimful of empathy and care this morning.' She caught sight of Cassie Holland barging into the waiting room. 'Oh, dear God, what fresh hell is this?'

'And she's all yours,' Alice said cheekily, slipping away with Coco at her heels to get the day started, noticeably brighter since Jamie's 'sickie' had been extended throughout the week to keep Connor company.

'Good morning, Cassie,' said Holly brightly. Okay, maybe not brightly, per se, but with as much pep as she could muster to see off any raptor-like tendencies from her patient. Showing weakness was not an option.

'Well, I'm glad you think so, Dr Graham. Since we obviously live in a town divided.' Cassie settled herself into a chair and folded her hands primly in her hessian-clad lap. 'The Haves and the Have-nots? Those included in town celebrations? Or supportive of madcap schemes to drag the town into ill-repute?'

'And what can I do for you this morning, Cassie?' Holly asked, unwilling to be drawn into Cassie's hissy fit about missing the wedding yesterday, or indeed the plans for Connor's festival.

'Well,' Cassie squirmed a little, clearly embarrassed, 'I don't want you to think this is something I do all the time, Dr Graham. It was only the once. But before we begin, I need your clear assurance that you won't judge me on my lifestyle choices? Understood?'

Holly paused, the little devil on her shoulder crowing – 'Oh my God, Cassie Holland has an STD!' – deliberately taking a moment to compose herself. For any one of her patients, this kind of appointment would be embarrassing enough, but for do-gooder Cassie it must be excruciating. 'Cassie, of course you have my word and any assurances you need. What you say in this room is completely confidential.'

'I know that,' Cassie sniped back. 'It doesn't stop you *thinking* it, though, does it?'

'You have me there,' Holly said gently. 'But, Cassie, there is very little about the human body that fazes me. And judgemental is not a word I would ever apply to how I think about my patients. Come on, out with it — what's causing you so much concern?'

Holly waited, poised for a sordid tale of Tinder and one-night stands, strange rashes and general debauchery.

'Well, I went to the nail salon,' said Cassie, struggling to maintain her composure. 'It was a gift certificate, okay. Not something I would ever have spent money on myself. You know I don't believe in that kind of thing ...'

Holly did a small double-take, her mouth hanging open briefly in shock. *This* was Cassie's mortifying secret?

'Well,' Cassie fidgeted. 'So, as I was saying, I went for this "manicure",' — she said the word in the same tone normally reserved for 'orgy' or 'opium den' — 'and the girl took one look at my left hand and told me to see a doctor.' She blushed deeply. 'She seems to think there's some kind of fungal situation going on with my thumbnail.'

Cassie released her clasp and held out her left hand, Holly only then aware that she had been hiding the offending nail out of sight.

'I only asked if she could use a dark colour — a burgundy or something — to cover this horrible stripe. She was most tactless, I'm afraid. And so, here I am. Not only have I succumbed to the vanity of the ignorant bourgeoisie, but also, it transpires, with a fungus.' She shuddered and Holly was left unclear which of the two most offended her patient.

She slipped on a pair of gloves and angled her lamp to illuminate Cassie's thumbnail more clearly, ready reassurances on the tip of her tongue that nail fungus was easily treatable and happened all the time. No biggie.

She paused and pulled open her desk drawer, rootling around for her magnifying glass. It wasn't as fancy as the one over by her treatment couch, but it had remarkable clarity. And clarity was what she needed right now.

'I think,' she began slowly, 'that going for a manicure might just turn out to be one of the best decisions you've ever made.' She switched off the lamp and turned to face Cassie, a little overwhelmed by the empathy she felt for this cantankerous woman and what she was about to endure. 'I'm guessing this dark line has been here for a while, yes?'

Cassie nodded. 'About six months,' she whispered, shedding all bravado in light of Holly's reaction.

'Then I don't think we should mess around. There's a condition called subungual melanoma, or cancer of the nail, if you prefer. Do you see here, where the black stripe has depth and is actually pressing down into the skin under your nail?' She pointed to the tip of Cassie's thumb, looking down the cross-section of her nail. 'Well, this is where the melanoma is extending. So I'm going to refer you across to the Oncology unit in Bath and I need you to prepare yourself for a bit of a whirlwind, okay?' She paused to check that Cassie was actually taking any of this information in.

'In all likelihood, they will want to do a biopsy of this and also your lymph nodes, just to get a feel for where we are.'

Cassie stared at her blankly. 'So, not a bruise? Not a fungus?'

'No, Cassie. This is something we need to take seriously.' She cradled Cassie's hand in her own, as Cassie stared down at the offending nail as if it were an intruder – which, in a way, it was. 'Is there someone who can go with you to the hospital, Cassie? A friend, a relative?'

Cassie shook her head, a stubborn set to her jaw that Holly knew only too well.

'Cassie? This is not a time to shut people out. What about the friend who bought you the gift certificate for the manicure? That was a lovely gesture – the kind of thing you do for someone you care about?'

A single tear released from Cassie's lashes as she blinked. 'It wasn't a friend. It was my brother, actually. But we don't really speak.'

'I'm not sure people who don't speak normally send thoughtful gifts, Cassie. Are you quite sure he wouldn't help you out?'

Cassie shrugged and then the floodgates opened. 'I don't speak to him, I mean. We disagree about everything. Everything. It's not a real relationship at all.'

'Siblings that don't agree? Sounds perfectly normal to me,' Holly said gently. 'And this isn't a question of organic food, or recycling, or natural childbirth, Cassie. This is your life. Let me call your brother for you, if it's just too awkward. You're going to need a little help and support.' Strike that, thought Holly, glancing down at the black mark and its incriminating thickness, a lot of help was actually more likely.

Cassie nodded. 'Okay, I'll call. At least he's local these days.' She looked up at Holly through tear-filled eyes. 'He's the head teacher at the primary school.'

'Oh!' gulped Holly, completely blindsided. Now *that* was something she hadn't seen coming. Glorious Alec French and his open, friendly demeanour, his rapport with the kids and parents alike – how on earth had they been cut from the same cloth? Although, it did go some way to explaining Cassie's disproportionate dislike of the poor man before he'd even got his name on the stationery.

*

Only four hours later and Holly was still reeling from the turn her morning had taken. She sat numbly in the squishiest armchair she could find in the doctors' lounge, hiding away while she processed the tangled web of Cassie Holland's life – no wonder the poor woman was so uptight. But then, as to which came first, she couldn't help but wonder.

'You okay there, Holly?' Alice asked gently, sitting down beside her and holding out a bacon sandwich on a plate. 'We saved you one of these if you're hungry?'

Holly shook her head, even as her stomach let rip with an ominous growl. She smiled. 'Well, maybe a little bit.' She took a bite, the ketchup oozing down her chin, and realised that sustenance was always the answer in a time of crisis. 'Thank you.'

She idly watched the nurses tie themselves into pretzels with a quick game of Twister, no doubt part of this bonkers league that Dan had devised to improve staff morale. She could only be grateful, she supposed, that strip poker had been struck from the list of challenges.

Alice remained beside her. 'Holly, is now a good time to ask you something?'

Holly nodded, her mouth full of crusty bread.

'It's just – well, you know how my mum has been nagging me to go home, back to the Orkneys? And that there's a job there waiting for me?' She stopped, and took a deep breath, her words then tumbling out as though she couldn't say them fast enough. 'Well, I'm wondering if she's got a point and I'm not really valued here and that I should just admit that and head north?'

Holly swallowed her mouthful with a jolt. 'Jesus, Alice. Where did all that come from?'

Alice looked pained. 'I guess, I see the partners coming and going as they please, and it's always me and Tilly covering their clinics. And then Tilly – Tilly, who's been here all of five minutes, shagged half the male population and caused scandals left, right and centre – is the one who's given her own project!' Her voice had gradually risen until the nurses in the kitchenette were beginning to stare.

Alice sighed. 'I mean, if I'm not going to be a valued team member, then why am I always the one going the extra mile? Coco too. If you can't all see that we bring something special to—'

'Alice,' Holly interrupted her, 'Alice, stop. I can see why, on some level, you might have drawn this conclusion, but it's just not accurate.' She plonked the plate down onto the coffee table, much to Coco's delight, as she wasted no time in snaffling a stray rasher of bacon, as Holly pulled Alice into a hug. Workplace etiquette and Patronising Patricia's advice be damned.

'Look, I know the partners have been taking the piss of late. There's been an awful lot going on in all our personal lives, but that's no excuse.'

'I suppose you are the bosses though, right?' Alice mumbled.

'All the more reason to lead from the front, I'd say,' Holly countered. 'But the Tilly situation doesn't reflect on you. It reflects on her need to relate to her patients, to feel as though she can make a difference, even outside a war zone or a famine. Look, you've known her an awfully long time – she needs to find her feet somewhere.' She paused. 'And you are the one, Alice, who suggested I be her mentor, don't forget.'

'I did. But I guess I didn't think it through.' She bit her lip and looked at Holly. 'I don't suppose you want to mentor me as well?'

Holly laughed. 'Oh, you daft muppet. You don't need a mentor. Your head is firmly screwed on. Normally.' She smiled at Alice, her gaze encompassing Coco chewing her bacon on the floor beside her. 'What you and Coco have achieved is phenomenal. And all the partners are so grateful that you've stayed here, and brought the canine clinic here. I guess maybe we thought you had your hands full already? But also, maybe we don't tell you enough just how indispensable you are to the team—' She held up a hand to stop Alice interrupting. 'And no, I don't just mean as emergency cover for when the partners are skiving off work.'

There was a ghost of a smile on Alice's face now, these worries having clearly been bothering her for some time.

'And if you miss your mum, and the Orkneys, then obviously we will let you go with our blessing. But, Alice, please don't. Please stay. There are so many changes on our horizon here at The Practice – some big, some small – but all of them are going to make this a better and happier place to work.'

'Give me an example?' Alice asked, obviously wary of having flattery turn her head.

'Okay. So, one of the big things I want to implement is that everyone will have their own area of responsibility, or research, that they feel passionate about, that they're accountable for. Tilly was my test balloon on this. When it comes to you, I have a particular project in mind, but I haven't had chance to talk to the people involved yet. So this is purely theoretical, okay?'

'O-kay,' agreed Alice, leaning forward fractionally.

'Well, I see you and Coco, and how fundamentally different your life is, simply for having her in it. And then I see children like Jess, like Lulu, even – children who have got through enormous challenges and traumas – and how they react to Banana, for example.'

'Emotional support animals,' breathed Alice, her eyes bright and her smile no longer tentative.

Holly nodded. 'There's loads of legislation and licensing to research. And you might need to consult with Jamie about the training side of things. But I genuinely cannot think of a better person to be the liaison and lead on this.'

'And you think I could do this alongside my usual clinics, and Coco's clinics?' Alice queried.

Holly nodded. 'There may only be two or three patients a year that this concerns, but those patients are going to need an awful lot of time and attention. What do you think? Am I on the right track for you?'

'Spot on,' said Alice, reaching automatically for Coco's soft ears. 'It's almost as if you know me all too well.'

Holly grinned, satisfied at last that even with a hangover she was finding her niche back at work once more. 'I'm not always the fastest at making change happen,' she said, 'but I like to think I'm generally pointing in the right direction.'

Chapter 42

Connor deliberately picked up his pace, as someone called his name across the Market Place. Old habits died hard.

Even as Matthew Giles jogged to catch up with him, Connor felt his pulse ricochet up a notch, braced instinctively for cameras and microphones and intrusive questions. 'All that rock music made you go a bit deaf, mate?' Matthew joked easily, as he fell into step beside Connor.

'Something like that,' Connor said, the faintest apology in his tone, as he wondered how often he'd recently snubbed people he knew, in his quest for evasion and privacy. 'Good of you to come along tonight, Matt. Really appreciate it.'

'Chuffed to be invited to be honest,' Matthew replied without guile. 'Mike from Bath Rugby's coming too, did you know? Dr Graham's definitely got a few ideas up her sleeve, but she was kind of cryptic when she called. Speak of the devil . . .'

Holly emerged from the wine shop on the Market Place, with a clanking bag of bottles. 'A little lubrication for the little grey cells,' she said by way of explanation. 'Hopefully an evening of brainstorming and vino will get the show back on the road.'

Connor coloured slightly under her none-too-subtle scrutiny as they walked together across to Number 42. 'I'm doing okay,' he said to her, avoiding the inevitable question, but somehow touched, rather than irked, by her concern. That was progress in itself, he thought, despite the dry mouth and nausea that seemed to accompany his new 'happy pills'. He could almost hear his new therapist cheering him on – 'Talk about it,' he would say, 'don't hide it.'

'Good,' said Holly simply, squeezing his hand in a way that was so reminiscent of Rachel that for a moment the breath caught in his throat. He squeezed back, just for a second, and then pulled his hand away.

Baby steps, human contact, learning how to breathe all over again.

Connor hung back as Holly pushed open the front door of Number 42 and stepped inside. The expression on Taffy's face as they all piled in was one that Connor recognised only too well, that of a man out of his depth and unwilling to admit it.

'Fun afternoon with the kids, darling?' Holly asked, kissing him lightly on the lips and passing him the bag of wine.

'Well, I can't say I wasn't warned,' Taffy replied, picking at the orange Play-Doh that seemed firmly welded to his eyebrow. 'Hi, guys, Holly roped you in too, has she?'

'The more the merrier,' said Mike Urquhart, catching them up as they congregated in the hallway. 'I, for one, can't wait to hear what you have in mind.'

'Me too,' Connor confessed, vacillating between a desire to throw in the towel on this festival completely, and his natural competitive drive to overcome any challenges in his path. Like it or not, Cassie Holland's sabotage had, in a way, also been the proverbial gauntlet . . .

As Mike slipped off his coat and hung it on the newel post,

he leaned in towards Connor. 'You know, you couldn't hope to have a better team on your side. What young Matthew has achieved with his support group is phenomenal – young carers, invisible disabilities – his efforts are going to change so many lives. Between you and me, I'm pulling together a consortium to fund his centre outright.'

'Impressive,' said Connor awkwardly. Was Mike hitting him up for a little investment too?

Mike walked towards the kitchen with a smile. 'You can blame Holly, really. She seems to have a knack for spending my money on things I didn't know I wanted.'

'Are you talking about me again?' Holly said, pouring out two glasses of wine and handing them across the kitchen island.

'Always,' Mike said easily. 'And at the Rugby Club Board Meeting just now, actually. We've been hearing a few interesting things on the grapevine about you, Holly, and about The Practice.' He paused to sip his wine and Connor frowned, wondering where this was heading. 'We wondered if you were in the market for a few more patients? It occurred to me that anything we could set up at the Club was only an imitation of what you're already doing, just down the road in Larkford.'

'Wow,' said Holly, clearly blindsided a little, turning to Taffy to gauge his reaction to the suggestion.

Taffy nodded. 'We might need to do a few sums, check out the funding allocations for new patients and whatnot, but—'

'I'm sure we can make it work,' interrupted Holly excitedly. 'And we could afford to keep Tilly on the payroll if we have more registered patients.'

Mike shrugged. 'Have a think and talk to the partners. Most of the guys and their families live in your catchment area anyway. It's one of the reasons I was so intrigued by your invitation tonight. Tell me, what's the plan?'

Several hours later, and well into the third bottle of wine, Connor, Holly, Taffy, Mike, Matthew, Lizzie and Elsie were all carving chunks of parmesan from the monolithic chunk that had arrived by Parcelforce from Plum's adoring parents. Since the 'care package' also included Parma ham, olives and salted, twisted grissini that melted in the mouth leaving a hint of rosemary, it was fair to assume that they had little faith in their daughter's transition to English cuisine.

On the other hand, Plum was so unbothered by its arrival that she had simply plonked it in the middle of the table and called it her contribution to the cause, thereby enabling her to duck out to the pub with Tilly with a clear conscience, their fledgling relationship growing stronger by the day, and with it, Tilly's confidence.

'Look, all I'm saying,' said Taffy, as he expertly whittled a roll of parmesan with the potato peeler, 'is that just because you *can* do something, doesn't always mean you should.'

Connor and Holly both looked at him with matching expressions of confusion. Such a notion was obviously anathema to both idealists.

'Why not, though?' said Connor with feeling. 'I *can* bring together an amazing experience for loads of punters. It *can* bring extra business and tourist money to Larkford, not to mention giving a little something back to the town that has, for the most part, welcomed a grieving grumpy guitar player with open arms.'

'For the most part,' Taffy reminded him.

Elsie had been uncharacteristically quiet all evening, even earning herself a few concerned glances from those around the table accustomed to her usual garrulous response to a few glasses of *vino bianco*.

When she did choose to speak, everyone fell silent to listen. 'You know,' Elsie said tentatively, 'I'm aware that some of this is my fault, and I can't imagine what I was thinking letting Cassie have her say on the radio, but I still think that what you have here is actually just a simple problem of perception.'

Connor turned, no longer scowling at Taffy, receptive to any and all suggestions.

'I mean, at no point have you actually told everyone of your plans in a transparent way – it's all coming out in dribs and drabs, half of it second-hand. The way it's being talked about in town, you'd think none of us were invited to come along – as though the residents and businesses of Larkford are just here to service the fancy-pants festival-goers who can actually afford an extortionate ticket. It only goes to feed into the notion of Them and Us.'

Connor frowned, noting that Elsie hadn't made it clear which camp she felt that she herself belonged to. He put down the sliver of Parma ham he had instinctively rolled into an attractive meat spliff. 'But how can that even be – when every resident is getting a free weekend pass?'

Elsie raised one perfectly pencilled eyebrow. 'That's as may be, young man, but have you actually told *them* that?'

'Bugger,' sighed Connor. 'You mean they don't know? I've been telling people that for weeks . . .'

'I think, mate,' said Taffy gently, 'that when people are really fired up about something, they don't necessarily listen to your answers. They just want you to hear their reservations.'

'True,' concurred Holly. 'If my day was anything to go by, there's an awful lot of me-me-me thinking and very little actual listening going on. Doesn't mean it's their fault, just that we need to find better ways to communicate our position. In my case, I should never have assumed that people would automatically understand the concept of help going to those in greatest medical need, on the basis that one day it might be them.'

'Hardly rocket science,' scoffed Elsie. 'Are you sure they didn't understand?'

Holly shrugged. 'I think if there's something better on offer, then it's human nature to want a piece of the action, a few minutes of special attention. Even if it is just for dandruff, or travel sickness.'

'To be fair,' mused Taffy, in danger of becoming an idealist himself after quite so much wine on a school night, 'half of these time-wasting reasons to come to The Practice are often a smokescreen for the real problem that's worrying them, though, don't you find? Hand on the doorknob, ready to leave, clock ticking around, "There was just *one* other thing, doctor . . ." You know what I mean.'

Connor nodded; after all, hadn't he himself often done something similar? It never ceased to amaze him how interconnected all their lives, their jobs, their issues were in this small town.

'You know,' Holly said after a moment's reflection, 'if people are against your festival on principle, because they think it's just a posh-nob's party in their own backyard, there is something you could do about that.'

Connor mouthed mutedly, clearly aghast at having his labour of love described so cynically.

'I'm not saying that's what it is — I'm saying that Elsie's right and that *perception* might be what's holding you back,' Holly clarified.

'Well, there's not a lot I can really do to change that, is there?' Connor said tiredly, feeling his enthusiasm almost physically leaching away. 'I'm already giving everyone free passes – that's no small kick to the bottom line, you know.'

'Ah well, there's the problem,' Elsie said, sitting back in her chair and sipping delicately at some sparkling water that Holly had carefully substituted for her wine glass as she'd reached for a top-up. 'You're already richer than Croesus. I'm guessing there's a school of thought that believes you making a profit on this folly at all is a little distasteful.'

'Folly? You'll be calling it a vanity project next,' Connor retorted crossly, taking her comments very personally indeed. Had she not got the memo that he was feeling a little fragile of late?

'Not my words, darling boy. Just keeping my ear to the ground, you know,' Elsie replied apologetically, her guilt making her outspoken and blunt.

'I have to pay the acts though, Elsie. They won't just come for the love of it, you know,' Connor said. 'It's hardly as though the profit margin is a mile wide, either. Contingency funds, public liability insurance – none of that comes for free.'

'What if they did come for free – your acts? Would there be a lot more profit then?' Lizzie mused, having been largely silent for most of the proceedings. It was her first proper night out since the operation and, much as Connor valued her support and her presence, he worried that she was overdoing it.

Connor frowned. 'Well, obviously. But—'

'You know the big festivals – like Glastonbury and Bestival and what's that other one, where it's all hippy dippy? Down in Cornwall? Well, they make a lot of money, yes? They're businesses in their own right,' Lizzie continued.

'Of course,' said Connor. 'They're well established and have a loyal clientele that go back year after year. I'm just starting out, so I need to open with a bang – with some big names to act as a draw. Like they do at the movies. It says Julia Roberts on the poster and you go, right, you don't necessarily even watch the trailer?'

'Sure,' interrupted Holly. 'But is this something you want to do year after year – are you trying to build a brand? I'm only asking because, to my mind, it makes a difference,' she said astutely.

Connor frowned as he pondered her question. Was this something he wanted to do every year – was this year simply the start of something? Or possibly even the end of something? Because, Holly was right – the answer to this question actually changed everything.

'If you're only doing it once, just for shits and giggles, you should really go big or go home,' said Elsie shrewdly. It was her standard go-to advice for almost anything from weddings, to cocktails, to the size of her fancy new Emperor bed.

'I think,' said Connor slowly, thinking his way forward tentatively, 'this is my way of saying goodbye to Rachel, to the life and the plans we had together.' He looked almost surprised by the words coming out of his mouth, as though he hadn't actually acknowledged his own motivation until that evening. 'I think my future involves a lot more goats and bees than chart-toppers or concerts.'

'Crikey,' said Taffy. 'You're no johnny-come-lately gentleman farmer, then? You're really going to walk away from the whole fame thing?'

Connor nodded slowly, as though making the decision in that moment, feeling the weight lift from his shoulders. 'D'you know, Taffs, I really am done. The thought of another world tour ... All that travel and upheaval and constant arse-kissing ...'

'Oh, I don't know,' butted in Elsie. 'Never underestimate the mood-boosting properties of a little sycophancy.'

'Not like this,' Connor disagreed. He looked around the table as though considering his audience. 'After Rachel, you know? Well, I did try to throw myself back into it all – but it's just no fun without her there taking the piss. The band all take everything so seriously – even down to how many groupies they can take back to their hotel room. It's like competitive shagging.' He gave a shudder. 'The last time I dated anyone was before I became "Somebody".' He made air-quotes with his fingers. 'And everything has changed. I mean, I did try to loosen up and enjoy the spoils of success but grass makes me paranoid, I'm terrified of coke, and the only one-night stand I had, it was like shagging Barbie. Seriously, this girl must have been waxed from neck to toe. Awful.' He offered up an apologetic smile. 'I just don't think I'm cut out for that life anymore.'

'So why even bother with this festival then?' asked Taffy, clearly a little thrown by Connor's heartfelt confession on the realities of life on tour.

'End of an era? Go out with a bang? I honestly don't know. It's just something I really wanted to do – I genuinely thought people would be pleased, as well. What an egomaniac! It was something a little different too, you know? With the Solstice and everything? I really thought the people of Larkford would embrace the idea—'

'Assuming they knew they were even invited,' Elsie cut in.

'Well, yes, obviously that was the first mistake in a litany of many.'

'Do you still want to try?' Holly asked. 'Only, I think

there's something we could look into that might yet turn everything around.'

Taffy groaned quietly; he'd seen that look on his wife's face before: the look that said she meant business. It was quite a pleasant change, he realised, to see it in a wider context again, rather than of late, applied at bath-time with the remit of bathing two sets of twins without casualties. Although he would never again underestimate the powers of persuasion and diplomacy *that* little task involved.

'Tell me more,' said Connor, refilling everyone's glasses. 'My God, this was a good idea,' he blurted suddenly. 'I've learned more about myself and my crazy broken heart in the last two hours than in all those months of grief counselling last year. Who knew I wanted to give Rachel a better send-off than standing over a rain-sodden grave, off my face on Valium – I can barely remember it, you know? And it's not like she was even religious – just hedging her bets, she always said. But she loved anything alternative or a bit Pagan and when I saw those stones, it was like ... Well, fate I suppose. So maybe this festival *is* a testament to her – to how she actually lived. Books, food and music – all created with passion. How did I not see that? Even when that slimy little journo point-blank asked me?'

'Grief is like wearing blinkers every day,' Elsie said quietly. 'It's not always intrusive, but it narrows your field of vision so you're only living half a life.' She reached for his hand, both their beringed fingers entwining. 'It doesn't stay that way, darling boy. This too shall pass.'

'Does the guilt fade too?' Connor murmured, focusing on their hands entwined. 'When your life continues, and theirs doesn't? When maybe you start having feelings for someone new? Does it get any easier?'

Elsie nodded. 'It does, but it takes time. Anyone worth loving, might be worth waiting for. Just so they get the *whole* you, not the fragmented pieces left over from your marriage.'

Connor looked up and saw that Taffy was about to leap in with questions, his lips almost already forming the shape of the word 'who', even as Holly shook her head gently. Connor had already shared so much this evening – he felt utterly spent – and he shot Holly a grateful glance. This at least could wait; he would tell them about his feelings for Kitty when he was ready.

'So,' Holly said, giving him a supportive smile, seemingly determined to steer the conversation onto safer ground, 'do you want to hear my fabulous idea, or not?'

Chapter 43

Holly and Alice wound in and out of the various stalls in the Market Place, sipping their coffees and browsing the sudden influx of all things 'Christmas' the next day. Fifteen minutes. That was all they could wrangle for their lunch hour, but staying inside and eating had never been an option. Not with the recent thaw bringing blue skies and fresh, crisp air.

'. . . and so, as I explained to Connor, if we rebrand his festival as a charity event, then not only can we actually make a fundamental difference, but he might not face so much opposition. What do you think?' Holly asked, running her fingers over a particularly soft knitted wrap on one of the displays and wondering whether Taffy's mum would deem it too decadent a gift.

Alice shrugged. 'Makes sense, I suppose. I mean, if he can get the acts to take a reduced fee or donate their time?' She looked a little confused. 'But, Holly, what's all this got to do with me?'

'Ah, yes, well I was just getting to that bit,' said Holly, well used to Alice's finely honed, Scottish, get-to-the-point sensibilities. 'Connor feels that to make the whole thing about Rachel is a little, well, self-indulgent – his words, not mine – so we're putting together a couple of local charities to run alongside the Air Ambulance, that might really resonate with the residents of Larkford. Matthew Giles's Young Carers' Drop-In Centre is already confirmed and . . .'

Holly paused, wanting to frame the suggestion in the most convincing way possible. 'Well, I also told him about your new role at The Practice, about all the commitments you were currently juggling, but that you'd taken it on because you felt so strongly about the importance of assistance animals.'

'We all feel strongly about it—' Alice interrupted.

'Exactly,' said Holly. 'In fact, can you think of a more unifying issue — think about it: Air Ambulance and Assistance Animals . . . The other AAs. Well, and Matthew.'

'Crikey,' breathed Alice. 'That could make all the difference, really. A little bit of operating capital.'

Holly nodded, an impish grin lighting up her face; she really was becoming a meddler of the highest order, Elsie's years of tuition having taught her well. 'And I had a thought about what you could spend some of it on.'

Alice merely waited, never one to supplicate.

'You'd have to register as an official charity, of course, but then you would need to hire a trainer,' suggested Holly. 'Maybe a dog trainer, who's in the market for local, yet meaningful employment? Maybe somebody who could really get the best out of the animals that we place and who you might be comfortable liaising with on a daily basis?'

'Oh!' managed Alice, one hand hovering over her mouth as she blinked to process the very thought. 'Bring Jamie home? Is that what you're suggesting? That's hardly charity.'

'Not for you, you daft muppet. For the project. You'll need some expertise if you're going to make a proper go of it. And, I was just thinking, it would dovetail nicely with that part-time position he was offered.'

'Well, he reckons he couldn't move back just for part-time work, although he's tempted just to hand in his resignation over there right now,' Alice mused. 'But then two halves do make a whole.' She swallowed hard and pulled Holly into such a rib-cracking hug that she gasped, still unclear whether the two halves in question were of the personal or professional variety.

Alice held on tight, clearly using their embrace to try and compose herself before she was spotted sobbing in the market. Again.

'More lesbians,' sniffed Gladys Jones as she walked by and gave them an appraising glance. 'Do you think we're missing a trick, Doreen? Based on the calibre of the menfolk around here, maybe they're on to something?'

Holly and Alice pulled apart and tried not to laugh, especially as Gladys tried to hold Doreen's hand and Doreen swatted her away with her straw shopper. 'I shall have to tell Plum and Tilly that one. They're clearly inspirational.'

'They always have been,' Alice supplied. 'Just for different reasons. I mean, have you ever stopped to look at how stunningly stylish your nanny is? It's enough to send me back to my shopping addiction, just to try and emulate her natural chic.'

'True,' replied Holly. 'I try not to focus on that too much or I'd never get dressed and leave the house. She's been rather disparaging about my leggings, to be honest. She and Elsie ganged up and chucked my favourite pair on the fire, can you believe it?'

'Were they the grey ones with the Smurf knees?' asked Alice. 'Because if so, I should jot them a note of thanks.' She grinned, an undeniable lift to her step that had not been put there by talk of leggings. 'Do you really think Connor could pull this off? Not just bringing Jamie home, obviously, I'm not that self-centred.' She gave a small self-deprecating laugh. 'But to change the focus of his festival so completely? I mean, he must have so many things already organised?'

'Ah, therein lies the key,' Holly replied, dropping her voice. 'Connor, I fear, is more of a thinker than a doer. He's got all the licences and things in place, and a few top-notch acts signed up, but it's like he ran out of steam when half of Larkford seemed against him. There's so much to do, it's almost mental. But thankfully, we have in our midst a very bored, very frustrated diva with a clipboard who has volunteered to step up as coordinator.'

'Lizzie,' they both said at the same time. It was the obvious solution and the perfect match, but for one thing.

'You don't think she's got the tiniest inappropriate crush on him though, do you?' Alice checked quietly, having borne witness to several episodes of Connor And Lizzie Go Mad In Larkford over the last few months.

'Nah, it's all good,' said Holly, with confidence. Lizzie was already rising to the challenge with this festival – even if still wearing pyjamas – all of her pent-up creative energies having finally found an appropriate outlet.

They continued to walk, occasionally stopping to buy a delicious pear, or a bunch of flowers. Each stall looked so inviting; the aroma of mulled wine, the promise of 'shopping local' for Christmas and the welcome sunshine had brought the residents of Larkford out in droves.

'You know,' said Alice, 'when I was up at Blackleigh Farm last night talking to Charlotte about Banana, I bumped into Kitty. And it occurred to me that she and Connor seem to be spending an awful lot of time together these days, what with the goats, and our mad dash down to Dorset and everything,' Alice said, fishing for the inside line from a different perspective.

'Ah well, he has just taken on Jamieson,' Holly pointed out equably, not giving too much away. Not that Connor had exactly confided his feelings for their lovely young vet, but Holly had noticed that mention of Kitty's name was the only thing guaranteed to bring a sparkle to his eye. 'And that has to be a labour of love – that poor dog is held together by fur and pharmaceuticals.'

'They'd make a gorgeous couple, don't you think? Can you imagine anything more romantic?' Alice looked rather taken by the notion. 'Falling in love over a new venture, setting up the farm together and nursing old Jamieson through his twilight years . . .'

'Dicky bladder and all,' said Holly drily.

'God, I hope you mean the wolfhound and not Connor,' Alice snorted. There was something about these illicit lunchtime liaisons – all in the name of work conversations – that made both women feel a little demob happy. Of course, it could have been the sheer volume of coffee they downed on their way around town. But they had both long since decided that multi-tasking was the way forward – Coco got her walk, they could have an uninterrupted conversation and a little fresh air to boot.

'Do you not have patients to get to, ladies?' asked the Major, tugging Grover's lead, before he attempted to devour the contents of Alice's shopping bag. Again.

'We do, we do, Major. But would you begrudge us a little merriment on such a lovely, festive day?' Holly said, holding up her newly purchased mistletoe and planting a kiss on his whiskery cheek, making him blush.

'I'll have what he's having,' catcalled Arnold the butcher

from under his stripy awning and shocking Alice. Not that it took very much to shock Alice these days. Finding out her oldest, bestest friend was batting for the other team had quite thrown her equilibrium.

As had finding out her mother's ulterior motive for wanting her home. Picking at the somewhat rustic-looking stollen she'd bought on their first lap of the stalls, Alice decided there was no time like the present to put her cards on the table.

'Holly, you know you have all these plans for The Practice?'

'Well, to be honest, I'd call them ideas or suggestions at this point,' Holly corrected her gently. 'I'm not naïve enough to think we can all get what we want, but I'm determined enough to try, if that helps?'

'Works for me,' said Alice. 'Look, the thing is ...' She floundered then, unable to clearly articulate what 'the thing' was, because it was still unformed in her own mind.

'Well, in a nutshell, I guess I'm asking whether you see me as a fixture here, and might consider me becoming a partner? I'd love to just get a sense of how you all think.'

'Yes,' said Holly simply. 'You're an integral part of the team and I, for one, can't imagine moving forward with our plans for expansion without you. I mean, it's going to take quite the leap of faith to put some of these ideas into practice, but you know you're vital to that process, Alice. At least, I hope you know.'

'Something for everyone, isn't that what you said? Find out everyone's aspirations and make sure their work fulfils them? I cannot tell you how much those words resonated with me, Holly. And now – with my cancer clinic with Coco, and overseeing the Assistance Animals pilot – well, you're ticking so many of my boxes, that I almost feel awkward asking for more – but I think I've reached the age where I need to know where I stand, professionally. And with Mum in my ear all the time to up sticks back to Orkney – well, it's focused my mind a little. I want to be a partner.'

'Okay then,' said Holly. 'Do you want me to discuss this with Taffy and Dan – test the water?'

Alice nodded. 'And in case it makes any difference. I can honour my buy-in with cash.'

Holly gaped for a moment, caught on the hoof. Nobody bought into a Partnership with cash. Loans were organised, mortgages repurposed ... It just wasn't ... 'Alice, have you been loaded all this time without telling us, or is your vintage clothing just worth a butt-load more than you realised?'

Alice twisted her mouth in embarrassment. 'Well, it turns out that my mum hadn't been entirely straight with me, when she said my dad hadn't left me anything. There's this trust, you see ...'

'You're a Trustafarian?' Holly blurted, pinking as she did so.

'Only in this particular instance, as it turns out. He wanted me to follow in his footsteps; to be a GP. So, he left funds invested so that I could do that. Apparently. And you have to understand, Holly, that this is all fresh information to me. I only found out two days ago. Something my mum let slip about needing an income to fund a trip. Turns out she's been sleeping with old Dr Sjorgen for the last ten years – they're quite the couple on the Island. So, if I head home and buy out his practice, she kills two birds with one stone – her daughter home and under her watchful eye once more, and a lovely nest egg for her and her beau to retire on.'

'You couldn't make it up. It's like Scotland Does Dynasty,' gasped Holly.

'It does feel a bit like that in my life at the moment, to be honest. First Tilly's renaissance, then you offering me my dream job and then Mum. If I was wearing shoulder pads then I'd know the metamorphosis was complete.'

'So do you have a plan?' Holly asked, holding out her gift bag of Cotswold fudge by way of support, forgetting that Taffy's dad was its intended recipient.

'I do,' said Alice. 'And ironically, Mum's made it so much easier to stay down south. I want to be a partner here, invested here – financially and emotionally.' She blushed. 'Jamie and I have already decided this is where we want to build our lives, maybe even have children, who knows? But at least now I can make my dad proud and myself happy with one decision. If you'll have me?'

Alice swallowed hard. She wasn't usually one for long speeches, but these words needed to be said, to be spoken out loud, if only to cement the notion in her own mind. Holly's professional belief in her had boosted Alice's self-esteem so much of late that she'd already been mulling over ways to make a commitment here, to prove to her mum that her life wasn't on those rocky windy islands that claimed to be her home but held none of her affections or loyalties, only desperate memories of winter storms and losing her father.

This legacy from her father, for that is what it was, felt like a lifeline – not just words of support for what Holly was trying to achieve, but money and action. Holly's concept of 'family medicine' was more in line with her own beliefs and ambitions than anyone she'd ever met, surely that was a better investment than becoming her mother's boyfriend's cash cow?

'Holly,' Alice said, as they neared The Practice and they both reached for their professional personas, 'I wanted to say thank you for being Tilly's mentor. It meant so much to her that you were prepared to take the time, make the effort. I'm sorry I was a bit jealous the other day.'

Holly grinned. 'She's a live wire that one. Reminds me of Elsie in a way – an unformed slip of a girl, just looking to find the shape she wants to be. Mark my words, she'll be the boss of us all one day.'

'I don't doubt it,' agreed Alice. 'And in the meantime, maybe The Practice can be moulded into the shape we feel family medicine should be?'

'I like that idea, Alice,' Holly replied. 'Any planning that involves Play-Doh automatically gets my vote. And Taffy's.'

They pushed open the door and the bright winter sunlight flickered behind them in the doorway for a moment, as though they were stepping through into a future filled with possibilities.

'Ah, Mrs Cavendish. You're bang on time, and look, Coco's so pleased to see you,' said Alice. 'Come on through and we'll take a look at those test results.'

Chapter 44

'Cassie, Cassie? Come on, my love. Don't cry. You're going to give yourself a blinding headache.' Holly offered yet more tissues and couldn't help the automatic glance at the clock as the minutes ticked by and her afternoon clinic ran more and more off piste.

It was fortunate in a way, that Holly had quietly started to trial the longer appointments. All very cloak and dagger actually, as she'd yet to clue the patients – or indeed some of the staff – in on the concept; instead, Lucy and Grace were making judgement calls as to which patients might benefit from a little extra time and booking them in with Holly accordingly. It was heartening to see that Holly's diary was already fully booked with deserving candidates. Imagine, she thought – as she attempted to soothe the snot-bubbling fountain of emotions that was Cassie Holland that afternoon – if all the doctors' diaries were opened up in that way? It would revolutionise their standard of care: she was convinced of it.

For every patient that was feeling frustrated for being rushed, she'd lay odds that their GP felt the same way. And really, what was the alternative? Just always to be running late, always running over? Booking in follow-up appointments that shouldn't really be necessary if there had been sufficient time in the first one? How could that be called efficiency? She was waiting on Tilly for the numbers, but a small part of her was hoping that they would show an actual cost to benefit ratio in her favour. Then, and only then, could she begin to clarify her proposals. She couldn't deny that an influx of new patients from the Rugby Club might have a positive impact, too, when it came to the bottom line.

Cassie looked up at her plaintively, her crying jag having burned itself out, and hiccuped her words. 'Isn't it bad enough that I've got cancer, Dr Graham? Cancer? Me? Do you know anyone else who lives as cleanly or holistically as I do? How can that be fair?'

'I'm not sure cancer is interested in fairness, Cassie. And this melanoma has nothing to do with lifestyle choices. It's awful, I know. But it's simply one of those things. And somebody *is* looking out for you – I mean, if you hadn't gone for that manicure?'

Cassie sniffed. 'You know me, Dr Graham, I've always been ready to take on the world, seize the day, grasp the nettle with both hands? And I was always determined to make my mark before I die. But now suddenly, with this cancer, there's not enough time,' she confided, as though she were the first person ever to experience that particular rollercoaster of emotions. 'Like the other week, when I went on the radio and I sorted that cocky Connor and his stupid festival. I made my mark then.' She sniffed again and Holly's stomach flipped disconcertingly at the sounds. 'But now I'm dealing with all this and I find that everybody's furious with me about it. Apparently,' she spat, 'they'd all been getting lots of new business off the back of it. All the B&Bs were booked solid and the pub was going to make lots of money from the extra people visiting Larkford. One minute, their scruples align with my own, and at the hint of some extra money, they all abandon their principles and *I'm* the bad guy?'

'But surely—' began Holly, wondering how Cassie could possibly be so blinkered, and whether she herself could reassure Cassie of the festival's future without breaking any confidences.

'Shunned. That's what I am now. A pariah in my own town. A pariah with cancer!' she wailed.

Holly discreetly pressed the button on her desk and breathed a sigh of relief when Jason knocked on the door. A male nurse at her beck and call would surely be enough for Cassie to take stock and pull herself together.

'Cassie? I need to see my other patients now,' Holly said gently, after all, there was no medical input required here. This was simply a hand-holding operation. Nevertheless she felt a lurch of guilt as she handed Cassie over into Jason's capable hands.

Cassie blinked up at Jason, like a scene from a Disney movie, her eyes wide and trusting. 'I'll be okay,' she said, standing up with disconcerting speed and taking Jason's out-stretched hand.

Cassie's remorse would be of no consequence to Connor, of course, Holly thought, even despite their fruitful meeting last night. The untold ripples of damage Cassie had caused by running her mouth off on air were still making themselves felt, even with their new plans in place.

Holly took a breath and checked her screen, all thoughts of Cassie falling from her mind as she saw Hannah Porter's name. If ever there was a patient deserving of a little extra time and attention it was Hannah.

'Hello,' Holly said, as Hannah walked nervously into her

consulting room, for once without her mother hovering beside her.

'Hi, Dr Graham,' Hannah managed, sitting down and folding herself into the smallest space she possibly could. She'd lost weight in the last few weeks, anyone could see that, no matter how many jumpers she had clearly layered on top of each other. And that despite The Practice's almost tropical central heating that was making Holly wilt.

'How are you doing?' Holly asked easily. She quietly noted the angry red stains on the poor girl's skin, the pock marks mottling her cheeks and the fine down that appeared to have thickened since last they met. In Holly's mind, alarm bells were ringing that they may yet have replaced one problem with another.

Hannah nodded, managing a twisted smile. 'Well, I haven't had the urge to top myself for a while, if that's what you're asking. So I think those horrible tablets are out of my system. And the people at the Nut House were terribly sweet with me.'

Holly shook her head. 'It's not a Nut House, Hannah. It was just to keep an eye on you while you found a little balance, yes?'

'You weren't there,' said Hannah darkly. 'But yeah, it got the job done. I guess I should be delighted that my skin is back to its hideous usual self.'

'Hannah, I know Daphne's not here, but if there's ever anything you want to share, maybe that you don't necessarily feel good about saying out loud, you know you can always come here, don't you? No judgement, no drama. Just someone to talk to?'

'I know.' Hannah tugged her sleeves down over her hands and sighed. 'I guess that's what I was thinking when I made this appointment actually. Mum's not been coping with me very well. She's shadowing my every move and it's so incredibly suffocating that, actually, it ends up having the opposite effect and I don't tell her things. Important things.'

'Like what?' said Holly, as casually as she could muster. Softly, softly.

'Well . . .' Hannah paused. 'I honestly don't want to top myself anymore.'

'Okay.'

'But even I can tell that some of my thoughts aren't real. Like they're not accurate or true, but I still believe them?' Hannah struggled to articulate what she'd clearly come here to ask. 'Does that mean I really am going mad?'

'Are you seeing things that aren't really there?' asked Holly, trying to get the measure of the situation. 'Having conversations by yourself, abrupt surges of rage, anything like that?'

'Not really. It's more beliefs, you know? Like that I'm always going to be alone because I'm so ugly? That maybe if I'm smaller, people will notice me less? And then once I thought that, I couldn't really manage my food – it got harder to swallow? So I've kind of stopped eating?'

There was a world of emotions and pain in the string of confidences formed as questions that told Holly so much about what Hannah was dealing with. She may have served her time at the Nut House, as she derisively called it, to deal with the drug-induced suicidal ideation, but Hannah's mental health was clearly still a precarious situation. Anorexia seemed like a probable outcome, if Hannah's jutting collarbones were any guideline – unless this disgust of food was actually a manifestation of sitophobia itself. Fear of food, rather than fear of nourishment.

It was the kind of diagnosis you might only ever find on the pages of a med school pop quiz, but nevertheless the word had long stuck with Holly. In some way it had offended her very sensibilities – after all, what was more intrinsic to life than the need to nourish our bodies, even our souls, by enjoying good food?

The look of revulsion on Hannah's face as she talked about eating was telling in itself.

There was no doubt in Holly's mind that Hannah needed some more professional counselling to get her back on track. But they'd been there before and Hannah had simply clammed up. Sure, it was progress that she'd come here today, sought out Holly for advice – even if Holly now found herself completely out of her depth, professionally.

Since she had absolutely no intention of playing fast and loose with Hannah's well-being while she attempted to learn on the job, no matter how intriguing her patient, Holly could only rely on her basic human empathy and her skills of persuasion.

As Hannah shut her down time and time again, Holly found herself beginning to grasp at straws. How could she persuade this gorgeous young girl to seek help if she was so adamant that any talking therapy was just 'a load of touchy feely bollocks'?

Holly frowned for a moment, as Hannah lapsed into silence. 'Hannah, can you give me just a second?' She angled her screen slightly so that her search of the NHS matrix was for her own eyes only. There was one avenue that she hadn't explored and she was now kicking herself for not going there first. After all, wasn't Hannah's current eating disorder a symptom, rather than the primary problem?

She took a deep breath, as the screen loaded and she double-checked the wording of the Access Statement.

'Look, Hannah, I'm going to talk to you like an adult, okay? So, I'm going to be blunt.'

Hannah managed the first smile since she'd walked in the door. 'Blunt I can do.'

'Look, we both know you need a little help right now. You need to talk to someone who is professionally trained to give you the best advice and a proper recovery programme. There is no doubt in my mind that taking the acne medication knocked you off balance, from a mental health perspective, and I know it must be distressing that your acne has flared up again so quickly and so badly.'

'Fucked either way, really,' offered Hannah, '– if we're still being blunt.'

'Quite,' replied Holly, without missing a beat. Living with Elsie had almost inured her to any cursing and blinding. 'So here's the thing. We know that laser treatment for acne can work very well, but it's not something the NHS covers—'

'And I know Mum can't afford it,' Hannah interrupted.

'Exactly. But what you may not know is that there are exemptions to that rule. There is – shall we say – a little leeway. And whether this is cheering to you or not, there is a caveat that it may be covered if the problem is causing the patient significant psychological distress.'

Holly paused, allowing Hannah to process what this might mean.

'You're saying that me going to the Nut House was actually a step in the right direction?' Hannah said eventually, her brow furrowed in deliberation.

'I'm saying that there are steps we need to take to make this happen. And the first one is to get a proper evaluation by a psychologist. And, in all likelihood, some ongoing therapy. But, Hannah, I can choose one for you who's likely to look kindly on our cause – however you'd have to actually go to the sessions and you'd have to engage – you can't just sit there and play on your phone for half an hour like last time. Whatever you do, please don't confuse stubbornness with strength, Hannah.' Holly's tone was stern but gentle, hoping to guide her patient into choosing this path herself, rather than having 'treatment' inflicted upon her.

In Holly's mind, that simple nuance could make all the difference to Hannah's compliance. And, if she wanted to qualify for the treatment that might deal with the underlying trigger for all of this, and ultimately change her whole life for the better, then compliance was about to become her new watch word.

As Holly accompanied Hannah out through the waiting room and waved her off, she was vaguely aware of mutterings echoing in their path. She leaned across the counter in reception and pinched one of Lucy's omnipresent mini Mars Bars.

'You're brave,' said Grace, popping her head up from one of the filing cabinets like a meerkat.

Holly flushed like a guilty pick-pocket. 'No, it's okay, Lucy said I could help myself any time.'

Grace laughed. 'No, you muppet, I meant walking the gauntlet through the waiting room. You wouldn't believe some of the conversations I've been hearing in there this afternoon.' She dropped her voice. 'Either way, it seems as though you've been rumbled.'

Holly looked at her quizzically as Grace stopped abruptly.

Holly became aware of a small, but disgruntled contingent of patients from the waiting room standing behind her. She smiled and made as though to walk back to her room, but Pru Hartley stepped sideways and stopped her. 'We want to switch doctors,' she said. 'We're not blind, Dr Graham. We can see how much extra time and attention you're spending on your patients while the rest of us are being hustled through with Madam in there like a conveyor belt.'

'Madam?' Holly queried, looking to Grace for understanding.

'Dr Campbell,' said Richard le Grange with feeling. 'She's seen six patients in the time you've spent with two. And you don't see her escorting her patients in and out like you do.'

'So we'd like to switch,' said Pru again, this time with an edge of firmness bordering on intimidation.

Holly bit her lip. It was too soon to talk about her trial. They had no data, they hadn't done the sums and the last thing she'd wanted to create was a two-tier system, whereby the majority felt short-changed. It was probably naïve of her not to see this coming, but in the back of her mind she'd begun to trust in Elsie's long-held truism that one wouldn't worry so much about what other people thought of you, once you realised how very rarely they actually did.

She obviously hadn't bargained on the residents of Larkford and their heightened powers of observation.

'Sometimes,' she said, by way of prevarication, 'certain patients need a little longer. One day that patient might be you, so do be considerate. A throat infection or a repeat prescription really doesn't take that long.' She didn't feel the need to elaborate.

On the other hand, she thought, as she walked back towards her consulting room, she had clearly been kidding herself about how long she could keep running a trial under their very noses. She couldn't deny that, in her head, she'd begun thinking of The Practice as a centre for health, rather than illness, still trying to work the elusive, holistic approach into NHS General Practice. It was clearly going to be easier said than done.

Taffy walked out into the corridor in front of her and she instinctively stepped straight into his arms for reassurance, wrapping her arms around his waist and laying her head on his chest.

His gentle laughter rumbled through her. 'So, I gather you've been sussed already. Old man Harris told me I needed to get patient care tips from my missus.'

'Oh God,' murmured Holly, not letting go. 'Sorry.'

'Don't apologise. It's become apparent already today how many of our patients had been feeling aggrieved by how little time we have to offer them. If anything, I reckon this means you're on the right track.'

'If we can make the sums add up,' Holly said, bolstered as always by Taffy's take on things.

'And we can hardly expect the patients themselves to decide whether they are worthy of a longer slot, now, can we? Some of them would talk for hours about their bunged-up nose or athlete's foot.'

'But then, for every one of those there's a patient like Hannah Porter. I could have spent an hour with her and it still wouldn't have been enough.'

'You sound surprised,' said Taffy, bemused. 'If you need an example of how actually communicating helps, you don't have to look very far.'

Holly smiled. 'We're doing okay now, you and me, aren't we?'

'Better than okay,' Taffy agreed. 'And to think all we needed was to have a proper conversation.'

'And a few lie-ins,' she reminded him with a loving smile, watching him swallow hard at the memory.

'Well, yes, I can't pretend that didn't help a little bit too.' He gave her a squeeze and let go. 'Now go and tend to your patients – just because you've got all the time in the world, doesn't mean that this poor desk jockey has time to be canoodling in corridors.' He paused, reluctantly releasing her hand. 'Maybe we could have an early night?'

Before Holly could reply, raised voices from reception put them both on high alert.

'Now, listen,' came Pru Hartley's angry voice echoing along the corridor, 'I've been waiting half an hour now about my stomach, Grace Allen, and all I need is the result of my autopsy.'

Everyone within earshot collapsed into laughter and Pru looked around in confusion. 'What?' she said. 'What did I say?'

'Biopsy, Pru,' said Grace gently, tears of mirth streaming unprofessionally down her face. 'You meant biopsy.'

Chapter 45

Dan slopped beer over his wrist as he attempted to flip down his seat in the grandstand and manoeuvre his pizza-pasty into his mouth at the same time. There really was nothing like a decent fixture at the Rugby Club with his best mate to take his mind off things and the legendary animosity between the Bath and Gloucester teams was sure to add a little off-pitch drama to the match.

'Right then, while this lot play silly buggers, are you going to fill me in or keep me guessing?' Taffy said, blowing on his hands for a little warmth against the chill breeze that whispered through the skyline of Bath – by half-time, they both knew all too well, they'd be freezing in their seats. Nevertheless it had been kind of Mike to think of them, and who in their right mind would say no to such cracking seats?

Dan chewed slowly, buying himself time to think. Even on the drive over he'd kept Taffy talking about nonsense just to avoid this moment.

'In all seriousness, for a minute,' Taffy said quietly, 'you need to give me something. You get married on the spur of the moment, then you all but drop off the radar with your new missus – even Lulu has been asking where you've been.'

'I've seen you at work,' Dan protested.

'Yeah – a fleeting hi–bye in the corridor hardly counts,' Taffy insisted. 'Now, either you fill me in, or I'm letting Holly loose to quiz Gracie. And she takes no prisoners at the moment, my wife. Whatever's going on, don't be an arse – let your friends into the loop. You never know, we might almost be useful.'

'There's a first for everything, I suppose.' Dan shrugged.

'Wanker,' said Taffy affectionately, punching him on the arm.

Dan grinned properly for the first time since they'd left Larkford. 'All right. But we are NOT spending the whole evening talking about this. Okay? I'll give you the edited highlights – frankly, just to shut you up – but then we are watching Gloucester get thrashed with a pint in our hands, okay?'

'Seems fair,' Taffy said reasonably.

Dan turned to face him, frowning as he sought the right words. 'Grace and I . . .' He stopped and frowned and started again. 'There's an awful lot to sort out about Lulu. Getting married was absolutely the right thing to do and Grace and I are both so happy we did.'

'Well, that's something,' Taffy said. 'You did have me worried for a bit there. You know, marry in haste and all that.'

'Yup,' said Dan with feeling. 'But actually, the more we talk it through, the more it feels like that was probably the only thing Keira asked of us that sat comfortably.' He sighed. 'It's perfectly natural for her to lay down the law about the kind of life she wants for her daughter and we're trying so hard to respect that, but nothing – not one thing – about this process is easy or joyful. The poor woman is dying, Taffs, and every time we go and see her, there's a little bit less spirit, and a little bit more fear. How can we possibly negotiate with that? In her eyes, either we want Lulu enough to make the commitments, or we don't. It's black and white.'

'And the reality?' Taffy asked. 'Between you and me?'

Dan nodded. 'Well, realistically, we can't promise to adopt another child until we've found our balance as parents, can we? I mean, we could promise to consider it – but that's not enough. And, if I'm being blunt, we don't want Elsie's house – no matter how incredibly generous she's being on the price. When we lost out on the sealed bids, Grace and I were both kind of relieved. It crystallised our thinking because we both realised we wanted something a little different, a little quirky – we'd had our hearts set on a doer-upper on the edge of town, with some land maybe and a few chickens ... But is that really a good enough reason not to tick the box for Keira and keep any hope of having Lulu?'

'And I suppose moving in there as a temporary measure wouldn't cut it?' Taffy suggested.

'Too dishonest. I couldn't do it. This is her child we're asking for. I can't quite believe I'm even hesitating,' Dan said, taking a bite of his pizza–pasty and chewing slowly, its taste no longer pleasing, merely sustenance.

'Actually, if it were me?' Taffy said after a moment's contemplation of the scrum taking place on the pitch below them. 'If you were looking to adopt *my* children as I died – well, I'd like to see you were committed obviously, but I'd be more impressed by someone with commitment *and* integrity – maybe someone who wasn't prepared to blindly jump through hoops, but could show me *their* game plan. *Their* ideals? Maybe they wouldn't be so very far apart in spirit, rather than in technicalities?'

Dan winced, as the Bath fly-half was knocked to the ground in a brutal tackle.

'Do you think so? Really? Because I have to tell you, mate, this is breaking my heart.' Dan swallowed hard. 'And what can I possibly say to Lulu when I see her – she knows nothing about any of this. But I still feel like I'm misleading her and she doesn't deserve that.'

Taffy drained his pint and wiped his mouth with the back of his hand, doing the matey thing by focusing on the game for a moment, while Dan recovered his equilibrium.

They both winced as another player hit the deck at speed.

'For what it's worth, I think staying away is worse. That little girl idolises you, Dan. You are in her life, one way or another. And I know, the ideal scenario has you being her new dad, but maybe Uncle Dan is better than nothing for now. She literally goes to the window to look for you every time a Land Rover drives by, or any other crappy, noisy car for that matter. She's all in, mate. She loves you. Don't leave her hanging.'

'But I thought—' Dan said, distressed by what he was hearing. So much for doing the right thing and not misleading her.

'Ah well, that's where you went wrong,' said Taffy easily.

Dan couldn't even muster the gall to swear at his long-suffering friend. Mainly because Taffy made a valid point. Several, actually. Dan sighed, knowing now that he was overthinking this. 'How do I show Keira how much I care, how much we care about her daughter? How do we prove that we are the right family for Lulu, even if we can't promise the things she's asked for?'

'Oh, that's easy,' said Taffy, shaking his head in frustration. 'She just needs to see you together. Honestly, mate, it's kind of heart-rending just watching you and Lulu interact – the absolute trust she has in you and Grace is like movie love. If that doesn't persuade her, nothing will.'

Dan punched Taffy's arm and nodded repeatedly, trying to catch hold of himself and not sob like a girl in front of rows of die-hard rugby fans.

'So we roll the dice,' he managed in the end.

'No time like the present,' said Taffy, annoying everyone in the rows behind him by standing up and starting to leave.

Dan gaped after him, his heart racing. There was friendship and there was leave-in-the-middle-of-the-match brotherhood. Taffy Jones truly was his Best Man in every sense of the word.

Driving back to Larkford, the atmosphere couldn't have been more different to the tense, stilted conversation on the way there. Grace had been phoned and, even now, was debating with Holly about what to wear and what games to bring to keep Lulu entertained as they made a group foray to visit Keira, their hearts on their sleeves for her to see.

'You know, we both have amazing wives,' said Dan, as he flicked the hands-free off.

'We do. Which, considering we're both utter wankers with the maturity of a pedigree panda, is not too shabby,' Taffy agreed.

'Notoriously immature, are they – pandas?' Dan clarified.

'Oh yes. I mean, not as bad as your lemurs – I mean, *they're* a regular fiesta of immature behaviour right through adult-hood,' Taffy said seriously.

Dan just shook his head. His thoughts were a little too distracted to fully engage in their usual mindless, but nevertheless relaxing, banter.

'So, if your wife gets her way, it'll be upheaval in every area of my life,' he said, indicating to overtake a procession of brightly coloured cyclists, red lights blinking from their helmets and with their bums in the air, approaching the hilly ascent over to the Larkford valley.

''Fraid so,' Taffy said, leaning across to honk the horn for no particular reason other than to make all the cyclists wobble. 'She's on quite the mission.' He paused. 'I think that might be our fault, though, actually. She's been feeling really sidelined being on maternity leave, so she's come back with a big stick and a basket of eggs determined to make waves.'

'And in English?' Dan queried, earning himself a grin from his mate.

'She reckons a little perspective has given her clarity. That she wants us to look at The Practice as a whole – not just as part of the community like before, but in what it brings to the staff's lives and by extension how we can improve that. Not just for the doctors, but for the patients too, obviously.'

'And I think she's on to something, I really do. And if anyone can make it work, it's Holly,' Dan said. 'I mean, everything that Bath job was offering – in terms of what it gave the patients and the doctors – that shouldn't be limited to private practice, should it? It should be what we're *all* aspiring to. Expansion really is the only way forward, although God knows how we'll fund it.'

'Holls reckons that if every member of the team had an area of responsibility that was theirs alone,' Taffy continued, 'that tied in with something they felt personally invested in, it would dramatically increase job satisfaction, not to mention efficiency, across the board.'

'I can see that. I mean, you never mind going the extra mile for something you feel really strongly about, do you? I mean, you've only got to look at Alice – do you think it still feels like overtime if she's learning about Banana's training?'

'I have an awful lot of time for young Alice, actually,' said Taffy. 'She's the kind of doctor I'd choose every time.'

'And you reckon she's still heading up to the Orkneys though, do you?'

Taffy shook his head. 'Not so much anymore. I think she may have reached the point where filial duty doesn't quite eclipse professional fulfilment anymore. Maybe we just need to give her a reason to stay?' Taffy frowned. 'Now you mention it, though, Holly said she wanted to talk to us both about Alice when we had time.'

'Well, if she's planning on leaving we'll stage an intervention,' proclaimed Dan. 'She's just too crucial to all our plans.'

'And actually just a really good egg. By my personal rulings, therefore, you never drop a good egg . . .'

'You never said what your dream project would be?' Dan said, intrigued to realise it was a question he couldn't automatically find the answer to.

'Easy,' said Taffy, surprising him. 'I'd love to have a sports medicine clinic – oh, I don't know, twice a week? Just sports injuries, proper therapies on site. Maybe even a dedicated physio to support the extra patients? Start small and build – now we've got all the rugby lads on our books, I don't think I'd be short of takers, even with their swanky Physio Suite on site at the club.'

'Do you know,' Dan said, not even a little bit surprised, 'I'd forgotten that about you – that was always your focus, wasn't it? When did that just slip quietly into the background?'

'Probably around the time I fell in love with Holly, and gained two sets of twins in under two years?' Taffy suggested, glancing out of the window at the woodland lining the winding road. 'It's not exactly straightforward, this parenting lark. You do know that, right? I mean, there's a reason that Holly and I both look permanently exhausted and we haven't been on a date in months. There's pictures of the kids in my wallet where my money used to be and I honestly couldn't be happier. But it's not one for the faint of heart, mate.'

'But your kids are great,' Dan countered, wondering whether in fact he had naïvely and selectively tailored his view of parenthood to suit an ideal in his mind, rather than the reality of the situation. Holly and Taffy always made it look so fun – even the impromptu suppers among macaroni-paintings and the yawning jokes about Holly's caffeine addiction. They made it look, if not effortless, then certainly life-affirming and do-able.

'They are great,' Taffy agreed. 'But they're still kids – noisy, demanding, unpredictable, expensive ... I have to tell you, it's a lot harder than I imagined it would be. Don't tell Holly, but these last few half-days have nearly finished me off. I've a whole new respect for what she's been dealing with. Are you and Grace quite sure you've thought this through?'

Dan smiled at the warmth of affection that filled his chest every time he so much as imagined the look on Lulu's face as she rushed to greet him and Grace at every visit. Right now, Taffy could have listed an encyclopaedia's worth of reasons *not* to do it, but they could never ever counter one simple fact: they loved her. As if she were their flesh and blood, and possibly even more so, watching her bravery at every hurdle life seemed determined to put in her path. Lulu was a hero-ine of the highest order in Dan's mind and he would move heaven and earth to make the rest of her childhood as joyful as it truly deserved to be.

As they crested the hills, the Land Rover exhaust billowing an unhealthy amount of fumes, the whole of Larkford lay spread out below them, almost like a model town.

'Do you ever think about how lucky we are to call this home – to have everyone we love together in this incredi-ble, crazy town?' Dan said, the lid on his bubbling emotions nowhere near re-affixed.

'Every single day, mate. Every single day,' Taffy replied, punching Dan's arm again for good measure as he changed gear.

Chapter 46

'Do you think it's being a parent that gives you a better insight into what our patients need? And the staff, for that matter?' asked Grace, as Lulu rolled happily on the floor with Eric, her fresh clean clothes already decorated with his paw marks. 'No matter what Patronising Patricia says, I think we all appreciate a bit of nurturing.'

Holly's heart went out to her friend. They'd been hovering by the door, suited and booted, for barely five minutes waiting for Taffy and Dan to pull up outside, but it was obvious the tension was getting to her. Never knowingly one for idle chit-chat, Grace had been scrabbling around for a topic that might hold her attention.

Holly was happy to oblige — this impromptu visit to Keira had thrown both of them for six. She herself was still a little ambivalent about Lulu's future — part of her wanted to wrap the small girl in her arms and refuse to let go; the other part — arguably the more rational part — told her that Lulu would remain in her life either way and that Dan and Grace would make glorious parents. That and the fact that she already had four children, a disgruntled hog and half an errant labradoodle in her care, not to mention a cantankerous pensioner and an emotionally needy nanny. When you looked at it that way . . .

'I don't think it's the parent thing, so much as the taking-time-out thing, really. I was only saying to Taffy last night how weird it is coming back – like I'm seeing everything afresh,' Holly said, slipping some playing cards and chocolate Matchmakers into her ever-expanding handbag of tricks.

'Or maybe you need to get your eyes checked,' laughed Grace nervously and then paused. 'But wait, you mean you've got *more* clarity, not less, don't you? I thought it was you that was supposed to have baby brain, not me.'

Holly shook her head. 'Based on what you've been telling me about how much of your "honeymoon" has been spent studying family law documents, I'd say you have a reasonable excuse. Do you know, if you'd asked me a year ago, I'd have told you, with absolute conviction, that there were certain pathways to being a doctor – the official ways, you know? But since I came back, I've realised that I actually did some of my best ever doctoring while I was on maternity leave.'

'Really?' asked Grace, pressing one hand to her chest. 'That's lovely.'

Holly smiled. 'I'm still quietly proud of myself actually. Saving a life at Toddler Tambourine isn't an everyday occurrence, or on live local radio. But even more so, it's the conversations I had, the time I had – to actually stop and listen to people. I'm convinced that it made a difference to their medical outcomes as well, seeing them now in clinic. I just question whether I would have seen the fundamental problems if I'd been rushing through morning surgery, juggling one patient after another. It's been quite the eye-opener in general, actually. I mean, have you ever noticed that it's always the big life decisions – the ones that require soul searching and proper consideration – that seem to get bumped in favour of the urgent, who's shouting loudest scenarios?'

'I think you're right,' said Grace, 'and if that's the case, then really the longer appointments have to be our priority, don't they? I know the individual projects are like the cherry on the cake, but surely we have to prioritise patient care over staff morale?'

'Grace Allen! I mean, Carter! Or do I?' Holly paused, confused. 'Look – you are the very last person I thought would ever say that. The two are so intrinsically linked – don't you think? It's obvious to me that happy, committed doctors make better, more empathetic decisions – why can't we have both?'

'Er – time, money, readiness . . . I'm not disagreeing with the concept, Holly. I'm just wondering whether it's realistic – and that maybe we should be doing this in baby steps . . .'

Holly couldn't help the quizzical look that passed over her face. Grace? Grace who had got married, seemingly was about to buy a house and adopt a child? All inside a week? Now talking – with a straight face – about baby steps?

Grace did at least look a little embarrassed at her emotive response. 'Ignore me, Holly. I'm distracted and nervous and secretly in awe of your boundless energy and positivity.'

Holly laughed and pulled her into a hug. 'Oh, Gracie,' she said. 'You have no idea how very wide of the mark you are . . .'

Lulu leapt to her feet to join the hug, tugging down her t-shirt that bore the sparkly legend *Bambina Bella* – it didn't take a rocket scientist to work out who'd been curating her new wardrobe.

Speak of the devil, Plum walked through into the hallway – a veritable Leaning Tower of Pisa of immaculately pressed miniature clothing in her arms. 'Have a lovely evening with your Mamma, Lulu. Now, do you have your beautiful painting for her to put beside her bed?' Plum effortlessly dropped to her knees, laundry in a single hand, and checked that this vital work of art was indeed tucked inside Lulu's bag. 'Remember, *mia tesorina – il cuore vuole quello che vuole*. Okay?' Plum kissed the little girl solemnly on both cheeks and then, to both Holly and Grace's eternal envy, Plum rose easily to standing without so much as a hand, a heave or a wobble.

'Good luck, *miei amici*!' she said, as she stepped nimbly over Eric and headed upstairs.

Holly turned and saw Lulu's eyes wide, following Plum's every step.

'What did she say to you, darling?' Holly asked.

Lulu smiled shyly, slipping her hand into Grace's. 'My heart – he wants what he wants,' she said, stumbling over the words, repeating them with Plum's Tuscan inflection in her voice.

Holly watched the tears, so easily on demand these days, fill Grace's eyes, as she leaned down to kiss Lulu on her cheek, Lulu's other hand drifting instinctively upwards to cup Grace's face.

Holly could only pray that Keira would make the right call – for, wherever they chose to live, however many children they chose to cherish, it was obvious to anyone that, in Grace and Dan's family, Lulu would be adored.

Holly sat with Taffy in the atrium of the Palliative Care Wing, trying not to check her watch every five minutes and wishing she hadn't been quite so considerate and polite in hanging back when Dan and Grace had suggested she accompany them into Keira's room. It was obvious to her that they needed a little time alone, just to talk and be together – but the waiting was killing her. She couldn't go home, because she'd promised Keira she'd stay – be on hand, talk things through, whatever she needed basically, at this stage.

'I can't believe this is what we're doing on a Friday night – does it get more real than this?' said Taffy, discreetly watching the comings and goings. There were no happy-ever-afters on this floor, as they both knew only too well, but Holly was aware that Taffy was taking this hard – his personal investment on so many levels, as Keira's diagnosing GP, as Dan's best friend and, perhaps more tellingly, as someone who had been equally prepared to open his home and his heart to one Louise Helen Fowler.

Lulu.

The reason they were all here – hoping, perhaps against hope, that no matter how tragic the circumstances, this young girl might yet buck the trend and leave this wing of the hospital with the possibility of a happy ending.

'You know, she's never lived with her mum,' Holly pondered aloud. 'I mean, briefly with both Keira and May as a baby, but she'll have no memories of that time. I even wonder whether she'll remember all this, looking back, and I can't actually decide whether that's a tragedy or for the best.'

'Let's go and get a coffee?' Taffy suggested, his voice husky with emotion. 'I don't think I can just sit here and wait, not knowing how it's even going in there. I mean, I'm assuming that Keira's still thinking clearly?'

Holly shrugged. 'Cancer or not, how clearly would you be thinking if you knew you had to say goodbye to the kids?'

'Fuck,' breathed Taffy and swallowed hard, his emotions never far from the surface since becoming a dad.

'Coffee,' said Holly, standing up and holding out a hand. There were some days when she just didn't feel qualified for anything – parenting, medicine, or frankly just being a grown-up. It was amazing how often, when difficulties arose,

Holly still looked around for the adult in the room to step in, before the realisation dawned that, these days, it was her.

'Silly question, by way of a change of topic,' said Taffy. 'I'm assuming we're okay with Tilly being at ours tonight? I mean, if Plum was dating some hot young male doctor, we wouldn't be quite so relaxed about her having her date over while she was on duty with the kids, would we?'

'Fair point,' Holly said, wondering whether she was guilty of double standards. 'But I think it has more to do with who it is, doesn't it? I mean, we know Tilly really well – we trust her. And obviously we trust Plum with the children . . .'

'But you have to admit that in combination they're a bit of an unknown quantity,' Taffy said.

'True. But I'm confident that they can exercise a little self-control. They're hardly going to be snogging on the sofa while the kids watch *Mary Poppins*.' She paused. 'I hope.'

'Yeah, you're right – I mean, if Plum was dating a bloke we knew really well – say Jason—' Taffy began.

Holly held up a hand. 'To be clear, I would categorically not use Jason as an example of self-control!'

Taffy laughed, their triathlete nurse was an incorrigible flirt, seemingly relaxed about his sexual preferences for both men and women and not known for his discretion or restraint. 'Valid point. Connor—'

Holly nodded. 'Yeah. I'd be okay with Connor. So, there you go, all above board.'

'No, I mean, look – there's Connor,' Taffy said, smiling at Holly's obvious confusion.

'All right, mate?' Taffy said, striding away to where Connor was sitting on a plastic chair outside the main hospital coffee shop, glancing disorientedly around him at the various Christmas decorations, and cradling a bandaged hand in his lap.

'It really is a small world round here,' said Connor with a twisted smile. 'No chance of keeping anything quiet.'

Taffy sat down beside him, as Holly joined them. 'What're you trying to keep quiet?' he asked tactlessly.

Connor gave him a sideways glance. 'Look, you can tell who you want, but I'd rather you didn't. I had a slight, erm, well, goat-related incident.'

Holly crouched down and lifted his injured hand. 'Is it broken?'

Connor shook his head. 'Just missing a sizeable chunk.' He gave a shudder as though the very thought made him nauseous.

'Can you still play the guitar?' Holly asked in concern.

'Oh my God, the guitar!' Connor said, his eyes widening, pupils already huge from a dose of prescription opiates no doubt. It was almost as though he genuinely hadn't even considered it. Perhaps his transition to gentleman farmer was almost complete.

'Kitty?' he said over their heads. 'What about my fecking guitar?'

Holly and Taffy swivelled as one to see Kitty walking out of the coffee shop, bearing two enormous hot drinks and a bag of doughnuts.

'Refined sugar is the cure for all ills in my book,' she said slightly defensively, catching Holly staring at the huge bag of doughnuts.

'I'm not judging,' said Holly, 'more yearning, actually.' She smiled as Kitty passed her the bag and wasted no time ripping into it and sharing the loot. 'So, what's the story?'

'– in Balamory . . .' Taffy hummed on autopilot before catching himself and blushing. 'Yeah, I mean, what did you do to that poor goat?'

Kitty grinned, clearly trying not to laugh. 'Well, I was giving Connor a milking lesson actually, and he may have been a little over-enthusiastic . . .'

'You said "tug", so I tugged!' countered Connor, his pride clearly as bruised as his hand. 'Bloody Maud. I should never have started with her – she's always so grouchy.'

Kitty nodded. 'Agatha would have been better.'

'Agatha Peal?' said Taffy, aghast. 'Bloody hell. That's a bit weird.'

'Agatha the goat,' Kitty corrected with a smile. 'Perry named them all after the matriarchs of Larkford. Don't worry, we didn't buy Elsie – thought that might be too close to home.'

'Yeah,' said Taffy drily, 'because milking Agatha sounds *so* much better.'

'Er, guys? About my guitar?' Connor tried again – the anxiety now hitting him despite his painkillers. 'How am I going to play at my own festival with a chunk missing out of my hand?'

Holly, Taffy and Kitty looked at each other, each hoping that someone else had an answer to his question.

'Do you ever think maybe this festival is doomed?' asked Kitty brightly, tactlessly. 'I mean it's just one thing after another after another.' She broke off at the aghast expression on all of their faces and smiled awkwardly. 'I mean, you have to wonder, right?'

'Maybe I'm cursed?' Connor said dismally.

'Bollocks,' said Kitty brightly, 'you're just a bit slow at taking a hint. Maybe the Universe thinks you should concentrate on one thing at a time – like, say, learning how to run a smallholding in the Cotswolds, before you become a festival magnet?'

'Magnate?' Connor suggested.

'Err, yeah that does make more sense,' Kitty accepted.

Holly watched the two of them chat back and forth – Kitty so completely underwhelmed by his fame and achievements that it bordered on the dismissive. But then that was Kitty Clarke: animals came first, second and third in her book – the occasional lucky human made her Top Ten but that in itself was a rarity.

Even the way she looked at Connor spoke volumes though, their affection and intimacy clear to see in this bizarre setting, without their habitual guards up, and Holly couldn't help but cross her fingers for a happy ending.

'We need more doughnuts!' Kitty declared, as she wiped her sugary fingers on her jeans, her enviably slim hips evidently more a testament to the miles she walked every day than any healthy diet.

'And now I'm torn,' said Taffy, 'because half of me really wants to know more about your goat injury so I can mock you about it, but the other half seriously wants to know what's afoot with you and the lovely Kitty?'

Connor's filters were down. There was only so much control he could exercise on the flipside of his potent medication. 'Isn't she great? I like her so much. And she gets me, you know?' He punched his good hand against his chest. 'In here? Like, she sees the real me.'

'Mate!' said Taffy with feeling and Holly could tell he'd been expecting tawdry tales of tumbles in haystacks, rather than an outpouring of obvious affection.

Connor nodded. 'I could spend all day with her and not get bored. And I don't just mean mucking about with the goats and the bees and Nigel.'

'Nigel?' Taffy mouthed across to Holly, looking perplexed.

'The donkey,' she whispered.

'That's right,' said Connor and sighed. 'I could write a million songs about her eyes and never do them justice. And she just picks up a hay bale, you know, like it weighs nothing – I never knew I liked that in a girl.'

Holly was actually rather relieved when Kitty came back. She couldn't help thinking that Connor might regret all these confidences in the cold light of day, not to mention that it was perfectly obvious from their every interaction that Kitty was still holding back. Or more precisely, had taken Connor at his word – after all, he hadn't been shy in stating his case – there would never be another woman for him like Rachel.

And maybe he had a point without realising it, Holly thought – for Kitty was absolutely nothing like Rachel. And therefore, possibly, exactly what Connor actually needed in his life.

Chapter 47

It probably wasn't quite the way that world–class rock star Connor Danes had hoped to capture the imagination and affection of the residents of Larkford, but nobody could deny it had been effective.

As word got out, as it inevitably did, about the nature of his wounded hand, something rather curious seemed to happen in the pubs and coffee shops and parks around the Larkford valley – Connor became human.

Of course, his celebrity history would never truly leave him, a faint burnished glow to his presence was always going to persist, but by losing his aura of infallibility, he had gained so much more – local affection and respect.

So many of his dissenters, it seemed, had simply assumed that Connor would hire in staff to keep his 'rural dream' ticking over, until he'd licked his wounds long enough, only to return to the world stage in his leather trousers, his time in Larkford merely a footnote of emotional rehab on his rock ascendancy.

'So,' said Pru Hartley, eyeing Connor's hand, 'you're really making a go of this farming lark, are you?'

'I am doing my level best, Mrs Hartley. And, of course, Clive and Kitty are teaching me the proper way to do things – no shortcuts,' said Connor deferentially, earning himself an approving smile from Pru behind the counter of the bakery, and from Holly standing behind him in the queue, as he hand-delivered the sheaf of personalised invitations to the festival.

Anyone looking at the swish graphics, enticing photos and glossy finish would be forgiven for not realising that it had been knocked up on Elsie's MacBook at the kitchen table. Her tech skills were continuing apace, even if the technical lingo defeated her on occasion – she'd put together a little YouTube video with absolute finesse, only to tell Connor she hoped it would go 'fungal'.

Holly couldn't quite believe the abrupt U-turn of feeling in the town. She'd quietly convinced herself it was down to the freebie festival passes, until Lizzie had pointed out the timeline. Could it really just be that Connor being bitten by a goat was all that was really required?

'You know,' said Holly, as they walked back to The Practice together, happy that she'd bumped into him on her morning croissant run – otherwise known as an excuse to dodge the central heating and take a breath of fresh air for just a few moments mid-morning – 'I'm beginning to think you might actually pull this off.'

'Cheers, mate,' said Connor. 'Good to know you never doubted me for a moment.' He paused and glanced around, dropping his voice. 'My new therapist is lovely, by the way. Good call that. Who knew that just saying all my crazy thoughts and mental machinations out loud would take so much of the pressure out of my brain?'

'Who knew?' shrugged Holly with a smile. 'Slowly does it, though, yes? Try and think of your recovery as a rebalance – some days you're going to wobble, but just try and keep your eyes on your focus . . .'

He nodded. 'And, in all seriousness, thank you for opening up your home the other night. It feels good to have a centre of operations and a little company.' He frowned. 'It's funny, because I genuinely thought that by setting up a really aspirational event on my new doorstep, it would help me get to know my new neighbours and really settle in. But that's only actually happened since things started going a bit pear-shaped.'

A bit pear-shaped was one way of describing the tangled mess that Connor had on his hands until barely forty-eight hours ago: no sponsor, a few big names still hanging on and willing to donate their time (mainly friends of his and Rachel's who could see what he was trying to achieve) and the spectre of thousands of festival-goers turning up to face disappointment at what was on offer. For that was one area where Connor had confounded all expectation: ticket sales were through the roof.

All he had to do now was deliver.

Easier said than done.

'Fecking hell,' said Connor, after they'd been waylaid by several of Larkford's more recalcitrant matrons, wishing him well and availing themselves of his tickets 'for their daughters'. 'If I'd known it was so easy to be accepted in this town, I'd have let Maud bite me weeks ago. She's the most ferocious of all my nanny goats, so surely I'd get even more brownie points for that?'

'Hmm?' murmured Holly distractedly, only half her attention – if that – on what he was saying. Running lists in her head, she couldn't escape the feeling that, when it came to the behemoth task of Christmas shopping this year, there was something vital she'd forgotten. Catching sight of Plum at the school gates, Olivia and Lottie in the pram, delivering what looked like Tom's forgotten gym kit in its distinctive red bag, she relegated the niggling thought for later. While she was quietly pleased that Plum hadn't let him escape his dreaded sports lesson, she felt somewhat divided on how best to proceed. She laid a hand on Connor's arm quietly. 'Hold fire here one minute. Once Plum's gone, I'm going to insist Tom gets his detention anyway. He'll never learn if we keep rescuing him.'

'Crikey,' said Connor, shocked. 'You're one hard-arse mummy, aren't you?'

'I'm really not,' Holly protested. 'But it's hardly fair if he misses his detention because the nanny brought his kit in, is it? The other working mums can't do that. If you think of it that way, then actually I'm saving him from social suicide.'

'You got all that in under sixty seconds?' Connor marvelled. 'I just thought, "Bad luck, mate, you're doing gym."'

Holly smiled. 'Well, there's method in my madness. And Lizzie found this out the hard way. There's a real mix of kids at the local primary – some of whom, bluntly, would be better at the posh prep up the road, and some on lunch-vouchers and benefits. It doesn't pay to be flashy, or different, when you're six. It's just basic tactfulness really, isn't it? Nobody wants to have their nose out of joint. So, in my book, Tom should have his detention.'

As hard as it was to watch Plum walk away across town with Holly's two baby girls, she forced herself to wait. Tactfulness applied to adults too and she didn't want Plum to feel censored or watched over.

'Mr French? Hi. Can I ask a favour?' Holly said, leaning over the locked school gates and nearly spilling her latte everywhere.

'I must be quite the popular chap this morning,' he said with a twinkle in his eye that did all sorts of unnecessary things to Holly's libido. 'I've had a veritable parade of Larkford ladies requiring my attention today.'

'Not hard to see why,' muttered Connor under his breath, earning him a hard stare from Holly.

'I've already had a lovely chat with your Dr Walker about having Banana come to school for a taster day. I know that Mrs Hearst has her heart set on boarding school for Jess, but I'm inclined to think that repeating Year Six and finding a balance health-wise is a very good suggestion, Dr Graham. I only hope I can persuade Mrs Hearst that, with a proven year in academia under Banana's belt – or should I say – girth, there will be much more support moving forward for Jess.'

Holly nodded. 'Thank you. It's a tricky one this, balancing the child's needs with the parent's aspirations.'

Mr French chortled – actually chortled – and Holly felt her whole self soften towards him immediately. He may look as though he fell off the pages of *GQ* magazine, but here was a very human, very dedicated teacher, whom she truly respected and liked. Surely that was more important than his undeniable appeal in other areas. Or his relatives.

As Holly outlined her quandary regarding Tom's dodged detention, he held up a hand to stop her. 'If I may, Dr Graham – Tom didn't remember his kit, your lovely nanny did. Detention stands. Think no more of it.'

'Thank you,' said Holly with feeling as he gave her an appraising glance, watching her that bit longer – surely – than was actually necessary.

'You surprise me, Dr Graham. Very pleasantly, if I may say. So many parents in your position tend to pander to their offspring. It's rather refreshing to see a slightly firmer line.'

'Well,' blustered Holly, much to Connor's amusement,

'there's not really much choice in our house. Even with the lovely Plum on board, we're still outnumbered.'

'I'm so sorry,' Mr French turned his attention to Connor, 'I don't think we've been formally introduced? I'm Alec, Alec French.'

'I'm Connor. I live at the old Peal house. No kids, I'm afraid, so no need of your professional services.' He laughed awkwardly.

'Fantastic to put a face to a name,' said Mr French, clearly not one of Connor's legion of fans. 'You must be the chap organising this festival extravaganza? You must say if you want the school choir to join in?' He paused, and allowed a stricken look of embarrassment to cross Connor's face before putting him out of his misery. 'I mean, if the crowds refuse to go home at the end of the weekend, I imagine a little tuneless carolling should see them nicely on their way?'

Connor grinned and shook his hand. 'Deal.'

'And I gather I have you to thank for my sister even deigning to talk to me,' said Mr French. 'She wanted a favour, of course, but we have to start somewhere. I'd love to know what you said to bring her around? We've been estranged for years – part of my reason for taking the position here actually. Try and build a few familial fences, you know.'

Connor looked confused. 'I haven't said anything to her.'

Holly was about to interject, correct poor Connor, after all, Mr French had clearly been talking to her, but the conversation carried on ambiguously around her.

'Ah well, maybe it was just good old-fashioned guilt, then. I know losing you your main sponsor sat pretty heavy on her conscience, so perhaps she just realised she'd taken things too far on the radio the other week? Still, all her efforts on your behalf seem to have made a difference, don't they?'

Holly and Connor looked at each other blankly.

'She's been garnering support among all the parents at the school gate? Not to mention at The Deli, the wholefoods place and that wonky yoga club she joined. Giving you her blessing, it seems.' He frowned. 'I have to tell you, I've known Cassie an awfully long time, as you can imagine, and she's behaving most oddly. Rather out of character.' He shook his head. 'But then maybe that's part of her charm? I have to say, I had no idea she was so influential around these parts or I'd have persuaded her onto the PTA.'

'I guess I shall have to find her and say thank you,' said Connor, blinking to try and process what he'd just been told.

'It's quite normal, you know,' Holly said quietly to Mr French, as Connor ambled over to pin one of his flyers on the school noticeboard. 'After a shock diagnosis like that, Cassie is bound to be looking at her life and her choices differently. I'm so glad you're here to give her and Tarquin some support. It's not going to be an easy year for her.'

It took barely a second for an horrific swooping sensation to unsettle her stomach and knock the world out from under her feet. Mr French's uncomprehending gaze said it all.

He didn't know.

Cassie hadn't told him.

And Holly had just violated her patient's confidentiality.

She quickly replayed the conversation in her head, and all she could find were her own assumptions . . .

'I'm so sorry,' she breathed, taking Alec French's hand, not a hint of flirtation even on the periphery of her mind. 'I hadn't realised that—'

'That my sister is a closed book?' He sighed. 'I know I can't ask you, but I'm assuming this isn't something minor?'

Holly bit her lip, hard, but instinctively shook her head.

He nodded, accepting. 'It was always going to be this way with my sister, Dr Graham. In many ways I should be grateful for your little slip. Rest assured, I won't breathe a word. But thank you. It was a timely reminder that I should perhaps be focusing a little less on the litter rota and a little more on building a relationship with my nephew.' He paused. 'If I may, I'd be grateful to talk to you in a professional capacity sometime?'

'Of course,' said Holly, the guilt overwhelming. 'When you phone, tell Grace that you'd like a trial appointment. Tell her I said it was okay.'

'How very cryptic,' said Mr French. 'I'll do just that.'

He walked away across the playground and Holly stood staring after him.

'Well, he's full of surprises,' said Connor, returning to her side and counting his flyers. 'Who knew we had Cassie Holland to thank? And here was me thinking goat-bites were the local currency to curry favour.'

Chapter 48

Grace squeezed Dan's hand tightly and swallowed hard. Even given the whirlwind of the last week, she couldn't quite believe they were doing this. 'Are you quite sure?' she whispered, her voice tremulous and filled with uncertainty.

Without once shifting his focus, Dan lovingly returned the pressure to her fingers. 'I don't mind jumping through hoops, Gracie, but this is one decision I can't bring myself to compromise on, no matter how generous Elsie's offer.'

He raised his wooden paddle in the air and Grace smiled, noting the number painted on the front – it had to be a sign – Thirteen. Unlucky for some, but not for her.

'Going once, going twice, and for the last time? Sold to Bidder Thirteen,' the auctioneer said, smacking his gavel down with authority.

'Bloody hell,' said Dan in a rather loud whisper. 'Congratulations, Mrs Carter – you're a homeowner.'

Grace clasped the hurriedly photocopied property particulars to her chest and tried not to whoop for joy. It was just too perfect. Assuming you overlooked the dry rot, and the hideous seventies bathrooms, and the dark, pokey kitchen . . . Nothing that a sledgehammer and a little vision couldn't fix.

They excused themselves from their row and slipped away to deal with the paperwork.

The whole day had been an exercise in serendipity – they never normally even drove out of Larkford on that particular lane. If they hadn't been avoiding one of the articulated lorries bearing Portaloos towards Connor's festival site, they might never have seen Heron Cottage, might never have known that their dream home was sitting, cold and neglected, frosted as though straight from a vintage Christmas card, and awaiting sale by auction. A sale with the least fanfare, and maximum expediency, by a repossession firm with little interest or no clue of the gem they had on their hands, or indeed the buoyancy of the Larkford property market. It was a steal, even considering the work that needed doing. Better still, it was a true family home in the making, with views across its rolling gardens, a cherry red Aga and four square bedrooms tucked under the eaves.

'It's everything I've ever dreamed of,' breathed Grace as she flicked through the particulars again as they queued up to hand over their combined life savings.

'We won the lottery this month, Gracie,' agreed Dan. 'The most beautiful wedding I could ever have imagined to the woman of my dreams, the prospect of a life with Lulu and now this . . .'

'Somebody's looking out for us, you know? Do you ever feel that, just as though somebody is moving all the chess pieces around on the board?' Grace shrugged, knowing it sounded crazy but unable to shake off the feeling that her life had recently taken on, well, a life of its own.

'Dr and Mrs Carter?' said the auction house clerk walking towards them with a clipboard. 'If you'd like to step this way?'

*

There was an inevitability to the phone call that was undeniable. That didn't mean it hadn't still come as a shock, emerging blinking into gentle flurries of powder soft snow, clutching the deeds to their new home, unable to believe their luck, when Grace's mobile had trilled intrusively from her pocket. And to think, she almost hadn't answered, wanting to savour this momentous occasion with her new husband for just a second longer.

'I understand,' she said, the bottom falling out of her world and blinking away the tears that sprang unbidden to her eyes. 'We'll be right there.'

She hung up and a tiny cry of desperation caught in the wind. She collapsed into Dan's arms and sobbed. 'It's too late, Dan. We never had time to tell her. Keira's lost consciousness — she's slipping away.'

Dan nodded, his own emotions written all over his face. He rubbed unconsciously at the light stubble on his chin. Their victory suddenly felt hollow. He pulled his car keys from his back pocket. 'Then it's another bit of serendipity that we're in Bath. Five minutes. That's all. And we'll be there to hold her hand, whatever she's decided. Nobody should ever leave this earth alone.'

Grace nodded and for the next five minutes neither of them spoke as Dan used every ounce of his never-forgotten army training to skilfully guide the car through the dense Bath traffic and screech to a halt outside the Palliative Care unit at the hospital, grateful for his Doctor's parking badge and for every green traffic light that had guided them there.

Wordlessly they ran through the corridors, Grace unable to escape the feeling that they were too late — too late to hold Keira's hand in this last moment, too late to secure a loving future for Lulu — too late.

The double doors swung closed behind them as they burst through in tandem and then froze, unsure of the protocol in these situations – it was somewhat outside the sphere of their everyday experience and certainly not one they wished to repeat ever again.

Twenty-five was just too young – too short a life, too little time.

It took Grace a moment to register that a soft-spoken nurse had come over to greet them, gently guiding them towards Keira's room, updating them on her condition, tenderly adjusting the sheets on Keira's bed as she lay quiet and still, the trace monitor's flickering numbers the only sign of life.

'You're just in time,' she said, slowly but clearly – obviously realising that Grace was barely able to process what she was saying – pulling over a chair beside the bed and guiding Grace to sit down. 'She's drifting in and out, so do talk to her. I'm sure she can hear you.'

Grace reached out and took Keira's fragile hand in her own, all other thoughts flying from her head, as the instinctive mother in her came to the fore. May Fowler couldn't be here for her daughter, but she could. She could be here for this precious girl, just as she would for her own boys in the same, heart-wrenching situation ... The very thought was enough for the words to start flowing. 'I'm here, my darling, it's Grace. You're not alone. We're here – me – and Dan. And the snow is just starting to fall outside your windows, Keira. It's so beautiful and so quiet and everyone who loves you is thinking of you – being grateful for you. Every extra moment they spent with you is a precious gift they will never forget.'

Keira's eyelids flickered for a moment and her hand moved perceptibly. 'Grace,' she managed, her throat dry and the sound faint. A flicker of a smile crossed her face. 'You're here.'

'I'm not going anywhere,' Grace reassured her.

'I want—' Keira began. 'I—'

Grace leaned across and moistened one of the tiny sponge 'lollipops' that were beside the bed, passing it gently over Keira's parched lips. 'It's okay,' she said, desperate to hear Keira's words, but knowing it might just be too much.

'You're my guardian angel,' said Keira, a lone tear escaping from her lashes. 'Love my baby, Grace, won't you?' she said, a sudden urgency in her words, her tone, as she even made as though to sit up, before falling back onto the nest of pillows supporting her delicate frame. 'Love her, please.'

Grace was unable to stop the tears that were flowing down her face now, dampening her cheeks. In the corner of her eye, she caught sight of the bundle of legal papers that Keira had seemingly been reaching for. Either way, there was nothing to be done now, other than to make a promise she had every intention of keeping.

'I will love her as though she were my own,' Grace said, leaning forward to kiss Keira's cheek. 'I will love her always and for ever – no matter what. You have my word.'

'Love her,' murmured Keira, already slipping back into unconsciousness and leaving Grace uncertain how much of their conversation Keira had really been aware of.

Even several hours later, as the hills over Bath were daubed a soothing white and the monitor beside them flickered ever more erratically, Grace still held her hand. Her promises to Lulu and Keira meant the world, but right now, her promise to herself, not to let this brave young woman slip away without a loving presence at her side, seemed even more important.

*

There was an almost visceral confusion in Grace's heart that left her reeling. To witness the intimacy of Keira's death, ultimately gentle in its simplicity, her last thoughts, fittingly, being of her daughter – and to do so on the very day when all of her hopes and dreams were being realised? Bittersweet didn't even begin to cover it.

She slipped her hand into Dan's, seeking warmth and comfort, despite the winter wonderland that now surrounded them and the festive, almost frolicsome atmosphere that seemed to pervade their home town at the imminent prospect of not only Connor's Solstice festival, but also the hope of a white Christmas with their nearest and dearest.

How could it be that on such a day, they were about to deliver news that would undoubtedly break the heart of the person they had grown to love most in the world?

The property particulars for Heron Cottage, their cottage, their family-home-in-waiting were crumpled in the bottom of Grace's handbag, now pinned down by the weight of legal documents from Keira's bedside.

Signed, witnessed, official.

Lulu was theirs.

Their daughter in every legal sense except biology.

But then, what was a little DNA between friends? A half-strangled laugh escaped Grace's lips and she felt instantly ashamed. Her new and wonderful husband by her side, building a home and raising a daughter together – it was everything she had ever wished for ... And yet, somehow, it felt as though their future happiness had been built on a foundation of someone else's suffering.

Be careful what you wish for, she reminded herself, her own words coming back to haunt her – 'I could never adopt someone's child if there was the possibility of them changing their mind'. Well, against all odds, that was the situation they now faced. And a part of her craved the opportunity to go back, insist that Lulu spent more time with Keira, even knowing how much the little girl had hated the hospital, hating the enforced intimacy with this woman, this girl herself, that Lulu hardly knew.

Nothing about this situation was ideal.

Except perhaps for one thing, she realised. Keira had passed away knowing that her daughter would be loved and cherished and raised by two adoring parents in her home town. That in itself had to be something.

'I'm going to need some maternity leave,' Grace said to Dan out of nowhere, as they slipped across the snowy Market Place towards Number 42, hands clammy, pulses racing.

'Me too,' he said. 'Let's take it in turns, week by week, until we're settled? Holly and Taffy style?'

'But without the months of sniping and soul-searching and total lack of communication?' Grace suggested with a soft smile.

'Obviously. We'll be far too busy making our own mistakes,' he replied, squeezing her hand. 'Are you ready for this?'

Grace nodded. The whole day had been choreographed long in advance, plans made, best options considered – but now, in the making, Grace's mind still skittered around, hoping that they hadn't missed something, misjudged something else, made the wrong call . . .

'Do you think we should have been the ones to tell her?' Grace said quietly, her voice cracking.

'I honestly don't know. But we asked the counsellor for her advice – this is what she does – all day every day. It seems the height of arrogance to then ignore it. And let's not forget, Lulu has been living with Holly and Taffy for months now.

She trusts them absolutely. If she has to hear about her mum dying from anyone, it makes sense that it comes from them. And then gradually to introduce the idea of you and me, of us as a family, once she can process the idea of a future without her mum in it.'

Grace nodded. There was no doubt that this was good advice. On paper. Theoretically. It just didn't cover how it would make her, Grace, actually feel. It seemed plain wrong that this little soul would be hearing all this life-changing news without Dan there to hold her in his arms, or Grace on hand to smooth away her worries and whisper sweet endearments.

'This isn't about us, anyway,' Dan continued gruffly, the emotion making his voice husky and deep. 'This is about Lulu. How we feel about this doesn't matter. Parenting 101, right? Do what's right for them, and then we're the grown-ups, so we just have to adapt.'

Grace nodded, relieved a little that she wasn't alone in feeling this way as they walked ever closer to Holly's house, with no idea of what they were walking into. Tears, drama, a mute and unresponsive child?

They held hands on the doorstep of Number 42, each of them seemingly waiting for the other to knock on the door.

They needn't have worried. Holly yanked the door open before them, almost as though she'd been hovering in the hallway, awaiting their arrival. 'Did you get my message?' she whispered.

Dan and Grace looked at each other. 'No,' they said in tandem. 'Is everything okay?'

Holly shrugged. 'I have no idea. This is all new to me as well.' She glanced over her shoulder, her voice barely audible, so keen was she not to be overheard. 'I did everything we said. She knows. She just didn't seem terribly surprised. She sat on my lap for a cuddle for a bit and then wanted to play in the snow with the boys.'

They all looked at each other in confusion, whatever they'd been expecting, it certainly wasn't this calm acceptance of her mother's passing.

'Maybe she didn't really understand?' Grace said after a moment.

Holly held out a slightly wonky drawing that took a little concentration to discern. But once the sky and the stars and the little angel that looked like Yoda became clear, there was no denying the message. 'She said "*Mamma angelo*" when she gave it to me.'

'Plum,' said Dan, nodding, immediately spotting the influence of the Catholic Italian in their midst. 'I think she's been laying the groundwork for weeks.'

'We all have,' agreed Holly. 'But we never thought any of it had actually gone in. I mean, it's not as though she says much.'

'Is she upset at all?' Grace asked, still finding her way through this moral maze of a day.

Holly shook her head. 'Not really. But I'm sure it will come, with time.' She paused. 'In fact, the only thing that's caused a problem so far today, is that you weren't here to do her plaits, Grace. Apparently I don't do it right.'

A tiny comment, a moment, really. And surely Holly had no idea how much it resonated deep within Grace's heart? But nevertheless, Grace had to swallow hard – it had been difficult at first, watching the love affair between Lulu and Dan evolve. At times, she had begun to wonder if she herself would always be surplus to requirements, the mutual adoration between the two of them seemingly so all-encompassing.

That simple thought, that Lulu needed her too, lifted her heart and appeased any last traces of doubt.

The kitchen door flew open, making them all jump, and a sticky-fingered Lulu appeared in the hallway, a slightly mangled mince pie in one hand. It fell from her fingers, no longer of importance. 'My Grace,' she said simply, almost sounding relieved, trotting towards her and pressing sticky hands around her as Grace instinctively dropped to her knees to hug her.

After a moment, Lulu glanced up, safe from within the circle of Grace's arms, her eyes wide and wise for one so young. A tentative smile crossed her face, as she looked up. 'My Dan?' she asked, a wealth of hope and expectation in her small voice.

As Dan kneeled down beside them, he wrapped his arms around them both, his voice choked with feeling. 'Always,' he replied without hesitation.

Chapter 49

'I still can't quite believe this,' Connor said, that weekend, looking around at the snow-frosted meadows behind his home, a trail of Tiki torches lighting a path up to the remains of the ancient stone circle that had been his inspiration. The car park was full and families had turned out in droves to celebrate the Winter Solstice together. The large sound stage set up at the end of the valley, backed by huge screens, looked a little incongruous right now, but Connor knew that it would literally light up the moment The Hive stepped out. Even the mammoth yurt for the 'local acts' was decorated in swathes of seasonal greenery and bunting and the smells emanating from the 'food court' – aka the stable yard – were enough to make anyone's mouth water.

He brushed a sneaky tear from his eye, unable to articulate to Lizzie and Will standing beside him just how much this moment meant to him, how much Rachel would have adored the spectacle. And perhaps even more so, how proud she would have been that they had taken the decision to go non-profit. In a way, he couldn't believe he hadn't gone that route from the outset – after all, it was much more in keeping with Rachel's entire ethos.

Having the Young Carers' Yurt dedicated to local musicians

had been another stroke of genius on Lizzie's part. Sure, the majority of them were seriously not great, but who knew whether there was a young talent out there today who would look back on this festival as their Big Break. Just another way of paying it forward – The Larkford Way.

'You know you have to give some press interviews after you officially open the show, don't you?' Lizzie reminded him, checking her detailed checklist on her clipboard and then eyeing his bandaged hand in dismay. 'I can't believe I don't get to hear you play live, after all these years – The Hive are opening in my own backyard and they subbed in Gary!'

Connor scowled at her. 'Rub it in, why don't you?'

It was an act.

In truth, he felt so overwhelmed by the festival and the sudden wave of local support, he wasn't sure he could even have rustled up a decent attempt at 'Smoke on the Water' – injury or no injury. It was quite a relief to let Gary, their ever-eager tour manager and wannabe rock star, step in as he took his first tentative steps towards recovery, both physical and mental.

'Ah yes, but without Agatha taking a chunk out of his hand, would we even be here today? Would you ever have got the locals onside?' Will said astutely.

'It was Maud, actually,' said Connor, defensive of his ladies' individual characters already, although nobody seemed to listen.

'Lady Peal been biting the hand that feeds?' guffawed the Major, ambling over towards them. 'Sounds about right, but I thought she'd hightailed it to Zurich the moment your cheque cleared? I even heard she had a new Swiss chappie on the hook. A doctor, I heard.'

Connor smiled and shook his hand. 'Peregrine. So pleased you could make it. No Marion today?'

The Major bent down and scooped up Grover. 'Chaps' day out, isn't it, Grover?'

'Good plan,' said Connor, barely having to reach downwards to scruff Jamieson's tufty ears. 'We had much the same idea ourselves.' There was something incredibly grounding about the soulful look on Jamieson's face; his sheer adoration of Connor and his absolute, unblinking focus certainly made it hard to look away. In fact, if there hadn't been so many people calling his name and demanding his attention, it wasn't so hard to imagine simply wandering among the punters with his giant dog by his side and drinking in the feeling of having achieved a worthy goal. Anonymity was not something that Connor could arrange, though — not here, when his name, his band, his efforts, had been the main allure for many of their guests.

Connor glanced up at Jamieson's baritone 'woof' as Kitty wove through the crowds towards him; there was something to be said for a fresh start too. Kitty gave him a cheerful smile and bestowed kisses upon Jamieson's head, his heavy tail beating a tattoo against Connor's leg. He swallowed a ridiculous surge of envy. 'You made it!' he said, kissing her chastely on each cheek and breathing in the intoxicating scent of vanilla that wafted from her hair as she turned.

'I wouldn't miss it for the world,' she said happily, crouching down to look Jamieson in the eye. 'And how's my favourite gentleman? You look so much brighter.' She kissed his nose. 'I am *very* pleased with you.'

She stood up again, stretching her back. 'And with you, Conn. Thank you for taking such good care of him, even with all this malarkey going on.'

Lizzie's head shot round. Only very close friends called him 'Conn' as a rule.

'And how long is Jamieson staying with you, *Conn*?' she asked, the proprietorial emphasis on his name making Kitty's eyebrows dance upwards in amusement.

'Oh, I think we're in it for the long-haul, aren't we, mate?' replied Connor easily. 'Once you've shared your bed with an Irish wolfhound, a setter, a spaniel and a beagle there really is no going back. I ought to be grateful the little yappy ones can't jump up that high.' He saw no reason to let on that he gently picked them up, one by one, and popped them on the bed with the other, bigger dogs, so they wouldn't feel left out.

Kitty chuckled. 'Not quite the rock-and-roll orgies of old, eh?'

Connor looked shocked. 'I am *far* too square to go in for stuff like that.' It suddenly felt very important that Kitty knew that. 'Serial monogamy is more my style,' he said, dropping his voice slightly. He knew that on some level, inviting The Hive and his old life into his new one might create tension; he just hadn't stopped to think that it might also change the way people around here viewed him.

Kitty, in particular.

He had come to rather like the bumbling, trainee farmer that he had become, in her eyes at least.

'Right then, you ol' fucker!' Gary barrelled towards them in his skin-tight leather trousers, his Cockney twang jarring slightly. 'Shall we get this show on the road?' He grimaced, as he lost his footing for a moment on a patch of icy mud and flamboyantly made a show of wiping it off in the long grass. 'Don't know how you live around 'ere, mate. Too much bloody nature for my taste.' He gave Kitty and Lizzie a somewhat salacious smile. 'Although I can see already that it has its compensations. All right, ladies?'

Connor felt a quiver of embarrassment. It wasn't that he

was ashamed of his old bandmates, it was more that he had forgotten that they came with pointy corners and loud opinions – it was almost as though he himself had been softened by his months in the countryside.

Everything today felt too loud, too jarring – basically just too much. Maybe he should have taken up his therapist's offer of some additional, softening pharmaceutical support, just until he was feeling less fragile? Somehow though, in his mind, there was no road to recovery that included drugs that blurred and clouded his feelings; he'd been running away from them for long enough already.

He wanted this festival to feel authentic – to feel in touch with himself as much as with the Universe – a beautiful lyric already forming in his head, as the North Pole tilted away from the sun only to return to the light. The symbolism was perfect and he wanted to embrace every moment.

He breathed out slowly, calming his nerves, and handed Jamieson's lead to Kitty. 'I've left the other dogs in the house with Mary – I mean Janet. I wasn't sure if they'd cope with the noise, but this old fella wouldn't leave my side. I hope he'll be okay with the speakers and things?'

Gary tugged at his sleeve. 'Mate, it's just a dog. Let's get on, shall we?' He strode away across the valley, cursing yet again as his McQueen Chelsea boots took another hit.

'Oh, thank God,' breathed Holly, bumping towards them with the double pram. Taffy had Ben and Tom tightly in his grasp and they both looked extremely frazzled. 'I thought we'd missed the big opening. Elsie's abandoned us in favour of your celebrity entourage.'

'And Plum and Tilly needed a little quality time together. What can you do, eh, young love? And what better place to go on your first "official date" apparently than here?' Taffy said affectionately, looking around. 'Even if it has been a little chaotic at our house today.'

'Is that why Holly's wearing her dungarees?' Lizzie pointed out wryly, trying not to laugh at the dismay on Holly's face.

'Bugger. I did *mean* to get changed. Obviously.' Holly glanced around the milling hordes and a smile flitted across her face. 'But it looks like I'm not the only one. Not like you to miss a trend there, Lizzie.'

She made a valid point and Lizzie's face dropped as she clocked several beautiful young girls in stylish, chunky roll-necks complementing their own dungaree ensembles. Her own skinny jeans suddenly looked dated and a trifle middle-aged. She turned to Will, barely missing a beat. 'If I don't go back to work soon, I'm going to lose what's left of my mind,' she informed him. 'We'll get ourselves a nice lesbian nanny, like Holly did, and then I can actually have a life that extends beyond mashed potato, Valium and finger painting.' Her tone was confrontational and a little aggressive and poor Will looked utterly thrown.

'You won't get any complaints from me,' he ventured in the end. 'You're much easier to live with when you've got a project on the go.'

Lizzie opened her mouth to protest, before realising he had a valid point and closing it again.

'Do you want to run my new Charitable Trust?' Connor offered easily. 'You'd have to work alongside me – and I'm probably not the easiest boss. But the pay would be good and you can still skive off for sports days and all those endless orthodontist appointments.'

They all fell silent and stared at him.

'Did I not mention?' he asked with a smile, knowing only too well this was fresh information. He shrugged. 'Well, it can't be too much of a surprise. I mean, look at me today – I'm like a fish out of water. I've made it official: I can't go back to touring – mainly because I don't really want to. My life is here, with my goats and my dogs and my bees. So, what do you think?'

'Are you really just walking away from all this?' Will asked.

'Yup. This festival is only the beginning. I'm going to start with the three causes closest to my heart – the Air Ambulance, obviously, the Assistance Animals situation has to be worth some investment, and Mike Urquhart has already roped me into his consortium to help Matthew Giles set up this support centre for Young Carers he's been working on. Seems like a good idea to start local. Maybe use this fame thing you lot keep going on about to my advantage for once?'

Holly leaned forward and kissed him on both cheeks before pulling him into a hug. The others piled on and soon Connor was gasping for air. 'Calm down, you daft sods. It's only a concept at the moment. But it seems like a good choice.' He couldn't help catching Kitty's eye. 'I seem to be making quite a few of those at the moment.'

She smiled back and for that one brief moment, there was a world of promise in their gaze.

'Oi, wanker! We're on in two!' heckled Gary across the paddock, to the amusement of festival-goers and friends alike.

'Go and be fabulous then,' Lizzie said, giving him a shove. 'Knock their socks off one last time, Boss.'

Connor grinned, the nerves ramping up, as he loped across to where Gary was holding out his radio mic.

'Hello, Larkford!' shouted Connor as he bounded to the stage, his charisma lighting up the front rows of fans, and a wave of cheers and hollers echoed around the valley. 'Are you ready for some music?'

Chapter 50

Holly sat back on the straw bales that had been thoughtfully arranged in little clusters around wrought-iron braziers throwing out heat and light across the darkening festival site, taking in as many little details as she possibly could, while wrangling four excitable children, each anticipating the warm cinnamon buns and hot chocolates that Taffy was now queuing for. For the last half an hour, at least, both Ben and Tom had been completely enthralled by the presence of their very favourite author, not to mention her willingness to read scenes from her books in a variety of captivating voices, and Holly had been able to relax for a while and savour the atmosphere.

She wasn't sure quite how Connor had managed it, although the whirlwind of energy that was Lizzie Parsons may have had a large part to play, but this truly was a very special festival. Somehow, possibly by accident, he had struck a balance between old and young, between locals and visitors, and what's more, the weather had happily complied, cold and crisp, yet dry, showcasing Larkford at her wintery finest. Even the stars had aligned so that Saturn was visible in the sky to look down on their very own attempt at Saturnalia. In the final rush towards the finish line, it was as though everything had simply fallen into place – not without effort of course – but certainly without hitting hurdles at every stride as before. Almost as though it were meant to be.

Food. Music. Friends.

It was a winning combination.

She looked up at the sound of her name and saw Jamie and Alice walking towards her, holding hands, Alice cradling the epically hideous trophy from The Practice's Game-Off – who knew she was such a demon at Monopoly? 'If you fancy a hot chocolate or some mulled wine, speak now or for ever hold your peace,' said Holly. 'Taffy's nearly at the front of the queue and he's been there for like a year.'

Jamie bounded across to place their order with Taffy and Alice sat down on the straw bales beside the boys, Coco tumbling instantly over their legs in a bid to lick them all in greeting. 'I can't quite believe all this,' she said, glancing around at the little packs of festival-goers with their Courchevel-meets-Coachella vibe, slick gloss Hunter boots, and youthful enthusiasm, countered in the glamour-stakes perhaps by Pru Hartley and the rest of the Larkford WI in their quilted Puffa jackets and sensible shoes. 'It shouldn't work; but somehow, it just does, right?'

Holly nodded. 'He's a clever old bean, our Connor.'

Alice beamed. 'He really is *our* Connor now, isn't he? I mean, you can't doubt his commitment to the place after this, can you? Did he tell you about this Larkford Fund he's setting up and that the Assistance Animals is one of his seed charities?' Alice breathed out happily. 'I can't believe how things have turned around for me in the last week or so.'

'And of course that has *nothing* to do with your Jamie handing in his notice and hightailing it home from Donegal for good?' checked Holly teasingly. 'No correlation there at all?'

Alice simply smiled; the kind of secretive smile in fact that made Holly wonder if there was more to Jamie's gallant, white-knight re-entry to Larkford life than she was privy to. 'I know we shouldn't talk shop today, but your partnership contracts are all ready and waiting for you to sign on the dotted line,' Holly said, wondering if the promotion in rank could be behind Alice's serene happiness.

'Perfect,' said Alice easily. 'I'll get that all sorted on Monday.' She quietly guided Coco away from the family sitting beside them, who seemed a little bemused by the doe-eyed spaniel in her assistance jacket. 'Oh, and remind me to talk to you later, when all this calms down?' Alice said with an enigmatic smile.

'Who wants food?' said Jamie boisterously, as he and Taffy approached, laden with warm drinks and cinnamon-scented boxes of steaming pastries; hunter-gatherers of the Cotswold style.

'Me! Me! Me!' clamoured the children. Well, and Holly. And for a few short moments there was a happy lull in conversation, filled by munching and giggling and general enjoyment. Holly watched Alice over the top of her mulled wine, seeing how her eyes danced with every word from Jamie's lips, trying not to second-guess what she might have to say.

She glanced over at Taffy, his face illuminated by the flickering brazier, wondering when that first flush of love matured into something deeper and more meaningful, only for him to catch her gaze and deliberately pull a silly face, giving Olivia and Lottie a severe case of giggle-itis.

The music had been going on all afternoon, but from Holly's point of view, the joy of the festival had been the food and the chance to see so many local people enjoying themselves. She was hardly a connoisseur of popular music at the best of times, but she knew what she liked, and appreciated that the bands had been chosen for maximum appeal.

Watching Hannah Porter dancing with her friends in the deepening twilight, plaits twirling as they spun around to the music, was possibly the best gift of all. Yes, she was still too thin, and they had a hundred and one hurdles to jump in getting her truly well, but still – she was here, with friends and enjoying the moment – and that felt like a significant victory to Holly.

'Hey, shh! Shh! You guys, they're going to announce the winner of the Yurt competition,' Taffy said, as everyone around them turned to face the main stage where Connor was holding the microphone as the music fell silent.

'Well, I hope you're all enjoying the festivities and each other's company, maybe getting a little taste of this life that I love?' Whooping cheers from the crowd brought a smile to his face. 'Now there's a very special award that I need to present this evening. And thanks to Bath Rugby's sponsorship of our very own Young Carers' Charity – and to the formidable Matthew Giles and his determination to get things up and running – I have in my hand an award to celebrate the very best of local talent. Every act in the Young Carers' Yurt today has been watched and enjoyed by my Music Management Team – although obviously we didn't tell them that!' He laughed, knowing how terrifying the prospect of performing would then have been. 'And it is my honour, and my privilege to announce the winner.'

He reached into his back pocket for an envelope – not a gold shiny one like at the Oscars, but a Mr Men one, courtesy of Ben and Tom's stationery set, sourced at the last minute. The front few rows of the crowd laughed, Molly Giles among them, her proud face beaming at what her wonderful son had

achieved. 'Oh yes,' Connor said, in response to a little heck-
ling, 'I am *all* about the glamour and the branding these days.
And,' he began, ripping open the envelope, 'I'm delighted to
announce that the winner is . . .'

Just as he paused for a drumroll from his bandmate,
Orlando, there was a scuffle and kerfuffle in the wings of the
stage, Nineteen and Nigel possessively barging their way over
to find their master. Flanking him, centre stage, making a
bid for stardom, Nigel reached out with his lips to snaffle the
results from Connor's hand, happily chewing them to a pulp,
as Nineteen grunted excitedly, and stood directly on the loop
pedal set up for the next act.

Holly laughed so hard that her mulled wine went up her
nose and made her eyes stream. Only in Larkford, she thought.

It took quite a while for Connor to stop laughing and
rescue the results from a reluctant Nigel, and it was a dead
cert which images would be splashed all over the tabloids the
next day. But looking at the elation and hilarity on his face,
Holly was fairly confident he wouldn't care less.

From the corner of her eye, she caught sight of Cassie
Holland, sitting on another cluster of bales, with her brother
Alec on one side, and Tarquin on the other. And wonder of
wonders, they were all eating candyfloss. Cassie may be a pain
in the proverbial, but she was also human, just like the rest of
them, with baggage and neuroses, and Holly made a little pact
with herself, there and then, to take the rough with the smooth,
through Cassie's chemo and the challenges that lay ahead.

'Right!' said Connor, finally composing himself, as a
blushing Kitty escorted Nigel and Nineteen from the stage.

'You had one job!' heckled her colleague Rupert from the
crowd, much to the locals' amusement and Kitty's increasing
embarrassment.

'And the winner – for most promising local artist – in a country-and-western style, I believe – Ms Cassie Holland!' Connor blinked at the slightly masticated paper in his hand, as though he himself couldn't quite believe it, before his professionalism reasserted itself and he led the applause with aplomb.

Cassie, pink of cheek, and looking uncharacteristically nervous, made her way up on stage and shook his hand. 'Thank you,' she said, her words echoing around the valley from his mic. 'This award is all the more special, actually, because without my lovely brother, I would never have dared take part. Thank you, Alec,' she said and swiftly left the stage, disappearing into the wings, leaving all the local parents mouthing at each other in disbelief. There was, after all, only one Alec in Larkford.

'Dear God,' said Taffy, to whom this wasn't news, 'she's going to be just unbearable now . . .'

'Ah, but did you hear her sing?' Jamie countered. 'Voice of an angel.'

Alice nodded her agreement and Holly leaned forward. 'You were going to tell me something, just now?'

'Oh yes,' Alice said, turning to face her excitedly. 'Well, it's not just my news to share, but Jamie and I—'

Holly held her breath, glancing automatically down at Alice's washboard stomach. 'Yes? Don't leave me hanging.'

Alice blushed. 'Well, we wanted you to be the first to know, that we've got Banana's certification through. In record time. We can't quite believe it ourselves. Isn't it wonderful?'

Holly almost felt the cogs in her head recalibrate, so certain had she been that Alice and Jamie's news had been of a different type altogether. 'That's wonderful. My God, that's just fabulous,' said Holly, throwing her arms around Alice in a heartfelt, if slightly delayed reaction. 'Jess must be over the moon?'

Alice nodded, standing up. 'In fact, she's doing a little interview for *Larkford Life* in a minute. A proper glossy photo shoot in the yurt as well. I said I'd go and hold her hand. One way or another, we're going to get Lavinia on board, so I thought, why not play to her interests?'

'Genius,' said Holly, particularly touched that Alice was already going the extra mile for her patients. 'Will you give them a big hug from me?'

'Me too,' squealed a small excited voice, as a Lulu-shaped blur came running through the crowds and threw herself into Holly's arms, a bundle of furry onesie and affection. 'Hello,' she said seriously, her entire face painted like a tiger and her stripy cheeks already slightly smudged with chocolate. 'I'm a scary tiger.'

'You are,' agreed Holly, kissing her on the end of her nose. 'A very happy tiger, by the looks of it.'

Lulu snuggled onto her lap, deftly moving Holly's omnipresent kit bag to make more space. 'Happy tiger,' she confirmed, popping her thumb in her mouth and leaning back against Holly in complete relaxation.

Dan and Grace were only a few paces away, watching, thoughtfully giving Holly the moment she hadn't known she needed. It seemed she wasn't alone, as Ben quietly took Lulu's hand, almost on autopilot, as though she'd never been away. One way or another, Lulu had become part of the very fabric of their family.

'So,' said Taffy, eyeing up his mate's rather rumpled appearance, 'how's parenthood going?'

'Exhausting, exhilarating, confusing and wonderful,' Dan

said, stifling a yawn and lovingly putting his arm around Grace's shoulders.

'Excellent,' said Taffy happily, seemingly delighted to finally have his mate in the same boat.

'Err, excuse me, guys?' said one of Connor's security team. 'I don't suppose you're the family of Elsie Townsend, are you? Only she's made herself rather at home on the tour bus and, well, she's refusing to leave.'

'I'll come and get her,' said Dan, barely batting an eyelid as his 'family' seemed to expand by the day in Larkford. He gave Holly a look. 'But if she's all tipsy and flirting, I'm handing her straight over to you, okay?'

Holly nodded. 'She's probably just winding them up.'

Dan walked away and Grace knelt down beside Holly and Lulu. 'I hope she's not too hurt that we turned down her generous offer with the house and everything?'

Holly shook her head. 'Really not. In fact, although she'd never say it, I think she was a little relieved, actually. Number 44 was kind of her dream home – a real project from the heart. It's quite the endorsement of your little family that she was prepared to give it up, I reckon.'

'The Elsie Townsend seal of approval is not one to be taken lightly, either,' said Taffy on the fringes of their conversation. 'But I for one am delighted she's next door. And not just for her Thursday night poker game.'

Holly smiled at him appreciatively, always taking their tumultuous life in his stride. Okay, so they'd hit a few potholes along the way, but the main truth remained. She loved him. Absolutely and unconditionally. And she couldn't imagine raising her family with anyone else.

'Now,' he said, reading the emotive expression in her eyes like a book, and reaching into his pocket for a small tissue paper parcel, 'don't you go getting all emotional on me. I can't promise this kind of serendipity for your Christmas present every year.'

He leaned across and kissed her firmly, lovingly on the lips, before sitting back on his heels and smiling as she unfurled the soft lilac tissue to reveal an exquisite moonstone Solstice pendant. 'Better than the kettle last year, yes? Or the hole punch?' He shrugged. 'I know I'm rubbish at buying presents, Holls, but it doesn't mean I love you any the less.'

He paused, taking in his wife's stricken expression. 'You've just worked out who you forgot to buy a present for, haven't you?' He leaned forward and kissed her again. 'Maybe there's something else I could unwrap instead?' he whispered with a cheeky smile. 'Plus, you know, this may actually be the best Christmas present ever: my wife – the woman who never forgets anything – on the back foot. Oh, I do love you, Toots.'

'I love you too,' she managed, blown away by how the tables had turned.

'I'm guessing my second present might actually be a little overkill, then?' he said with an unapologetic grin, as The Hive took to the main stage once more and Holly heard their names being mentioned in the introduction, just before the opening chords of the Van Morrison classic, and Holly's ultimate feel-good song, 'Brown-Eyed Girl', began.

All eyes were on their little group, a family in so many ways, as Holly swallowed hard and sought Taffy's hand with her own. They may have all their eggs in one very small basket, she thought, but she'd never felt quite so contented or at one with herself in her whole life.

Not such a shabby basket, after all.

Her children clapped and her friends cheered as Taffy led her by the hand into a small empty patch of grass and twirled her around to the music, catching her and kissing her to whoops and applause.

'Happy Christmas, Taffs,' she said, trying to catch her breath from dancing and laughing at the same time.

'Better than the hole punch?' he checked, twirling her around once more.

'Definitely,' she replied.

Acknowledgements

It's somewhat fitting, I always think, that — in true Larkford style — it really does take a village to bring this book from my imagination to your bookshelf and there is no way that I could do it alone. Nor indeed would I want to.

My team at Books And The City — Simon & Schuster (under the guidance of Editor-extraordinaire Jo Dickinson and the wonder that is Sara-Jade Virtue) and at Curtis Brown (where the fabulous Cathryn Summerhayes holds my hand) are truly magicians, not to mention downright lovely people and I am incredibly grateful for their support, their belief in my work, not to mention their friendship.

Similarly, the wonderful whirlwind that is my writing life is enhanced in *every* way by my author mates — who are always there for the ups and the downs, whether in person or online. My Cotswold posse are an incredible source of joy and I wouldn't be anywhere else: Katie Fforde, AJ Pearce, Caroline Sanderson, Nikki Owen and Kate Riordan — you are all wonderful and fabulous and I love you; not to mention the sisterhood among my fellow Schusters is hard to beat: Milly Johnson, Bernie Strachan, Dany Atkins, Patricia Scanlan, Sarah Vaughan, Catherine Isaac, Kate Furnivall, Paige Toon, Heidi Swain and Holly Hepburn — you make 'work' parties an absolute joy and I'm so grateful to have you at the end of an email.

My ever-tolerant friends and family are now getting used to me disappearing into my fictional world, but their support is nonetheless vital in my attempts to keep a little balance. I owe you all new Post-its, replenished gin supplies, and heaps of love and hugs. Always.

And no Tiggerish round-up of thank yous would ever be complete without thanking the booksellers and bloggers, reviewers, readers and buyers who took a leap of faith with my first book and have been waving the Larkford pom-poms ever since – you're all amazing and so very much appreciated . . . I quite literally couldn't do this without you.

Px